PUFFIN BOOKS

Blood Witch
and
Dark Magick

Books by Cate Tiernan

BOOK OF SHADOWS and THE COVEN
BLOOD WITCH and DARK MAGICK

Blood Witch

Cate Tiernan

PUFFIN

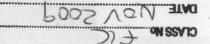

PUFFIN BOOKS

Published by the Penguin Group

Penguin Books Ltd, 80 Strand, London WC2R ORL, England
Penguin Group (USA) Inc., 375 Hudson Street, New York, New York 10014, USA
Penguin Group (Canada), 90 Eglinton Avenue East, Suite 700, Toronto, Ontario, Canada M4P 2Y3
(a division of Pearson Penguin Canada Inc.)
Penguin Ireland, 25 St Stephen's Green, Dublin 2, Ireland (a division of Penguin Books Ltd)
Penguin Group (Australia), 250 Camberwell Road, Camberwell, Victoria 3124, Australia
(a division of Pearson Australia Group Pty Ltd)
Penguin Books India Pvt Ltd, 11 Community Centre, Panchsheel Park, New Delhi – 110 017, India
Penguin Group (NZ), 67 Apollo Drive, Rosedale, North Shore 0632, New Zealand
(a division of Pearson New Zealand Ltd)
Penguin Books (South Africa) (Pty) Ltd, 24 Sturdee Avenue, Rosebank, Johannesburg 2196, South Africa

Penguin Books Ltd, Registered Offices: 80 Strand, London WC2R ORL England

puffinbooks.com

First published as separate editions in the USA in Puffin Books, a division of Penguin Group (USA) Inc.,
as *Sweep: Blood Witch* and *Sweep: Dark Magick* 2001
Published as separate editions in Great Britain in Puffin Books 2002
First published in one volume 2008

4

Copyright © 17th Street Productions, an Alloy Online, Inc. company, and Gabrielle Charbonnet, 2001
All rights reserved

17th Street Productions and associated logos
are trademarks and/ or registered trademarks of Alloy Online, Inc.

Made and printed in England by Clays Ltd, St Ives plc

British Library Cataloguing in Publication Data
A CIP catalogue record for this book is available from the British Library

ISBN: 978-0-141-32532-3

www.greenpenguin.co.uk

Penguin Books is committed to a sustainable future
for our business, our readers and our planet.
The book in your hands is made from paper
certified by the Forest Stewardship Council.

With love to my circle

1.
Secrets

May 4, 1978

Today for the first time I helped Ma cast a circle for Belwicket. In time I'll be high priestess. Then I'll be leading the circles as she does now. Already people come to me for charms and potions, and me only seventeen! Ma says it's because I have the Riordan sight, the Riordan power, like my grandma. My own ma is a very powerful witch, stronger than anyone in Belwicket. She says I'll be stronger than that yet.

And then what, I wonder. What will I do? Make our sheep healthy? Make our fields more fertile? Heal our ponies when they go lame?

I have so many questions. Why would I have such power, the power to shake mountains? My granny's Book of Shadows says that our magick is just to be used here, in this village, this place in the country, so far away from other towns and cities. Is that so? Maybe the Goddess has a purpose for me, but I cannot see it.

— Bradhadair

For a moment the name hung in the air before me, wavering like a black insect in front of my eyes. Bradhadair! Also known as my birth mother, Maeve Riordan. I was holding her Book of Shadows, started when she first joined her mother's coven, when she was fourteen. Her Wiccan name, Bradhadair, was Gaelic for "fire starter." And I was reading words she had written in her very own hand—

"Morgan?"

I glanced up, startled. And then I felt a jolt of alarm.

My boyfriend, Cal Blaire, and his mother, Selene Belltower, stood at the entrance of the secret library. Their bodies were backlit by a shaft of light from the hall. Their faces were blank masks, hidden in shadow.

My breath caught in my throat. I had entered this room without permission. Not only had I kept Cal and our other friends waiting, I had trespassed in a private area of Selene's house. I had no business being in this room, reading these books. This I knew. A hot flush of shame made my face burn.

But I couldn't help myself. I was desperate for more knowledge—about Wicca, about my birth mother. After all, I'd only recently uncovered extraordinary secrets: that I'd been adopted, that my birth mother, a powerful witch, had been murdered, burned to death in a barn. But so many questions still remained unanswered. And now I had found Maeve Riordan's Book of Shadows: her private book of spells, thoughts, and dreams. The key to her innermost life. If the answers I sought were anywhere, they were in this book. Subconsciously—in spite of my guilt—my hands tightened around it.

"Morgan?" Cal repeated. "What are you doing in here? I've been looking all over for you."

"I'm sorry," I said, the words rushing out. I looked around, wondering how I could explain being in this place. "Uh—"

"The others went on to the movie," Cal interrupted. His voice hardened. "I told them we'd try to catch up with them, but it's too late now."

I glanced at my watch. Eight o'clock. The movie theater was at least a twenty-minute drive from here, and the movie started at eight-fifteen. I swallowed. "I'm really sorry," I said. "I just—"

"Morgan," Selene said. She stepped farther into the room. For the first time I saw tense lines on her youthful face, so like Cal's. "This is my private retreat. No one is allowed in here except me."

Now I was nervous. Her voice was calm, but I sensed the leashed anger underneath. Was I in real trouble? I stood up at her desk and closed the book. "I—I know I shouldn't be in here, and I didn't mean to intrude. But I was walking along the hall, and then suddenly I just fell against this door, and it opened. Once I was inside, I couldn't stop looking at everything. It's the most amazing library. . . ." My voice trailed off.

Selene and Cal gazed at me. I couldn't read their eyes, nor could I get any sense of what was going through their minds, and that made me even more nervous. I wasn't lying, but I hadn't told them the whole story, either. I had also been trying to avoid Sky Eventide and Hunter Niall, two English witches who were here tonight to take part in one of Selene's circles. For some reason, these two guests of Selene's filled me with inexplicable dread. When I'd heard them coming along the hall, I had tried to avoid them—and had ended up stumbling into this secret library. It had been an accident.

That's right, I thought. It *had* been an accident. Nothing

to be ashamed of. Besides, I wasn't the only one who had some explaining to do. I had a few questions for Selene.

"This is Maeve Riordan's Book of Shadows," I found myself saying. My voice sounded loud, harsh in my ears. "Why do you have it? And why didn't you tell me you had it? You both know I've been trying to find out about her. I mean . . . don't you think I'd want to see something that belonged to her?"

Cal seemed surprised. He glanced at his mother.

Selene reached behind her and shut the door, closing us all inside the secret room. No one walking down the hall would ever notice the door's almost invisible line. Her beautiful eyebrows arched as she came closer to me.

"I know you've been trying to find out about your mother," she said. In the golden halo of the lamplight her expression seemed to soften. She glanced at the book. "How much have you read?"

"Not a lot." I chewed my lip anxiously.

"Have you come across anything surprising?"

"Not really," I said, watching her.

"Well, a Book of Shadows is a very personal thing," Selene said. "Secrets are revealed there, unexpected things. I was waiting to tell you about it because I know what it contains, and I wasn't sure you were ready to read it." Her voice fell to a whisper. "I'm not sure you're ready now, but it's too late."

My face tightened. Maybe I had been violating a private area of her house, but I had a right to know about my mother. "But it's not really your decision to make," I argued. "I mean, she was *my* mother. Her Book of Shadows should be mine. That's what you're supposed to do with Books of Shadows, pass them down to your children. It *is* mine."

Selene blinked at my strong words. She glanced at Cal again, but he was looking at me. Once more my fingers tingled as they traced the book's worn leather cover.

"So why do you have it?" I repeated.

"I got it by accident," Selene said. A fleeting smile crossed her face. "Though of course most witches don't believe in accidents. My hobby is collecting Books of Shadows—really, I collect almost any book having to do with witchcraft, as you can see." She waved an elegant hand at the shelves in the room. "I work with several dealers, mostly in Europe, who have standing orders to send me whatever books they have of interest—any Book of Shadows, no matter what its condition. I find them fascinating. I take them with me wherever we go and set them up in a private study, as I did here when we moved in this past summer. To me, they're a window into the human side of the craft. They're diaries, records of experiments; they're people's histories. I have over two hundred Books of Shadows, and Maeve Riordan's is just one of them."

I waited for her to elaborate, but she didn't. Her response sounded strangely voyeuristic—especially from a high priestess, someone who was otherwise so in touch with people's feelings. Why couldn't she see that Maeve Riordan's book wasn't just another Book of Shadows? At least not to me.

My initial guilt and nervousness were giving way to anger. Selene had read my mother's private words. But right then Cal stepped across the room and put his hand on my shoulder, rubbing gently. He seemed to be saying he was on my side, that he understood. So why couldn't his mother? Did she think I was too much of a child to handle my mother's secrets?

"Where did you get *this* Book of Shadows?" I asked insistently.

"From a dealer in Manhattan," Selene said. Once again her tone was impossible to read. "He had acquired it from someone else—someone who had no credentials, who may have stolen it or found it in a second-hand store somewhere." She shrugged. "I bought it about ten or eleven years ago, sight unseen. When I opened it, I realized it was by the same young witch who I'd read about dying in a fire, not far from here. It's a special Book of Shadows, and not just because it's Maeve's."

"I'm going to take it home," I said boldly, surprising myself again.

For a long moment silence hung thick in the air. Again my heart started to race. I'd never challenged Cal's mother before; I hardly ever challenged adults at all . . . and she was a powerful witch. Cal's eyes flashed between the two of us.

"Of course, my dear," Selene finally said. "It's yours."

I let my breath out silently. Selene added, "After Cal told me your story, I knew one day I would give it to you. If, after you read it, you have any questions or concerns, I hope you'll come and talk to me."

I nodded. "Thanks," I mumbled. I turned to Cal. "You know, I really just want to go home now." My voice was shaky.

"Okay," Cal said. "I'll drive you. Let's get our coats."

Selene stepped aside to let us pass. She remained in the study, probably to look around at what else I had touched or examined. Not that I could blame her. I didn't know what to feel. I hadn't meant to abuse her trust, but there was no denying the reward: I now possessed an intimate record of my birth mother's life, written in her hand. No matter what mysteries lay inside, I knew I could handle them. I *had* to handle them.

Cal squeezed my shoulder as we walked down the hall, reassuring me.

Outside, the November wind whipped through my hair, and I brushed it out of my face. Cal opened his car and I climbed in, shivering against the cold leather seats and pushing my hands deep inside my pockets. The Book of Shadows was zipped up inside my jacket, next to my chest.

"The heater will warm things up in a minute," Cal said. He turned the key and punched buttons on the dash. His handsome face was just a silhouette in the dark of night. Then he turned to me and brushed his hand, surprisingly warm, against my cheek. "Are you okay?" he asked.

I nodded, but I wasn't sure. I was grateful for his concern, yet I was all wrapped up in the mystery of the book and still uneasy about what had just happened with Selene.

"I wasn't trying to spy or sneak around," I told him. The words were true, but they sounded even less convincing the second time around.

He glanced at me again as he turned the Explorer onto the main road. "That door is spelled shut," he said thoughtfully. "I still have to get Mom's permission to go in—I've never been able to open the door by myself. And believe me, I've tried." His grin was a white flash in the darkness.

"But that's weird," I said, frowning. "I mean, I didn't even try to open the door—it just popped open, and I almost fell down."

Cal didn't respond. He concentrated on the road. Maybe he was trying to figure out how I had gotten in there, wondering if I'd used magick. But I hadn't, at least not consciously. Maybe I had been destined to find my way into that study, to find my mother's book.

Snow had started to fall, and now it brushed against the windshield, not sticking anywhere. It would be gone by morning. I couldn't wait to get home, to run upstairs to my room and start reading. For some reason, my thoughts turned to Sky Eventide and Hunter Niall. I had instantly disliked both of them: their piercing gazes, their snotty English accents, the way they looked at Cal and at me.

But why? Who were they? Why did they seem so important? I'd only seen Sky once before, in the cemetery a few days ago. And Hunter—Hunter upset me in a way I couldn't explain. I was still thinking about it when Cal pulled into my driveway and switched off the engine.

"Are your folks home?" he asked.

I nodded.

"Are you okay? Do you want me to come in?"

"That's all right," I said, appreciating his offer. "I think I'll just hole up and read."

"Okay. Listen, I'll be home all night. Just call me if you want to talk."

"Thanks," I said, reaching for him.

He came into my arms, and we kissed for a few moments. The sweetness momentarily washed away any confusion and uncertainty I was feeling about my encounter with Selene. Finally, reluctantly, I untangled myself and opened the car door.

"Thanks," I said again. "I'll call you."

"Okay. Take care." He gave me a smile and didn't leave until I was inside.

"Hi!" I called. "I'm home."

My parents were watching a movie in the family room. "You're early," said Mom, looking at the clock.

I shrugged. "We missed the movie," I explained. "And I just decided to come home. Well, I'll be upstairs." I fled up to my room, ditched my coat, and flopped down on my bed. Then I pulled out a *Scientific American* magazine and got it ready in case I suddenly needed to cover the Book of Shadows. My parents and I had reached an uneasy truce—about Wicca, about my birth mother, about all the deception. It was best not to disturb that. I didn't want to have to explain anything painful to them.

Maeve Riordan's own words, I thought.

My hands trembling, I opened my mother's Book of Shadows and began to read.

2.
Picketts Road

What to write? The pressure inside me is building until my head pounds. Until recently I've always wanted to do what I needed to do. Now for the first time these two paths are diverging. She is blooming like an orchid: transforming from a plain plant into something crushingly beautiful, a blossom that cries out to be picked.

But now, somehow, the thought bothers me. I know it's right, it's necessary, it's expected. And I know I'll do it, but they keep hounding me. Nothing is turning out the way I had envisioned. I need more time to tie her to me, to join with her mentally, emotionally, so she'll see through my eyes. I even find myself liking the idea of joining with her. I'll bet the Goddess is laughing at me.

As to craft, I've found a variant reading of Hellorus that describes how sitting beneath an oak can bend the will of Eolh. I want to try it soon.

—Sgàth

Saturday morning I didn't exactly leap out of bed. I'd been up until the wee hours, reading Maeve's Book of Shadows. She'd started it when she was fourteen years old. So far, I couldn't figure out what Selene meant about finding out something upsetting. Aside from unpronounceable Gaelic words and lots of spells and recipes, I hadn't found anything really disturbing or strange. I knew that Maeve Riordan and Angus Bramson, my birth parents, were burned to death after they came to America. I just didn't know why. Maybe this book would explain it somehow. But I was reading slowly. I wanted to savor every word.

When I finally woke up and groped my way downstairs, my eyes were slits. I stumbled toward the refrigerator for a Diet Coke.

I was working on a couple of Pop-Tarts when Mom and Mary K. breezed in, having taken a brisk mother-daughter walk in the chill November air.

"Wow!" said Mom, her nose pink. She clapped her gloved hands. "It's nippy outside!" She came over and gave me a kiss, and I flinched as her icy hair brushed against my face.

"It's pretty, though," Mary K. added. "The snow is just starting to melt, and all the squirrels and birds are on the ground, looking for something to eat."

I rolled my eyes. Some people are just too cheerful in the morning. It isn't natural.

"Speaking of something to eat," Mom said, taking off her gloves and sitting down across from me, "can you two hit the grocery store this morning? I'm showing a house at ten-thirty, and we're out of almost everything."

Mentally I reviewed my blank calendar. "Sure," I said. "Got a list?"

Mom plucked it off the fridge and started adding items to it. Mary K. put the last bagel in the toaster. The phone rang, and she whirled to get it.

Cal, I thought, my heart picking up a beat. Happiness washed over me.

"Hello?" answered Mary K., sounding perky and breathless at the same time. "Oh, hi. Yeah, she's here. Just a sec."

She handed the phone to me, mouthing, "Cal."

I knew it. Ever since I'd discovered Wicca, since I'd discovered Cal, I'd always been able to tell who was calling. "Hi," I said into the phone.

"How are you?" he asked. "Did you stay up all night, reading?"

He knew me. "Yes . . . I want to talk to you about it," I said. I was very aware of my mother and Mary K. sitting right there, especially since Mary K. was patting her heart and making swooning gestures at me. I frowned.

"Good—I'd like that," Cal said. "Want to drive up to Practical Magick this afternoon?"

Practical Magick was a Wicca store in the nearby town of Red Kill, and one of my favorite places to spend a spare hour or two. "I'd love to," I said. My frown melted into a smile. All my senses were waking up.

"I'll come get you. Say, one-thirty?"

"Okay. See you then."

I hung up the phone. My mom lowered the newspaper and looked at me over her reading glasses.

"What?" I said self-consciously, a big grin on my face.

"Everything going all right with Cal?" she asked.

"Uh-huh," I said. I could feel my cheeks reddening. It felt

weird to talk to my parents about my boyfriend—especially since he was the one who had introduced me to Wicca. I'd always been able to discuss my life with Mom and Dad, but Wicca was a part of it they wanted gone, forever. It had created a wall between us.

"Cal seems nice," Mom said brightly, trying to put me at ease and fish for information at the same time. "He's certainly good-looking."

"Um . . . yeah, he's really nice. Let me go take a shower," I mumbled, standing up. "Then we'll go to the store."

I fled.

"Okay, first stop, coffee shop," Mary K. directed a half hour later. She folded Mom's grocery list and stuck it in her coat pocket.

I wheeled Das Boot—my massive, submarinelike old car—into the parking lot of the small strip mall that boasted Widow's Vale's one and only coffee emporium. We dashed from the car to the café, where it smelled like coffee and pastry. I looked at the board and tried to decide between a grande latte or a grande today's special. Mary K. leaned over the glass case, gazing longingly at the bear claws. I checked my cash.

"Get one if you want," I said. "My treat. Get me one, too."

My sister flashed me a smile, and I thought again that she looked so much older than fourteen. Some fourteen-year-olds are so gawky: half formed, childlike. Mary K. wasn't. She was savvy and mature. For the first time in a long while, it occurred to me that I was lucky to have her as my sister, even if we didn't share the same blood.

The door swung open, bells jangling. Bakker Blackburn

came in, followed by his older brother, Roger, who had been a senior at Widow's Vale High last year and was now at Vassar. My insides clenched. Mary K. glanced up, eyes wide. She looked away quickly.

"Hey, Mary K., Morgan," Bakker mumbled, avoiding my gaze. He probably hated me. About a week earlier, I'd kicked him out of our house in no uncertain terms when I'd found him pinning Mary K. down on her bed, practically raping her. He also probably thought I was an alien, since those terms had included hitting him with a ball of crackly blue witch fire—without even meaning to. I still didn't know how I'd done it. My own power constantly surprised me.

Mary K. nodded at Bakker. She clearly didn't know what to say.

"Hey, Roger," I said. He was two years older than me, but Widow's Vale is a small town, and we all pretty much know each other. "How's it going?"

Roger shrugged. "Not bad."

Bakker's eyes remained glued to Mary K.

"We'd better go," I stated, heading toward the exit.

Mary K. nodded, but she took her time following me out the door. Maybe she secretly wanted to see if Bakker would say anything. Sure enough, he approached her.

"Mary K.," he began pleadingly.

She looked at him but turned and caught up to me without a word. I was relieved. I knew he'd been groveling hard since The Incident, and I could tell that Mary K. was weakening. I was afraid that if I spoke too harshly, it might drive her back to him. So I kept my mouth shut. But I had promised myself that if I got the slightest inkling of his forcing himself on her again, I would tell my parents, his parents, and everyone I knew.

And Mary K. would probably never forgive me, I thought as we got into the car.

I started Das Boot's engine and pulled out onto the street. Thinking about Mary K.'s love life made me think about my own. I started to smile and couldn't stop. Was Cal my mùirn beatha dàn—the Wiccan term for soul mate, life partner? He seemed to believe so. The possibility sent a shiver down my spine.

At the grocery store we stocked up on Pop-Tarts and other necessities. In the snacks aisle I lifted twelve-packs of Diet Coke into the cart while Mary K. piled bags of pretzels and chips on top. Farther down the shelf were boxes of Fudge Therapy, Bree's favorite junk food.

Bree. My former best friend.

I swallowed. How many times had Bree and I smuggled boxes of Fudge Therapy into a movie theater? How many boxes had we consumed during sleep overs as we lay in the dark, spilling our secrets to each other? It still seemed bizarre that we were enemies, that our friendship had broken up because she had wanted Cal and he had wanted me. In the past few weeks I had wished again and again that I could talk to her about all that I'd learned. Bree didn't even know I was adopted. She still thought I was a Rowlands by birth, like Mary K. But Bree was being such a bitch to me now, and I was being cold to her. Oh, well. For now, there was nothing I could do about it. It seemed best not to dwell on what I couldn't change.

Mary K. and I checked out and loaded up the car. I stifled a yawn as we climbed back in. The gray, cheerless weather seemed to sap my energy. I wanted to go home and nap before Cal came over.

"Let's go down Picketts Road," said Mary K., adjusting the car's heater vents to blow right on her. "It's so pretty, even if it takes longer."

"Picketts Road it is," I said, taking the turn. I preferred this route, too: it was hilly and winding, and there weren't many houses. People kept horses back here, and though most of the trees were now bare, colorful leaves still littered the ground, like the patterns on an oriental carpet.

Up ahead were two cars parked by the side of the road. My eyes narrowed. I recognized them as Matt Adler's white jeep and Raven Meltzer's beat-up black Peugeot . . . parked right next to each other on a road few people used. That was odd. I hadn't even realized that they spoke to each other. I looked around but didn't see either one of them.

"Interesting," I muttered.

"What?" said my sister, fiddling with the radio dial.

"That was Matt Adler's jeep and Raven Meltzer's Peugeot," I said.

"So?"

"They're not even friends," I said, shrugging. "What are their cars doing out here?"

Mary K. pursed her lips. "Gosh, maybe they killed someone and are burying the body," she said sarcastically.

I smirked at her. "It's just kind of unusual, that's all. I mean, Matt is Jenna's boyfriend, and Raven . . ." Raven doesn't care if a guy is someone's boyfriend, I finished silently. Raven just liked to get guys, chew them up, and spit them out.

"Yeah, but they both do this Wicca stuff with you, right?"

said Mary K., flipping down the sun visor mirror to check her appearance. It was obvious that she didn't want to look me in the eye. She'd made it very clear that she disapproved of "this Wicca stuff," as she liked to call it.

"But Raven's not in our coven," I said. "She and Bree started their own coven."

"Because you and Bree aren't talking anymore?" she asked pointedly, still looking in the mirror.

I bit my lip. I still hadn't explained very much about Bree and Cal to my family. They had noticed, of course, that Bree and I weren't hanging out and that Bree wasn't calling the house nine times a day. But I'd mumbled something about Bree being busy with a new boyfriend, and no one had called me on it till now.

"That's part of it," I said with a sigh. "She thought she was in love with Cal. But he wanted to be with me. So Bree decided the hell with me." It hurt to say it out loud.

"And you chose Cal," my sister said, but her tone was forgiving.

I shook my head. "It's not like I chose Cal *over* her. Actually, she chose him over me first. Besides, I didn't tell Bree she had to get out of my life or anything. I still wanted to be friends."

Mary K. flipped the visor back up. "Even though she loved your boyfriend."

"She *thought* she loved him," I said, getting prickly. "She didn't even know him, though. She still doesn't. Anyway, you know how she is about guys. She likes the thrill of the chase and the conquest much more than any long-term thing. Use them and lose them. And Cal didn't want to be with her." I sighed again. "It's complicated."

Mary K. shrugged.

"You think I shouldn't go out with Cal just because Bree wanted him?" I asked. My knuckles whitened on the steering wheel.

"No, not exactly," said Mary K. "It's just, I feel kind of sorry for Bree. She lost you *and* Cal."

I sniffed. "Well, she's being a total bitch to me now," I muttered, forgetting how much I had been missing Bree just minutes ago. "So she obviously isn't all broken up about it."

Mary K. stared out the window. "Maybe being a bitch is just how Bree acts sad," she murmured absently, watching the barren trees pass. "If you were my best friend for about twelve years and you left me for a guy you just met, maybe I would be a bitch, too."

I didn't answer. Just stay out of it, I thought. Like my fourteen-year-old sister knew anything. She'd allowed herself to get involved with a sleazebag like Bakker, after all.

But deep down, I wondered if I was irritated because Mary K. was right.

3.
Woodbane

Litha, 1998

    This is the time of year when I am most sad. Sad and angry. One of the last circles that I did with my mum and dad was for Beltane, eight years ago. I was eight, Linden was six, and Alwyn was only four. I remember the three of us sitting with the other kids, sons and daughters of the coven's members. The warmth of May was trying to steal in and banish April's cold, dreary wetness. Around our maypole the grown-ups were laughing and drinking wine. We kids danced, weaving our ribbons in and out of each other, gathering magick to us in a pastel net.

    I felt the magick inside me, inside everything. I was so impatient. I didn't know how I'd ever make it till I was fourteen, when I could be initiated as a full witch. I remember the sunset glowing on Mum's hair, and she and Dad held each other, kissing, while the others laughed. The other kids and I groaned and covered our faces. But we were only pretending to be embarrassed. Inside, our spirits were dancing. The air was full of life, and everything was glowing and swelling with light and wonder and happiness.

And before Litha, seven weeks later, Mum was gone, Dad was gone—vanished, without a trace, without a word to us, their children. And my life changed forever. My spirit shriveled, shrank, twisted.

Now I'm a witch and almost full-grown. Yet inside, my spirit is still a mean, twisted thing. And even though I have since learned the truth, I am still angry—in some ways, more than I have ever been. Will it always be that way? Maybe only the Goddess knows.

—Giomanach

After lunch I was in my room, twisting my long hair into a braid, when I felt Cal's presence. A smile spread across my face. I focused my senses and felt my parents in the living room, my sister in the bathroom—and then Cal, coming closer, tickling my nerves as he approached. By the time I snapped an elastic around my braid, he was ringing the doorbell. I dashed from my room and down the stairs.

Mom answered the door.

"Hello, Cal," she said. She'd met him once before, when he'd come to visit after Bree had practically broken my nose with a volleyball during gym. I could feel her giving him the standard maternal up-and-down as he stood there.

"Hi, Mrs. Rowlands," Cal replied easily, smiling. "Is Morgan—oh, there she is." Our eyes met, and we grinned foolishly at each other. I couldn't hide the pleasure that I took in seeing him, not even from my mom.

"Will you be back for dinner?" Mom asked, unable to resist giving me a quick kiss.

"Yes," I said. "And then I'm going to Jenna's tonight."

"Okay." Mom took a deep breath, then smiled at Cal again. "Have a good time."

I knew that she was trying hard not to ask Cal to drive safely, and to her credit, she managed it. I waved good-bye and hurried out to Cal's car.

He climbed in and started the engine. "Still want to go to Practical Magick?" he asked.

"Yes." I settled back in my seat. My thoughts instantly turned to the night before, to finding Maeve's Book of Shadows.

As soon as we were out of eyesight of my house, Cal pulled the car over and reached across to kiss me. I moved as close to him as I could in the bucket seats and held him tightly. It was so strange: I had always counted on Bree and my family for grounding, for support. But now Bree was out of my life, and my family and I were still coming to terms with the fact that I was adopted. If it weren't for Cal . . . well, it seemed best not to think of that.

"Are you okay?" he asked, pulling back to kiss my face again. "No worries with the BOS?"

"Not yet," I told him, shaking my head. "It's really amazing, though. I'm learning so much." I paused. "Your mom isn't mad I took it, is she?"

"No. She knows it's yours. She should have told you about it." He smiled ruefully. "It's just—I don't know. Mom is used to being in charge, you know? She leads her coven. She's a high priestess. She's always helping people solve problems, helping them with stuff. So sometimes she acts like she's got to protect the whole world. Whether they want her to or not."

I nodded, trying to understand. "Yeah. I can see that. I guess I just felt that it wasn't really her business, you know? Or maybe it could be, but it should be my business first."

There was a flash of faint surprise in Cal's eyes, and he gave a dry laugh. "You're funny," he said. "Usually people are swarming all over my mom. Everyone is so impressed with her power, her strength. They blurt out all their problems and tell her everything, and they want to be as close to her as possible. She's not used to people challenging her."

"But I like her a lot," I said, worried that I'd sounded too harsh. "I mean, I—"

"No, it's okay," he interrupted, nodding. "It's refreshing. You want to stand on your own two feet, do things yourself. You're your own person. It makes you interesting."

I didn't know what to say. I blushed slightly.

Cal pulled my braid out from underneath my coat. "I love your hair," he murmured, watching the braid run through his fingers. "Witch hair." Then he gave me a lopsided grin and shifted the car into gear.

Now I knew my face must be bright red. But I sat back, feeling happy and strong and unsure all at once. My eyes wandered out the window as we drove. The clouds had darkened, moving sluggishly across the sky as if trying to decide when to start dumping snow. By the time we reached

Red Kill, they let loose with big, wet flakes that stuck to everything in clumps.

"Here we go," said Cal, turning on his windshield wiper. "Welcome to winter."

I smiled. Somehow the falling snow and thumping wipers made the silence inside the car even more peaceful. I was so glad to be here right now, in this moment, with Cal. I felt like I could tackle anything.

"You know, there's something I meant to tell you before," I said. "The other day I followed Bree because I wanted to have it out with her once and for all."

Cal glanced over at me. "Really?"

I nodded. "Yeah—but it didn't end up that way. Instead I saw her and Raven meeting Sky Eventide."

His hand darted away, and he shot another quick glance at me. His brow was furrowed. "Sky?"

"Yeah, the blond witch I met last night at your mom's." The really good-looking one, I thought with an odd pang of jealousy. Even though I knew Cal loved me, that he had chosen me, I still felt insecure, especially when we were around pretty girls. It was just that he was so handsome, with his golden eyes and tall frame and perfect body. And I . . . well, I wasn't so perfect. A flat-chested girl with a big nose could hardly be called perfect.

"Anyway, I saw Sky with Bree and Raven," I continued, shoving my insecurities aside. "I bet she's the blood witch they have in their coven."

"Hmmm," said Cal. He gazed forward at the road, as if thinking intently. "Really. Yeah, I guess it's possible."

"Is she . . . bad?" I asked, for lack of a better term. "I mean, I feel like you dislike her and Hunter, too. Are they, I don't know, from the dark side?" I stumbled over the words. They sounded so melodramatic.

Cal laughed, startled. "Dark side? You've been watching too many movies. There's no dark side to Wicca. It's just a big circle. Everything magickal is part of that circle. You, me, the world, Hunter, Sky, everything. We're all connected."

I frowned. It seemed a strange thing to say, considering the way he'd glared at Hunter and Sky. "Last night you guys seemed to not like each other," I persisted.

Cal shrugged. He turned onto Red Kill's main street and cruised slowly, looking for a parking spot. After a few moments' silence he finally said, "Sometimes you just meet people who rub you the wrong way. I met Hunter a couple of years ago, and . . . we just can't stand each other." He laughed as if it were no big deal. "Everything about him pisses me off, and it's mutual. That doesn't sound very witchy, I know. But I don't trust him."

"What do you mean? Trust him as a person or a witch?"

Cal parked the car at an angle and turned off the engine. "There isn't a difference," he muttered. His expression was distant.

"What about the big circle?" I asked, unable to help myself. "If you're connected, then how can he piss you off so much?"

"It's just . . . ," he began, then shook his head. "Forget it. Let's talk about something else." He opened his door and stepped out into snowfall.

I opened my mouth, then closed it. Pursuing the conversation seemed important. After all, Hunter and Sky had both had a profound effect on me, and I couldn't figure out why. But if Cal wanted to leave it alone, I could respect that.

There were things I didn't want to talk about with him, either. I hopped out of the car and slammed the door behind me, then ran to catch up with him.

"It's too bad you don't have anything else of your mom's," Cal remarked as we walked toward the cozy little shop. We both buried our faces in our coats to protect ourselves from the cold. "Like the coven's tools, its athame, or wand, or maybe your mom's robe. Those things would be great to have."

"Yeah," I agreed. "But I guess all that stuff's long gone by now."

Cal swung open Practical Magick's heavy glass door, and I ducked inside. Warm air wafted over us, rich with the scent of herbs. We stamped the snow off our shoes, and I took off my gloves. I smiled. Automatically I started scanning book titles on the shelves. I loved this store. I could stay here and read all day. I glanced at Cal. He was already reading book spines, too.

Alyce and David, the two store clerks, were both in the back, talking quietly to customers. My eyes immediately flashed from David—with his short gray hair, his unusually youthful face, and his piercing dark eyes—to Alyce. I'd felt a connection with Alyce the first time I had met her. It was Alyce who had told me the story of my birth mother, how her coven had been completely destroyed. From Alyce, I'd learned that Maeve and my father had fled for America and settled in Meshomah Falls, a town about two hours from here. In America they had renounced magick and witchcraft and lived quietly by themselves. Then, about seven months after I was born, they gave me up for adoption. Soon after that they had been locked in a barn, and the barn was set on fire.

"Have you read this?" Cal asked, breaking into my thoughts. He reached for a book on a shelf near the register. Its title was *Gardens of the Craft.* "My mom has a copy of it. She uses it a lot."

"Really?" I took it from him, intrigued. I hadn't remembered seeing it in Selene's library. Then again, there had been hundreds of books. "Oh, this is incredible," I murmured, flipping through the pages. It was all about laying out an herb garden to maximize its potential, to get the most out of healing plants and plants for spells. "This is exactly what I want to do—"

I broke off. At the very back of the book there was a chapter titled "Spells to Cross Foes." An unpleasant tingling sensation crept across my neck. What did that mean, exactly? Could the plants' magick be used to harm people? It didn't seem right somehow. On the other hand, maybe a witch needed to know about the negative possibilities of herbal magick—in order to guard against them. Yes. Maybe that knowledge was a crucial part of the big circle of Wicca that Cal had mentioned only moments ago.

Gently Cal took the book from me and tucked it under his arm. "I'll get it for you," he said, kissing me. "As a pre-birthday present."

I nodded, feeling my concerns evaporate in a wash of pleasure. My seventeenth birthday was still eight days away. I was surprised and thrilled that Cal was thinking about it already.

We started walking through the store. I'd never been here with Cal, and he showed me hidden treasures I'd never noticed before. First we looked at candles. Each color of candle had different properties, and Cal told me about which ones were used in which rituals. My mind whirled with all of the names. There was so much to learn. Next we examined sets of small bowls. Wiccans used them to hold salt or other ritual substances, like water or incense. Cal told me that when he lived in California, he and Selene had spent a whole summer gathering ocean water and evaporating it for the salt. They saved the salt and used it to purify their circles for almost a year afterward.

After that we saw brass bells that helped charge energy fields during a circle, and Cal pointed out magickally charged twine and thread and ink. These were everyday objects, but they had been transformed. Like me, I thought. I almost laughed aloud with pleasure. Magick was in everything, and a truly knowledgeable witch could use literally anything to imbue spells with power. I'd had glimpses of this knowledge before, but with Cal here—really showing it to me—it seemed more real, more accessible, and infinitely more exciting than it ever had before.

And everywhere there were books: on runes, on how the positions of the stars affected one's spells, on the healing uses of magic, on how to increase one's power. Cal pointed out several he thought I should read but said he had copies and would lend them to me.

"Do you have a magickal robe yet?" he suddenly asked. He gestured to one on a rack near the rear of the store. It was made of deep blue silk that flowed like water.

I shook my head.

"I think that by Imbolc we should start using robes in our circles," he said. "I'll speak to the others about it. Robes are usually better than street clothes for making magick: you wear them only when you're doing magick, so they don't get contaminated with the jangled vibrations of the rest of your life. And they're comfortable, practical."

I nodded, brushing my hand against the fabric of the different robes. The variety was astounding. Some were plain; some were painted or sewn with magickal symbols and runes. But I didn't see any that I felt I absolutely had to have, though they were all beautiful. That was okay, though; Imbolc wasn't until the end of January. I had plenty of time to find one.

"Do you wear a robe?" I asked.

"Uh-huh," he said. "Whenever I do a circle with my mom or by myself. Mine is white, a really heavy linen. I've had it a couple of years. I sort of wish I could wear it all the time," he added with a grin. "But I don't think the people of Widow's Vale are ready for that."

I laughed, picturing him casually walking into Schweickhardt's drugstore in a long, white robe.

"Sometimes robes are passed down from generation to generation," Cal continued. "Like tools. Or sometimes people weave the cloth and sew them themselves. It's like anything else—the more thought and energy you put into something, the more it stores up magickal energy and the more it can help you focus when you do spells."

I was beginning to understand that, although I knew I would spend a lot of time meditating on how I could start applying it to my own magickal doings.

Cal stepped across the aisle and reached for something on an upper shelf. It was an athame: a ceremonial dagger, about ten inches long. The blade was made of silver, so brightly polished, it looked like a mirror. Its handle was carved with silver roses. There was a skull joining the handle and the blade together.

"It's beautiful, isn't it?" Cal murmured.

"Why does it have a skull on it?" I asked.

"To remind us that in life, there is always death," he said quietly, turning it in his fingers. "There is darkness in light, there is pain in joy, and there are thorns on the rose." He sounded solemn and thoughtful, and I shivered.

Then he glanced up at me. "Maybe a certain lucky some-one will get it for her birthday."

I wiggled my eyebrows, looking hopeful, and he laughed.

It was getting late, and I had to get home. Cal checked out, buying some green candles, some incense, and the book on gardening for me. I felt Alyce's eyes on me.

"Nothing for you?" she asked in her gentle way.

I shook my head.

She hesitated, then cast a quick glance at Cal. "I have something I think you should read," she said to me. Moving with surprising grace for a short, round person, she left the counter and walked down the aisle of books. I shrugged at Cal—and then Alyce was back, her lavender skirts swishing. She handed me a plain, dark brown book.

"*Woodbane, Fact and Fiction*," I read aloud. A chill shot through my body. The Woodbanes were the darkest of the seven ancient Wiccan clans, notorious for their quest for power at any cost. The evil ones. I looked at her, baffled. "Why should I read this?" I asked.

Alyce met my gaze squarely. "It's an interesting book that

debunks many of the myths surrounding the Woodbanes," she said, ringing it up. "It's useful for any student of the craft."

I didn't know what to say, but I pulled out my wallet and counted out money, pushing the bills across the counter. I trusted Alyce. If she thought I should read this, I would. But at the same time I was aware of tension tightening Cal's body. He wasn't angry, but he seemed hyperalert, watching Alyce, watching me, measuring everything. I put my arm around his waist and gave him a reassuring squeeze.

He smiled.

"Good-bye, Alyce," I said. "Thanks."

"My pleasure," she replied. "Good-bye, Morgan. Good-bye, Cal."

I held my two new books under my arm as we walked to the door—one book I wanted to read, one I didn't. Yet I would read them both. Although I had been studying witchcraft for barely two months, I had already learned a valuable lesson: Everything had two sides. I had to take the good with the bad, the fun with the discomfort, the excitement with the fear. The thorns with the rose.

Cal pushed open the door, and the bells jingled.

He stopped so suddenly that I walked right into his back.

"Oof," I said, steadying myself. I peeked around him.

That was when I saw what had made him pause.

It was Hunter Niall, crouched in the street, looking under Cal's car.

4.
Spell

Litha, 1990

I'm frightened. I woke up this morning to the sound of weeping. Alwyn and Linden were in my room. They were crying because they could not find Mum and Dad. I was angry and told them that they weren't babies anymore. I said Mum and Dad would be back soon. I thought they must have run to town for something we needed.

But night has fallen and we are still alone. I've heard no word from our neighbors, none from Mum and Dad's coven. I went to Siobhan's house, and to Caradog Owens's house over in Grasmere, to ask if they knew where Mum and Dad were. But there was no one home.

And there's something else. When I was making my bed I found Dad's lueg under my pillow—the stone he uses to scry with. How did it get there? He always keeps it safe with the rest of his magickal tools. He never even let me touch it before.

So how did it get under my pillow? I have a bad feeling....

Dad has often told me that when he and Mum are on their errands, I am master of the house. It is my job to watch over my brother and sister. But I am not a man like him. I am only eight years old. I won't be a witch for many years yet. What can I do if there is trouble?

What if something happened to them? They have never left us alone like this. Did someone take them away? Are they being held prisoner somewhere?

I must sleep, but I can't. Alwyn and Linden can sleep for me. I must be strong for them.

Mum and Dad will come back to us soon. They will. I know it. Goddess, bring them home.

—Giomanach

As if he sensed our approach, Hunter stood quickly. His green eyes were puffy and bloodshot. His face was pale from the cold, and snowflakes had settled on his hat. But aside from the redness of his eyes, he looked like he was carved of marble—still and somehow dangerous. Why was he looking under the car? More important, why did I find him so threatening? I didn't know the answers, but I knew that as a blood witch, I should trust my instincts. I shuddered inside my coat.

"What are you doing, Niall?" Cal demanded. His voice was so low and steady that I hardly recognized it. I looked at him and saw that his jaw was tight. His hands were clenched at his sides.

"Just admiring your big American car," Hunter said. He sniffed, then pulled a handkerchief from his pocket. He must have a cold, I thought. I wondered how long he'd been out here in the snow.

Cal flicked his gaze to the Explorer, sweeping it from bumper to bumper, as if scanning for something out of place.

"Hello, Morgan," Hunter murmured. With his sickly nasal voice the greeting sounded like an insult. "Interesting company you keep."

The falling snowflakes were cold against my hot skin.

I shifted my books to my other arm and gazed at Hunter, confused. Why should he care?

Hunter stepped onto the sidewalk. Cal turned to face him, placing himself between me and Hunter. My hero, I thought. But a part of me still felt a palpable fear as well. Hunter scowled, his cheekbones so sharp that snowflakes seemed to glance off them.

"So Cal is teaching you the secrets of Wicca, is he?" he asked. He leaned nonchalantly against the hood of the car, and Cal didn't take his eyes off him for a second. "Of course, he has quite a few secrets of his own, eh?"

"You can leave now, Niall," Cal spat.

"No, I think not," Hunter replied evenly. "I think I'll be around for a while. Who knows, I might have to teach Morgan a thing or two myself."

"What is that supposed to mean?" I asked.

Hunter just shrugged.

"Get away from me," Cal commanded.

Hunter stood back with a slight smile, his hands in the air as if to show he was unarmed. Cal glanced from him to the car. I'd never seen Cal so angry, so on the verge of losing control. It frightened me. He was like a tiger, waiting to pounce.

"There is one thing you should learn, Morgan," Hunter remarked. "Cal isn't the only blood witch around. He'd like to think he's a big man, but he's really just small fry. One day you'll realize that. And I want to be there to see it."

"Go to hell," Cal spat.

"Look, you don't *know* me," I told Hunter loudly. "You don't know anything about me. So shut up and leave us alone!" I stomped angrily to the car. But as I pushed past Hunter, barely brushing against him, a sickening rush of energy hit me in my stomach—so hard that I gasped. He's put a spell on me, I thought in a panic, groping for the door handle. But he'd said nothing; he'd done nothing that I could see. I blinked hard.

"Please, Cal," I whispered, my voice shaking. "Let's go."

Cal was still staring at Hunter as if he'd like to rip him apart. His eyes blazed, and his skin seemed to whiten.

Hunter stared back, but I felt his concentration break: he was shaken for a moment. Then he steeled himself again.

"Please, Cal," I repeated. I knew something had happened to me; I felt hot and strange and desperate to be gone, to be at home. My voice must have alerted Cal to my distress because he took his eyes off Hunter for a second. I stared at him pleadingly. Finally he pulled his keys from his pocket, slid into the car, and opened my door.

I collapsed inside and put my hands over my face.

"Good-bye, Morgan!" Hunter called.

Cal gunned the engine and sped backward, shooting snow and ice toward Hunter. I peeked through my fingers and saw Hunter standing there with an indecipherable expression on his face. Was it . . . anger? No. Snow swirled around him as he watched us leave.

It wasn't until we were almost at my house that it suddenly hit me.

The look on his face had been hunger.

5.
Dagda

Beltane, 1992

I feel like punching everyone and everything. I hate my life, hate living with Uncle Beck and Aunt Shelagh. Nothing has been the same, not since Mum and Dad disappeared that day two years ago, and it never will be.

Today Linden fell off Uncle Beck's ladder and bloodied his knee. I had to clean him up and bandage the wound, and all the while he wept. And I cursed Mum and Dad while I did it, I cursed them for leaving us and leaving me to do their job. Why did they go? Where did they go? Uncle Beck knows, but he won't tell me. He says I am not ready. Aunt Shelagh says he's only thinking of my good. But how can it be good not to know the truth? I hate Uncle Beck.

In the end, when I was finished with Linden, I made a face, and he laughed through his tears. That made me feel better.

But only for a while. No happiness lasts very long. That's what I've learned. Linden would do well to learn it, too.
     —Giomanach

Mom came into my room that night as I was getting dressed to go to Jenna Ruiz's for the circle. "Are you guys going to a movie?" she asked. She automatically began straightening the pile of rejected clothes on my bed.

"No," I said, and left it at that. When it came to Wicca, silence was the best policy. I turned in front of the mirror, frowning. As usual, I looked hopeless. I pulled open the bathroom door and yelled, "Mary K.!" Having an endlessly trendy sister had its perks.

She appeared at once.

I held out my arms. "Help."

Her warm brown eyes skimmed me critically, then she shook her head. "Take it all off," she ordered.

I obeyed meekly. Mom grinned at us.

While Mary K. pawed through my closet, Mom tried to wheedle more information from me. "You said you were going to Jenna's? Will Bree be there?"

I paused for a moment. Both Mary K. and Mom had mentioned Bree today. I wasn't really surprised; she had been a virtual fixture at our house for years—but talking about her was painful. "I don't think so," I finally said. "It's just going to be our regular group, getting together. You know, I've never been to Jenna's house before." A lame attempt to change the subject, I knew. Mary K. threw a pair of skinny jeans at me, and I obediently shimmied into them.

"We never see Bree anymore," Mom commented as Mary K. disappeared into her room.

I nodded, aware of Mom's eyes on me.

"Did you guys have a fight?" Mom asked straight out.

Mary K. returned, holding an embroidered cotton sweater.

"Kind of," I said with a sigh. I really didn't want to get into this, not now. I pulled off my sweatshirt and tugged on the sweater. It fit smoothly, to my surprise. I'm taller and thinner than Mary K., but she inherited my mom's curvy chest. My adoptive mom, that is. I wondered fleetingly if Maeve Riordan had been built like me.

"Did you fight over Wicca?" Mom pried with the subtlety of an ax. "Does Bree not like Wicca?"

"No," I said, pulling my hair out of the sweater and examining my new look. It was a big improvement, which lifted my mood a little. "Bree does Wicca, too." I sighed again, finally giving in to Mom's interrogation. "Actually, we fought over Cal. She wanted to go out with him, but he wanted to go out with me. Now she pretty much hates me."

Mom was quiet for a moment. Mary K. stared at the floor.

"That's too bad," Mom said after a moment. "It's sad when friends fight over a boy." She laughed gently, reassuringly. "Usually the boys aren't worth it."

I nodded. A lump had formed in my throat. I didn't want to talk about Bree anymore; it hurt too much. I checked the clock. "I wish it didn't have to be like this. Anyway, I'm late; I better go." My voice was strained. "Thanks, Mary K." I kissed the air beside Mom's cheek—then I was down the stairs and out the door, pulling on my coat and shivering in the cold.

In a few moments, though, the sadness over Bree began to melt away. I felt a tingle of anticipation. It was circle night.

Jenna lived not far from me in a small, Victorian-style house. It was charmingly run-down, with an overgrown yard. The paint was peeling, and one shutter was missing a hinge.

As soon as I walked up the steps to the porch, a cat greeted me. It meowed and rubbed its head against my legs.

"What are you doing out here?" I whispered as I rang the doorbell.

Jenna opened the door right away, her cheeks flushed, blond hair pulled back, a big smile on her face.

"Hi, Morgan!" she said, then looked down at the cat squeezing its way inside. "Hugo, I told you it was freezing out there! I called you! You ignored me. Now your paws are cold."

I laughed and glanced around to see who was here. No Cal, not yet. Of course, I knew that already; I hadn't seen his car outside, hadn't felt his presence. Robbie was examining Jenna's stereo system, which had a real turntable. A stack of old vinyl records was piled haphazardly next to the fireplace.

"Hey," he said.

"Hi," I answered. I was amazed that this was Jenna's home. Jenna was by far one of the most popular girls in school and thoroughly up-to-date, like Mary K.—but her house looked like a throwback to the 1970s. The furniture was comfortably shabby, with plants hung in front of every window, some needing water. There seemed to be dust and cat hair everywhere. And dog hair, I amended, seeing two basset hounds snoring on a dog bed in a corner of the dining room. No wonder Jenna has asthma, I found myself thinking. She'd have to live in a plastic bubble in this house to breathe clean air.

"Want some cider?" Jenna asked, handing me a cup. It was warm and smelled deliciously spicy. I took a sip as the doorbell rang again.

"Hey!" It was Sharon Goodfine. She shrugged off her thick black leather coat and hung it on the stairs' newel post. "Hugo! Don't even think about it!" she cried as the cat reached up to pat her coat with his fat white paws. Obviously she had been here before.

Ethan Sharp came right after Sharon, looking under-dressed in a thin fatigue jacket.

Sharon handed him a cup of cider. "Apparently you lack the gene that allows you to dress for the weather," she teased.

He grinned at her, looking vaguely stoned, even though I knew he didn't smoke pot anymore. She smiled back. I tried not to roll my eyes. When would they realize that they liked each other? Right now they sort of sniped at each other childishly.

Cal arrived next, and my heart lifted as he walked through the door. I was still upset about what had happened with Hunter at Practical Magick; Cal and I had hardly said two words to each other on the way home. But seeing him now made me feel much better, and when he met my eyes, I could tell he had missed me in the hours we had been apart.

"Morgan, can I talk to you for a second?" he asked, hesitating near the door. He didn't have to add "alone." I could see it in his face.

I nodded, surprised, and stepped toward him.

"What's up?" I asked.

Turning his back on the living room, he pulled a small stone from his pocket. It was smooth, round, and gray—about the size of a Ping-Pong ball. Inscribed on it in black ink was a rune. I had been reading about runes, so I recognized it instantly: it was Peorth, the rune for hidden things revealed.

"I found this stuck into the suspension of my car," Cal whispered.

My head jerked up in alarm. "Did Hunter . . . ?" I didn't finish.

Cal nodded.

"What does it mean?" I asked.

"It means that he's using dirty tricks to spy on us," he muttered, shoving the stone back into his pocket. "It's nothing to worry about, though. If anything, it proves that he doesn't have much power."

"But—"

"Don't worry," Cal said. He flashed me a reassuring smile. "You know, I don't even know why I bothered showing this to you. It's not a big deal. Really."

I watched him as he headed to the living room to say hi to the others. He wasn't being completely honest with me; I could feel that even without using my heightened witch senses. Hunter's little trick did concern him, at least to some degree.

What is Hunter up to? I wondered again. What does he want with us?

It was already nine o'clock, when we usually got started. We drank cider. Robbie played music. I tried to forget about the stone. Looking at the pets soothed me: the dogs snored and twitched in their sleep, and the cats rubbed our legs in quiet demands for attention. I realized that the only one of us missing was Jenna's boyfriend, Matt. Jenna kept glancing at the tall grandfather clock in the foyer. As the minutes went by, she seemed increasingly ill at ease.

Her parents wandered in, met us, totally unconcerned with the fact that we were here to perform a Wiccan circle. It must be nice not to worry about making your parents mad, I thought. They headed upstairs to watch TV and told us to have a good time.

"Well, I'll get started with the circles," Cal said finally, opening his bag and settling down on the floor. "We'll give Matt ten more minutes."

"It's not like him to be late," Jenna murmured. "I called his cell phone, but it went straight to voice mail."

I suddenly remembered seeing Matt's car, parked next to Raven's. Was that only this morning? It had been a long day. I stifled a yawn as I sat on the worn green couch in the living room, watching Cal work.

"What are you doing?" I asked. Usually he drew a simple, perfect circle in salt. When we stepped in, he closed it and purified it with earth, air, fire, and water. But tonight's circle was different.

"This is more complicated," Cal explained.

Slowly the others drifted over to watch him. He was drawing circles within circles, leaving an opening in each one. There were three geometrically perfect circles now, the largest one taking up every inch of available space in Jenna's living room.

At the four compass points of the circles Cal drew a rune in chalk and also in the air: Mann, the rune for community and interdependence; Daeg, symbolizing dawn, awakening, clarity; Ur, for strength; Tyr, for victory in battle. Cal named them as he drew them but didn't offer any explanation. Before we could ask, the front door blew open and Matt breezed in, looking uncharacteristically disheveled and scattered.

"Hi, everyone. Sorry I'm late. Car trouble." He kept his head down, not meeting anyone's eye. Jenna looked at him, first in concern, then in confusion as he threw off his coat and came to watch Cal. For a moment Jenna hesitated. Then she walked up to him and took his hand. He gave her a brief smile but ignored her otherwise.

"Okay, everyone, step inside, and I'll close the circles," Cal instructed.

We did. I stood between Matt and Sharon. I tried never to stand next to Cal at a circle—I knew from experience that it would be too much to handle or control. Sharon and Matt were safe.

"Tonight we're working on personal goals," Cal continued, standing up. He handed Ethan a small bowl of salt and told him to purify the circle. Next he asked Jenna to light the incense, symbolizing air, and Sharon to touch each of our foreheads with a drop of water from its matching bowl. There was a fire in the living-room fireplace—and we used it for fire, naturally. My tiredness started to fade as I glanced around at everyone united for the same purpose. This circle felt special somehow, more important, more focused.

"During our breathing exercises," Cal said, "I want you each to concentrate on your own personal goals. Think about what you want out of Wicca and what you can offer to Wicca. Try to make it as simple and pure as possible. Stuff like 'I want a new car' isn't it."

We laughed.

"It's more like, I want to be more patient, or I want to be more honest, or I want to be braver. Think about what that means to you and how Wicca can help you achieve it. Any questions?"

I shook my head. There were so many things about myself I wanted to improve. I pictured myself as a smiling, confident person—open and honest and giving: a poster girl for Wicca. Feeling no anger, no envy, no greed. I sighed. Yeah, right. Accomplishing all that was a pretty ambitious project. Maybe too ambitious.

"Everyone take hands, and let's begin our breathing exercises," said Cal.

I reached for my neighbors. Matt's hand was still cool from being outside. Sharon's bracelets jingled against my wrist. I began to breathe slowly and deeply, trying to let all the day's negativity and tensions drain from my body, trying to draw in all the positive energies I could. I consciously relaxed every muscle, starting at the top of my head and working my way down. Within a few minutes I felt calm and focused, in a meditative state where I was only semiaware of my surroundings. This was good.

"Now think about your goals." Cal's voice seemed to float from everywhere at once. Unbidden, we began to move in a circle, first slowly, then more quickly and smoothly. My eyes opened, and I saw Jenna's living room as a series of dark smudges, a wild blur as we spun around and around. The fireplace marked our turns, and I looked into the fire, feeling its warmth and light and power.

"I want to be more open," I heard Sharon murmur, as if on a breeze.

"I want to be happy," said Ethan.

There was a moment of silence while I thought about what I wanted, and then Jenna said, "I want to be more lovable."

I felt Matt's hand clench mine for an instant, and then he said, "I want to be more honest." The words sounded reluctant and pained.

"I want to be strong," Cal whispered.

"I want to be a good person," said Robbie—and I thought, But you are.

I was last. I could feel the seconds ticking by. I still didn't know what I needed to work on the most. Yet words seemed to explode from my mouth, as if by their own accord. They hung on the air like smoke from a bog fire.

"I want to realize my power."

As soon as I said it, a current ran through the circle, like a wind whipping a rope. It was electric: it charged me, so that I felt I could fly or dance above the earth.

A chant came to my lips, one I didn't remember ever hearing or reading. I had no idea what it meant, but I let it flow from me, as my wish had flowed from me.

> *An di allaigh an di aigh*
> *An di allaigh an di ne ullah*
> *An di ullah be nith rah*
> *Cair di na ulla nith rah*
> *Cair feal ti theo nith rah*
> *An di allaigh an di aigh.*

I chanted it by myself, very softly at first—then more loudly, hearing my voice weaving a beautiful pattern in the air. The words sounded Gaelic and ancient. Someone was speaking through me. I lost myself, but I wasn't frightened. I was exhilarated. I threw my arms up in the air and swirled in circles within our circle. Together the coven spun in orbit; they were planets around a shining star—and the shining star was me. Silver rain was sprinkling down on my head, making me a goddess. My hair came undone from its tidy braid and whirled in a stream, catching the firelight. I was all-powerful, all-knowing, all-seeing—a goddess indeed. It came to me that the words must have been a spell, an ancient spell, one that called power.

It had called power to me tonight.

"Let's take it down."

The voice belonged to Cal. Again his words seemed to come from everywhere and nowhere at once. In answer to his bidding I slowed my whirling and let myself come to a wavering stop. I was as old as time itself; I was every woman who had ever danced for magick under the moon, every goddess who had celebrated life and death and the joy and sorrow in between.

Hunter Niall's face suddenly flashed into my mind, his superior, contemptuous smirk. Look at me, Hunter! I wanted to shout. Look at my power! I am a match for you or any witch!

Then, all at once, with no warning, I felt frightened, no longer in control. Without Cal telling me, I immediately lay face down on Jenna's wooden floor—with my hands flat by my shoulders to ground my energy. The wood was warm and smooth beneath my cheek, and energy flowed over and around me like water.

Slowly, very slowly, my breathing returned to normal. The fear fluttered, weakening. I became aware that someone was taking my right hand.

I blinked and glanced up. It was Jenna.

"Please," she said, placing my hand on her breastbone. I knew that she wanted me to help her. A week ago I had sent energy into her and eased her asthma. But I didn't think I had the power left now to do anything. Still, I closed my eyes and concentrated on light . . . white, healing light. I gathered it within me and sent it coursing down my arm, through my hand, into Jenna's constricted lungs. She breathed deeply, exclaiming slightly at the warmth.

"Thank you," she murmured.

I was lying on my side now. Suddenly I noticed that everyone was staring at me. Once again I was the center of attention. Self-consciously I pulled my hand away, wondering why a minute ago it was so natural to dance alone in front of everyone while now I felt embarrassed and shy. Why couldn't I hold on to those wonderful feelings of strength?

Matt put his hands on Jenna's shoulders, the most attention he'd shown her since he'd arrived. He was panting slightly from the effort of the dance.

"Did Morgan help your breathing?" he asked.

Jenna nodded, a blissful smile on her lips.

Cal crouched by my side, his hand on my hip.

"Everything all right?" he asked. He sounded excited, breathless.

"Uh . . . yeah," I murmured.

"Where did the chant come from?" he asked, brushing my hair off my shoulder. "What did it do?"

"I don't know where it came from, but it seemed to call power to me," I said.

"It was so beautiful," said Jenna.

"Pretty witchy," said Sharon.

"It was really cool," said Ethan.

I looked at Robbie, and he gazed calmly back at me, warm satisfaction on his face. I smiled at him. At that moment I was perfectly content—but the mood was abruptly broken when I felt nails on the back of my legs.

"Ow!" I muttered.

Half sitting up, I looked over to see the fuzzy, triangular head of a tiny gray kitten.

It mewed in greeting, and I laughed.

Jenna grinned. "Oh, sorry. One of our cats had kittens two months ago. We're trying to get rid of them. Anyone want a cat?" she joked.

I picked him up. He looked back at me intently, a world of feline wisdom in his baby blue eyes. He was solid gray, shorthaired, with a fat baby's belly and a short spiky tail that stuck straight up like an exclamation mark. He mewed in my face again and reached out a paw to pat my cheek.

"Hello," I said, remembering Maeve's kitten from her Book of Shadows. His name had been Dagda. I gazed at Jenna's cat in wonder, suddenly knowing that he was meant for me, that this was a perfect way to end the evening.

"Hi," I said softly. "Your name is Dagda, and you're going to come home and live with me. All right?"

He mewed once more, and I fell in love.

6.
Communion

Imbolc, 1993

    A Seeker is here. He came two days ago and took a room above the pub on Goose Lane. He talked with Uncle Beck a good while yesterday. Uncle Beck says he'll talk with everyone and that we all have to be honest. But I don't like the man. His skin is white and he doesn't smile, and when he looks at me, his eyes are like two black holes. He makes me feel cold as frost.

    —Giomanach

"A rat!" Mary K. screeched the next morning, right in my face. Not the best way to wake up. "Oh God, Morgan, there's a rat! Don't move!"

Of course by now I was stirring in my bed, and little Dagda was, too. He huddled next to me, small ears flat, body hunkered down. But he summoned enough courage to give Mary K. a good hiss. I wrapped my hand around him protectively.

Mom and Dad ran into my room, wide-eyed.

"It isn't a rat," I croaked, clearing sleep out of my throat.

"It isn't?" Dad asked.

I sat up. "It's a kitten," I said, stating the obvious. "Jenna's cat had kittens, and they were trying to get rid of them, so I took one. Can I keep him? I'll pay for his food and litter and everything," I added.

Dagda rose up on his little legs and eyed my family curiously. Then, as if to prove how cute he really was, he opened his mouth and mewed. They all melted at once. I hid a smile.

Mary K. sat on my bed and gently extended her hand. Dagda cautiously made his way across my comforter and licked her finger. Mary K. giggled.

"He's very sweet," said my mom. "How old is he?"

"Eight weeks," I said. "Old enough to leave his mom. So—is it okay?"

Mom and Dad exchanged a glance.

"Morgan, cats cost more than just food and litter," my dad said. "They need shots, checkups. . . ."

"He'll need to be neutered," my mom added.

I grinned. "Fortunately, we have a vet in the family," I said, referring to my aunt Eileen's girlfriend. "Besides, I have money saved from working last summer. I can pay for all that."

Mom and Dad both shrugged, then smiled.

"I guess it's okay, then," said Mom. "Maybe after church we can go to the store and get the stuff he needs."

"He's hungry," Mary K. announced, holding him to her chest. She immediately hopped up and dashed from the room, cradling him like a baby. "There's chicken left over from last night. I'll get him some."

"Don't give him milk," I called after her. "It'll upset his tummy. . . ."

I leaned back against my pillow, happy. Dagda was an official member of our family.

It was the second-to-last Sunday before Thanksgiving, so our church was decorated with dried leaves, pyracantha branches with bright red berries, pinecones, and rust-colored mums in pots. The atmosphere was beautiful, warm, and inviting. I decided it would be nice to find natural decorations like that for our own house at Thanksgiving.

In some way, I guess because I still wasn't sure about how coming to church fit in with Wicca, I felt strangely detached from everything going on around me. I stood when I was supposed to and knelt at the right time; I even followed along in the prayers and sang the hymns. But I did it without being a part of the congregation. My thoughts roamed freely, without restraint.

A thin, wintry sunlight had broken through the clouds. Yesterday's snow had mostly melted, and the church's stained-glass windows glowed with fiery reds, deep blues, pure greens, and crystalline yellows. There was a faint aroma of incense, and as I sank deeper within myself, I felt the weight of the people all around me. Their thoughts began to intrude, their hearts beating incessantly. I took a deep breath and shut my eyes, closing myself off to them.

Only when I had walled them out of my senses did I open my eyes again. I felt peaceful and full of gladness. The music was lovely, the ecclesiastical words moving. It all seemed timeless and traditional. It wasn't the bark and earth and salt of Wicca, nor was it the grounding of energy and the working of spells. But it was beautiful, in its own way.

I rose automatically when it was time to take communion. I followed my parents and sister up to the railing in front of the altar. The tall altar candles burned brightly, reflecting off the brass fixtures and dark polished wood. I knelt on the flat needle-work pillow that had been embroidered by the women's guild. My mom had made one of these pillows a couple of years ago.

My hands clasped, I waited as Father Hotchkiss said the wine blessing for every person in the row. I felt at peace. Already I was looking forward to going home to see Dagda, read Maeve's Book of Shadows, and do some more rune research. Last night when Cal had drawn runes in the air around our circle, it seemed to focus our energy in a whole new way. I liked runes and wanted to find out more about them.

Next to me Mary K. took a sip of wine. I caught a whiff of the fruity scent. A moment later it was my turn. Father Hotchkiss stood in front of me, wiping the large silver chalice with a linen cloth.

"This is the blood of Christ our Lord," he murmured. "Drink this in his name, that you may be saved."

I tilted my head forward to sip.

With an unexpected stumble Father Hotchkiss lurched toward me. The chalice slipped from his hands. It dropped to the white marble floor with a metallic clang, and Father Hotchkiss gripped the wooden rail that separated us.

I put my hand on his, searching his face. "Are you okay, Father?" I asked.

He nodded. "I'm sorry, my dear. I slipped. Did I splash you?"

"No, no." I looked down, and sure enough, my dress was wine free. Deacon Carlson was hurrying to get another blessed chalice, and Father Hotchkiss stepped away to help him.

Mary K. was waiting for me, looking uncertain. I stayed kneeling, watching the dark red wine flow across the white marble floor. The contrast of color was mesmerizing.

"What happened?" Mary K. whispered. "Are you okay?"

That was when the thought came to me: What if I was the one who had made Father Hotchkiss stumble? I almost gasped, with my hand over my mouth. What if, in the middle of all my Wicca thoughts, a force had decreed that my taking communion was not a good idea? Quickly I stood, my eyes large. Mary K. headed back to our pew and our parents, and I followed her.

No, I thought. It was just a coincidence. It didn't mean anything.

But inside me a witchy voice said sweetly: There are no coincidences. And everything means something.

So what did it mean, exactly? That I should stop taking communion? That I should stop coming to church altogether? I glanced at my mother, who smiled at me with no awareness of the confusion that was raging inside me. I was thankful for that.

I couldn't imagine cutting church out of my life completely. Catholicism was part of the glue that held our family together; it was a part of me. But maybe I should hold off on taking communion for a while, at least until I figured out what it all meant. I could still come to church. I could still participate. Couldn't I?

I sighed as I sat back down beside Mary K. She looked at me but didn't say anything.

With every door that Wicca opened, I thought, another door seemed to shut. Somehow I had to find balance.

After lunch at the Widow's Diner we stopped at the grocery store. I bought a litter box and a scoop, a box of cat litter, and a bag of kitten food. Mom and Dad pitched in for a couple of cat toys, and Mary K. bought some kitty treats.

I was really touched, and I hugged them all, right in the pet aisle.

Of course, when we got home, we found that Dagda had peed on my down comforter. He had also eaten part of Mom's maidenhair fern and barfed it up on the carpet. Then he had apparently worked himself into a frenzy sharpening his tiny but amazingly effective claws on the armrest of my dad's favorite chair.

Now he was asleep on a pillow, curled up like a fuzzy little snail.

"God, he's so *cute,*" I said, shaking my head.

7.
Symbols

I had to draw a spell of protection tonight. I invoked the Goddess and drew the runes at the four points of the compass: Ur, Sigel, Eolh, and Tyr. I took iron nails and buried them at the four corners, wearing a gold ring. And from now on, I will carry a piece of malachite for protection.

A Seeker is here.

But I am not afraid. The first blow has already been struck, and the Seeker is weakened by it. And as the Seeker weakens, my love grows stronger and stronger.

—Sgàth

On Monday, Mary K. and I were late for school. I had stayed up late reading Maeve's BOS, and Mary K. had stayed up late having a heartfelt, tortured talk with Bakker—and so we both overslept. We signed ourselves in at the office and got our tardy slips: the New York Public School System's version of the Scarlet Letter.

The halls were empty as we split up for our lockers and headed toward our respective homerooms. My mind swam with what I had been reading. Maeve had loved the herbal side of Wicca. Her BOS was filled with several long passages about magickal uses for plants—and how they're affected by time of year, amount of recent rainfall, position of stars, and phases of the moon. I wondered if I was a descendant of the Brightendale clan, the clan that farmed the earth for healing powers.

In homeroom I slithered into my desk chair. Out of habit I glanced at Bree, but she ignored me, and I felt irritated that it still caused me grief. Forget her, I thought. I'd once read somewhere that it takes about half as long to recover from a deep relationship as the relationship lasted. So in Bree's case, I would still be upset about her a good six years from now. Great.

I thought about Dagda and how Bree would adore him: she'd loved her cat Smokey and had been devastated when he died, two days after her fourteenth birthday. I'd helped her bury him in her backyard.

"Hey. Slept late?" my friend Tamara Pritchett called softly from the next desk. It seemed as if I barely saw her anymore, now that Wicca was taking up so much of my time.

I nodded and started organizing my books and notebooks for my morning classes.

"Well, you missed the big news," Tamara went on. I looked up. "Ben and Janice are officially going out. Boyfriend and girlfriend."

"Really? Oh, cool," I said. I glanced across the room at the lovebirds in question. They were sitting next to each other, talking quietly, smiling at each other. I felt happy for them. But I also felt removed—they, too, were friends I'd hardly seen in recent weeks.

My senses prickled, and I glanced across to see Bree's dark eyes on me. I was startled by their intense expression, and then we both blinked and it was gone. She turned away, and I was unsure if I had imagined it or not. I felt unsettled. Cal had said there was no dark side to Wicca. But aren't two sides of a circle opposite each other? And if one side was good, what was the other? I had disliked Sky as soon as I had met her. What was Bree doing with her?

The bell rang for first period. I felt sour, as if I shouldn't be there—and thought enviously of Dagda at home, wreaking feline havoc.

During American lit it started to drizzle outside: a depressing, steady stream that was trying hard to turn into sleet but not quite making it. My eyelids felt heavy. I hadn't even had time for a Diet Coke yet. I pictured my bed at home and for just a moment considered getting Cal, skipping out, and going home to be alone with him. We could lie in my bed, reading Maeve's BOS and talking about magick. . . .

Major temptation. By lunchtime I was really torn, even though I never skipped school. Only the knowledge that my mom sometimes popped home in the middle of the day prevented me from bringing up the idea to Cal when I saw him.

"You bought lunch?" he asked, eyeing my tray as I slid it onto our lunch table. He met my eyes. As clear as the rainfall, I heard the words *I missed you this morning* inside my head.

I smiled and nodded, sitting down across from him, next to Sharon. "I overslept, so I didn't have time to make anything at home."

"Hey, Morgan," Jenna said, brushing her wheat-colored hair over her shoulder. "You know what I've been thinking about? Those words you said the other night. They were so amazing. I still can't get them out of my mind."

I shrugged. "Yeah, it's funny. I don't know where they came from," I said, popping the top off my soda. "I haven't had time to research it, either. At the time I thought it felt like a spell, calling power to me. But I don't know. The words sounded really old."

Sharon smiled tentatively. "It was kind of creepy, to tell you the truth," she murmured. She opened her container of soup and took out a crusty roll. "I mean, it was beautiful, but it's weird to have words you don't even know coming out of your mouth."

I looked up at Cal. "Did you recognize them?"

He shook his head. "Uh-uh. But later I thought about it, and I felt like I had heard them before. I wish I had taped our circle. I could play it for Mom and see if she knew what it was."

"Cool, you're speaking in tongues," Ethan joked. "Like that girl in *The Exorcist.*"

I pursed my lips. "Great," I said, and Robbie laughed.

Cal shot me an amused glance. "Want some?" he asked, handing me a slice of his apple.

Without thinking, I took a bite. It was astonishingly

delicious. I looked at it: it was just an apple slice. But it was tart and sweet, bursting with juice.

"This is a *great* apple," I said, amazed. "It's perfect. It's the *über*-apple."

"Apples are very symbolic," said Cal. "Especially of the Goddess. Look." He took his pocketknife and cut his apple again—but across the middle instead of top to bottom. He held up a piece. "A pentacle," he said pointing to the pattern made from the seeds. It was a five-pointed star within the circle of the apple's skin.

"Whoa," I said.

"Awesome," said Matt. Jenna glanced at him, but he didn't meet her eye.

"Everything means something," said Cal lightly, taking a bite of the apple. I looked up at him sharply, reminded of what had happened yesterday in church.

Across the lunchroom I saw Bree sitting with Raven, Lin Green, Chip Newton, and Beth Nielson. I wondered if Bree was enjoying hanging out with her new crowd . . . people she had once referred to as stoners, wastoids. Her old crowd—Nell Norton, Alessandra Spotford, Justin Bartlett, and Suzanne Herbert—were sitting at a table near the windows. They probably thought Bree was crazy.

"I wonder how their coven's circle went on Saturday," I mumbled, half to myself. "Bree's and Raven's. Robbie, do you know? Did you talk to Bree?"

Robbie shrugged and finished his piece of pizza.

"It went really well," said Matt absently. Then he blinked and frowned a tiny bit, as if he hadn't expected to say anything.

Jenna looked at him. "How do you know?" she asked.

Matt's face turned slightly pink. He shrugged, his attention on his lunch. "Uh, I talked to Raven during English," he said finally. "She said it was cool."

Jenna regarded Matt steadily. She started to gather up her tray. Once again I remembered seeing Matt's car and Raven's car on the side of the road. As I wondered what it could mean, I heard Mary K.'s laughter, a few tables away. She was sitting next to Bakker with her friend Jaycee, Jaycee's older sister, Brenda, and a bunch of their friends. Mary K. and Bakker were looking into each other's eyes. I shook my head. He had won her over. But he'd better watch his step.

"What are you doing this afternoon?" Cal asked in the parking lot after school. The rain had all but stopped, and an icy wind was blowing.

I glanced at my watch. "Besides waiting for my sister? Nothing. I have to get dinner together."

Robbie snaked his way through a few cars, heading toward us. "Hey, what's going on with Matt?" he called. "He's acting all squirrelly."

"Yeah, I thought so, too, " I said. "Almost like he wants to break up with Jenna but doesn't want to at the same time. If that makes any sense."

Cal smiled. "I don't know them as well as you guys do," he said, putting his arm around me. "Is Matt acting that different?"

Robbie nodded. "Yeah. Not that we're bosom buddies or anything, but he seems kind of off to me. Usually he's really straightforward. He's always just right there." He gestured with his hands.

"I know," I agreed. "Now he seems to have something else going on." I wanted to mention the Matt-Raven car thing but thought it would be too gossipy. I wasn't even sure if it meant anything. I suddenly wished Bree and I were still close. She would have appreciated the significance.

"Morgan!" called Jaycee. "Mary K. asked me to tell you that she was catching a ride with Bakker." Jaycee waved and trotted off, her blond ponytail bouncing.

"Damn!" I said, disengaging myself from Cal. "I have to get home."

"What's the matter? Do you want me to come with you?" Cal asked.

"I would love it," I said gratefully. It would be nice to have an ally in case Bakker needed to be kicked out of the house again.

"See you, Robbie," I called, hurrying off to my car. Damnation, Mary K., I thought. How stupid can you be?

8.
Muirn Beatha Dàn

Ostara, 1993

Aunt Shelagh told me she saw someone under a braigh before, when she was a girl, visiting her granny in Scotland. A local witch had been selling potions and charms and spells to cause harm. When Aunt Shelagh was there one summer, the Seeker came

Shelagh says she woke in the night to screams and howls. The whole village turned out to see the Seeker take away the herbwife. In the moonlight, Shelagh saw the glint of the silver braigh around the herbwife's wrists, saw how the flesh was burned. The Seeker took her away, and no one saw her again, though they whispered she was living on the streets in Edinburgh.

Shelagh doesn't think the woman was ever able to do magick again, good or bad, so I don't know how long she would have wanted to live like that. But Shelagh also said that one sight of that herbwife under the braigh was enough to make her promise to never ever misuse her power. It was a terrible thing, she said. Terrible to see. She told me this story last month, when the Seeker was here. But he took no one away with him, and our coven is placid once more.

I am glad he's gone.

—Giomanach

I drove home as quickly as I could, considering that the streets were basically one big ice slick. The temperature kept dropping, and the air was miserable with the kind of bone-drenching chill that Widow's Vale seems to specialize in.

"I thought Mary K. broke up with Bakker after what happened," said Cal.

"She did," I grumbled. "But he's been begging her to take him back, it was all a mistake, he's so sorry, it'll never happen again, blah blah blah." Anger made my voice shrill.

My tires skidded a bit as I turned into our driveway. Bakker's car was parked out front. I slammed the car door and crunched up our walk—only to find Mary K. and Bakker huddled together on the front steps, shaking and practically blue with cold.

"What are you doing?" I exclaimed, relief washing over me.

"I wanted to wait for you," Mary K. muttered, and I silently applauded her good sense.

"Come on, then," I said, pushing open the front door. "But you guys stay downstairs."

"Okay," Bakker mumbled, sounding half frozen. "As long as it's warm."

Cal started making hot cider for us all while I stayed outside and salted the front walk and the driveway so my parents wouldn't have a hard time when they got home. It was nice to get back inside, and I cranked up the thermostat, then headed to the kitchen. It was my night to make dinner. I washed four potatoes, stabbed them with a fork, and put them in the oven to bake.

"Hey, Morgan, can we just run upstairs for a sec?" Mary K. asked tentatively, clutching her mug. Since I'd met Cal, I'd begun drinking a ton of cider. It was incredibly warming on cold days. "All my CDs are in my room."

I shook my head. "Tough," I said shortly. I blew on my cider to cool it. "You guys stay downstairs, or Mom will have my ass."

Mary K. sighed. Then she and Bakker brought their stuff to the dining-room table and self-righteously started to do their homework. Or at least they pretended to do their homework.

As soon as my sister was gone, I waved my left hand in a circle, deosil, over my cider, and whispered, "Cool the fire." The next time I took a sip, it was just right, and I beamed. I loved being a witch!

Cal grinned and said, "Now what? Do we have to stay downstairs, too?"

I let my mind wander tantalizingly over the possibilities if I didn't practice what I preached but finally sighed and said, "I guess so. Mom would go insane if I was upstairs with an evil boy while she wasn't home. I mean, you've probably got only one thing on your mind and all."

"Yeah." Cal raised his eyebrows and laughed. "But it's one good thing, let me tell you."

Dagda padded into the kitchen and mewed.

"Hey, little guy," I crooned. I put my cider down on the counter and scooped him up. He began to purr hard, his small body trembling.

"He gets to go upstairs," Cal pointed out, "and he's a boy."

I grinned. "They don't care if *he* sleeps with me," I said.

Cal let out a good-natured groan as I carried Dagda into the family room and sat on the couch. Cal sat next to me, and I felt the warmth of his leg against mine. I smiled at him, but his face turned solemn. He stroked my hair and traced the line of my chin with his fingers.

"What's wrong?" I asked.

"You surprise me all the time," he said out of the blue.

"How?" I was stroking Dagda's soft triangular head, and he was purring and kneading my knees.

"You're just—different than I thought you would be," he said. He put his arm across the back of the couch and leaned toward me as if trying to memorize my face, my eyes. He seemed so serious.

I didn't know what to think. "What did you expect me to be like?" I asked. I could smell the clean laundry scent of his shirt. In my mind I pictured us stretched on the couch, kissing. We could do it. I knew that Mary K. and Bakker were in the other room, that they wouldn't bother us. But suddenly I felt insecure, remembering again that I was almost seventeen and he was the first boy who'd ever asked me out, ever kissed me. "Boring?" I asked. "Kind of vanilla?"

His golden eyes crinkled at the edges, and he tapped my

lips gently with one finger. "No, of course not," he said. "But you're so strong. So interesting." His forehead creased momentarily, as if he regretted what he'd said. "I mean, right when I met you, I thought you were interesting and good-looking and the rest of it, and I could tell right away you had a gift for the craft. I wanted to get close to you. But you've turned out to be so much more than that. The more I know you, the more you feel equal to me, like a real partner. Like I said, my muìrn beatha dàn. It's kind of a huge idea." He shook his head. "I've never felt this way before."

I didn't know what to say. I looked at his face, still amazed by how beautiful I found it, still awed by the feelings he awoke in me. "Kiss me," I heard myself breathe. He leaned closer and pressed his lips to mine.

After several moments Dagda shifted impatiently in my lap. Cal laughed and shook his head, then drew away from me as if deciding to exercise better judgment. He reached down and pulled a pad of paper and pen out of his book bag and handed them to me.

"Let's see you write your runes," he said.

I nodded. It wasn't kissing, but it was magick—a close second. I began to draw, from memory, the twenty-four runes. There were others, I knew, that dated from later times, but these twenty-four were considered the basics.

"Feoh," I said softly, drawing a vertical line, then two lines that slanted up and to the right from it. "For wealth."

"What else is it for?" asked Cal.

"Prosperity, increase, success." I thought. "Things turning out well. And this is Eolh, for protection," I said, drawing the shape that was like an upside-down Mercedes logo.

"It's very positive. This is Geofu, which stands for gift or partnership. Generosity. Strengthening friendships or other relationships. The joining of the God and Goddess."

"Very good," said Cal, nodding.

I kept on until I had drawn all of them, as well as a blank space for the Wyrd rune, the undrawn one, the symbol that signified something you ought not know: dangerous or hurtful knowledge, a path you should not take. In rune sets it was represented by a blank tile.

"That's great, Morgan," Cal whispered. "Now close your eyes and think about these runes. Let your fingers drift over the page, and stop when you feel you should stop. Then look at what rune you've stopped on."

I loved this kind of thing. I closed my eyes and let my fingers skim the paper. At first I felt nothing, but then I focused my concentration, trying to shut out everything except what I was doing. I tuned out the murmur of Mary K. and Bakker's voices from the dining room, the ticking of the cuckoo clock my dad had built from a kit, the gentle hum of the furnace kicking in.

I don't know how long it was before I realized that my fingertips were picking up impressions. I felt feathery softness, a cool stone, a warm prickle . . . were these the images of the runes? I let myself go deeper into the magick, losing myself in its power. *There.* Yes, there was one place where I felt a stronger sensation. Each time my fingers passed it, it called to me. I let my hand drift downward to rest on the paper and opened my eyes.

My fingers were on the rune called Yr. The symbol for death.

I frowned. "What does this mean?"

"Hmmm," said Cal, looking at the paper, his hand on his chin. "Well, you know, Yr can be interpreted many different ways. It doesn't mean that you or someone you know is going to die. It may simply mean the ending of something and the beginning of something new. Some sort of big change, not necessarily a bad one."

The double-fishhook symbol of Yr shone darkly on the white paper. Death. The importance of endings. It seemed like an omen. A scary omen. A jet of adrenaline surged through me, making my heart thud.

All at once I heard the back door open.

"Hello?" came my mom's voice. "Morgan? Mary K.?" There were footsteps in the dining room. My concentration evaporated.

"Hey, sweetie," she said to Mary K. She paused. "Hello, Bakker. Mary K., is your sister here?" I knew she meant: For God's sake, you're not here alone with a boy, are you?

"I'm in here," I said, tucking the paper of runes into my pocket. Cal and I walked out of the family room. Mom's eyes flashed over us, and I could immediately see the thoughts going through her mind. *My girls, alone in the house with two boys.* But we were all downstairs, we had our clothes on, and Mary K. and Bakker were at least sitting at the dining-room table. I could see Mom consciously decide not to worry about it.

"Are you baking potatoes?" she asked, sniffing.

"Yep," I said.

"Do you think we could mash them instead?" she asked. "I've asked Eileen and Paula to dinner." She held up a folder. "I've got some hot prospects for them housewise."

"Cool," I said. "Yeah, we can mash them, and then

there'll be enough. I'm making hamburgers, too, but there's plenty."

"Great. Thanks, sweetie." Mom headed upstairs to change out of her work clothes.

"I'd better go," I heard Bakker say reluctantly. Good, I thought.

"Me too," said Cal. "Bakker, do you think you could give me a lift back to school? That's where my car is."

"No prob," said Bakker.

I walked Cal outside, and we hugged on the front porch. He kissed my neck and whispered, "I'll call you later. Don't get all bent about the Yr thing. It was just an exercise."

"Okay," I whispered back, although I still wasn't sure how I felt. "Thanks for coming over."

Aunt Eileen arrived first. "Hi!" she said, coming in and taking off her coat. "Paula called and said she was running a few minutes late—something about a Chihuahua having a difficult labor."

I smiled awkwardly in the front hall. I hadn't seen her since I had demanded to know why she hadn't told me I was adopted, at a family dinner two weeks ago. I felt a little embarrassed to see her again, but I was sure Mom had been talking to her, keeping her up-to-date with everything.

"Hi, Aunt Eileen," I said. "I . . . uh, I'm sorry about making a scene last time. You know."

As if to answer, she swept me up in a tight hug. "It's okay, sweetie," she whispered. "I understand. I don't blame you a bit."

We pulled back and smiled at each other for a moment. I

knew Aunt Eileen would make everything okay again. Then she glanced down and gasped, pointing urgently to my dad's La-Z-Boy, where a small gray butt and tail were sticking out from under the skirt.

I laughed and scooped Dagda out.

"This is Dagda," I said, rubbing him behind his ears. "He's my new cat."

"Oh, my goodness," said Eileen, stroking his head. "I'm sorry. I thought he was a rat."

"You should know better," I joked, putting him back on the chair. "You *date* a vet."

Aunt Eileen laughed, too. "I know, I know."

Soon afterward Paula arrived, her sandy hair windblown, her nose pink with cold.

"Hey," I greeted her. "Is the Chihuahua okay?"

"Fine, and the proud mom of two pups," she said, giving me a hug. "Oh! What a beautiful kitten!" she said, spotting Dagda on Dad's chair.

I beamed. *Finally!* Somebody who knew what a treasure Dagda was. I'd always liked Aunt Eileen's new girlfriend, but now it struck me that they were a perfect match. Maybe Paula was even Eileen's muìrn beatha dàn.

Thinking about it brought a smile to my face. Everybody deserved somebody. Not everyone was as lucky as I was, of course. I had Cal.

9.
Trust

The magick is working, as I knew it would. The Seeker no longer frightens me as much. I believe I am the stronger of us two, especially with the power of the others behind me.

Soon I will join with my love. I do understand the urgency, though I wish they would trust me to do it my way, at my pace. More and more, lately, I want to do this for my own sake. But the timing must be perfect. I dare not frighten her; there is too much at stake.

I have been reading the ancient texts, the ones about love and union. I have even copied down my favorite passage from <u>Song of the Goddess</u>: "To give pleasure to yourself and to others, that is my ritual. To love yourself and others, that is my ritual. Celebrate your body and spirit with joy and passion, and as you do so, you worship me."

    —Sgàth

"I hope you know that you can't trust Bakker," I said to Mary K. the next morning. I tried not to sound snotty, but it came out that way anyhow.

Mary K. didn't answer. She just looked out her car window. Frost covered everything in lacy, powdered-sugar patterns.

I drove slowly, trying to avoid the hard patches of black ice where the newly plowed roads had puddled and frozen. My breath came out in a mist inside Das Boot.

"I know he's really sorry," I went on, in spite of my sister's stiff face. "And I believe he really cares about you. But I just don't trust his temper."

"Then don't go out with him," Mary K. muttered.

Alarm bells went off in my brain. I was criticizing him, and she was defending him. I was doing what I feared: pushing them closer together. I took a deep breath. Goddess, guide me, I said silently.

"You know," I said finally, several blocks from school. "I bet you're right. I bet it was just a onetime thing. But you guys have talked, right?" I didn't wait for an answer. "And he *is* really sorry. I guess it will never happen again."

Mary K. looked over at me suspiciously, but I kept my face neutral and my eyes on the road.

"He *is* sorry," my sister said. "He feels terrible about it. He never meant to hurt me. And now he knows he has to listen to me."

I nodded. "I know he cares about you."

"He does," said Mary K.

She looked transparently self-assured. Inside, my heart throbbed. I hated this. Maybe everything I had just said was true. But I couldn't help fearing that Bakker would try again to force Mary K. into doing something she didn't want to do.

If he did, I would make him pay.

I got to school early enough to see Cal before the bell rang. He was waiting for me by the east entrance, where our coven gathered during better weather.

"Hey," he said, kissing me. "Come on, we found a new place to hang out. It's warmer."

Inside, we passed the steps leading to the second floor and turned a corner. There another set of steps led down to the building's cellar. No one was supposed to go down here except the janitors. But Robbie, Ethan, Sharon, and Jenna were sitting on the steps, talking and laughing.

"Morganita," Robbie said, using a nickname he had given me in fifth grade. I hadn't heard it for years, and I smiled.

"We were just talking about your birthday," said Jenna.

"Oh!" I said in surprise. "How did you know about it?"

"I told them," said Robbie, drinking from a carton of orange juice. "Let the cat out of the bag."

"Speaking of cats, how's Dagda?" Jenna asked.

Matt's long, black-jean-clad legs obscured my view for a moment as he came and sat on the step above Jenna. She gave him a faint smile but didn't respond when he rubbed her shoulder.

"He's great," I said enthusiastically. "And he's growing really fast!"

"So your birthday's this weekend?" Sharon asked.

"Sunday," I said.

"Let's have a special birthday circle on Saturday, then," said Jenna. "With a cake and all."

Sharon nodded. "That sounds good," she said.

"Um, I can't make it Saturday night," Matt mumbled. He ran a hand through his thick black hair, lowering his eyes.

We all looked at him.

"I've got family stuff to do," he added, but the words were empty.

He is the worst liar in the world, I thought, seeing Jenna staring at him.

"Actually, could we do the birthday thing some other time?" Robbie asked. "I'm thinking I wouldn't mind skipping Saturday night's circle, too."

"Why?" I asked.

"Bree's been after me to come to one of their circles," Robbie admitted. I was surprised by his honesty, not in a bad way—but I felt a renewed rush of anger toward Bree. Robbie shrugged. "I don't want to join their coven, but it wouldn't be a bad idea for me to go to one of their circles, see what they're doing, scope it out."

"Like spying?" Jenna asked, but her tone was soft.

Robbie shrugged again, his hair falling onto his forehead. "I'm curious," he said. "I care about Bree. I want to know what she's doing."

I swallowed and forced myself to nod. "I think that's a good idea," I said. I couldn't believe that Bree would try to poach from our coven, but on the other hand, I was glad that Robbie wanted to keep an eye on her to make sure she wasn't doing anything crazy.

"I don't know," said Cal, shifting and stretching his legs out two steps below. "A lot of what's important in Wicca is continuity. It's about getting in touch with the day-in, day-out stuff, the cycle of the year, the turn of the wheel. Meeting every Saturday, being committed to that, is part of it. It's not something you should skip whenever you want to."

Matt stared at the floor. But Robbie looked back at Cal calmly.

"I hear what you're saying," Robbie said. "And I agree with it. But I'm not doing this just for me, and it isn't just because I feel lazy or I want to watch the game. I need to know what's going on with Bree and her coven, and this is how I can find out."

I was impressed with the air of quiet confidence Robbie projected. His acne and glasses had been gone ever since I'd put a healing spell on him. But something seemed to have healed inside him as well, something that didn't have anything to do with my magick. After years of being a somewhat awkward geek, he was growing into himself and finding new sources of strength. It was great to see.

Cal was silent for a while, and he and Robbie regarded each other. A month ago I would never have thought that Robbie would be a match for someone as strong as Cal, but now they didn't seem that different in a way.

Finally Cal nodded and let out a breath. "Yeah, okay. It won't kill us to take a break. Since there's only seven of us, if two of us can't make it, the circle will be kind of unbalanced. So let's all just take Saturday night off, and we'll meet again the week after."

"And *that's* when we'll have Morgan's birthday cake," said Robbie, smiling at me.

Sharon cleared her throat. "Um . . . I guess this isn't a good time to mention that next Saturday I'll be in Philadelphia for Thanksgiving."

Cal laughed. "Well, we'll just do the best we can. It's always tough around the holidays, with everyone having family stuff. How about you, Matt? Can you make it the following week?"

Matt nodded automatically, and I wondered if he'd even heard what Cal had said. The bell rang, and we all stood. Jenna put her hand in Matt's, staring into his face. He looked drawn, tense. I wished I knew what was going on.

As I headed to homeroom, the halls rapidly filled with streams of students, and Cal tugged on my coat sleeve.

"This Saturday we can have a birthday circle, just us two," he whispered into my ear. "This could be a good thing."

I shivered with delight and looked up at him. "That would be great."

He nodded. "Good. I'll plan something special."

In homeroom I noticed that Tamara was absent. Janice told me she had a cold. Everyone seemed to have colds lately.

Bree was absent, too, or so I thought before I saw her stop outside the class door. She was dressed all in black and was wearing vivid dark makeup, like Raven. It obscured her naturally beautiful face and made her seem anonymous somehow, as if she were wearing a mask. It filled me with an uneasy feeling. She stood outside, talking in a low voice to Chip Newton, and then they both came in and sat down.

I swallowed. Chip was cute and seemed like a pretty nice guy. He was brilliant in math, too—way better than me, and I'm pretty good. But Chip was also our school's biggest dealer. Last year Anita Fleming had gone to the hospital after overdosing on Seconal that she had gotten from him. Which made me wonder just how nice he really was.

What are you doing with him, Bree? I asked silently. And what's your coven up to?

Later that morning, while I was in the first-floor girls' bathroom, I heard Bree's voice, then Raven's, outside my stall. Quickly I pulled up my feet and braced them against my door so nobody could tell that the stall was occupied. I just didn't feel up to facing the two of them, having them sneer at me, right now.

"Where are we meeting?" Raven asked. I heard Bree rustling in her purse, and in my mind's eye I could picture her fishing out lipstick.

"At Sky's place," answered Bree. My interest perked up. They must be talking about their new coven.

"It's so cool that they have their own place," said Raven. "I mean, they're barely older than we are."

I breathed silently, intent on their voices.

"Yeah," said Bree. "What do you think of him?"

"He's hot," said Raven, and they laughed. "But it's Sky who knocks me out. She knows everything, she's so cool, and she's got awesome powers. I want to be just like that." I heard more rustling, then one of them turned on the water for a moment.

"Yeah," said Bree. "Did you think it was weird, what she was talking about on Saturday?"

"Not really," Raven said. "I mean, everything has a light side and a dark side, right? We have to be aware of it."

"Yeah." Bree sounded thoughtful, and I wondered what

the hell Sky had been talking about. Was Sky pulling them toward dark magick? Or was she just showing them part of Wicca's big circle, like Cal had said? It didn't seem—

"You got the hair, didn't you?" Raven asked.

"Yeah," Bree answered. Now she sounded almost . . . depressed. I couldn't follow the conversation at all. What hair?

"What's wrong?" Raven demanded. "Sky promised no one would get hurt."

"I know," Bree mumbled. "It's just, you know, I found the hair in this old comb—"

"Morgan will be *fine*," Raven interrupted.

"That's not what I was talking about," Bree snapped. "I'm not worried about her."

My eyes flew open wide. I bit my lip to keep from gasping as everything fell into place. Bree was talking about *my* hair. I couldn't believe it. She was turning over a strand of my hair to a strange girl—a witch—behind my back.

There could be only one reason: Sky wanted my hair to put a spell on me. So why had Bree gone through with it? Did she really believe that Sky didn't intend to harm me? Why *else* would she want the hair?

Or did Bree want me to be harmed? I wondered miserably.

"We need more people," Raven stated in the silence.

"Yeah. Well, Robbie's going to come. And we might get Matt, too."

Raven laughed. "Yeah. Matt. Oh God, I can't wait to see Thalia's face when Robbie walks in. She'll probably jump him right there."

I frowned. Who was Thalia?

"Really?" Bree asked.

"She just broke up with her boyfriend, and she's trolling," Raven said. "And Robbie's really hot now. I wouldn't mind hooking up with him myself."

"Oh, Jesus, Raven," said Bree.

Raven laughed again, and I heard a purse being zipped shut. "Just kidding. Maybe."

Silence. I held my breath.

"What?" said Raven as the door opened.

"Thalia's not his type," Bree said as sounds from the outside hall filtered into the room.

"If she wants him, she's his type."

The bathroom door closed again, and air exploded from my lungs. I got to my feet, shaking with reaction. So Sky was manipulating Bree. They were definitely trying to get Matt and Robbie to leave our coven and join theirs. And Sky had her own place, where they were meeting. Did she live with Hunter? Was that who Raven thought was hot? Maybe. Then again, Raven thought most breathing males were hot. And they knew somebody named Thalia who was going to jump Robbie. For some reason, Bree had sounded less than thrilled by that idea—as she had about turning over my hair to Sky. But her reluctant tone was small consolation.

I hated everything that I had just overheard. But more than that, now I was afraid.

10.
Magesight

Things are starting to heat up, and not just because of the Seeker. We have been having many visitors. Many I've never seen before—others I remember from all over the world: Manhattan, New Orleans, California, England, Austria. They come and go at all hours, and I keep coming across little knots of people huddled in this room or that, heads together, discussing, arguing, making magick. I don't know all of what's going on, but it's clear that our discovery here has set many things in motion. And the circles! We are having them almost every day now. They are powerful and exhilarating, but they leave me tired the next day.

—Sgàth

After school I wanted to talk to Cal about what I had overheard, but he was already gone. He'd left a note on my locker, saying he'd had to go home and meet with one of his mother's friends. So for now I was on my own with my questions about Bree and Raven and their coven. Even Mary K. wasn't coming home with me. As I was getting into Das Boot, she ran up to tell me she was going to Jaycee's house.

I nodded and waved, but I couldn't bring myself to smile. I didn't want to be alone. Too much was troubling me.

Luckily Robbie sauntered over to the car. "What's up?" he asked.

I shielded my eyes from the pale November sunlight and looked at him. I wasn't sure whether or not I should tell him what was on my mind. I decided not to. It was too complicated. Instead I merely said, "I was thinking about going to Butler's Ferry park and gathering some pinecones and stuff for Thanksgiving."

Robbie thought for a moment. "Sounds cool," he said. "Do you want some company?"

"Absolutely," I said, unlocking the passenger-side door.

"So, do you have family coming in for Thanksgiving?" he asked.

I nodded as I pulled out of the driveway, picking up speed on the open road. "My mom's parents, my dad's brother and his family. And then everyone who lives in town. We're having dinner at our house this year."

"Yeah. We're going to my aunt and uncle's," Robbie said without enthusiasm. "They'll be yelling at the football game on TV, the food will suck, and then my dad and Uncle Stan will both get plastered and end up taking a swing at each other."

"Well, they do that every year," I said, trying to inject some humor in a not-so-humorous situation. I'd heard about this from Robbie before, and it always made me sad. "So it's almost, like, traditional."

He laughed as I turned onto Miltown Pike. "I guess you're right. Tradition is a good thing. That's something I've learned from Wicca."

Soon I was pulling into the empty Butler's Ferry parking lot and cutting the engine. I retrieved a basket with a handle from the trunk. Despite the cold the sun was trying hard to shine, and it glittered off the leaves crumpling under our feet. The trees were bare and sculptural, the sky wide and a pale, bleached blue. The peace of the place began to steal over me, calm me down. I felt suddenly happy to be here with Robbie, whom I'd known for so long.

"So are there any herbs or anything around this time of year?" Robbie asked.

"Not a lot." I shook my head. "I checked my field guide, and we might see some stuff, but I'm not counting on it. I'll have to wait till spring. I'll be able to collect plants in the wild then and also start my own garden."

"It's weird that you're so powerful in Wicca, isn't it?" Robbie asked suddenly. But it wasn't a mean or probing question.

For a moment my breath stopped, and I thought about telling him everything that I had learned about myself in the past month. Robbie didn't even know I was adopted. But I just couldn't tell him. He'd been my friend for so long; he'd listened to me complain about my family, and he'd always pictured me as one of them: a Rowlands. I wasn't up to dealing with the emotional backlash of spilling the whole story *again*. I knew I would tell him sometime. We were too close for me to have this huge a secret. But not today.

"Yeah, I guess," I said finally, keeping my voice light. "I mean, it's amazing. But who would've thunk it?"

We grinned at each other, and I found a pretty pine branch on the ground that had three perfect little cones on it. I also stopped to pick up a few oak twigs that had clumps of dried leaves on them. I love the shape of oak leaves.

"It's really changed everything," Robbie murmured, picking up a likely branch and handing it to me. I accepted it, and it joined the others in my basket. "Magick, I mean. It's completely changed your life. And you completely changed my life." He gestured to his face, his skin. I felt a brief stab of guilt. All I'd meant to do was try a tiny healing spell to clear up the acne that had scarred his face since seventh grade. But the spell had continued to perfect him. He didn't even need glasses anymore. Every once in a while the whole thing spooked me all over again.

"I guess it has," I agreed quietly. I leaned down to study a small, fuzzy vine climbing a tree. It had a few withering, bright red leaves on it.

"Don't touch that," said Robbie. "It's poison ivy."

I laughed, startled. "Great witch I'll make." We smiled at each other in the deepening twilight, the silence of the woods all around us. "I'm glad there's no one else besides you here," I added. "I know you won't think I'm a complete idiot."

Robbie nodded, but his smile faded. He bit his lip.

"What's wrong?" I asked.

"Do you miss Bree?" Robbie asked out of the blue.

I stared at him, unable to answer. I didn't know what to say. But I knew what he was feeling: here we were, having fun as we'd done so many times in the past—only Bree wasn't here to share the fun with us.

"I'm in love with her, you know," he said.

My jaw dropped open. Wow. I'd had some suspicions about his feelings for her, but I'd never imagined they were so strong. Nor did I ever expect him just to put them out there like that.

"Uh, I guess I sort of figured you liked her," I admitted awkwardly.

"No, it's more than that," Robbie said. He looked away and tossed an acorn off into the bushes. "I'm in love with her. Crazy about her. I always have been, for years." He smiled and shook his head. I stole a quick glance at him, and any regrets I had about healing his face vanished. I'd done a good thing. He was handsome, secure; his jaw was smooth and strong. He looked like a model.

"Years?" I asked. "I didn't know that."

He shrugged. "I didn't want you to. I didn't want anyone to know, especially Bree. She's always gone for the dumb, good-looking types. I've been watching her be with one jerk after another, knowing I never had a chance." His smile faltered. "You know she told me about when she lost her virginity?" He turned to me, his blue-gray eyes glinting in fading sunlight. He shook his head again, remembered pain on his face. "She was all happy and excited. The best thing since mocha latte, she said. And with that loser, Akers Rowley."

I frowned. "I know. Akers was an ass. I'm sorry, Robbie."

"Anyway," Robbie went on, his smile returning, "have you looked at me lately?"

"You're gorgeous," I said instantly. "You're one of the best-looking guys in school."

Robbie laughed, sounding for a moment like his old awkward and self-conscious self. "Thanks. But, um, do you think maybe I have a shot now?"

I bit my lip. Now, there was a loaded question. I mean, totally apart from the fact that Bree might be getting involved in dark magick, it was so odd to think of her and Robbie as a couple. They'd been friends for so long. "I don't know," I said after a minute. "I don't know how Bree sees you. Yeah, you're good-looking, but she might think of you more as a brother. You sort of know her too well to put a spell on her. Or vice versa." I grinned. "Nonmagickally speaking."

Robbie nodded, kicking his boots through the leaves. His forehead was creased.

We walked deeper into the woods. We had only about twenty minutes before it would be dark; soon we'd have to turn around.

I threaded my arm through his. "There's something else," I said. I felt I needed to warn him, to put him on his guard. "Today I heard Bree and Raven talking about their new coven."

I told him the gist of what I had overheard in the bathroom, leaving out the part about my hair. That was something I had to deal with myself, with Cal's help. Besides, I wasn't even sure what the strand of hair meant. I didn't want Robbie to feel any more torn between me and Bree than he already did. But at the same time I didn't want her to use him.

"Yeah, I know they want to recruit new members," he acknowledged. "Don't worry, I'm not interested. But I am going to go and see what's going on."

Here with Robbie, in the woods, my thoughts about Bree and Raven and their coven began to seem a little paranoid. So what if they wanted to have their own coven? That wasn't necessarily bad or evil. It was just different, another spoke on the wheel. And the hair . . . well, who knew what that was about? Sky had told them no one would get hurt, and they seemed to trust her. But most of all, I just couldn't see Bree as evil. She'd been my best friend for so long. I'd know if there was something really warped about her. Wouldn't I?

I shook my head. It was too hard to think about. Then I remembered something else that I'd overheard. "Do you know someone named Thalia?" I asked Robbie. "She's in Bree and Raven's coven."

He thought and shook his head. "Maybe she's a friend of Raven's."

"Well, my informants tell me she may make a move on you," I said. I'd meant it as a joke, but the words came out sounding dark for some reason.

Robbie brightened. "Excellent," he said.

I laughed and poked him in the side as we walked along the park path.

"Just watch out, okay?" I said after a while. "I mean, with Bree. She tends to like guys she can control, you know? Guys she can intimidate, who'll do whatever she wants. They don't last long."

Robbie was silent. I didn't have to tell him all this; he knew it already.

"If Bree could care about you in the way you deserve," I went on, "it would be great. But I don't want you to get hurt."

"I know," he said.

I squeezed his arm a little tighter. "Good luck," I whispered.

He smiled. "Thanks."

For just a minute I wondered about love spells, love potions, and whether they ever worked. But Robbie broke into my thoughts, as if reading my mind.

"Don't you dare interfere with this magickwise," he warned me.

I feigned a hurt expression. "Of course not! I think I've done enough already. . . ."

Robbie laughed.

Suddenly I stopped short and pulled on his arm. He glanced at me quizzically. I raised a finger to my lips. My eyes scanned the woods. I saw nothing. But my senses . . . there was someone here. Two someones. I could feel them. But where were they?

After another moment I heard muffled voices.

Without thinking, we both dropped down behind a large boulder by the side of the path.

"You're wrong—I don't want to," someone was saying.

My eyes met Robbie's and widened. It was Matt's voice.

"Don't be silly, Matt. Of course you want to. I've seen how you look at me."

Of course. It was Raven—and she was trying to seduce Matt. It made perfect sense. I remembered how she'd said his name in the bathroom, how she'd laughed.

Without speaking, Robbie and I peeked over the top of the boulder. About twenty feet from us Matt and Raven were standing face-to-face. The sun was dropping rapidly now, the air turning colder. Raven moved closer to him, a smile playing on her lips. He frowned and stepped back but bumped into a tree. She moved in and pressed herself against him from chest to knee.

"Stop," he said weakly.

Raven wrapped her hands around his neck and stood on tiptoes to kiss him.

"Stop," he repeated, but the word had about as much force as Dagda's meowing. He resisted for a grand total of five seconds, then his arms went around her, his head slanted, and he pulled her to him tightly. Next to me Robbie dropped his head into his hands. I gaped at them for a little while longer—but when Matt unzipped Raven's coat and unbuttoned his own, I couldn't stand it anymore. Robbie and I leaned with our backs against the boulder. I heard a small moan and cringed. This was too embarrassing.

Robbie leaned closer and breathed into my ear. "Do you think they're gonna do it?"

I grimaced. "I don't know. I mean, it's freezing out here."

Robbie let out a muffled snort. Then I started giggling. For several seconds we crouched low and chewed on our coat sleeves, choking with laughter. Finally Robbie had to look. He eased his head around the boulder into the woods. "I can't see much," he complained in a whisper. "It's too dark in the trees."

I didn't want to look myself, though I knew I could have seen everything clearly. My night vision had improved dramatically; I could see easily in the darkness now, as if everything was illuminated slightly from within. I'd even found a reference to that power in a witchcraft book: it was called magesight.

"I don't think they're doing it," Robbie whispered, squinting.

"It looks more like heavy making out. They're still standing."

"Thank the God and Goddess," I muttered.

I heard Matt's voice: "We have to stop. Jenna . . ."

"Forget Jenna," Raven murmured beguilingly. "I want you. You want me. You want to be with me, in our coven."

"No, I—"

"Matt, please. Quit fighting it. Just give in and you can have me. Don't you want me?"

He gave a strangled moan. Now it was my turn to cover my face with my hands. I wished I could stop Matt somehow. Of course, I was also thinking he was a total jerk.

"You *do* want me," Raven coaxed. "And I can give you what you want. What Jenna can't do for you. We can be together, and we can make magick, strong magick, in my coven. You don't want to be with Cal anymore. He's a control freak."

I stiffened and frowned. What the hell did she know about Cal?

"In our circle you can do what you want," Raven continued. "No one will hold you back. And you can be with me. Come on. . . ."

Raven's voice had never sounded so sweet and pleading. A shiver went down my spine that had nothing to do with the cold.

"I can't," Matt answered. His voice was tortured. We could hear their footsteps in the fallen leaves. Luckily they were moving away from us.

"My ass is frozen," Robbie whispered. "Let's get out of here."

I nodded and stood. As quietly and swiftly as we could, we hurried back down the path to Das Boot. Without a word I dumped my basket of decorations in the trunk, and we hopped into the car.

"That was weird," Robbie finally muttered, blowing on his hands.

I nodded and jammed my key into the ignition. "Now we know why he's being strange," I said as I cranked the heater. I grinned. "Raven's totally hot for him."

Robbie didn't smile, and my own smile faded quickly. This wasn't funny. Not in the least. People could get hurt. I pulled Das Boot out of the parking lot and onto the road.

"Do we do anything about it?" I asked. "I feel sorry for Jenna. I even sort of feel sorry for Matt. He's just . . . lost."

"Do you think Raven's working a spell on him?" Robbie asked.

I shook my head. "I don't know. I mean, she isn't a blood witch. It would be different if she had been doing Wicca for years and was more in touch with her natural power. I don't really see it. Unless Sky did something to her that made her able to do something to Matt . . ."

"I guess it's enough to use the spell of sex," said Robbie dryly.

I thought back to how Cal had made me feel, to the few times we had been close and making out—how swept away I had been, how almost everything faded away except him.

"Yeah," I muttered. "So what do we do?"

Robbie thought. "I don't know. I can't see confronting either of them about it. In a way, it isn't our business. What if you told Cal? I mean, it's his coven they're trying to split up. Tell him the stuff you overheard at school."

I sighed, then nodded. "Good idea." I bit my lip. "Robbie—thanks for telling me about how you feel about Bree. I'm glad you trusted me. And I won't tell anyone else. But just . . . be careful, okay?"

Robbie nodded. "I will."

11.
The Council

Samhain Eve, 1995.

My cousins are having a costume party on Samhain, after we do the service. I'm going as the Dagda, the Lord of the Heavens, and high king of the Tuatha De Danaan. I'm going to carry my panpipes for music, my wand for magick, and a book for knowledge. It'll be fun. I've been helping Linden and Alwyn with their costumes, and we've laughed a lot.

I saw my cousin Athar kissing Dare MacGregor behind a tree in the garden. I teased her and she put a binding spell on me and I can't even tattle. I've been looking for the antispell for two days.

Next year I'll be making my initiation, and then I'll be a witch. The waiting will be over. I've been studying long enough. Seems like all I've done is study, since I came here. Aunt Shelagh is not so bad, but Uncle Beck is a slave driver. And it's even harder because Linden and Alwyn are always hanging onto me, running after me, asking questions that I have a hard time answering. My mind is always spinning, spinning—like a wheel.

But what I think of most, still, is Mum and Dad. Where are they, and why did they leave us? I have lost so much—my family, my trust. The anger never dies. In a year, I'll learn the truth. Another reason I can't wait for my initiation.

—Giomanach

"I tried to call you last night," I told Cal, pressing my face against his warm coat. The chill air swept across the parking lot, rustling my hair. I shivered. His hand stroked my back.

The morning bell was about to ring, but I didn't feel like sharing Cal with the others right now. I didn't want to see Matt and Jenna, either. My nerves felt jangled—both from the bizarre events of yesterday and from the awful dreams I'd had last night. Dreams of a dark cloud, like a swarm of black insects, that was chasing me, suffocating me. I'd woken up sweating and shaking, and I hadn't fallen back asleep until dawn. And then Mary K. had woken me up barely an hour later.

"I know," Cal whispered, kissing my temple. "I got your message. But I got back too late to call you. Was it important? I figured if you really needed me, you'd send a witch message."

I wrapped my arms tightly around his waist. "It was just . . . a bunch of weird stuff I wanted to talk to you about."

"Like what?"

For an instant I hesitated. We were leaning against his car, across the street from school, and it felt almost private. Not private enough, though. I glanced around to make sure we were alone. "Well, first I overheard Raven and Bree talking in the girls' bathroom. They were talking about trying to get Matt and Robbie to join their coven. I think they want to split us up. Sky is their leader. They meet at her place, wherever that is. Then Bree said something about how she found some of my hair to give to Sky. I was kind of . . . freaked out," I confessed. "I mean, what does Sky want with my hair?"

Cal's golden eyes narrowed. "I don't know—but I plan to find out." He took a deep breath. "Don't worry. No one is going to interfere with you, Morgan. Not while I'm around."

I was amazed at how comforting I found his words. I felt like a weight had been lifted from my shoulders.

"There's more," I told him. "Later, Robbie and I were in the park, and we saw Raven and Matt actually making out."

Cal's eyebrows rose. "Oh," he said.

"Yeah. It was totally by accident. Robbie and I were walking around, gathering pinecones and stuff, and we saw Raven practically roping and tying Matt, trying to get him to break up with Jenna and join their coven."

"Man," Cal said, frowning. "So you were right—Matt is acting squirrelly, and now we know why."

"Yep."

A thoughtful expression crossed Cal's face. "And Sky's definitely the leader of their coven? That makes sense since you saw her meeting with Bree and Raven."

I nodded. But I couldn't help wondering . . . if Sky was their leader, then what had she been doing at Cal's house with Selene, participating in one of Selene's circles the night I'd found Maeve's Book of Shadows? Was she some kind of Wiccan spy? Did Selene know Sky had her own coven? Did it even matter? My head was spinning. There was so much I didn't understand, so much I had to find out.

At that moment we heard the distant ringing of the homeroom bell, and we both groaned. Going to classes was not my number-one priority today.

With our arms around each other, we started slogging across the dead brown grass toward school. "Let me think about this," said Cal. "I need to talk to Sky, obviously. But I also need to figure out if I should talk to Raven, or Matt, or both."

I nodded. Part of me felt like a tattler. But mostly I was just relieved that Cal knew. I was thinking about talking to Matt myself, but I felt certain that Cal would take care of anything bigger, like with Sky. As we climbed the stone steps of the back entrance, I squeezed his hand good-bye. Yes, I would have to talk to Matt. He was a friend and still a part of our circle. I owed it to him.

"Matt?" I called down the hall. "Do you have a minute?"

It was after lunch and almost time to head to class. My lack of sleep was starting to catch up with me. My feet were definitely starting to drag. I would have given anything to just go curl up somewhere and take a nap. But this was the first chance I'd had to talk to Matt, and I wasn't going to let it slip.

"What's up, Morgan?" Matt asked. He stood in front of me, his face shuttered and remote, his hands in his pockets.

I took a deep breath, then decided just to get right into it. "I saw you and Raven yesterday," I stated baldly. "In Butler's Ferry park."

Matt's black eyes went wide, and he stared at me. "Uh . . . what are you talking about?"

"Come on," I said patiently. I pulled him over to one side

of the hallway so we could talk without being overheard by the occasional wandering student. I lowered my voice. "I mean, I *saw* you yesterday, with Raven, in the park. I know she's trying to get you to join her coven. I know you're fooling around with her."

"I'm not fooling around with her!" Matt insisted.

I didn't even answer. I just raised my eyebrows.

His gaze fell to the floor. "I mean, it hasn't gotten that far," he mumbled, finally giving in. "Jesus, I don't know what to do."

I shrugged. "Break up with Jenna if you want to go out with Raven," I said.

"But I don't want to go out with Raven," Matt said. "I don't want to join her coven. The thing is . . . I've always thought she was kind of hot, you know?" He shook his head as if to clear it. "Why am I even telling you this?"

A couple of freshman girls passed us. Though they were only two years younger, they seemed a world apart from me. They *were* a world apart. They belonged to the world of school and homework and boys. Mary K.'s world. Not mine.

"Why does she want you to join their coven?" I asked.

"I guess they need more people," Matt answered. He sounded miserable. "A bunch of people started coming, but they all dropped out or were kicked out. A lot of them didn't take it seriously."

"But why *you?*" I pressed.

He sniffed. "I don't think it's really me. I mean, I'm nobody. I'm just a warm body."

"You're also part of our coven," I muttered. Part of me wanted to console him, but the other part wanted to wring his neck. "So what are you going to do?" I asked. I crossed my arms and tried not to look too judgmental.

"I don't know."

I sighed. "Maybe you should talk to Cal about this," I suggested. "Maybe he could help you clarify your thoughts."

Matt didn't look so sure. "Maybe," he said doubtfully. "I'll think about it." He glanced up at me. "Are you going to tell Jenna?"

"No." I shook my head. "But she's not stupid. She knows something's wrong."

He laughed distantly. "Yeah. We've been going out for four years. We know each other so well. But we're not even eighteen yet." With that, he pushed himself off the wall and headed off to his class—without so much as even a backward glance.

I watched him leave, thinking about what he'd said. Did he mean he had gotten tied up with Jenna too early and wanted to date other people? As I pondered it, a short rhyme popped into my mind. I repeated the words quietly.

"Help him see the way to go
Help him know the truth to show
He is not the hunter here
Nor yet should he be the deer."

I shook my head and headed to my own class. What did it mean? I wondered. Who knew? These things didn't come with instructions and commentary.

That afternoon when Mary K. and I got home from school, there was a gray car parked in front of our house. I didn't think anything of it—people parked in front of our house all the time. It was probably one of my mother's clients. So I just followed my sister up the walkway.

"Morgan!"

I wheeled at that voice. Hunter Niall was getting out of the car.

"Who's the dish?" Mary K. asked, arching an eyebrow.

I glared at her. "Go inside," I commanded, my heart kicking up a beat. "I'll deal with it."

Mary K. grinned at me. "Ooh. I can't wait to hear all about *this*." She pounded up the porch steps, stomped the ice off her Doc Martens, and went inside.

"Hello, Morgan," Hunter said, approaching me. How did he manage to make a simple greeting sound menacing? I wondered. His cold seemed to have gotten worse, too. His nose was red, and his voice was very nasal.

"What do you want?" I asked, swallowing. I remembered my bad dream of last night, my overwhelming feelings of being smothered, the dark cloud that had been chasing me.

He coughed. "I want to talk to you."

"About what?" I slung my backpack up onto the porch, not taking my eyes off him. I watched his hands, his mouth, his eyes, anything that he could use to do magick. My pulse was racing; my throat felt tight. I wished hard that Cal would suddenly drive up out of the blue. I considered sending him a message with my thoughts, a witch message—but then I realized I should just turn around and go in. I could handle myself. I didn't even need to talk to Hunter.

But for some reason I just stood there as he strode toward me, cutting across our lawn, leaving black footprints in the half-melted ice. He was close enough now that I could see that his fair skin was completely unblemished and there were a few freckles across the bridge of his strong nose. His eyes were cold and green.

"Let's talk about *you*, Morgan," he said, and he pushed his leather cap farther back on his head. A few tufts of blond hair poked out beneath it. "You don't know what you're doing with Cal." He made this announcement firmly but casually, as if he were simply telling me it was four o'clock and time for tea.

I shook my head, feeling the anger rise. "You don't even know—"

"It's not your fault," he interrupted. "This is all new to you."

The anger welled in the pit of my stomach, turning to rage. What right did he have to be so condescending to me?

Hunter fastened his eyes on mine. "You can't be expected to know about Cal, and his mother, and who they are," he said. "No one blames you," he added.

"No one blames me for what?" I demanded. "What are you talking about? I don't even *know* you. Where do you get off telling me anything about people I know, people I care about?"

He shrugged. His manner was as cold as the air around us. "You're stumbling into something bigger and darker than you could possibly imagine."

Rage turned to sarcasm. Hunter definitely brought out the worst in me. "Oh," I said, trying to sound bored. "Stop, stop, you're scaring me."

His face tightened, and he stepped toward me. My stomach clenched, and adrenaline pumped through my veins. I resisted the urge to turn and bolt into the house.

"Cal's lied to you," Hunter snarled. "He isn't what or

who you think he is. Neither he nor his mother. I'm here to warn you. Don't be stupid. Look at me!" He gestured at his puffy eyes and red nose. "Do you think this is normal? Because it isn't. They're working magick on me—"

"Oh, are you kidding me?" I interrupted. "Are you actually telling me they're plotting against you? Give me a break!"

Who *was* this guy? Did he really think I would believe that Cal and Selene gave him a cold with dark magick? Or was he simply some paranoid nut? Maybe I should feel sorry for him—but I couldn't. All I felt was fury. I wanted to shove him as hard as I could, knock him down and kick him. I had never been so angry, not at my parents, or Bree, not even at Bakker. I spun to go inside.

Hunter darted forward and caught my arm in a painful grip. Feeling trapped, furious, I drew my fingers together and smacked his hand. A jolt of crackly blue light jumped from my hand and shocked him. He released me at once, looking startled.

"So that's it," he whispered, rubbing his hand. He nodded in astonishment. "That's why he wants you."

"Get the hell away from me!" I shouted. "Or do you want me to really hurt you?"

Hunter sneered. "Trying to show me just what a powerful Woodbane you are?"

Time seemed to freeze.

"That's right," he whispered. "I know your secret. I know you're Woodbane."

"You don't know anything," I managed. The words came out in a misty whisper.

"Maeve Riordan," he said, shrugging. "Belwicket. They were all Woodbane. Don't act like you don't know."

"You're lying," I spat, but I felt an awful sensation

bubbling inside me, like a boiling cauldron. I wondered if I was going to throw up.

A flash of surprise crossed his face, instantly replaced with suspicion. "You can't hide it," he said. Now he sounded more irritated than arrogant. "You can't pretend it away. You're Woodbane, Cal is Woodbane, and the two of you are dancing with fire. But it's going to stop. You have a choice, and he does, too. I'm here to make sure you make the right one."

Move, I told my body, my feet. Get inside. Move, dammit! But I couldn't.

"Who are you?" I asked. "Why are you doing this to me?"

"I'm Hunter," he said with a sudden, wolfish grin that made me draw in my breath. He looked feral and dangerous. "The youngest member of the International Council of Witches."

My breath was now coming in shallow gasps, as if I were facing death itself.

"And I'm Cal's brother," he said.

12.
The Future

I thank the God and Goddess for her. What a revelation she is, continually. When I was assigned to her, I had no idea she would be anything but an exercise in power. She has become so much more than that. She is a wild bird: delicate but possessing fierce strength. To move too soon would be to watch her take flight in fear.

For the first time in my life there is a chink in my armor, and it is my love.

    —Sgàth

I ran up the ice-crusted steps of our house and threw myself through the door. Somehow I knew Hunter wouldn't follow me. The house was wonderfully warm and cozy, and I almost sobbed with relief as I pounded up the stairs and crashed into my bedroom. I had enough presence of mind to lock my door, and when Mary K. knocked a minute later, I called, "I'll be down in a few minutes."

"Okay," she replied. A moment later her feet padded downstairs.

My head was spinning. The first thing I did was run into the bathroom and examine my face in the mirror. It was me, still the same old me, despite the haunted look in my brown eyes and my shock-whitened face. Was Hunter right? Was I Woodbane?

I threw myself onto my bed and pulled Maeve's Book of Shadows out from under my mattress, then started flipping pages. I'd thumbed through the entries before, reading bits here and there, but mostly I'd been plodding through slowly, savoring every word, letting each spell sink in, deepening my knowledge and my only link to the woman who had given birth to me.

Strangely enough, though, it didn't take me long to find what I was looking for. It was from when Maeve was still writing as Bradhadair. She wrote matter-of-factly: "Despite the Woodbane blood in our veins, the Belwicket clan has resolved to do no evil."

With the force of a wave crashing on a beach, Selene's words came back to me: "I know what it contains, and I wasn't sure you were ready to read it."

Selene knew Maeve had been Woodbane. Suddenly my eyes were drawn to a small volume on my desk—the book about Woodbanes that Alyce at Practical Magick had wanted me to read. So . . . Alyce knew, too? Hunter knew? How did everyone know except *me*? Did Cal know? It didn't seem possible.

Hunter was a liar, though. I could feel the fury gathering within me all over again, like storm clouds. Hunter had also said he was Cal's brother. I thought back. I knew that Cal's father had remarried and that Cal had half siblings in England. But Hunter couldn't be one of them—he and Cal seemed practically the same age.

Lies. All lies.

But why was Hunter here? Had he just decided to come to America and mess with my mind? Maybe he *was* Cal's half brother and he was out to get Cal for some reason. And he was attacking me in order to hurt Cal. He was doing a damn good job of it if that was the case.

The whole thing was giving me a horrible headache. I shut the book and pulled Dagda into my arms, listening to his small, sleepy purr. I stayed there until Mary K. called me to tell me dinner was ready.

The meal was practically inedible: a vegetarian casserole that Mary K. had concocted. I wasn't even hungry, anyway. I needed some answers.

Sidestepping a whispered question from Mary K. about Hunter, I told her I'd help her with the dishes later, then asked my parents if I could go to Cal's. Luckily they said yes.

It started to snow again as I pulled away from the house in Das Boot. Of course I was still upset about everything Hunter had said, but I tried not to let it affect my driving. The wipers pushed snow off the windshield in big arcs, and my brights illuminated thousands of flakes swirling down out of the sky. It was beautiful and silent and lonely.

Woodbane. When I got home tonight, I would read the book Alyce had given me. But first I needed to see Cal.

In the long, U-shaped driveway in front of Cal's house, I saw his gold Explorer and another car—a small, green vehicle

I didn't recognize. I plodded through the surface of the snowfall, feeling the ice crunch beneath my clogs. The wide stone steps had been shoveled and salted. I hurried up and rang the doorbell.

What would I say if Selene answered the door? The last time I had seen her, I was in her private library, basically stealing a book from her. On the other hand, the book was rightly mine. And she *had* allowed me to keep it.

Several seconds passed. There was no stirring inside, at least none that I could hear. I started to feel cold. Maybe I should have called first, I thought. I rang the doorbell again, then reached out with my senses to see who was home. But the house was a fortress. I received no answer. And then a thought occurred to me: It was spelled, deliberately shut off from magick.

Snowflakes gathered on my long hair, as if I wore a lace mantle that was slowly melting against my cheeks and eyelids. I rang again, beginning to feel unsure. Maybe they were busy. Maybe they were meeting with someone. Maybe they were having a circle or working magick or throwing a party . . . but at last the tall, heavy wooden door opened.

"Morgan!" Cal said. "I didn't even feel you come up. You look frozen. Come on in." He ushered me into the foyer and brushed his hand down my cold, damp hair. Light footsteps behind him made me pull back, and I looked up to see Sky Eventide.

I blinked, looking at her. Her face was closed, and I wondered what I had interrupted. Had Cal invited her here to ask her about her coven and my hair? I glanced at him for signs of irritation or wariness, but he seemed easy and comfortable.

"I should have called," I said, looking from Cal to Sky. "I didn't mean to interrupt anything."

Tell me what I'm interrupting, I thought as Sky reached for her heavy leather coat. She looked beautiful and exotic. Next to her I felt about as exciting as a brown field mouse. I had a tingle of jealousy. Did Cal find her attractive?

"It's all right," Sky said, zipping her coat. "I was just leaving." Her black eyes searched Cal's and held them. "Remember what I said," she told him, ignoring me. The words seemed to have an element of threat, but Cal laughed.

"You worry too much. Relax," he said cheerfully, and she just looked at him.

I watched as she opened the front door and left, not bothering to say good-bye. There was something strange going on here, and I needed to know what it was.

"What was all that about?" I asked point-blank.

Cal shook his head, still smiling. "I ran into her earlier and told her I wanted to talk to her about what she's up to with her coven. So she came over—but all she wanted was to be Hunter's messenger," he said, tugging on my coat so it came off. He draped it over a high-backed chair and then took my hand, rubbing its coldness away. "Hey, I tried to call you a few minutes ago, but the phone was busy."

"Someone must be on-line," I guessed, frowning. Was he trying to change the subject? "What kind of message did Sky have?"

"She was warning me," he answered simply. Still holding my hand, he led me through a pair of dark wooden doors that opened into a large, formal parlor. A fire was blazing in an enormous stone hearth, and in front of it a deep blue sofa beckoned. Cal sat and pulled me down to sit next to him.

"Warning you?" I pressed.

He sighed. "Hunter's out to get me, basically, and Sky was telling me to be on my guard. That's all."

I frowned into the fire. Usually I felt reassured by the heat and glow of flames—but not now. "Why is Hunter out to get you?"

Cal hesitated. "It's . . . um, kind of personal," he said.

"But why was Sky warning you? Isn't she with him?"

"Sky doesn't know what she wants," Cal answered cryptically. He hadn't shaved in a while, and the shadow of stubble across his face made him look older. Sexier, too. He was quiet for a few moments, and then he edged closer to me, so I felt his warmth from my shoulder to my hip. A memory swept over me: of how it had felt to lie next to him, to kiss him deeply, to have his hands touch me and to touch him back. But I couldn't allow myself to be distracted.

"Who *is* Hunter?" I asked.

Cal made a face. "I don't want to talk about him," he said.

"Well, he came to see me today."

"What?" Shock flared in Cal's golden eyes. I saw something else there, too. Concern, maybe. Concern for *me*.

"What's the International Council of Witches?" I pressed on.

Cal drew away from me, then sighed in resignation. He sat back against the couch and nodded. "You'd better just tell me everything," he said.

"Hunter came to my house and said I was Woodbane," I said. The words flowed from my mouth as if a dam had been broken. "He said *you* were Woodbane and that he was your brother. He said I was stumbling into danger. He said he was on the International Council of Witches."

"I can't believe this." Cal groaned. "I'm sorry. I'll make sure he leaves you alone from now on." He paused, as if collecting his thoughts. "Anyway, the International Council of Witches is just what it sounds like. Witches from all over the world getting together. It's kind of a governing body, though what they govern isn't really clear. They're kind of like village elders, but the village consists of all witches everywhere. I think there's something like sixty-seven countries represented."

"What do they do?"

"In the old days they often settled disputes about land, clan wars, cases of magick being used against others," Cal explained. "Now they mostly try to set guidelines about appropriate use of magick, and they try to consolidate magickal knowledge."

I shook my head, not quite understanding. "And Hunter's part of it?"

Cal shrugged. "He says he is. I think he's lying, but who knows? Maybe the council is really hard up for members." He gave a short laugh. "Mostly he's just a second-rate witch with delusions of grandeur."

"Delusions is right," I murmured, remembering how Hunter had claimed his cold was the result of a spell. That was so obviously ridiculous that maybe I should just forget about everything else he'd said, too. But somehow I couldn't.

Cal glanced at me. "He told you that you were Woodbane?"

"Yes," I said stiffly. "And I went inside and found it in Maeve's BOS. I *am* Woodbane. All of Belwicket was. Did you know?"

Cal didn't answer right away. Instead he seemed to weigh my words. He looked at the fire. "How do you feel about that?" he finally asked.

"Bad," I said honestly. "I would have been really proud to be Rowanwand or even anything else. But to be Woodbane . . . it's like finding out my ancestors are a long line of jailbirds and lowlifes. Worse, really. Much worse."

Cal laughed again. He turned to me. "No, it's not, my love. It's not that bad."

"How can you say that?"

"It's easy," he said with a grin. "Nowadays it isn't a big deal. Like I said, people have sort of a prejudiced view of Woodbanes, but they're ignoring all their good qualities, like strength, and loyalty, and power, and pursuit of knowledge."

I stared at him. "You didn't know I was a Woodbane? I'm sure your mom does."

Cal shook his head. "No, I didn't know. I haven't read Maeve's book, and Mom didn't discuss it with me. Listen, knowing you're Woodbane isn't a bad thing. It's better than not knowing your clan at all. Better than being a mongrel. I've always thought the Woodbanes have gotten a bad rap— you know, revisionist history."

I turned back to the fire. "He said you were Woodbane, too," I whispered.

"We don't know what we are," Cal said quietly. "Mom has done a lot of research, but it isn't clear. But if we were, would it matter to you? Would you not love me?"

"Of course it wouldn't matter," I said. The flames crackled with life before us, and I rested my head on Cal's shoulder. As upset as I had been, I was starting to feel better. I kicked off my shoes and stretched my feet out to the fire. My socks hung loose. The heat felt delicious on my toes, and I sighed. I still had more questions to ask.

"Why did Hunter say he was your brother?"

Cal's eyes darkened. "Because my dad's a high priest and very powerful. Hunter wants to be that way, too. And he *is* the son of the woman my father married after he left my mom. So we're at least stepbrothers."

I swallowed, wincing. "Ouch," I murmured. "I'm sorry."

"Yeah. Me too. I wish I'd never met him."

"How did you meet?" I asked cautiously.

"At a convention, two years ago," Cal answered.

I was startled into laughter. "A witch convention?"

"Uh-huh," said Cal, smiling a little. "I met Hunter, and he informed me we were only six months apart and brothers. Which would mean that my father had deliberately gotten another woman pregnant while my mom was pregnant with *me*. I hated Hunter for that. I still don't want to believe it. So no matter what Hunter says, I say that his father is someone else, not my dad. I can't accept that my father, total jerk that he is, would have done that." He put his arm around me, and I rested my chin on his chest, hearing the steady thumping of his heart, sleepily watching the fire.

"Is that why Hunter is acting this way?"

"Yeah, I think so. Somehow he's all . . . I don't know, bent and twisted. It must have something to do with his childhood. I know I shouldn't hate him—it's not his fault my dad's life is so messy. But he just—got off on telling me that my dad fathered him. Like he enjoyed hurting me."

I gently stroked Cal's wavy hair. "I'm sorry," I said again.

Cal gave a rueful chuckle, and I wanted to comfort him, the way he had comforted me so many times. Gently, I kissed him, trying to give him love he could be sure of. He almost purred with contentment and held me closer.

"Why was Hunter here, in your mother's house, that night when she had the circle?" I asked softly when I stopped for breath.

"He likes to keep in touch with us," Cal said sarcastically. "I don't know why. Sometimes I think he likes Mom and me to just remember he's alive, that he exists. Rubbing our faces in it, I guess."

I shuddered. "Ugh. He's horrible. I don't feel the least bit sorry for him. I just can't stand him—and I hate what he's doing to you. If he keeps on, he'd better watch out."

Cal grinned. "Mmmm, I like it when you talk tough."

"I'm serious," I told him. "I'll zap him with witch fire so hard, he won't know what hit him." I flexed my fingers, surprised at the violence of my own feelings.

Cal's smile broadened, but he said, "Look, let's just change the subject." He kissed me, then pulled away. "I have a question for you. What are you thinking about in terms of college?"

I furrowed my brow, surprised and bemused. "I'm not sure," I said. "For a while I thought I'd apply to MIT or maybe Cal Tech. You know, something for math."

"Brain," Cal teased affectionately.

"Why do you want to know?" I asked. It seemed so oddly normal, coming right after all this talk about a Council of Witches and ancient magickal clans.

"I've been thinking about our future," he said. His tone was very straightforward, relaxed. "I was thinking about going to Europe next year, maybe taking a year off to travel. I was also thinking, maybe I could get us a little place when I come back and we could both go to the same school."

My eyes widened with shock. "You mean . . . *live together?*" I whispered.

"Yes, live together," he said, flashing me a little half grin as if he were talking about doing our homework together or going to see a movie. "I want to be with you." He drew back and looked deeply in my eyes. "No one's ever wanted to protect me before, like you do."

My breath came fast at the thought. Laughing, I grabbed him, knocking him back on the sofa. I meant to kiss him, but we ended up toppling onto the floor with a thud.

"Ow," said Cal, rubbing his head. He smiled at me and I kissed him. But right at that moment I caught a glimpse of an old grandfather clock. My spirits sank. It was getting late. Mom and Dad would start to worry.

"I have to go," I said reluctantly.

"Someday you won't have to," he promised.

Then I was getting into my coat, melting with happiness, and Cal was walking me out. I didn't even feel the cold until I was almost home.

13.
Dark Side

Litha, 1996

Until now my life has been winter. But last night, at my initiation, spring broke through the ice. It was magick. Aunt Shelagh and Uncle Beck led the rite. The coven elders gathered around. I was blindfolded and given wine to drink. I was tested and I answered as best I could. In my blindness I made a circle and drew my runes and cast my spells. The warmth of the summer night fled before the cold draughts of the North Sea, blowing off the coast. Someone held the sharp point of a dagger to my right eye and told me to step forward. I tried to remember if I'd seen any coven members with ruined eyes, and I couldn't, so I stepped smartly forward, and the sharp tip faded away.

I sang my song of initiation alone, in the darkness, with the weight of the magick pressing in on me, and my feet stumbling in the rough heathers of the headland. I sang my song, and the magick came to me and lifted me up, and I felt huge and powerful and bursting with joy and knowledge. Then I was unblindfolded and the initiation was complete. I was a witch and a full-grown man in the eyes of the craft. We drank wine and I hugged everyone. Even Uncle Beck, and he hugged me back and told me he was proud of me. Cousin Athar teased me but I just grinned at her. Later I hunted Molly F. down and gave her a real kiss, and she pushed me away and threatened to tell Aunt Shelagh.

I guess I wasn't as much of a man as I thought.

—Giomanach

On Friday when I woke up, the remnants of disturbing dreams fluttered in my mind like torn banners. I stretched several times, trying to snap myself out of it—and then they faded, and I had no idea what they'd been: there were no lingering images or clear emotions to give me a clue. I just knew they'd been bad.

I had stayed up too late the night before, reading both Maeve's Book of Shadows and the book about Woodbanes that Alyce had given to me. It was still very strange for me, knowing Maeve was my birth mother and now knowing she was also Woodbane. Throughout my entire life I had felt just a bit different from my family, and I had wondered why. The odd thing was, now that I knew my origins, I felt more like a Rowlands and less like an Irish witch.

I could tell it was cold and disgusting outside just from looking out the window. And I was snug in my bed, and I had beside me a small kitten who was completely adorable and sound asleep.

So there was no way I was getting up.

"Morgan, you have to hurry!" Mary K. shouted, sounding frantic. A second later she burst into my room and tugged at my comforter. "We have ten minutes to get to school, and it's snowing and I can't ride my bike. Come on!"

Damn, I thought, giving in. One day I would really have to act on my desire to skip school.

We made it just as the late bell rang, and I skittered into class just as my name was called for roll.

"Here!" I said unnecessarily, panting and sliding into my seat. As Tamara smirked at me, I pulled out my brush and began untangling my hair. Across the room Bree sat talking to Chip Newton. I thought about Sky and Raven and their coven, about Sky telling them about the dark side. I still didn't have a clear idea of what the dark side was except for some vague paragraphs in one of my Wicca books. I would have to do more research. I would have to finish reading the book Alyce had given me about the Woodbanes. Cal had said there was no dark side per se, there was only the circle of Wicca. Maybe I should ask Alyce about it.

I glanced over at Bree, as if looking at her would tell me what she was doing or thinking. I used to be able to look in her eyes and know exactly what was going on with her—and also tell her exactly what was going on with me. Not anymore. We spoke different languages now.

It was an odd day.

At school Matt wouldn't meet my eyes. Jenna seemed nervous. Cal was fine, of course; we both knew we had reached a new level of closeness. We'd made plans for the future. Every time we saw each other, we smiled. He was a ray of light to me. Robbie was his usual comforting self, and it was interesting to see how girls who'd never noticed him before were now going out of their way to talk to him, to walk next to him, to pepper him with questions about home-work and chess problems and what kind of music he liked. Ethan and Sharon were still circling each other flirtatiously.

Yet the whole day I felt on edge somehow. I hadn't got-ten enough sleep, and I had too many questions ricocheting around my brain. I couldn't relax and pay attention in class. In my mind I kept going over what I had read in Maeve's book. Then my thoughts would flash to Hunter's bizarre behavior—and then to lying with Cal in front of the fire at his house, feeling so full of love for him. Why couldn't I focus? I needed to be alone or, better yet, with Cal—to meditate and focus my energy.

After school I waited for Cal by his car. He was talking to Matt, and I wondered what they were saying. Matt looked uncomfortable, but he was nodding. Cal seemed to be mak-ing him feel better. That was good. But I also hoped he was letting Matt know that it was very uncool to mess around with Raven behind Jenna's back.

Finally Cal saw me. He strolled right over and put his arms around me, pinning me to his car. I was aware of Nell Norton walking by, looking envious, and I enjoyed it.

"What are you up to right now?" I asked. "Can you hang out?"

"I wish I could," he said, holding a handful of hair and kissing my forehead. "Mom has some people in from out of town, and she wants me to meet with them. People from her old coven in Manhattan."

"How many covens has she had?" I asked, curious.

"Hmmm, let's see," Cal said, counting under his breath. "Eight, I think. She forms a coven in a new place and makes sure they're really strong, then she trains a new leader, and when they're ready, she moves on." He smiled down at me. "She's like the Johnny Appleseed of Wicca."

I laughed. Cal kissed me again and got into his car, and I headed for Das Boot. A minivan slowed next to me, and the window went down. "Going home with Jaycee!" Mary K. called. She waved, and I waved back. I saw Robbie pull away in his car, and down the block Bree climbed into her BMW and drove off. I wished I knew where she was going but didn't have the emotional or physical energy to follow her.

Instead I headed for Red Kill.

Practical Magick smelled like steam and tea and candles burning. I stepped in and felt myself relax for the first time since I had pried myself out of bed this morning.

For a moment I stood just inside the door, warming up, feeling my chest expand and my fingers thaw. My hair was slightly damp from the snow, and I shook it out so it would dry. David looked up from the checkout counter and regarded me with his full attention. He didn't smile but somehow he conveyed the impression of being glad to see me. Maybe I was finally used to him, because it felt like seeing an old friend. I hadn't felt an immediate connection with him as I had with Alyce, and I wasn't sure why. But maybe I was getting over it.

"Hello, Morgan," he said. "How are you?"

I thought for a moment, then shook my head with a tired smile. "I don't know."

David nodded, then stepped through a curtained door in back of the counter, revealing a small, cluttered room. I saw a tiny, battered table with three chairs, a rusty apartment-size fridge, and a two-burner hot plate. A teakettle was already starting to whistle there. Strange, I thought. Had he somehow known I was coming?

"You look like you could use some tea," he called.

"Tea would be great," I said sincerely, deciding to accept the friendship he seemed to be offering. "Thanks." I stuffed my gloves into my pockets and looked around the store. No one else was here. "Slow day?" I asked.

"We had some people in this morning," David replied from behind the curtain. "But it's been quiet this afternoon. I like it this way."

I wondered if they made any money doing this.

"Um, who owns this store?" I asked.

"My aunt Rose, actually," said David. "But she's very old now, and doesn't come in much anymore. I've been working here for years—on and off since right after college." I heard some clinking of spoons in mugs, and then he ducked back through the curtain, carrying two steaming cups. He handed one to me. I took it gratefully, inhaling its unusual fragrance.

"Thanks. What kind of tea is this?"

David grinned and sipped his own. "You tell me."

I looked at him uncertainly, and he just waited. Was this a test? Feeling self-conscious, I closed my eyes and sniffed deeply. The tea had several scents: they blended together into a sweet whole, and I couldn't identify any of them.

"I don't know," I said.

"You do," David encouraged quietly. "Just listen to it."

Once again I closed my eyes and inhaled, and this time I let go of the knowledge that this was tea in a mug. I focused on the odor, on the qualities carried by the water's steam. Slowly I breathed in and out, stilling my thoughts, relaxing my tension. The more still I became, the more I felt part of the tea. In my mind's eye I saw the gentle steam rising and swaying before me, dissolving in the slightest breath of air.

Speak to me, I thought. Show me your nature.

Then, as I watched inside my mind, the steam coiled and separated into four streams, like a fine thread unraveling. With my next breath I was alone in a meadow. It was sunny and warm, and I reached out to touch a perfect, rounded pink blossom. Its heavy aroma tickled my nose and bathed me in its beauty.

"Rose," I whispered.

David was quiet.

I turned to the next steam thread and followed it, saw it being dug from the ground, black dirt clinging to its rough skin. It was washed and peeled, and when its pink flesh was grated, a sharp tang was released.

"Oh, ginger," I listed, nodding.

The third strand drifted from rows and rows of low-growing, silver-green plants covered with purple flowers. More bees than I had ever seen buzzed over the plants, creating a vibrant, living mantle of insects. Hot sun, black earth, and the incessant drone filled me with a drowsy contentment.

"Lavender."

The last thread was a woodier scent, less familiar and also less pretty. It was a low-growing, crinkle-leafed plant, with slender stalks of miniature flowers. I crushed some of the leaves in my hand and smelled them. It was earthy and different, almost unpleasant. But intertwined with the other three scents, it made a beautifully balanced whole: it added strength to their sweetness and tempered the pungent odor of the ginger.

"I want to say skullcap," I said tentatively. "But I'm not sure what that is."

I opened my eyes to find David watching me.

"Very good," he said with a nod. "Very good indeed. Skullcap is a perennial. Its flowering stems help diminish tension."

By now the tea had cooled a bit, and I took a sip. I didn't notice the actual flavors so much; I was more aware of drinking the different essences, allowing them to warm me and infuse me with their qualities of healing, soothing, and calming. I perched on a stool next to the counter. But then, without warning, all the unsettled aspects of my life crept up and made me feel like I was suffocating again. Matt and Jenna, Sky and Bree and Raven, Hunter, being Woodbane, Mary K. and Bakker . . . it was overwhelming. The only thing that was going right was Cal.

"Sometimes I feel like I don't know anything," I heard myself blurt out. "I just want things to be straightforward. But things and people have all these different layers. As soon as you learn one, then another pops up, and you have to start all over again."

"The more you learn, the more you need to learn,"

David agreed calmly. "That's what life is. That's what Wicca is. That's what you are."

I looked at him. "What do you mean?"

"You thought you knew yourself, and then you found out one thing and then another thing. It changes the whole way you see yourself and see others in relation to you." He sounded very matter-of-fact.

"You mean, *one* does these things or me in particular?" I asked carefully.

Outside, the weak afternoon sun gave up its struggle and faded behind a bank of gray clouds. I could make out the hulking shape of Das Boot, parked in front of the store entrance, and I saw that it was already covered by at least an inch of snow and tiny rocks of ice.

"Everyone is like that," he said with a smile, "but I was speaking of you in particular."

I blinked, not quite understanding. David had once said that I was a witch who pretended not to be a witch.

"Do you still think I pretend that I'm not a witch?" I asked.

He didn't seem concerned that I knew what he had said. "No." He hesitated, forming his thoughts. He looked up at me, his dark eyes steady. "It's more that you don't present yourself clearly because you aren't yet sure who you are, *what* you are. I've known I'm a witch my whole life— thirty-two years. And I've also always known—" He paused again, as if making up his mind. Then he said quietly, "I'm a Burnhide. It's not only who I am, it's what I am. I'm the same thing on the inside as I am on the outside. You're different in that you've only recently discovered—"

"That I'm Woodbane?" I interrupted.

He gazed at me. "I was about to say, discovered you're a witch at all. But now you know you're Woodbane. You've hardly begun to discover what this means to you, so it's almost impossible for you to project what it should mean to others."

I nodded. He was beginning to make sense. "Alyce once told me that you and she were both blood witches, but you didn't know your clans. But you're a Burnhide?"

"Yes. The Burnhides settled mostly in Germany. My family was from there. We've always been Burnhides. Among most blood witches your clan is considered a private matter. So many people lost all knowledge of their house that nowadays most people say they don't know their clan until they know someone well enough."

I felt pleased that he had trusted me. "Well, I'm Woodbane," I said awkwardly.

David grinned without prejudice. "It's good to know what you are," he said. "The more you know, the more you know."

I laughed at that and drank my tea.

"Are there any ways to really identify the clans?" I asked after a moment. "I read that Leapvaughns tend to have red hair."

"It's not incredibly reliable," David answered. The phone rang, and he cocked his head for a moment, concentrating, then didn't answer it. In the back room I heard the answering machine pick it up.

"For example, lots of Burnhides have dark eyes, and lots of them tend to go gray early." He gestured to his own silvery hair. "But that doesn't mean every dark-eyed, gray-haired person is a Burnhide nor that all Burnhides look like this."

I had a sudden thought. "What about this?" I asked, and

pulled up my shirt to show him the birthmark on my side, under my right arm. My need to know outweighed my embarrassment.

"Yeah, the Woodbane athame," David said matter-of-factly. "Same thing. Not all of you have them."

It was somehow shocking to hear so casually that I had been marked this way my whole life, marked with the symbol of a clan, and that I had never known.

"What about . . . the International Council of Witches?" I asked, my brain following a series of thoughts.

The brass bells over the door jangled, and two girls about my age came in. Without deliberately deciding to, I sent out my senses and picked up the fact that they seemed nonmagickal: just girls. They walked through the store slowly, whispering and laughing, looking at all the merchandise.

"It's an independent council," David said softly. "It's designed to represent all the modern clans—there are hundreds and hundreds who aren't affiliated with any of the seven houses. Its main function is to monitor and sometimes punish the illegitimate use of magick . . . magick used to gain power over others, for example, or to interfere with others without their knowledge or agreement. Magick used to harm."

I frowned. "So they're sort of like the Wicca police."

David raised his eyebrows. "There are those who see the council that way, certainly."

"How do they know if someone is using magick for the wrong reasons?" I asked. Behind us the girls had left the book aisle and were now oohing and aahing over the many beautiful handmade candles the store stocked. I waited to hear them come across the penis-shaped candles.

"Oh my God," whispered one, and I grinned.

"There are witches within the council who specifically look for people like that," David explained. "We call them Seekers. It's their job to investigate claims of dark magick or misuse of power."

"Seekers?" I said.

"Yeah. Wait a second. I can tell you more about them." David ducked out from the counter and headed down the book aisle. He paused for a moment in front of a shelf, then chose an old, worn volume and pulled it out. He was already thumbing through pages when he got back to me. "Here," he said. "Listen to this."

I stared at him as he began to read, sipping my tea.

" 'I am sad to say that there are those who do not agree with the wisdom and purpose of the High Council. Some clans exist who wish to remain separate, secretive, and insulated from their peers. Certainly no one could fault a clan for guarding private knowledge. We all agree that a clan's spells, history, and rituals are their province alone. But we have seen in these modern times that it is wise to join together, to share as much as we can, to create a society in which we can fully participate and celebrate with others of our own kind. This is the purpose of the International Community of Witches.' "

He paused for a moment and glanced at me.

"That sounds like a good thing," I said.

"Yes," he said, but there was an odd tone in his voice. His eyes flashed back down to the page. " 'One cannot help but question those who refuse to participate, who work against this goal and use magick that the council has decried.

In the past such apostasy was the undoing of countless numbers. There is little strength in being alone and little joy in unsanctified magick. That is why we have Seekers.'"

There was something about the way he said *seekers* that gave me a chill. "And what do they do, exactly?" I pressed.

"'Seekers are council members who have been selected to find witches who have strayed beyond our bounds,'" he continued. "'If they discover witches who are actively working against the council, working to harm themselves or others, then they have been given license to take action against them. It is better that we police our own, from within, before the rest of the world chooses once again to police us from without.'" David closed the book and looked at me again. "Those are the words of Birgit Fallon O'Roark. She was high priestess of the High Council from the 1820s to the 1860s."

My tea was starting to get cold. I finished it all in a big gulp and placed the mug on the counter. "What do the Seekers do if they find the witches working against the council?" I asked.

"Usually they put binding spells on them," said David, looking troubled. His voice sounded strained, as if the words themselves were painful to say. "So they can't use their magick anymore. There are things you can do, certain herbs or minerals that you can make them ingest . . . and they can no longer get in touch with their inner magick."

A cold wind seemed to pass over me. My stomach twisted. "Is that bad?" I asked.

"It's very bad," said David emphatically. "To be magickal and not be able to use your magick—it's like suffocating. Like being buried alive. It's enough to make someone lose their mind."

I thought of Maeve and Angus, living in America for years, renouncing their powers. How had they borne it? What had it done to them? I thought about my suffocating dream—how intolerable it had been. Was that what their everyday life had been like for them without Wicca?

"But if you're abusing your power, a Seeker will come for you sooner or later," said David, shaking his head, almost as if to himself. His face seemed older, lined with memories I didn't think I wanted to know about.

"Hmmm." Outside it was dark. I wondered who Cal was meeting and if he would call me later. I wondered if Hunter was really from the council. He seemed more like one of the bad witches the council would send a Seeker to track down.

I wondered if Maeve and the rest of Belwicket had been successful in renouncing the dark side. Would the dark side allow itself to be renounced?

"Is there a dark side?" I said the words tentatively, and felt David draw back.

"Oh, yes," he said softly. "Yes, there's a dark side."

I swallowed, thinking of Cal. "Someone told me there was no dark side—that all of Wicca was a circle and everything was connected to each other, all part of the same thing. That would mean there aren't two different sides, like light and dark."

"That's true, too." David sounded thoughtful. "We say bright and dark when talking about magick used for good and magick used for bad, or evil—to give it a common name."

"So they're two different things?" I pressed.

Slowly David ran his finger around the circular rim of his cup. "Yes. They are different but not opposite. Often they're right next to each other, very similar. It has to do with philosophy and how people interpret actions. It has to do with the spirit of the magick, with will and intent." He glanced up at me and smiled. "It's very complicated. That's why we have to study our whole lifetimes."

"But can you say that someone is on the dark side and that they're evil and you should stay away from them?"

Again David looked troubled. "You could. But it wouldn't be the whole picture. Are there witches who use magick for the wrong purposes? Yes. Are there witches who deliberately hurt others for their own gain? Yes. Should some witches be stopped? Yes. But it usually isn't that simple."

It seemed that nothing in Wicca was simple, I thought. "Well, I'd better get home," I said, pushing my mug across the counter. "Thanks for the talk. And for the tea."

"It was my pleasure," said David. "Please come back any time you need to talk. Sometimes Alyce and I . . . feel concerned about you."

"Me?" I asked. "Why?"

A slight smile turned up the corners of David's mouth. "Because you're in the middle of becoming who you will be," he said gently. "It isn't going to be easy. You may need help. So feel free to ask us for it."

"Thanks," I said again, feeling reassured but still not quite understanding what he meant. With a little wave I left the warmth of Practical Magick and went out to my car. My tires slid a tiny bit as I backed up, but soon I was on the road heading back to Widow's Vale, my headlights illuminating each unique, magickal snowflake.

14.
Scry

Litha, 1996

    Early this morning Uncle Beck and I sat on the edge of the cliff and watched the sun come up, my first sunrise as a witch, and he told me the truth about Mum and Dad. In all the years since they disappeared, I have fought back tears at every turn, telling myself not to give in to childish grief.

    But today the tears came, and it's strange, because now I am supposed to be a man. Still, I wept. I wept for them, but mostly for me—for all the anger I have wasted. I know now that Uncle Beck had good reasons for keeping the truth from me, that Mum and Dad had to disappear in order to protect me, Linden, and Alwyn. That he's heard from them only once, two years ago. That he hasn't even ever tried to scry for them.

    And I know why.

    And now I also know what to do with myself, where I'm

going, what I'll be, and it's funny, because it's all in my name anyway. I am going to hunt down those who ripped my family apart, and I won't stop until I draw Yr on their faces with their blood.

—Giomanach

I was barely two miles from my house when I saw the headlights behind me. First there was nothing, not another car in sight. Then I rounded a corner, and suddenly the lights were right there in my rearview mirror, blinding me, filling my car as if it were lit from within. I squinted and flashed my brakes a few times, but whoever it was didn't pass or turn off the brights. The headlights drew closer.

I slowed Das Boot, sending the message of "get off my tail," but the other car glued itself to my bumper, tailgating me. Mild road rage started to build. Who could be following me like this? Some practical joker, a jerk kid with his dad's car? I jammed my foot on the gas, but the car sped up as I did. The tires skidded slightly as I rounded another corner. The car matched my movement. A prickle of nervousness shot down my spine. My wipers were click-clicking away— matching my pulse—clearing away the falling snow. I couldn't see any other lights on the road. We were alone.

Okay. Something was definitely wrong. I'd heard stories about car jackers . . . but I was in a '71 Valiant. No matter how much I loved it, I doubted anyone would try to steal it from me by force, especially not in the middle of a snowstorm. So what was this idiot doing?

My eyes shot to the rearview mirror. The headlights

bored into my pupils. I blinked, trying to clear my vision of a sea of purple dots. Anger began to turn to fear. I could barely see a thing in the darkness . . . nothing except those lights, the lights that seemed to grow in strength with each passing second. But for some reason, I couldn't hear the other car's engine. It was as if—

Magick.

The word slithered into my thoughts like a snake.

I bit my lip. Maybe that wasn't a car behind me at all. Maybe those two lights were some manifestation of a magickal force. I had a sudden, vivid memory of Hunter Niall peering under Cal's Explorer, of Cal showing me that rune-inscribed stone. We knew Hunter had tried to use magick on us once already. What if he was doing it again now, to me?

Home, I thought. I just needed to get home. I flipped up my mirror so the light wouldn't blind me. But there was about another mile and a half of road until I made it to my street. That was actually pretty far. "Crap," I muttered, and my voice shook a little. With my right hand I drew signs on my dashboard: Eolh, for protection; Ur, for strength; and Rad, for travel. . . .

The lights seemed to flash even brighter in my mirror. My left hand jerked involuntarily on the steering wheel. All at once I felt something bumpy under my wheels.

Before I knew it, I was sliding sideways out of control into the deep drainage ditch. *Goddess!* I screamed silently. Fear and adrenaline pierced my body, a slew of invisible arrows. My hands gripped the steering wheel. I had lost control; the tires screeched. Das Boot lurched sideways on an ice slick, like a heavy white glacier.

The next few seconds unfolded in slow motion. With a sickening crunch the car's nose rammed a pile of ice and snow. I jerked forward and heard the shattering of a headlight. Then silence. The car was no longer moving. But for a few seconds I sat there—paralyzed, unable to move. I was conscious only of my own breathing. It came in quick, uneven gasps.

All right, I finally said to myself. I'm not hurt.

When I lifted my head, I thought I saw the briefest flash of two red taillights, vanishing into the night.

My eyes narrowed. So . . . it *had* been a real car after all.

With a trembling sigh I turned off the engine. Then I threw open the door and hoisted myself out of the driver's seat—no easy feat, considering Das Boot was skewed at a crazy angle. It was hard to concentrate, but I called on my magesight and peered down the road in the direction that the car had disappeared. All I saw, though, were trees, sleeping birds, the faint glow of living nocturnal creatures.

The car was gone.

I leaned against my door, breathing hard, my fists clenched inside my pockets. Even though I was pretty sure those lights hadn't been magickal, the fear didn't subside. Somebody had run me off the road. Das Boot was hopelessly lodged in the ditch. A lump formed in my throat. I was on the verge of bursting into tears, shaking like a leaf. What was going on? I remembered the runes I had drawn on the dash right before the wreck, and now I redrew them in the chill air around me. Eolh, Ur, Rad. The brisk movement helped calm me slightly, at least enough for me to try to figure out what to do.

Actually, there was pretty much only one option. I had to walk the rest of the way home. I didn't have a cell phone, so

I couldn't call anyone for help. And I didn't exactly feel like waiting around in the darkness on this frozen, lonely road all by myself.

Heaving open the driver's door again, I fished inside for my backpack and carefully locked Das Boot. I shook my head. It was going to be a long, miserable march to my house. But as I heaved the backpack across my shoulder, a flash of dim light illuminated the snowflakes around me, and I heard the faint rumble of a motor. I turned to see a car slowly approaching . . . from the same direction the lights had vanished.

The flash of relief I'd briefly felt at the possibility of being rescued evaporated as the car rolled to a stop, not fifteen feet from where I stood. The headlights weren't nearly as bright, but for all I knew, this was the same car. Maybe the person driving had decided to turn around and finish me off, or—

My insides clenched. The license plate, the grating of the tan BMW . . . I recognized it even before the passenger window unrolled. It was Bree's car.

Bree looked across from the driver's seat, her eyes outlined in black, her skin pale and perfect. We regarded each other silently for a few moments. I hoped I didn't look as freaked out and disheveled as I felt. I wanted to radiate strength.

"What happened, Morgan?" she asked.

I opened my mouth, then closed it. My eyes narrowed as a horrible thought struck me. Could Bree have been the one who'd run me into the ditch?

It was possible. There were no other cars on the road. She could have made a U-turn up ahead and come back to see what had happened to me. But . . . Bree? Hurt me?

Remember what you heard in the bathroom, a voice

inside chimed. *She gave your hair to a witch.* Remember.

Maybe things had changed permanently. Maybe Bree no longer cared about me at all. Or maybe Sky Eventide had put her up to this—as a stunt to scare me, the same way that Sky had forced her to turn over a lock of my hair. A thousand thoughts pounded against my skull, aching to be let out, to be heard: Oh God, Bree, don't let them fool you! I'm worried about you. I miss you. You're being so stupid. I'm sorry. I need to talk to you. Don't you know what's happened to me? I'm adopted. I'm a blood witch. I'm Woodbane. I'm sorry about Cal—

"Morgan?" she prodded, her brow furrowed.

I cleared my throat. "I hit a patch of ice," I said. I gestured unnecessarily to Das Boot.

"Are you okay?" she asked stiffly. "Did you hurt yourself?"

I shook my head. "I'm fine."

She blinked. "Do you want a ride home?"

I took a deep breath but shook my head again. I couldn't get into her car. Not when she might have been the one who had run me off the road in the first place. Even though I could hardly believe I was having such horrible thoughts about someone who had once been my best friend, I didn't dare risk it.

"Are you sure?" she pressed.

"I'll be fine," I mumbled.

Without another word she rolled up her window and took off. I noticed that she accelerated slowly so she wouldn't splatter me with snow and slush.

My chest ached as I walked home.

My parents fussed over me, which was nice. I told them I'd skidded off the road on a bad patch of ice, which was true in a way, but I left out the part about the other car behind me. I didn't want to worry them any more than necessary. I called a tow truck company, who agreed to get Das Boot and bring it home later that night. Thank the Goddess for Triple A, I thought and decided to ask for a cell phone for Christmas.

"Are you sure you don't want to come for Chinese with us?" Mom asked, after making sure I had thawed. My parents were heading out to meet Aunt Eileen and Paula, to drive by several houses that were for sale in the area, then to get dinner. They wouldn't be back till late. Mary K. was at Jaycee's, and I was sure she was meeting Bakker later.

"No, thanks," I said. "I'll just wait for the tow truck."

Mom kissed me. "I am so thankful you're okay. You could've been hurt so easily," she said, and I hugged her back. It was true, I realized. I really could have been hurt. If it had happened at another section of the road, I could have gone into a thirty-foot ravine. An image popped into my mind of Das Boot tumbling down a rocky cliff, then bursting into flames—and I cringed.

After Mom and Dad left, I set a pot of water on to boil for frozen ravioli. I grabbed a Diet Coke, and the phone rang. I knew it was Cal.

"Hello there," he said. "We're taking a little break. What are you doing?"

"Fixing some dinner." It was incredible: I still felt a little shaky, even though the mere sound of Cal's voice worked wonders. "I, um, had a little accident."

"What?" His voice was sharp with concern. "Are you okay?"

"It wasn't anything," I said bravely. "I just went off the road and ended up in a ditch. I'm waiting for the tow truck to bring Das Boot home."

"Really? Why didn't you call me?"

I smiled, feeling much better as I dumped a bunch of ravioli into the water. "I guess I was still recovering. I'm okay, though. I didn't hurt anything except my car. And I knew you were busy, anyway."

He was quiet for a moment. "Next time something happens, call me right away," he said.

I laughed. If it had been anyone else, I would have said they were overreacting. "I'll try not to do it again," I said.

"I wish I could come see you," he said, sounding frustrated. "But we're doing a circle here and it's about to start. Lousy timing. I'm sorry."

"It's fine. Don't worry so much." I sighed and stirred the pot. "You know, I . . ." I left the sentence hanging. I was going to tell him about seeing Bree, about all of my terrible fears and suspicions, but I didn't. I couldn't bear to reopen the wound, to allow all those painful emotions to come flooding back.

"You what?" Cal asked.

"Nothing," I murmured.

"You're sure?"

"Yeah."

He sighed, too. "Well, okay. I should probably go. My mom is starting to do her stuff. I'm not sure how late this will go—I might not be able to call you later. And you know we don't pick up the phone if it rings during a circle, so you won't be able to call me."

"That's okay," I said. "I'll see you tomorrow."

"Oh, tomorrow," said Cal, sounding brighter. "The famous pre-birthday day. Yeah, I have special plans for tomorrow."

I laughed, wondering what plans he had made. Then he made a silly kissing noise into the phone, and we hung up.

Alone and quiet, I ate my dinner. It felt soothing to be by myself and not have to talk. In the living room I noticed a basket full of fatwood by the fireplace. In just a few minutes I had a good blaze going, and I fetched Maeve's BOS from upstairs and settled on the couch. My mom's one crocheting attempt had resulted in an incredibly ugly afghan the size and weight of a dead mule. I pulled it over me. Within moments Dagda had scrambled up the side of the couch and was stomping happily across my knees, purring hard and kneading me with his sharp little paws.

"Hey, cute thing," I said, scratching him behind his ears. He settled on my lap, and I started reading.

July 6, 1977

Tonight I'm going to scry with fire. ; My witch sight is good, and the magick is strong. I used water once, but it was hard to see anything. I told Angus and he laughed at me, saying that I was a clumsy girl and might have splashed some of the water out of the glass. I know he was teasing, but I never used it again.

Fire is different. Fire opens doors I never knew were there.

Fire.

The word rolled around my head, and I glanced up from the page. My birth mother was right. Fire *was* different. I'd loved fire since I was little: its warmth, the mesmerizing golden red glow of the flames. I even loved the noise fire made as it ate the dry wood. To me it had sounded like laughter—both exciting and frightening in its hungry appetite and eager destruction.

My eyes wandered to the burning logs. I shifted carefully on the couch, trying not to disturb Dagda, though he could probably sleep through almost anything. Facing the flames, I let my head rest against the back of the couch. I set the BOS aside. I was one hundred percent comfortable.

I decided to try to scry.

First I released all the thoughts circling my brain, one by one. Bree, looking at me standing in the snow by the side of the road. Hunter. His face was hard to get rid of—and when I pictured it, I got angry. Over and over I saw him, silhouetted against a leaden gray sky, his green eyes looking like reflections of Irish fields, his arrogance coming off him in waves.

My eyelids fluttered shut. I breathed in and out slowly. The tension drained from each muscle in my body. As I felt myself drift more completely into a delicious concentration, I became more and more aware of my surroundings: Dagda's small heart beating quickly as he slept, the ecstatic joy of the fire as it consumed the wood.

I opened my eyes.

The fire had transformed into a mirror.

There in the flames I saw my own face, looking back: the long sweep of brown hair, the kitten in my lap.

What do you want to know? the fire whispered to me. Its voice was raspy and sibilant—seductive yet fleeting, fading away in acrid curls of smoke.

I don't understand anything, I answered. My face was

serene, but my silent voice cried out in frustration. *I don't understand anything.*

Then in the fire a curtain of flame was drawn back. I saw Cal, walking through a field of wheat as golden as his eyes. He swept out his hand, looking beautiful and godlike, and it felt like he was offering the entire field to me as a gift. Then Hunter and Sky came up behind him, hand in hand. Their pale, bleached elegance was beautiful in its own way, but I felt a terrible sense of danger suddenly. I closed my eyes as if that might blot it out.

When I opened them again, I found myself walking through a forest so thickly grown that barely any light reached the ground. My bare feet were silent on the rotting leaves. Soon I saw figures standing in the woods, hidden among the trees. One of them was Sky again, and she turned and smiled at me, her white-blond hair glowing like an angel's halo around her. Then she turned to the person behind her: it was Raven, dressed all in black. Sky leaned over and kissed Raven gently, and I blinked in surprise.

Many disjointed images flowed over each other next, sliding across my consciousness, hard to follow. Robbie kissing Bree . . . my parents watching me walk away, tears running down their faces . . . Aunt Eileen holding a baby.

And then, as if that movie were over and a new reel began, I saw a small, white clapboard house, set back on a slight rise among the trees. Curtains fluttered from the open windows. A neat, tended garden of holly bushes and mums lined the front of the house.

Off to one side was Maeve Riordan. My birth mother.

I drew in my breath. I remembered her from another

vision I'd had, a vision of her holding me when I was an infant. She smiled and beckoned to me, looking young and goofy in her 1980s clothes. Behind her was a large square garden of herbs and vegetables, bursting with health. She turned and headed toward the house. I followed her—around the side, where a narrow walk separated the house from the lawn. Turning to face me again, she knelt and gestured underneath the house, pointing.

Confusion came over me. What was this? Then a phone began ringing from far away. Although I tried to keep concentrating, the scene began to fade, and my last image was of my birth mother, impossibly young and lovely, waving good-bye.

I blinked, my breathing ragged.

The sound of a phone still filled my ears. What was going on? Several seconds passed before I realized that it was *our* phone, not a phone in my vision. The images were all gone now. I was alone in our house again—and somebody was calling.

15.
Presence

September 4, 1998

    Uncle Beck hit me last night. Today I have a shiner and a split lip. It looks really impressive, and I'm going to tell people I got it defending what's left of Athar's honor.

    Two years ago, on the dawn after my initiation, Uncle Beck told me why Mum and Dad disappeared. How Mum had seen the dark cloud coming when she was scrying, and how it had nearly killed her, right through the vision. And how, right after they escaped and went into hiding, their coven was wiped out. I remember all the witches in the coven, how they were like aunts and uncles to me. Then they were dead, and Linden and Alwyn and I came to live with Beck and Shelagh and Athar and Maris and Siobhan.

    Since then I've been trying to find out about the dark wave, the force of evil that destroyed my parents' coven and made them go into hiding. I know it's got something to do with Woodbanes. Dad is—or was—Woodbane. The last time I was in London, I went to all the old bookshops where they sell occult books. I visited the Circle of Morath, where they keep a lot of the old writings. I've been reading and searching for two years. Finally last night, Linden and I were going to try to call on the dark side, to get information. Since Linden's initiation last month, he's been pestering me to let him help, and I had to say yes, because they were his parents too. Maybe in two years, when Alwyn's initiated, she'll want to work with us. I don't know.

Anyway, Uncle Beck found us in the marshes a mile from the house. We hadn't even got far in the rite, and suddenly Uncle was storming up, looking huge and terrible and furious. He broke through our circles, kicked out our candles and our fire, and knocked the athame from my hand. I've never seen him so angry, and he hauled me up by my collar as if I was a dog and not sixteen and as tall as him.

"Call on the blackness, will you?" he growled, while Linden jumped to his feet. "You bloody bastard! For eight years I've fed you and taught you and you've slept under my roof, and you're out here dealing with blackness and leading your young brother astray?" Then he punched me, knocked me down, and I hit the ground like an unstrung puppet. The man has a fist like a ham—only harder.

We had words, we thrashed it out, and at the end, he understood what I wanted, and I understood that he'd rather *kill me than let me do it, and that if I involved Linden again I would need to find another place to live. He's a good man, my uncle, and a good witch, though we often clash. Mum is his sister and I know now that he desires to right the wrong done to her as much as I. The difference is that I was willing to cross the line to do it, and Beck isn't.*

—Giomanach

"Hello?" I said into the receiver. I realized that I had no sense of who it was, even though I usually did before I picked up the phone.

Silence.

"Hello?" I said again.

Click. Drone of dial tone.

Okay, I knew, of course, that people get wrong numbers all the time. But for some reason, maybe because I was still caught up in images, emotions, and sensations from the fire, this silent phone call unnerved me. Every spooky movie I had ever seen came back to haunt me: *Scream, Halloween, The Exorcist, Fatal Attraction, Blair Witch.* My only thought was: Someone was checking to see if I was home. And I was. Alone.

I punched in star sixty-nine. Nothing happened. Finally a computerized female voice told me that the number I was trying to reach was blocked.

Feeling tense, I slammed the phone down on the hook. Then I began to race around the house, locking the front and back doors, the basement door, locking windows that had never been locked in my memory. Was I being stupid? It didn't matter. Better stupid and safe than smart and dead. I turned on all the outside lights instead of just the dim yellow glow of the front porch fixture.

I didn't know why I felt so afraid, but my first sense of alarm was rapidly growing into pure terror. So I retrieved my trusty baseball bat from the mudroom, locked that door, scooped up Dagda, and scampered upstairs to my room, glancing over my shoulder. Maybe it was still the aftermath of the accident, but my hands were clammy. My breath came quickly. I locked my bedroom door, then locked the door that led from the bathroom to Mary K.'s room.

I sat down on my bed, clenching and unclenching my fists. Cal, was all I could think. Cal, help me. I need you. Come to me.

I sent the witch message out into the night. Cal would get it. Cal would save me.

But the minutes ticked by, and he didn't come. He didn't even call to say he was on his way. I thought about calling him, but then I remembered what he'd said about not answering the phone during the circle.

Didn't he get my message? I wondered frantically. Where is he?

I tried to calm myself down. Mom and Dad would be home soon. So would Mary K. Anyway, it was just a phone call. A wrong number. Maybe it was Bree calling to apologize, and she'd lost her nerve.

But why would Bree's number have been blocked? It could have been anyone, though: a prank call by some pimply sixth grader whose mom caught him just before he spoke. Or maybe it was a telemarketer. . . .

Calm down, calm down, I ordered myself. Breathe.

A faint prickling at the edge of my senses made me sit up straight. I cast out my senses, searching as hard as I could. Then I knew what it was. Someone was on the edge of the property. Fear oozed through me like burning lava.

"Wait here," I whispered idiotically to Dagda.

I crept soundlessly to my darkened window and peered out into the yard. As I looked out, the outside lights all blinked off. *Shit.* Who had gotten to them?

I could make out the leaves of the shrubs, the swooping shadow of an owl, the crusts of ice hanging on our fence.

That was when I saw them: two dark figures.

I squinted, using my magesight to make out their features, but for some reason I couldn't focus on their faces. It didn't matter, though. For a moment the night's cloud cover broke and allowed the not quite half-moon to appear. The glint of moonlight reflected off pale, shining hair, and I knew who was here. Sky Eventide. The person with her wore a dark knit cap and was too tall to be either Bree or Raven. Hunter. I felt sure it was Hunter.

Where was Cal?

I watched from my crouching position on the floor as they faded into the house's shadows. When I could no longer see them, I closed my eyes and tried to follow them with my senses. I felt them moving around the perimeter of the house slowly, pausing here and there. Would they try to come in? My fingers tightened on the bat, even though I knew it would be of zero use against witches in full possession of their powers. And Sky and Hunter were blood witches.

What did they want? What were they doing?

And then it came to me: of course. They were putting a spell on my house, on me. I remembered reading about how Maeve and her mother, Mackenna Riordan, had put spells on people. They had often needed to walk around a house or a person or a place. To surround something with magick is to change it.

Sky and Hunter were surrounding *me*.

They were circling my house, and I couldn't stop them— I didn't even have any idea what they were doing. It must have been one of them who had called earlier, to make sure I was home. And maybe they had blocked my call to Cal somehow. He might not be coming at all. . . .

I looked at Dagda to see if he was nervous or upset, if his senses had picked up on the vibrations of danger and magick.

He was asleep: tiny mouth slightly open, blue eyes shut, ribby little side rising and falling with sleep-slowed breaths. So much for the power of animals. I scowled, then looked out the window again. The shadowy figures were no longer visible but still present. Feeling terribly alone, I sat on my floor and waited. It was all I could do.

Three times Hunter and Sky moved around the house. I heard nothing and saw nothing, but I sensed them. They were there.

Almost half an hour later they left. I felt them leave, felt them close a circle behind them . . . felt them send one last line of magick out toward the house and toward me. Soon after that I heard the quiet purr of an engine as it faded down the street. The outside lights all flickered back on. But there was no way I was going outside to see what they had done. No. I was going to stay put.

With my baseball bat at my side, I went back downstairs and watched television until the tow truck driver showed up with Das Boot. Mom and Dad came home a few minutes later. I hurried upstairs to my room before they walked through the front door. I was too wrung out to act normal around them.

Cal never came.

"Hi, honey," Mom said when I stumbled into the kitchen the next morning. "Sleep well?"

"Uh-huh," I said, moving purposefully toward the refrigerator for a Diet Coke. But I was lying. The truth was, I hadn't slept well at all. I'd dozed fitfully, my fleeting dreams filled with images from the fire and the silhouettes of Sky and whoever else had been on our lawn. Finally I'd given up on sleep altogether. I glanced at the kitchen clock. Only eight-thirty. I wanted to call Cal, but it was too early, especially for a Saturday morning.

"Does anyone have plans for today?" Dad asked, folding back the newspaper.

"Jaycee and I are going to Northgate Mall," said Mary K. She fiddled with a box of Pop-Tarts, still in her pajamas. "The pre-Thanksgiving sales are starting."

"I'm going to be getting ready for tomorrow," said Mom. She flashed a meaningful smile at me. "Morgan, do you want an ice-cream cake this year?"

Suddenly I remembered that the next day was my birthday. Wow. Until this year I'd always eagerly looked forward to my birthday, anticipating it for months and months. Of course, until this year I'd had no idea that I was an adopted blood witch from the Woodbane clan. Nor, in previous years, was I being stalked by other witches. Things had changed a little.

I nodded and sipped my Diet Coke. "Chocolate cake on the bottom, mint-chip ice cream on top," I instructed, summoning up a smile.

"And what do you want for dinner tomorrow night?" Mom asked, starting to make a list.

"Lamb chops, mint jelly, roasted potatoes, fresh peas, salad," I rattled off. The same birthday dinner I always wanted. It was comforting somehow. This was my house, my family, and we were going to celebrate my birthday— same as always.

"Are you going to be busy tonight?" Mom asked, averting her eyes. She knew we usually had circles on Saturday nights.

"I'm seeing Cal," I said.

She nodded and thankfully left it at that.

As soon as I was dressed, I went outside and walked around the house. As far as I could tell, I couldn't feel the effects of a spell's magick. Which could very well be *part* of the spell, of course. Slowly I circled our entire house. I saw no sign of anything. No hexes spray painted on the house, no dead animals hanging from trees. Then again, I knew the signs would be infinitely more subtle than that.

Weirdly enough, even the snow-covered ground betrayed no footprints, though it hadn't snowed since before my visitors had arrived. I searched and searched but saw no trace of anyone's having been in our yard at all—except me, just now. Frowning, I shook my head. Had it all been an illusion? Had it been part of my scrying? How much could I trust my own perceptions? But I remembered the images I had seen—so clearly, too—the sights, sounds, and smells that had accompanied my fire scrying.

Most of all I remembered Maeve, standing by her house, smiling and pointing.

Maeve had lived in Meshomah Falls, two hours away. I glanced at my watch, then went inside to call Cal.

"What happened to your car?" Robbie asked half an hour later. We were in the front seat of Das Boot; I had just picked him up. Thankfully the car still worked, although the right headlight had been shattered and there was a massive dent in the front bumper. When I had called Cal, he hadn't been home—Selene had said he was out shopping, and she wasn't sure when he'd be back. Somehow, speaking to Selene calmed me down. I thought of asking her if he'd gotten my witch message, but my mom was in the room and I didn't want to bring it up in front of her. I'd ask Cal later.

Fortunately Robbie had been home, and he was a happy second choice for the road trip I had planned.

"I went into a ditch last night," I said with a grimace. "Slid on the ice." I didn't mention the lights I'd seen. That was something I'd only talk to Cal about. Whatever was going on, I didn't want to drag Robbie into it.

"Man," said Robbie. "Were you hurt?"

"No. But I have to get my headlight fixed. Big pain."

Robbie opened a map across the dashboard as I pulled away from his house. The day was rapidly clearing: I had a hope of actual sunshine before too long. It was still cold, but the snow and ice were melting slowly, and the streets were wet, the gutters running with water.

"You're looking for a town called Meshomah Falls. It should be north, right up the Hudson," I told him, turning onto the road that would lead to the highway. "About two, two and a half hours away."

"Oh, okay," he said, tracing his finger over the map. "I see it. Yeah, take Route 9 north until we get to Hookbridge Falls."

After a quick stop for gas and a supply of junk food, we were on our way. Bree and I used to go on road trips all the time: just day trips to malls or cool places to hike or little artists' colonies. We had felt so free, so unstoppable. But I tried not to dredge up those memories. Now they just filled me with pain.

"Want a chip?" Robbie offered, and I dug a hand into the bag.

"Have you talked to Bree yet?" I asked, unable to tear my mind from her. "About how you feel?"

He shook his head. "I've sort of tried, but it hasn't actually come up. I guess I'm a coward."

"No, you're not," I said. "But she can be hard to approach."

He shrugged. "You know, Bree asks about you, too," he said.

"What do you mean?"

"I mean, you always ask about her. Well, she asks about you, too. I mean, she never says anything nice about you, you both say mean things about the other one, but even a total idiot could tell that you two miss each other."

My face felt stiff as I stared out the window.

"Just thought you should know," he added.

We didn't say another word for the next sixty miles—not until we saw a sign for the Hookbridge Falls exit. By then the sky had cleared, and it was open and blue in a way it hadn't been for what seemed like weeks. The sun's warmth on my face lifted my spirits. I felt like we were on a real adventure.

Robbie consulted the map. "We get off here and head east on Pedersen, which leads right into Meshomah Falls," he said.

"Okay."

A few minutes after we'd turned off the highway, I saw the sign announcing Meshomah Falls, New York.

A shiver ran down my spine. This was where I had been born.

I drove down Main Street slowly, staring at the buildings. Meshomah Falls was a lot like Widow's Vale, except not quite as old and not quite as Victorian. It was a cute town, though, and I could see why Maeve and Angus had decided to settle here. I picked a side street at random and turned onto it, slowing even more as I looked carefully at each house. Next to me, Robbie chewed gum and drummed his fingers along to the radio.

"So, when are you going to tell me why we're here?" he joked.

"Uh . . ." I didn't know what to say. I guess I had been planning to pass this off as a simple joyride, just a chance to get out and do something. But Robbie knew me too well. "I'll tell you later," I whispered, feeling unsure and vulnerable. To tell him one part of the story would mean telling him everything—and I had yet to come fully to terms with that.

"Have you ever been here before?" Robbie asked.

I shook my head. Most of the houses were pretty modest, but none was immediately recognizable as the house I'd seen in my vision. And they were fewer and farther between now;

we were heading into the country again. I started to wonder what the hell I was doing. Why on earth did I think I'd be able to recognize Maeve's house? And if by some miracle I found it, what would I do then? This whole idea was stupid—

There it was.

I slammed on the brakes. Das Boot squealed to an abrupt halt. Robbie glared at me. But I hardly noticed. The house from my vision, my birth mother's house, stood right before my eyes.

16.
Hidden

January 12, 1999

I've been ill, apparently.

Aunt Shelagh says I have been out for six days. Raving, she told me, with a high fever. I feel like death itself. I don't even remember what happened to me. And no one will say a word. I don't understand any of it.

Where is Linden? I want to see my brother. When I awoke this morning, eight witches from Vinneag were around my bed, working healing rites. I heard Athar and Alwyn in the hall, sobbing. But when I asked if they could come in to see me, the Vinneag witches just gave each other grave glances, then shook their heads. Why? Am I that ill? Or is it something else? What is happening? I must know, but no one will tell me a thing, and I am as weak as a hollow bone.

—Giomanach

The house was on the right side of the road, and as I glanced through Robbie's window, it was as if a cool breeze suddenly washed across my face. I pulled up alongside it.

The walls were no longer white but painted a pale coffee color with dark red accents. The neat garden in front was gone, as was the large herb and vegetable patch to one side. Instead some clumpy rhododendrons hid the front windows on the first floor.

I sat there in silence, drinking in the sight of the place. This was it. This was Maeve's house, and my home for the first seven months of my life. Robbie watched me, not saying anything. There were no cars in the driveway, no sign that anyone was home. I didn't know what to do. But after several minutes I turned to Robbie and took a deep breath.

"I have something to tell you," I began.

He nodded, a somber expression on his face.

"I'm a blood witch, like Cal said a couple of weeks ago. But my parents aren't. I was adopted."

Robbie's eyes widened, but he said nothing

"I was adopted when I was about eight months old. My birth mother was a blood witch from Ireland. Her name was Maeve Riordan, and she lived in that house." I gestured out the window. "Her coven was wiped out in Ireland, and she and my biological father escaped to America and settled here. When they did, they swore never to use magick again."

I took another deep, shaky breath. This whole story sounded like a movie of the week. A bad one. But Robbie nodded encouragingly.

"Anyway," I went on, "they had me, and then something happened—I don't know what—and my mother gave me up for adoption. Right after that, she and my father were locked in a barn and burned to death."

Robbie blinked. His face turned slightly pale. "Jesus," he muttered, rubbing his chin. "And who was your dad?"

"His name was Angus Bramson. He was a witch, too, from the same coven in Ireland. I don't think they were married." I sighed. "So that's why I'm so strong in Wicca, why that spell I did for you worked, why I channel so much energy at circles. It's because I come from a line of witches that's hundreds or thousands of years old."

For what seemed like a long time Robbie just stared at me. "This is mind-blowing," he mumbled finally.

"Tell me about it."

He offered a sympathetic smile. "I'll bet things have been crazy at your house lately."

I laughed. "Yeah, you could say that. We were all freaked out about it. I mean, my parents never told me, not in sixteen years, that I was adopted. And all my relatives knew and all their friends. I was . . . really angry."

"I'll bet," Robbie murmured.

"And they knew how my birth parents died and that witchcraft was involved, so they're really upset that I'm doing Wicca because the whole thing scares them. They don't want anything to happen to me."

Robbie chewed his lip, looking concerned. "No one knows why your birth parents were killed? They were murdered, right? I mean, it wasn't suicide or some ritual gone wrong."

"No. Apparently the barn door was locked from the outside. But they must have been scared about something because they gave me up for adoption right before they died. I can't find out why it happened, though, or who could have done it. I have

Maeve's Book of Shadows, and she says that after they came to America, they didn't practice magick at all—"

"How did you get your birth mother's Book of Shadows?" he interrupted.

I sighed again. "It's a long story, but Selene Belltower had it, and I found it. It was all a bunch of weird coincidences."

Robbie raised his eyebrows. "I thought there weren't any coincidences."

I looked at him, startled. You're absolutely right, I thought.

"So why are we here?" he asked.

I hesitated. "Last night I had a dream . . . I mean, I had a vision. Actually, I scryed in the fire last night."

"You scryed?" Robbie shifted in his seat. Creases lined his forehead. "You mean you tried to divine information, like magickal information?"

"Yes," I admitted, staring down at my lap for a moment. "I know, you think I'm doing stuff I shouldn't be doing yet. But I think it's allowed. It's not a real spell or anything."

Robbie remained silent.

I shook my head and glanced out the window again. "Anyway, I was watching the fire last night, and I saw all sorts of weird images and scenes and stuff. But the most realistic scene, the clearest one, was about this house. I saw Maeve standing outside it and pointing underneath it. Pointing and smiling. Like she wanted to show me something underneath this house—"

"Wait a second," Robbie cut in. "Let me get this straight. You had a vision, so now we're here, and you want to crawl under that house?"

I almost laughed. It didn't sound bizarre; it sounded utterly insane. "Well, when you put it that way . . ."

He shook his head, but he was smiling, too. "Are you sure this is the house?"

I nodded.

He didn't say anything.

"So do you think I'm crazy, coming here?" I asked. "Do you think we should turn around and go home?"

He hesitated. "No," he said finally. "If you had that vision while you were actually scrying, then I think it makes sense to check it out. I mean, if you actually want to crawl under there." He glanced at me. "Or . . . do you want *me* to crawl under there?"

I smiled at him and patted his arm. "Thanks. That's really sweet. But no. I guess I'd better do it. Even though I have no idea what I'm looking for."

Robbie turned to the house again. "Got a flashlight?"

"Of course not." I smirked. "That would make me too well prepared, wouldn't it?"

He laughed as I slid out of the car and zipped up my coat. I hesitated only a moment before I unlatched the chain-link gate, then headed up the walk. Under my breath I whispered: "I am invisible, I am invisible, I am invisible," just in case anyone was watching from one of the neighboring houses. It was a trick Cal had told me about, but I'd never tried it before. I hoped it worked.

On the left side of the house, past the shaggy rhododendrons, I found the place where Maeve had been standing in my vision. There was an opening between the low brick foundation and the floor supports. The opening was barely twenty inches high. I glanced back at the car. Robbie was leaning against it in case he suddenly needed to come to my aid. I smiled and gave him a thumbs-up. He smiled back reassuringly. I was lucky. He was a good friend.

Crouching down, I peered underneath the house and saw only a dense, inky blackness. My heart was pounding loudly, but my senses picked up no people above or around me. For all I knew, I would find dead bodies and crumbling bones in there. Or rats. I would freak if I came face to face with a rat. I pictured myself screaming and scrambling to get out from under the house as fast as I could. But there was no sense in waiting. My magesight would guide me. I crept forward on my hands and knees. As soon as I had edged under the house, I paused to give my eyes time to adjust.

I saw a lot of junk, glowing faintly with time: old insulation foam, an ancient, dirt-encrusted sink, old pipes and chunks of sheet metal. I maneuvered my way carefully through this maze, looking around, trying to get some idea of what I could be looking *for*. I could feel the cold dampness seep through my jeans. I sneezed. It was dank under here. Dank and musty.

Again the questions festered in my mind. Why was I here? Why had Maeve wanted me to come here? Think, think! Could there be something about the house itself? I glanced upward to see if runes or sigils were traced on the bottom of the floor supports. The wood was old and dirty and blackened, and I saw nothing. I swept my gaze from side to side, starting to feel incredibly stupid—

Wait. There was something. . . . I blinked, rapidly. About fifteen feet in front of me, next to a brick piling, there was something. Something magickal. Whatever it was, I could sense it more than I could see it. I crawled forward, ducking low under water pipes and phone wires. At one point I had to shimmy on my belly beneath a sewer line. I was going to look like hell when I got out of here—I could feel my hair dragging in the dirt and cursed myself for not tying it up.

Finally I slithered out and could crawl normally again. I sneezed and wiped my nose on my sleeve. There! Tucked between two supports, practically hidden behind the piling, was a box. In order to get to it, I had to stretch my arms around the piling; the supports blocked my path.

Tentatively I reached for it. The air around the box felt thick, like clear Jell-O. My fingertips pushed through it and reached icy cold metal. Gritting my teeth, I tried to pry it out of the dirt. But it wouldn't budge. And in my awkward position I couldn't get any leverage to give it a good wrench. Again I yanked at it, scratching my fingers on its rusted, pitted surface. There was no use, though. It was stuck.

I felt like screaming. Here I was, on my hands and knees in the mud, under a strange house, *drawn* here—and I was helpless. I leaned forward and squinted at the box, concentrating hard. There, carved into the lid and barely visible under years of dust, were the initials M. R. Maeve Riordan. To me they were as clear as if I were seeing them in sunlight.

My breath came fast. This was it. This was why my mother had sent me here. I was meant to have it—this box that had remained hidden for almost seventeen years.

A memory suddenly flashed through my mind: that day not so long ago, right when we had all first discovered Wicca, when a leaf had fallen on Raven's head and I'd willed it to hover there with my thoughts. It had been nothing more than a flight of whimsy and a gesture of defiance against her for being cruel to me. But now it took on a deeper significance. If I could move a leaf, could I move something heavier?

I closed my eyes, focusing my concentration. Again I

stretched forward and touched the dusty box with my fingertips. My mind emptied, all my thoughts vanishing like water down a drain. Only one thought remained: What had once belonged to my birth mother now belonged to me. The box was mine. I would have it.

It jumped into my hands.

My eyes flew open. A smile crossed my face. I'd done it! By the Goddess, I'd done it! Clutching the box under one arm, I scrambled out of there as fast as I could. Outside, the sunlight seemed overly bright, the air too cold. I blinked and stood, my muscles cramped, then stamped my feet and brushed off my coat as best I could. Then I hurried forward.

A middle-aged man was walking up the sidewalk toward the house. He dragged a fat dachshund behind him by a leash. As he caught sight of me coming around from the back of the house, he slowed and then stopped. His eyes were sharp with suspicion.

I froze for an instant, my heart thumping. I am invisible, I am invisible, I am invisible. I hurled the thought at him with as much force as I could.

A moment later his gaze seemed to lose its focus. His eyes slid aside, and he began walking again.

Wow. I felt a spurt of elation. My powers were growing so strong!

From his vantage point beside Das Boot, Robbie had seen it all. He opened the back door without a word, and I gently placed the box in the backseat. Then he slid smoothly behind the wheel, I got in, and we drove off. Over my shoulder I watched the little house grow smaller until finally we went around a bend and it disappeared from sight.

17.
Treasure

January 14, 1999

I am sitting up. Today I ate some broth. Everyone is tip-toeing around me, and Uncle Beck looks at me with a coldness in his eyes the likes of which I've never seen. I keep asking about Linden, but no one will answer. They finally let Athar in today, and I caught her hand and asked her, too, but she just looked at me with those deep, dark eyes. Then they let Alwyn in to see me, but she just sobbed and clutched my hand till they took her away. I realized she's almost fourteen—three months away from her initiation.

Where is Linden? Why has he not come to see me?

Council members have been in and out of the house all week. A net of fear is closing about me. But I dare not name what I fear. It is too horrible.

—Giomanach

"What's in the box?" Robbie asked after a few minutes. He glanced at me. I had cobwebs in my hair, and I was filthy and smelled musty and dirty.

"I don't know," I said. "But it has Maeve's initials on it."

Robbie nodded. "Let's go to my house," he said. "My folks aren't there."

I nodded. "Thanks for driving," I said.

The drive back to Widow's Vale seemed endless. The sun dropped out of the sky shortly after four-thirty, and we drove the last half hour through chilly darkness. I was aching to open the box, but I felt I needed complete security to do it. Robbie parked Das Boot outside his parents' tiny, run-down house. As long as I had known Robbie, they had never repainted their house, or repaired the walk, or done any of the usual homeowner-type stuff. The front lawn was ragged and in need of mowing. It was Robbie's job and he hated it, and his parents didn't seem to care.

I'd never liked coming here, which is why the three of us had usually hung out at Bree's house, our favorite, or my house, our second favorite. Robbie's house was to be avoided, and we all knew it. But for now, it was fine.

Robbie flicked on lights, illuminating the living room, its dingy floor, and the permanent odor of stale cooking and cigarette smoke.

"Where are your folks?" I asked as we walked down the hall to Robbie's room.

"Mom's at her sister's, and Dad's hunting."

"Ugh," I said. "I still remember that time I came over and you had a deer hanging from the tree in your front yard."

Robbie laughed, and we passed through his older sister

Michelle's room. She was away at college, and her room was maintained as a kind of shrine in case she ever came home. Michelle was his parents' favorite, and they made no effort to conceal it. But Robbie didn't resent her. Michelle adored Robbie, and the two of them were very close. I caught a glimpse of a framed school picture of him up on her shelf, taken last year. His face was almost unrecognizable: his skin covered with acne, his eyes concealed by glasses.

Robbie flicked on a lamp. His room was less than half the size of Michelle's, more like a big closet. There was barely enough space for his twin-size bed, which was covered with an old Mexican blanket. A large chest of drawers topped with bookshelves was wedged into a corner. The shelves were overflowing with books, most of them paperbacks, all of them read.

"How's Michelle?" I asked, setting the box carefully on his bed. I was nervous and took my time unbuttoning my coat.

"Fine. She thinks she'll be on the dean's list again."

"Good for her. Is she coming home for Christmas?" My pulse was racing again, but I tried to calm myself. I sat down on the bed.

"Yeah." Robbie grinned. "She's going to be surprised by my looks."

I glanced at him. "Yeah," I said soberly.

"Well, are you gonna open this thing?" he asked, sitting at the other end of his bed.

I swallowed, unwilling to admit how anxious I was. What if there was something awful in there? Something awful or—

"Do you want me to do it?" he asked.

I shook my head quickly. "No—no. I'll do it."

I picked up the box. It was about twenty inches long by sixteen inches wide and about four inches tall. Outside, the metal was flaking off. Two metal clasps held the box shut. They were rusted almost solid. Robbie jumped up and rummaged around in his desk for a screwdriver, then handed it to me. Holding my breath, I wedged it under the lid and pried the clasps free. The lid opened with a pop, and I dug my fingers underneath it and flung it open.

"Wow!" Robbie and I exclaimed at the exact same time.

Though the outside of the box was worn and rusted, the inside of the box was untouched by age or the elements. The interior was shiny and silver. The first thing I saw was an athame. I picked it up. It was heavy in my hand, ancient looking, with an age-worn silver blade and an intricately carved ivory handle. Celtic knots encircled the handle, finely carved but with the unmistakable look of handwork. This hadn't been made in a factory. Turning it over, I saw that the blade itself had been stamped with rows of initials, eighteen pairs of them. The very last ones were M. R. The ones above those were M. R.

"Maeve Riordan," I said, touching the initials. "And Mackenna Riordan, her mother. My grandmother. And me." I felt a rush of happiness. "This came to me from my family." A deep sense of belonging and continuity made me beam with satisfaction. I set the athame carefully on Robbie's bed.

Next I took out a package of deep green silk. When I held it up, it fell into the folds of a robe.

"Cool," said Robbie, touching it gently.

I nodded in agreement, awed. The robe was in the shape

of a large rectangle, with an opening for the head and knots of silk that held the shoulders together.

"It looks like a toga," I said, holding it up to my chest. I blinked, seeing Robbie's questioning face. I smiled at him, knowing that I would try on the robe—but at home, behind locked doors.

The embroidery was astounding: full of Celtic knots, dragons, pentacles, runes, stars, and stylized plants worked in gold and silver thread. It was a work of art, and I could imagine how proud Maeve would have been to inherit it from her mother, to wear it the first time she presided over a circle. As far as I knew, Mackenna had still been high priestess of Belwicket when it was destroyed.

"This is incredible," said Robbie.

"I know," I echoed. "I know."

Folding the robe gently, I laid it aside. Next I found four small silver bowls, embossed again with Celtic symbols. I recognized the runes for air, fire, water, and earth and knew that my birth mother had used these in her circles.

I took out a wand, made of black wood. Thin gold and silver lines had been pounded into the shaft, and the tip was set with a large crystal sphere. Four small red stones circled the wand beneath the crystal, and I wondered if they were real rubies.

Beneath everything, jumbled on the bottom, were several other large chunks of crystal as well as other stones, a feather, and a silver chain with a claddagh charm on it: two hands holding a heart topped with a crown. It was funny: Mom—my adoptive mom—had a claddagh ring that Dad had given her on their twenty-fifth anniversary, last year. The chain felt warm and heavy in my hand.

My gaze swept over all the tools. So much treasure, so much bounty. It was mine: my true inheritance, filled with magick and mystery and power. I felt full of joy but in a way that I could never explain to Robbie . . . in a way I couldn't explain even to myself.

"Two weeks ago I had nothing of my birth mother's," I found myself saying. "Now I have her Book of Shadows and all this besides. I mean, these are things she touched and used. They're full of her magick. And I have them! This is amazing."

Robbie shook his head, his eyes wide. "What's really amazing is that you found out about them by scrying," he murmured.

"I know, I know." Excitement coursed through my veins. "It was like Maeve actually chose to visit me, to give me a message."

"Pretty weird," Robbie acknowledged. "Now, did you say that they didn't do magick while they were in America?"

I nodded. "That's what I've gotten from her Book of Shadows. I mean, I haven't finished reading it yet."

"But she brought all of this with her, anyway? And didn't use it? That must have been really hard."

"Yeah," I said. An inexplicable sense of unease began to cloud my happiness. "I guess she couldn't bear to leave her tools behind, even if she couldn't use them again."

"Maybe she knew she would have a baby," suggested Robbie, "and thought that in time she could pass the tools on. Which she did."

I shrugged. "Could be," I said thoughtfully. "I don't know. Maybe I'll find some explanation in her book."

"I wonder if she thought not using them would protect her somehow," Robbie mused. "Maybe using them would have given away her identity or her location sooner."

I gazed at him, then back at all the stuff. "Maybe so," I said slowly. The unease began to grow. My brows came together as I went on. "Maybe it's still dangerous to have these things. Maybe I shouldn't touch them—or maybe I should put them back."

"I don't know," said Robbie. "Maeve told you where to find them. She didn't seem to be warning you, did she?"

I shook my head. "No. In my vision it felt positive. No warning signs at all." I carefully folded the robe and placed it back in the box, followed by the wand, the athame, and the four small cups. Then I closed the lid. I definitely needed to talk to Cal about this, and also Alyce or David, the next time I saw them.

"So, are you getting together with Cal tonight?" Robbie asked. He grinned. "He's going to flip over all this."

My excitement began to return. "I know. I can't wait to hear what he says about it. Speaking of which, I better go. I have to get cleaned up." I bit my lip, hesitating. "Are you going to Bree's circle tonight?"

"I am," Robbie said easily. He stood and started walking back down the hall. "They're meeting at Raven's."

"Hmmm." I put on my coat and opened the front door, the box tucked securely under my arm. "Well, be careful, okay? And thanks so much for coming with me today. I couldn't have done it without you." I leaned forward and hugged Robbie hard, and he patted my back awkwardly. Then I smiled and waved, and headed out to my car.

My birth mother's tools, I thought as I cranked the engine. I actually had the same tools that had been used by my birth mother, and *her* mother, and her mother's mother, and so on, for possibly hundreds of years . . . if the initials on the athame represented all the high priestesses of Belwicket. I felt a sense of belonging, of family history—one that I knew had somehow been lacking in my life until now. I wished that I could go to Ireland to research their coven and their town and find out what really happened. Maybe someday.

18.
Sigils

January 22, 1999

Now I know. Linden, my brother, barely fifteen years old, is dead. Goddess help me, I am all alone, but for Alwyn. And they say I murdered him.

I look at the words I just wrote, and I cannot make sense of them. Linden is dead. I am accused of Linden's murder.

They say my trial is starting soon. I can't think. My head aches all the time, what I eat my body rejects. I've lost more than two stone and can count my ribs.

My brother is dead.

When I looked at him I saw Mum's face. He is dead, and I am being blamed, though there is no way I would have done it.
—Giomanach

When I got home, no one else was around. I was glad to be by myself; I'd had an idea while I was driving back from Robbie's, and I wanted to test it in private.

First, though, it was time to take some precautions. I got a Phillips-head screwdriver from Dad's toolbox in the mud-room. Then I carried the box with Maeve's tools up to the second-floor landing. Unscrewing the HVAC vent cover, I pulled it out from the wall and set the box inside the vent. When I screwed the cover back on, it would be totally invisible. I knew because I'd used this spot as a hiding place over the years—I'd kept my first diary here, and Mary K.'s favorite doll when I hid it from her after a huge fight.

Before I closed the vent, though, I took out the athame, the beautiful, antique athame with my mother's initials on it. I loved the fact that my initials were the same as hers and my grandmother's. I ran my fingers gently over the carved handle as I carried the athame downstairs.

About a week before, I'd been looking for information about Wicca on-line, and I'd come across an old article by a woman named Helen Firesdaughter. It described the traditional witch's tools and their uses. The athame, the article had said, was linked with the element of fire. It was used to direct energy and to symbolize and bring about change. It was also used to illuminate, to bring hidden things to light.

I pulled on my coat, then stepped outside into the frigid dusk and closed the front door behind me. A quick glance up and down the street assured me that no one was watching. Holding the athame in front of me like a metal detector, I began to walk around my house. I swept the ancient blade over windowsills, doors, the clapboard siding, whatever I could reach.

I found the first sigil on the porch railing, around to the side. To the naked eye there was nothing there, but when the athame swept over it, the rune glowed very faintly, with an ethereal bluish witch light. My throat tightened. So— there it was. Proof that Sky and Hunter had worked magick here last night. I traced its lines and curves with my finger. Peorth. It stood for hidden things revealed.

I breathed deeply, trying to stay calm and rational. Peorth. Well, that didn't tell me much about their plans, one way or the other. I'd have to keep looking.

As I circled the house, more and more sigils glowed under the athame's blade. Daeg, for awakening and clarity. Eoh, the horse, which means change of some kind. Othel, for birthright, inheritance. And then, on the clapboards directly below my bedroom window, I found the one I'd been dreading to see: the double fishhook of Yr.

I stared at it and felt like a fist was squeezing my lungs. Yr. The death rune. Cal had told me that it didn't always have to mean death—that it could mean some other kind of important ending. I tried to take comfort in that possibility. But I was having a hard time convincing myself.

Then I felt a tingle at the edge of my senses. Someone was nearby. Watching me.

I spun around, peering into the dim winter twilight. A lone street lamp cast a cone of yellow light outside our yard. But I could see no shadowed form, no flicker of movement anywhere, not even when I used my magesight. Nor could I feel the presence any longer. Was I imagining it? Sensing things that weren't really there?

I didn't know. All I knew was that suddenly I couldn't

bear to be outside, alone, for one second longer. Turning, I bolted into the house and locked the door behind me.

By the time Cal came to pick me up, I had calmed down enough that I was feeling excited about my special birthday celebration.

"What's changed about you?" Cal asked as I pulled the front door closed. He smiled at me, puzzled. "You look different. Your eyes are different."

I batted my lashes at him. "I'm wearing makeup," I said. "Mary K. finally got her mitts on me. I figured, why not? It's a special occasion."

He laughed and took my arm, and together we walked to his car. "Well, you look incredible, but don't think you have to wear it on my account." He opened my door and then went around to the driver's side.

"Did you get my messages?" I asked as he started the engine.

He nodded. "Mom said you called." He didn't mention the witch message. "Sorry I missed you. I had some errands to do." He wiggled his eyebrows at me. "Mysterious errands, if you know what I mean, Birthday Girl."

I smiled briefly, but I was impatient to tell him about the events of the last 24 hours. "I had a pretty eventful day without you. In fact, I've had *two* pretty eventful days." I hunkered lower in my coat.

"What happened?" he asked.

I opened my mouth, and before I knew it, everything was tumbling out of me like an avalanche: the headlights behind me that had made me wreck, scrying into the fire, seeing Sky and Hunter outside my house the night before. Cal kept shooting glances at me, some baffled, some shocked, some worried. Then I offered up my pièce de résistance, finding Maeve's tools.

"You found your mother's tools?" he cried. The car swerved. I wondered for a second if it was going to end up like Das Boot. Luckily, though, we were turning into his driveway.

I threw up my hands and grinned. "I can't believe it myself," I said.

He cut the engine and sat there, staring at me in amazement. "Did you bring them?" he asked eagerly.

"No," I admitted. "I hid them behind the HVAC vent. And then when I was leaving, Dad was fixing an electrical outlet in the hall and I couldn't get to them."

Cal gave me an amused, conspiratorial look. "Behind the HVAC vent," he repeated, and I couldn't help laughing with him. It was a pretty silly hiding place for a bunch of magickal tools, come to think of it.

"Oh, well, no big deal. You can show them to me tomorrow," he said. I nodded.

"So—what do you think about my accident?" I asked.

"I don't know," he murmured. He shook his head. "It could have been just some jerk who was in a hurry. But if you were scared, I say you should trust your instincts—and we should start asking some questions." His eyes seemed to harden, but then his face melted in a worried smile. "Why didn't you tell me about this last night? And about Hunter and Sky being at your house?"

"I sent you a witch message," I told him. "But you

never came. I was wondering if Sky could have blocked it somehow."

Cal frowned. Then he smacked his forehead. "No, that's not it. I know exactly what it was. Mom and I did a powerful warding spell before our circle, just in case people like Sky or Hunter were trying to snoop on us. That would have blocked your message. Wow, I am so sorry. It never occurred to me that you might try to reach me."

"It's okay," I told him. "Nothing happened to me." A shudder ran through me as I remembered my terror last night. "At least, nothing permanent."

We got out of the car, shivering, and hurried up his front steps together.

We met Selene on her way out. She was wrapped in a black velvet cloak that swept to the ground and wore shining purple amethysts around her neck and on her ears. As always, she looked stunning.

"Good evening, my dears," she said with a smile. A delicious scent wafted off her, giving me an impression of maturity, of richness. It made my own dab of patchouli oil seem naive and hippyish—girly, almost.

"You look beautiful," I said sincerely.

"Thank you, Birthday Girl. So do you," she said, pulling on black gloves. "I'm going to a party." She shot Cal a meaningful look. "I won't be back till quite late, so be on your best behavior."

I felt embarrassed, but Cal laughed easily. As Selene left through the wide front door, we started to climb the stairs to his room on the third floor.

"Um, what does your mom think we might do?" I asked

clumsily. My steps were muffled by the thick carpet on the stairs.

"I guess she thinks we might make love," Cal said. Judging from his tone, it sounded like he was talking about spending the evening playing board games. He flashed a casual smile.

I nearly fell down the stairs. "Uh—would she . . . you know, be upset?" I stammered, struggling to sound calm but failing miserably. All of my friends' parents would have a cow if they thought their kids were doing that under their own roof. Well, maybe not Jenna's. But everyone else's.

"No," said Cal. "In Wicca, making love doesn't have the same kind of stigma as it does in other religions. It's seen as a celebration of love, of life—an acknowledgment of the God and Goddess. It's beautiful. Something special."

"Oh." Blood pounded through me. I nodded, trying to look confident.

Cal closed the door behind him. Then he pulled me to him and kissed me. "I'm sorry I wasn't there for you last night," he breathed against my lips. "I know I've been really tied up with Mom's business lately. But from now on I'm going to make sure I'm more available."

I reached up and draped my arms around his neck. "Good," I said.

He held me for a moment longer, then gently disengaged my arms and grabbed some matches from the nightstand by his bed. As I watched, he lit candles around his room, one by one, until there were tiny flames everywhere. The candles lined the mantel, the top of every bookcase, stood in holders on the floor; there was even an old-fashioned iron chandelier that held candles, hanging from the ceiling. When he

turned off the overhead light, we found ourselves surrounded in a glowing fiery cocoon. It was dreamy, beautiful,
romantic.

Next Cal walked over to his dark wooden desk, where a
bottle of sparkling cider stood next to a bowl filled with perfect, amazingly red strawberries and another bowl of dipping
chocolate. He poured two glasses of cider and brought
me one.

"Thank you," I said happily. "This is incredible." The light,
golden cider tickled my throat with its starry little bubbles.

He came and sat down next to me again, and we drank
our cider. "I can't wait to see Maeve's tools," he said,
stroking the hair along my temple. "The historical value
alone—it's like finding King Tut's tomb."

I laughed. "The Wiccan version of King Tut's tomb.
Which reminds me. I kept one thing out, and brought it with
me." Putting my glass down on the nightstand, I hopped up
and went to my jacket, where I took out the athame from
the breast pocket. I had wrapped it in a handkerchief. Silently
I handed it to Cal, watching his face as I nestled back down
with him again.

"Goddess," he whispered as he unwrapped it. His eyes
were shining, and an eager smile played about his lips. "Oh,
Morgan, this is beautiful."

I laughed again at his excitement. "I know. Isn't it
amazing?"

His fingers traced the lines of initials carved into the
blade. "Tomorrow," he said absently, then looked up at me.
"Tomorrow," he said more firmly, "I'm going to have a busy
day. First I have to find Hunter and Sky and tell them to leave

you the hell alone. Then I have to go to your house and remove all their sigils, if I can. Then I have to salivate over your mother's tools."

"Oh, that's a lovely image," I said, laughing. "Thank you."

He laughed, too, then we were leaning together, kissing and sipping cider. Magick, I thought dreamily, staring at him.

Cal kissed me again, his golden eyes intent, and then he blinked and pulled back.

"Presents!" he said, motioning across the room.

It took a second to spot the pile of beautifully wrapped gifts that waited for me on a large table pushed against the wall.

"What have you done?" I asked, putting my hand to my throat, where his silver pentacle still nestled warm against my skin. It was the first thing he'd ever given me, and I treasured it for that.

He grinned and stood, carrying the presents back to the bed and spreading them before me on the mattress. I took another sip of my cider, then placed it on the nightstand again.

First was a rectangular box. I started pulling off the paper.

"This is kind of redundant now," he said.

My face melted in a smile. Inside the box was the silver athame we had seen at Practical Magick, the one carved with roses and a skull. I turned to him.

"It's lovely," I said, running my fingers across it.

"It can be your backup," he said cheerfully. "Or a cake knife. Or a letter opener."

"Thank you," I whispered.

"I wanted you to have it," Cal said. "Next."

He held out a small box, and I held my breath as I opened it, revealing a gorgeous pair of silver earrings set with golden tigereyes. The gems looked so much like Cal's eyes that I had to glance up at him just for the sake of comparison.

"These are so beautiful." I shook my head.

"Put them on," he encouraged, "and it will be like I'm always with you." He brushed back my hair to expose my earlobe.

I held the earrings, not knowing what to say.

"Your ears aren't pierced," Cal said in surprise.

"I know," I mumbled apologetically. "My mom took me and Bree to have it done when we were twelve, but I chickened out."

"Oh, Morgan, I'm sorry," he said, laughing. "It's my fault. I can't believe I didn't notice before now. I should have gotten you something else. Here—I'll take them back and exchange them."

"No!" I said, pulling the box close. "I love them—they're the most beautiful things I've ever seen. I've been wanting to get my ears pierced, anyway. This will be my inspiration."

Cal looked at me assessingly but appeared to take my word. "Hmmm. Well, okay." He nodded at another present.

Next was a beautifully bound and illustrated book about spell weaving. It included a short history of spell making and had a whole section of sample spells and how to use them as well as how to individualize them for your particular situation.

"Oh, this is fabulous," I said with enthusiasm, leafing through it. "This is perfect."

"I'm glad you like it," he said, grinning. "We can go over some of them if you want, practice them."

I nodded eagerly, like a child, and he laughed again.

"And last," he said, handing me a medium-size box.

"More?" I couldn't quite believe this. I was beginning to feel spoiled. Inside this box was a batik blouse in muted shades of lavender and purple and plum. It looked like a storm-shot sunset. I stared at it, touching the cloth with my fingers, drinking in the colors, practically hearing the rumble of thunder and rain.

"I love it," I said, leaning over to hug him. "I love all of it. Thank you so much for this." My throat tightened with a rush of emotion. Once again I felt a sense of belonging, of pure contentment. "These are the best birthday gifts anyone has ever given me."

Cal gave me a sweet smile, and then I was in his arms and we were lying on the bed. I held his head tightly, my fingers laced through his dark hair as we kissed.

"Do you love me?" he whispered against my mouth. I nodded, overwhelmed, holding him hard against me, wanting to be closer.

The cider, the candles all around us, the slight scent of incense, the feel of his smooth skin under my hands—it was as if he were weaving a spell of love around me, making me drowsy and full of a physical longing and ache. And yet . . . and yet. I still held the end of a line between us. Despite my love for him, despite the dark wave of yearning he had awoken in me, I felt myself holding back.

Dimly, as we kissed, I came to the surprising realization that I wasn't quite ready to completely give myself to him. Even though we were probably *mùirn beatha dàns,* still, I wasn't ready to make love with him, to go all the way in joining ourselves together physically and mentally. I didn't know the reason, but I had to trust my feelings.

"Morgan," Cal said softly. He raised up on one elbow and looked at me. He was incredibly beautiful, the most beautiful male I had ever seen. His cheeks were flushed, his mouth a dark rose color from kissing. There was no way he and Hunter could be brothers, I thought distantly—and I wondered why Hunter had even popped into my thoughts. Hunter was mean and dangerous, a liar.

"Come on," Cal said, his voice husky, his hand stroking my waist through my black jumper.

"Um . . ."

"What's wrong?" he whispered.

I let out my breath, not knowing what to say. He draped one leg over me and pulled me closer, curling his hand around my back and snuggling. He nuzzled my neck, and his hand drifted up my waist to just below my breast. It felt incredible, and I willed myself to give in to it, to let the wash of sensation carry me to a new place. I would be seventeen tomorrow: it was time. But somehow I just couldn't. . . .

"Morgan?" His voice sounded questioning, and my eyes flew to his. His hand stroked my hair away from my face. "I want to make love to you."

19.
Circle of Two

They are pushing me to join with her. And I want to do it. Goddess, how I want to do it. She is a butterfly, a flower in bloom, a dark ruby being cut from dusty stone. And I can make her better than that. I can make her catch fire, so her power illuminates all who stand near. I can teach her, I can help her reach the deep magick within. Together we will be unstoppable.

Whoever would have thought this could happen? One look at her would not have revealed the tigress waiting inside. Her love devours me, her constancy humbles me, her beauty and power make me hunger.

She will be mine. And I will be hers.

—Sgàth

I stared at Cal, loving him but feeling utterly lost.

"I thought you wanted me, too," he said quietly.

I nodded. That was true—partially, anyway. But what my brain wanted and my body wanted were two different things.

"If you're worried about birth control, I can take care of it," he said. "I wouldn't ever hurt you."

"I know." I could feel tears welling up in my eyes, and I willed them to stop. I felt like a complete failure, and I didn't know why.

Cal rolled away from me, his arm resting across his forehead as he looked at me. "So what is it?" he said.

"I don't know," I whispered. "I mean, I want to, but I just can't. I don't feel ready."

He reached out his other hand and held mine, absently stroking his thumb across my palm. Finally he shifted and sat up cross-legged in front of me. I scrambled into a sitting position opposite him.

"Are you angry?" I asked.

He smiled wryly. "I'll live. It's okay. Don't worry about it. I . . ." He left the sentence unfinished.

"I'm sorry," I said miserably. "I don't know what's wrong with me."

He leaned over and pushed my hair off my neck to kiss my nape gently. I shuddered at the warmth of his lips. "Nothing is wrong with you," he whispered. "We have our whole future together. There's no hurry. Whenever you're ready, I'll be here."

I swallowed, worrying that if I opened my mouth again, I would definitely start crying.

"Look, let's do a circle," he said, rubbing the tension out of my neck. "Not a *circle* circle, but just like a joined meditation. It's another way for us to be close. Okay?"

I nodded. "Okay," I choked out.

I reached for him, and we held hands loosely, with our knees touching. Together we closed our eyes and began to systematically shut everything down: emotions, sensations, awareness of the outside world. I felt embarrassed about not wanting to sleep with him, but I deliberately released those feelings. It was almost as if I could see them falling away from me. My eyes stopped stinging; my throat relaxed.

Gradually our breathing, in sync, slowed and quieted. I had been meditating almost every day, and it was easy for me to slip into a light trance. I lost the sensation of touching Cal: we felt joined, breathing as one, drifting as one into a place of deep peace and restfulness. It was a relief.

I became aware of the strength of Cal's mind, aligning with mine, and it was very exciting and intimate. It was amazing that we could share this, and I thought of all the nonwitches in the world who would probably never be able to achieve such closeness with their lovers. I breathed a long sigh of contentment.

In our meditation I felt Cal's thoughts; I read the intensity of his passion, felt his desire for me, and my flesh broke out in goosebumps. I felt his admiration of my strength in the craft, as well as eagerness for me to progress—to get stronger and stronger, as strong as he was. I tried to share my own thoughts with him, unsure if he was reading me as well. I expressed my desires and hopes for our future together; I tried to let waves of pure emotion convey my feelings in a way that words never could.

Eventually we drifted apart, like two leaves separating as they fell toward earth. I slipped back into my self, and we remained there for a while afterward, gazing at each other. It was the most intensely connected I had ever felt to another person. I knew it. But knowing this also made me feel vulnerable and nervous.

"Was it good for you?" I asked, trying to lighten the moment.

He smiled. "It was great for me."

I looked into his face for a while longer, allowing myself to get lost in his eyes, enjoying the silence and the glow of the candles. Dimly I became aware of the ticking of a clock nearby. I glanced at it.

"Oh my God, is it one o'clock?" I gasped.

Cal looked, too, and grinned. "Hmmm. Do you have a curfew?"

I was already climbing off the bed. "Not officially," I said, searching for my shoes. "But I'm supposed to call if I'm later than midnight. Of course, if I call now, I'll wake them up." Quickly I gathered my presents into a pile. I found Maeve's athame and put it back inside my coat. We trotted downstairs. A pang of longing welled up inside me; I wanted to stay *here,* in the warmth and coziness of Cal's room, with him.

Cold wind blasted my face when we stepped through the front door.

"Ugh," I moaned, gripping the neck of my coat tighter.

Heads down, we hurried out to Cal's Explorer. "Maybe we should call your folks and tell them you're having a sleepover," he suggested with a grin.

I laughed, thinking of how well that would go over with Mom and Dad, then carefully placed my beautiful birthday presents on the backseat. But as I was about to climb into the front, the sound of a car arriving made me pause. I glanced at Cal. His eyes had narrowed. He looked alert and tense, his hand on the car door next to me.

"Is it your mom?" I asked.

Cal shook his head. "That's not her car."

Using magesight, I squinted into the approaching head-lights, staring right past them. My heart lurched. It was a gray car. Hunter's car.

He pulled to a stop in front of us.

"Oh God, what's he doing here?" I groaned. "It's one in the morning!"

"Who knows?" Cal said tersely. "But I need to talk to him, anyway."

Hunter left his car running as he stepped out and faced us. The headlights put him in silhouette, but I could see that his green eyes were solemn. His cold seemed to have gotten better. His breath was like white smoke.

"Hello," he said precisely. Just hearing him speak made me clench up. "Fancy meeting the both of you here. How inconvenient."

"Why?" Cal asked, his voice low. "Were you going to put sigils on my house, like you did Morgan's?"

A glimmer of surprise crossed Hunter's face.

"Know about that, do you?" he said, shifting his gaze to me.

I nodded coldly.

"What else do you know?" Hunter asked. "Like, do you know what Cal wants from you? What you are to him? Do you know the truth about *anything*?"

I glared at him, trying to think of a scathing reply. But

again the only thought I had was: Why is he tormenting us like this?

Beside me Cal clenched his fists. "She knows the truth. I love her."

"No," Hunter corrected him. "The truth is, you *need* her. You need her because she has incredible, untapped powers. You need her so you can use her power to take over the High Council, and then you can start to eliminate the other clans, one by one. Because you're a Woodbane, too, and frankly, the other clans just aren't good enough."

My eyes flashed to Cal. "What is he talking about? You're not a Woodbane, are you?"

"He's raving," Cal muttered, staring at Hunter with pure contempt. "Saying anything he can think of to hurt me." Cal put his arm around me. "You can forget breaking us up," he said. "She loves me, and I love her."

Hunter laughed. The sound of it was like glass shattering. "What a crock," he spat. "She's your lightning rod—the last surviving member of Belwicket, the destined high priestess of one of the most powerful of the Woodbane clans. Don't you get it? Belwicket renounced the dark arts! There's no way Morgan would agree to what you want!"

"How would *you* know what I would do?" I shouted, infuriated by how he was speaking as if I weren't there.

Cal just shook his head. "There's no point to this," he said. "We're together, and there's nothing you can do. So you can go back to where you came from and leave us alone."

Hunter chuckled softly. "Oh, no, I'm afraid it's much too late for that. You see, the council would never forgive me if I left Morgan in your clutches."

"What?" I practically screeched. What the hell did the council care who I dated? I hardly even *knew* about the council. How could they know so much about me?

"You should know about forgiveness," Cal snapped. "After all, the council has never quite forgiven you for killing your brother, right? You're still making up for that, aren't you? Still trying to prove it wasn't your fault."

I stared at the two of them. I had no idea what Cal was talking about, but his tone terrified me. He sounded like a stranger.

"Go to hell," Hunter snarled, his body tightening.

"Wiccans don't believe in hell," Cal whispered.

Hunter started toward us, his face stiff with fury. All at once Cal ducked into the car and snatched the athame he'd given me from the pile of gifts. My pulse shot into overdrive. This isn't happening, I thought in panic. This can't be happening. I watched, immobile, as Cal backed away from me. Hunter glanced between the two of us.

"You want me?" Cal taunted Hunter. "You want me, Hunter? Then come get me." With that, he turned and sped straight for the dark woods bordering the property. I blinked, and he was out of sight, hidden by trees and darkness.

Hunter was wild-eyed as he scanned the woods' edge.

"Stay here!" he commanded me, then he raced off after Cal.

I stopped for just a moment. Then I ran after them.

20.
The Seeker

February 12, 1999

    With help, now, I can walk across a room. But I am still weak, so weak.

    My trial is starting tomorrow.

    I have been telling my story over and over, what I remember of it. I woke in the night and saw Linden was gone. I tracked him to the fell, and found him in the middle of calling a <u>taibhs</u>, a dark spirit. It is something we had talked about in the past year, in our search for answers about our parents. But I had not counseled Linden to do it, nor would I have ever condoned his trying to summon the evil thing alone.

    I saw Linden, his arms upstretched, a look of joy on his face. The dark taibhs moved toward him, and I rushed forward. I could not get through the circle without magick so I conjured a break in the force. The rest of what I remember is a nightmare of reaching for Linden, of finding him and having him sag in my arms, of being surrounded by a choking wraith, then being smothered, unable to breathe, and sinking down to the cold ground to embrace death.

Next I woke in my bed at Uncle Beck and Aunt Shelagh's, with witches around me praying for my recovery, after six days of unconsciousness.

I know I did not kill my brother, but I know that my quest to redress the harm done my family is what caused his death. For this I could be sentenced to death. Except that I know Alwyn would grieve for me, I would welcome it, for there is no life for me here anymore.

—Giomanach

By the time I reached the edge of the woods, it had started to snow again. While Cal and I were inside, the sky had been consumed by thick gray clouds that blotted out the moon and the stars.

"Dammit," I whispered. Cal had obviously led Hunter away to protect me, but how could he expect me to stand around, waiting to see what happened? I didn't know what was going on between the two of them. All I knew was that I would never forgive Hunter if he hurt Cal.

The woods were dense and untamed, the undergrowth thick and impossible to run through. I ran into a low-hanging branch, and I stopped. I had no idea where Cal and Hunter had gone. It was absolutely black here, and for a moment I trembled. I had to breathe slowly, to focus and concentrate. I clenched and unclenched my fists and squeezed my eyes shut.

"One, two, three," I counted. I breathed in and out.

A moment later I opened my eyes and found that my magesight had kicked in and I could see. Trees stood out as dark verticals, the undergrowth was defined, and the few nocturnal animals and birds who weren't hibernating glowed with a pale yellow light. Okay. I scanned the area, and easily picked up the rough track Hunter and Cal had made as they crashed through the woods: the forest floor was scraped and disturbed, and small branches were snapped.

As quickly as I could, I followed their trail. My feet and nose were freezing, and snow began to fall and bleach the surroundings. Slowly I became aware of a dim, rhythmic pounding. It wasn't the blood in my veins. Then it came to me: of course. Selene and Cal lived at the edge of town; their house was practically on the Hudson River. The surging waters were dead ahead. I quickened my pace, grabbing trees to push me forward, stumbling against rocks, cursing.

"You're bidden to come with me!"

It was Hunter's voice. I stopped silent, listening—then rushed forward and came out into a narrow, treeless strip that ran parallel with the river. Hunter was backed against the edge of the cliff, and Cal, holding my athame in front of him, was moving forward. I was lost in a swirl of fear and confusion.

"Cal!" I shouted.

They both turned, their faces unreadable in the snow and darkness.

"Stay back!" Cal ordered me, flinging out his hand. To my utter shock I stopped hard, as if I'd struck a wall. He had used a spell against me.

The next instant Hunter hurled a ball of witch light, and it knocked the athame from Cal's hand. Cal's jaw dropped. I struggled to believe that this was real, my real life, and not just a screen full of computer-generated effects. Hunter leaped away from the edge and onto Cal, who was scrambling back toward the knife. As I tried to move forward, I felt like I was wrapped in a thick wool blanket. My legs were made of stone. The two of them rolled over in the new-fallen snow, light hair and dark flashing against the ground and the background of night.

"Stop it!" I shouted as loud as I could, but they ignored me.

Cal pinned Hunter on the ground, then closed his fist and smashed it into Hunter's face. Hunter's head whipped sideways. A bright ribbon of blood streamed from his nose. The redness on the snow reminded me of the spilled communion wine last Sunday, and I shuddered. This was wrong. This shouldn't be happening. This kind of anger, of long-held hatred, was the antithesis of magick. I had to separate them.

Gathering all my strength, I pictured myself breaking out of an eggshell and then tried to shove my way out of Cal's binding spell. This time I was able to move. A few feet away I saw the athame, and I lunged for it—at the very moment Hunter shoved Cal off him. We all stumbled to our feet at the same time, panting heavily.

"Morgan, get out of here!" Hunter yelled at me, not taking his eyes off Cal. "I'm a Seeker, and Cal has to answer to the council!"

"Don't listen to him, Morgan!" Cal retorted. I saw flecks of Hunter's blood on his fist. "He's jealous of anything I have, and he wants to hurt me. He'll hurt you, too!"

"That's a lie," Hunter spat angrily. "Cal's Woodbane, Morgan, but unlike Maeve, he hasn't renounced the dark side. Please, just get out of here!"

Cal turned to me, and his hot golden eyes caught mine. A fuzzy softness clouded my brain. I blinked. Hunter said something, but it was muffled, and time seemed to slow. What was happening to me? I watched helplessly as Hunter and Cal circled each other, their eyes burning, their faces stony and pale.

Hunter spoke again, waving his arm, and it fluttered through the air slowly. His voice was like the deep growl of an animal. They came softly together—as if their movements were choreographed—and Hunter's fist connected with Cal's stomach. Cal doubled over. I winced, but I was trapped in a nightmare, powerless to stop the fight. I clutched the athame to my chest. There was a small knot of heat at my throat. I touched the warm silver of the pentacle hanging there. But I couldn't move toward them.

Cal straightened. Hunter swung again at him but missed. Then Cal kicked the back of Hunter's knee, and Hunter crumpled to the ground, the blood on his face smearing the snow. Memories flashed through my mind as Hunter staggered to his feet and threw himself on Cal . . . Hunter telling me Cal was Woodbane, Hunter in the dark outside my house, Hunter being so snide and hateful.

I remembered Cal kissing me, touching me, showing me magick. Showing me how to ground myself at circles, giving me presents. I thought of Bree yelling at me in her car by the side of the road, so long ago. Sky and Hunter together. The images made me unbearably weary. All I wanted to do was lie down in the snow and fall asleep. I sank to my knees, feeling a smile form on my lips. Sleep, I thought. There must have been magick at work, but it didn't seem to matter.

In front of me Cal and Hunter rolled over and over, toward the river.

"Morgan."

My name came to me softly, on a snowflake, and I looked up. For just an instant I met Cal's eyes. They stared pleadingly at me. Then I saw that Hunter was holding Cal down, his knee on Cal's chest. He had a length of silver chain and was binding Cal's hands with it while Cal writhed in pain.

"Morgan."

I received a sharp flash of his pain. I gasped and grabbed my chest, falling forward onto the snow. As I blinked rapidly, my head suddenly seemed clearer.

"He's killing me. Help me. Morgan!"

I couldn't hear the words, but I felt them inside my head, and I pushed myself to my feet with one hand.

"You're through," Hunter was gasping angrily, pulling the silver chain. "I've got you."

"Morgan!" Cal's shout ripped through the snowy night and shattered my calm. I had to move, to fight. I loved Cal, had always loved him. I struggled to my feet as if I had been asleep for a long, long time. I had no plan; I was no match for Hunter, but suddenly I remembered I was still clutching the athame, my birthday athame. Without thinking, I hurled it at Hunter as hard as I could. I watched as it sailed through the air in a gleaming arc.

It struck Hunter's neck, quivering there for a second before falling. Hunter cried out and clapped his hand to the wound. Blood began to spout from the flesh, blooming red like a poppy. I couldn't believe what I had done.

In that second Cal drew up his knees and kicked Hunter as hard as he could. With a cry of surprise Hunter staggered back, off balance, still clutching his wound . . . and then I was screaming, "No! No! No!" as he toppled clumsily and disappeared over the edge of the cliff.

I stared at the emptiness, dumbstruck.

"Morgan, help!" Cal cried, startling me. "Get this off! It's burning me! Get it off!"

Numb, I hurried to Cal and pulled at the silver chain looped around his wrists. I felt nothing but a mild tingle when I touched it—but I saw raw, red blistering welts on Cal's skin where it had touched him. Once it was off, I threw down the chain and scrambled to the edge of the cliff. If I saw Hunter's body at the bottom, on the rocks, I knew I would throw up, but I forced myself to look, already thinking about calling 911, about trying to climb down there, wondering if I remembered CPR from my baby-sitting course.

But I saw nothing. Nothing but a jumble of rocks and the gray, turbulent water.

Cal staggered up beside me. I met his eyes. He looked horrified, pale and hollow and weak. "Goddess, he's already gone," Cal murmured. "He must have hit the water, and the current . . ." He was breathing hard, his dark hair wet with snow and traces of blood.

"We have to call someone," I said softly, reaching out to touch him. "We have to tell someone about Hunter. And we have to take care of your wrists. Do you think you can get back to the house?"

Cal just shook his head. "Morgan," he said in a broken voice. "You saved me." With fingers swollen from hitting Hunter, he touched my cheek and said tenderly, "You saved me. Hunter was going to kill me, but you protected me from him, like you said you would. I love you." He kissed me, his lips cold and tasting of blood. "I love you more than I ever knew I could. Today our future truly begins."

I didn't know what to say. My thoughts had stopped swirling; they had vanished altogether. My mind was a void. I put my arm around him as he began to limp back through the woods, and I couldn't help glancing over my shoulder to the cliff's edge. It was all too much to take in, everything that had happened, and I concentrated on putting one foot in front of the other, feeling Cal rest some of his weight on me as we slogged through the snow.

And then I remembered: it was November 23.

I wondered what time it was—I knew it was very late. I had been born at two-seventeen in the morning on November 23. I decided I must already be officially seventeen. I swallowed. This was the first day of my seventeenth year. What would tomorrow bring?

Dark Magick

Cate Tiernan

PUFFIN

For my mùirn beatha dàn

1.
Falling

November 1999

The council pronounced me not guilty of killing Linden. The vote of the seven elders of the Great Clans was not unanimous, though. The Vikroth representative and the Wyndenkell, my mother's own clanswoman, voted against me.

I had almost hoped they would condemn me, for then at least my life's path would be certain. And in a way, I was guilty, was I not? I filled Linden's head with my talk of vengeance, and opened his mind to the idea of calling on the darkness. If I had not actually killed my brother, then I knew he had found his way to his death along a path I had shown him.

When I was found innocent, I felt lost. I knew only that I would spend the rest of my life atoning for Linden's death.

—Giomanach

Snowflakes mixed with sleet whipped at my cheeks. I stumbled through the snow, supporting my boyfriend Cal's weight against me, my feet growing leaden and icy in my clogs. Cal stumbled, and I braced myself. In the moonlight I peered up at his face, alarmed by how white he looked, how beaten, how ill. I trudged through the dark woods, feeling like every step away from the cliff took an hour.

The cliff. In my mind, I saw Hunter Niall falling backward, his arms windmilling as he went over the edge. Bile rose in my throat, and I swallowed convulsively. Yes, Cal was a mess, but Hunter was probably dead. Dead! And Cal and I had killed him. I drew in a shuddering breath as Cal swayed against me.

Together we stumbled through the woods, accompanied only by the malevolent hiss of the sleet in the black branches around us. Where was Cal's house?

"Are we headed the right way?" I asked Cal. The freezing wind snatched the words from my throat.

Cal blinked. One eye was swollen shut and already purple. His beautiful mouth was bloody, and his lower lip was split.

"Never mind," I said, looking ahead. "I think this is it."

By the time Cal's house was in view, we were both soaked through and frozen. Anxiously I scanned the circular driveway for Selene Belltower's car, but Cal's mother was still out. Not good. I needed help.

"Tired," Cal said fuzzily as I helped him up the steps. Somehow we made it through the front door, but once inside, there was no way I could get him up to his attic room.

"There." Cal gestured with a hand swollen from punching Hunter. Feeling unbearably weary, I lurched through the parlor doors and helped Cal collapse on the blue sofa. He toppled over, curling to fit on the cushions. He was shaking with cold, his face shocked and pale.

"Cal," I said, "we need to call 911. About Hunter. Maybe they can find him. It might not be too late."

Cal's face crinkled in a grotesque approximation of a laugh. His split lip oozed blood, and his cheek was mottled with angry bruises. "It's too late," he croaked, his teeth chattering. "I'm positive." He nodded toward the fireplace, his eyes shut. "Fire."

Was it too late for Hunter? A tiny part of me almost hoped it was—if Hunter was dead, then we couldn't help him, and I didn't even have to try.

But was he? A sob rose in my throat. Was he?

Okay, I thought, trying to calm down. Okay. Break down the situation. Make a plan. I knelt and clumsily piled newspaper and kindling on the grate. I chose three large logs and arranged them on top.

I didn't see any matches, so, closing my eyes, I tried to summon fire with my mind. But my magickal powers felt almost nonexistent. In fact, just trying to call on them made my head ache sharply. After nearly seventeen years of living without magick, to find myself bereft of it now was terrifying. I opened my eyes and looked wildly around. Finally I saw an Aim 'n' Flame on the mantel, and I grabbed it and popped its trigger.

The paper and kindling caught. I swayed toward the flames, feeling their healing warmth, then I glanced at Cal again. He looked wretched.

"Cal?" I helped him sit up enough to tug him out of his leather jacket, taking care not to scrape his wrists, which were raw and blistered where Hunter had tried to bind them with a strange magickal chain. I pulled off Cal's wet boots. Then I covered him up with a patchwork velvet throw that was draped artistically over one end of the couch. He squeezed my fingers and tried to smile at me.

"Be right back," I said, and hurried to the kitchen. I felt horribly alone as I waited for water to boil. I ran upstairs and rummaged through the first bathroom I found for bandages, then went back down and fixed a pot of herb tea. A pale face with accusing green eyes seemed to form in the steam that rose from the top of the teapot. Hunter, oh, God, Hunter.

Hunter had tried to kill Cal, I reminded myself. He might have tried to kill me, too. Still, it was Hunter who had gone over the edge of the cliff into the Hudson River, the river filled with ice chunks as big as his head. It was Hunter who had probably been swept away by the current and Hunter whose body would be found tomorrow. Or not. I clamped my lips together to keep from sobbing as I hurried back to Cal.

Slowly I got Cal to drink a whole mug of goldenseal-and-ginger tea. His color looked better when he had finished it. I gently swabbed his wrists with a damp cloth, then wrapped them with a roll of gauze I had found, but the skin was blistered, and I knew it must hurt incredibly.

After the tea Cal lay down again and slept, his breathing uneven. Should I have given him Tylenol? Should I hunt around for witch-type medicine? In the short while I had known Cal, he had been the strong one in our relationship. I had counted on him. Now he was counting on me, and I didn't know if I was ready.

The mantel clock above my head struck three slow chimes. I stared at it. Three o'clock in the morning! I set my mug down on the coffee table. I was supposed to be home by one. And I didn't even have my car—Cal had picked me up. He was clearly in no shape to drive. Selene wasn't back yet. Dammit! I said to myself. Think, think.

I could call my dad and have him come get me. Very unappealing option.

It was too late to call the only taxi service in Widow's Vale, which was in essence Ed Jinkins in his old Cutlass Supreme hanging out at the commuter station.

I could take Cal's car.

Five minutes later I let myself out of the house carefully. Cal was still asleep. I had taken the keys from his jacket, then written a note of explanation and tucked it in his jeans pocket, hoping he would understand. I stopped dead when I saw Hunter's gray sedan sitting in the driveway like an accusation. Crap! What to do about his car?

There was nothing I could do. Hunter had the keys. And he was gone. I couldn't push the car anywhere by myself and anyway, that seemed so—methodical somehow. So planned.

My head spun. What should I do? Waves of exhaustion flowed over me, almost making me weep. But I had to accept the fact that I couldn't do anything about this. Cal or Selene would have to deal with Hunter's car. Trembling, I climbed into Cal's gold Explorer, turned on the brights, and headed for home.

Cal had used spells on me tonight, spells of binding so I couldn't move. Why? So I wouldn't interfere in his battle with Hunter? So I wouldn't be hurt? Or because he didn't trust me? Well, if he hadn't trusted me before, he knew better now. I clamped my teeth together on a semihysterical giggle. It wasn't every girl who would throw a Wiccan ceremonial dagger into the neck of her boyfriend's enemy.

Hunter had tried to kill Cal, had bound his hands with spelled silver chain that had started to sizzle against Cal's flesh as soon as it touched him. That was when I'd hurled the athame at him and sent him over the cliff's edge. And probably killed him. Killed him.

I shuddered as I turned onto my street. *Had* we actually killed him? Did Hunter have a chance? Maybe the wound in his neck wasn't as horrific as it had seemed. Maybe, when he went over the cliff, he had landed on a ledge. Maybe he was found by a park ranger or someone like that.

Maybe.

I let the Explorer drift to a halt around the corner from my house. As I pocketed the keys, I noticed all the birthday gifts Cal had given me earlier, piled up on the backseat. Well, almost all. The beautiful athame was gone—Hunter had taken it over the cliff with him. With a sense of unreality I gathered up the other gifts and then ran home down the shoveled and salted walks. I let myself in silently, feeling with my senses. Again my magick was like a single match being held in a storm wind instead of the powerful wave I was used to feeling. I couldn't detect much of anything.

To my relief, my parents didn't stir as I went past their bedroom door. In my own room I sat for a moment on the edge of my bed, collecting my strength. After the nightmarish events of tonight my bedroom looked babyish, as if it belonged to a stranger. The pink-and-white-striped walls, flowered border, and frilly curtains had never been me, anyway. Mom had picked everything out and redone the room for me as a surprise while I was at camp, six years ago.

I threw off my clammy clothes and sighed with relief as I pulled on sweats. Then I went downstairs and dialed 911.

"What is the nature of the emergency?" a crisp voice asked.

"I saw someone fall into the Hudson," I said quickly, speaking through a tissue like they did in old movies. "About two miles up from the North Bridge." This was an estimate, based on where I thought Cal's house was. "Someone fell in. He may need help." I hung up quickly, hoping I hadn't stayed on the phone long enough for the call to be traced. How did that work? Did I have to stay on for a minute? Thirty seconds? Oh, Jesus. If they tracked me down I would confess everything. I couldn't live with this burden on my soul.

My mind was racing with everything that had happened: my wonderful, romantic birthday with Cal; almost making love but then backing out; all my gifts; the magick we shared; my birth mother's athame, which I had shown Cal tonight and was now clutching like a security blanket; then the battle with Hunter, the horror as he fell. And now it was too late, Cal said. But was it? I had to try one last thing.

I put on my wet coat, went outside, and walked around the side of my house in the darkness. Holding my birth mother's athame, I leaned close to a windowsill. There, glowing faintly beneath the knife's power, shimmered a sigil. Sky Eventide and Hunter had surrounded my house with the charms; I still didn't know why. But I hoped this would work.

Once more closing my eyes, I held the athame over the

sigil. I concentrated, feeling like I was about to pass out. Sky, I thought, swallowing. Sky.

I hated Sky Eventide. Everything about her filled me with loathing and distrust, just as Hunter did, though for some reason Hunter upset me more. But she was his ally, and she was the person who should be told about him. I sent my thought out toward the purplish snow clouds. Sky. Hunter is in the river, by Cal's house. Go get him. He needs your help.

What am I doing? I thought, beyond weariness. I can't even light a match. I can't feel my family sleeping inside my house. My magick is gone. But still I stood there in the cold darkness, my eyes closed, my hand turning to a frozen claw around the knife handle. Hunter is in the river. Go get him. Go get Hunter. Hunter is in the river.

Tears came without warning, shockingly warm against my chilled cheeks. Gasping, I stumbled back inside and hung up my coat. Then I slowly mounted the steps, one by one, and was dimly surprised when I made it to the top. I hid my mother's athame under my mattress and crawled into bed. My kitten, Dagda, stretched sleepily, then moved up to coil himself next to my neck. I curled one hand around him. Huddled under my comforter, I shook with cold and wept until the first blades of sunlight pierced the childish, ruffled curtains at my window.

2.
Guilty

November 1999

Uncle Beck, Aunt Shelagh, and Cousin Athan held a small celebration for me back at the house, after the trial. But my heart was full of pain.

I sat at the kitchen table. Aunt Shelagh and Alwyn were swooping around, arranging food on plates. Then Uncle Beck came in. He told me that I'd been cleared of the blame and I must let it go.

"How can I?" I asked. It was I who'd first tried to use dark magick to find our parents. Though Linden had acted alone in calling on the dark spectre that killed him, he wouldn't have had the idea if I hadn't put it into his head.

Then Alwyn spoke up. She said I was wrong, that Linden had always liked the dark side. She said he liked the power, and that he'd thought making herb mixtures was beneath him.

Her halo of corkscrew curls, fiery red like our Mum's, seemed to quiver as she spoke.

"What are you on about?" I asked her. "Linden never mentioned any of this to me."

She said Linden had believed I wouldn't understand. He'd told her he wanted to be the most powerful witch anyone had ever seen. Her words were like needles in my heart.

Uncle Beck asked why she hadn't told us sooner, and she said she had. I saw her jut her chin in that obstinate way she has. And Aunt Shelagh thought about it, and said, "You know, she did. She did tell me. I thought she was telling stories."

Alwyn said no one had believed her because she was just a kid. Then she left the room, while Uncle Beck, Aunt Shelagh, and I sat in the kitchen and weighed our guilt.

—Giomanach

I woke up on my seventeenth birthday feeling like someone had put me in a blender and set it to chop. Sleepily I blinked and checked my clock. Nine. Dawn had come at six, so I had gotten a big three hours' sleep. Great. And then I thought—is Hunter dead? Did I kill him? My stomach roiled, and I wanted to cry.

Under the covers, I felt a small warm body creeping cautiously along my side. When Dagda poked his little gray head out from under the covers, I stroked his ears.

"Hi, little guy," I said softly. I sat up just as the door to my room opened.

"Morning, birthday girl!" my mom said brightly. She crossed my room and pushed aside the curtains, filling my room with brittle sunlight.

"Morning," I said, trying to sound normal. A vision of my mom finding out about Hunter made me shudder. It would destroy her.

She sat on my bed and kissed my forehead, as if I was seven instead of seventeen. Then she peered at me. "Do you feel all right?" She pressed the back of her hand against my forehead. "Hmmm. No fever. But your eyes look a bit red and puffy."

"I'm okay. Just tired," I mumbled. Time to change the subject. I had a sudden thought. "Is today really my actual birthday?" I asked.

Mom stroked my hair back from my face with a gentle hand. "Of course it is. Morgan, you've seen your birth certificate," she reminded me.

"Oh, right." Until a few weeks ago I had always believed I was a Rowlands, like the rest of my family. But when I met Cal and began exploring Wicca, it became clear that I had magickal powers and that I was a blood witch, from a long line of blood witches—witches from one of the Seven Great Clans of Wicca. That's how I'd found out I was adopted. Since then it had been pretty much of an emotional roller-coaster ride here at home. But I loved my parents, Sean and Mary Grace Rowlands, and my sister, Mary K., who was their biological daughter. And they loved me. And they were trying to come to terms with my Wiccan heritage, my legacy. As was I.

"Now, since today is your birthday, you can do what you

want, more or less," Mom said, absently tickling Dagda's bat-like gray ears. "Do you want to have a big breakfast and we'll go to a later mass? Or we can go to church now and then do something special for lunch?"

I don't want to go to church at all, I thought. Lately my relationship with church had seemed like a battle of wills as I struggled to integrate Wicca into my life. I also couldn't face the idea of sitting through a Catholic mass and then having lunch with my family after what had happened the night before. "Um, is it all right if I just sleep in today?" I asked. "I am feeling a little under the weather, actually. You guys do church and lunch without me."

Mom's lips thinned, but after a moment she nodded. "All right," she said. "If that's what you want." She stood up. "Do you want us to bring you back something for lunch?"

The idea of food repulsed me. "Oh, no thanks," I said, trying to sound casual. "I'll just find something in the fridge. Thanks, anyway, though."

"Okay," Mom said, touching my forehead again. "Tonight Eileen and Paula are coming over, and we'll do dinner and cake and presents. Sound good?"

"Great," I said, and Mom closed the door behind her. I sank back on my pillow. I felt as if I had a split personality. On the one hand, I was Morgan Rowlands, good daughter, honor roll student, math whiz, observant Catholic. On the other hand, I was a witch, by heritage and inclination.

I stretched, feeling the ache in my muscles. The events of the night before hovered over my head like a storm cloud. What had I done? How had I come to this? If only I knew for sure whether or not Hunter was dead. . . .

I waited until I heard the front door close behind my family. Then I got up and began pulling on my clothes. I knew what I had to do next.

I drove my car to the back road that ran behind Cal's house and parked. Then I crunched across the snow to the cliff's rocky edge. Carefully I stretched out on my stomach and peered over. If I saw Hunter's body, I would have to climb down there, I warned myself. If he was alive, I would go for help. If he was dead . . . I wasn't sure what I would do.

Later I would go up to Cal's house and see how he was, but first I needed to do this, to look for Hunter. Had Sky gotten my message? Had 911 responded?

The ground around this area was churned and muddy, evidence of the horrific battle Hunter and Cal had fought. It was awful to think about it, to remember how helpless I had been under Cal's binding spell. Why had he done that to me?

I leaned over farther to try to see beneath a rocky ledge. The icy Hudson swept beneath me, clean and deadly. Sharp rocks jutted up from the riverbed. If Hunter had hit them, if he'd been in the water any length of time, he was surely dead. The thought made my stomach clench up again. In my mind I pictured Hunter falling in slow motion over the edge, his neck streaming blood, an expression of surprise on his face. . . .

"Looking for something?"

I turned quickly, already scrambling to my feet as I recognized the English-accented voice. Sky Eventide.

She stood fifteen feet away, hands in her pockets. Her

pale face, whitish blond hair, and black eyes seemed etched against the painful blue of the sky.

"What are you doing here?" I said.

"I was about to ask the same thing," she said, stepping toward me. She was taller than me and as thin. Her black leather jacket didn't look warm enough for the cold.

I said nothing, and she went on, a razor's edge in her voice. "Hunter didn't come home last night. I felt his presence here. But now I don't feel it at all."

She hasn't found Hunter. Hunter's dead. Oh, Goddess, I thought.

"What happened here?" she went on, her face like stone in the cold, bright sun. "The ground looks like it was plowed. There's blood everywhere." She stepped closer to me, fierce and cold, like a Viking. "Tell me what you know about it."

"I don't know anything," I said, too loudly. *Hunter's dead.*

"You're lying. You're a lying Woodbane, just like Cal and Selene," Sky said bitterly, spitting out the words as if she were saying, You're filth, you're garbage.

The world shifted around me, became slightly unreal. There was snow beneath my feet, water below the cliff, trees behind Sky, but it was like a stage set.

"Cal and Selene aren't Woodbane," I said. My mouth was dry.

Sky tossed her head. "Of course they are," she said. "And you're just like them. You'll stop at nothing to keep your power."

"That's not true," I snapped.

"Last night Hunter was on his way to Cal's place, on council business. He was going to confront Cal. I think you were there, too, since you're Cal's little lapdog. Now tell me what happened." Her voice rang out like steel, actually hurting my ears, and I felt the strength of her personality pressing on me. I wanted to spill out everything I knew. All of a sudden I realized she was putting a spell on me. A flash of rage seared through me. How dare she?

I straightened up and deliberately walled off my mind.

Sky's eyes flickered. "You don't know what you're doing," she said, her words chipping away at me. "That makes you dangerous. I'll be watching you. And so will the council."

She whirled and disappeared into the woods, her short, sunlight-colored hair riffling in the breeze.

The woods were silent after she left. No birds chirped, no leaves stirred, the wind itself died. After several minutes I went back to my car and drove it up to Cal's house. Hunter's car was no longer there. I climbed the stone steps and rang the doorbell, feeling a fresh wash of fear as I wondered what I might find, what might have happened to Cal since I left.

Selene opened the door. She was wearing an apron, and the faint scent of herbs clung to her. There was a wealth of warmth and concern in her golden eyes as she reached out and hugged me to her. She had never hugged me before, and I closed my eyes, enjoying the lovely feeling of comfort and relief she offered.

Then Selene withdrew and looked deeply into my face. "I heard about last night. Morgan, you saved my son's life," she said, her voice low and melodious. "Thank you." She looped her arm through mine and drew me inside, shutting out the rest of the world. We walked down the hallway to the large, sunny kitchen at the back of the house.

"How is Cal?" I managed.

"He's better," she said. "Thanks to you. I came home and found him in the parlor, and he managed to tell me most of what happened. I've been doing some healing work with him."

"I didn't know what to do," I said helplessly. "He fell asleep, and I had to get home. I have his car at my house," I added inanely.

Selene nodded. "We'll come get it later," she said, and I dug in my pocket and gave her the keys. She took them and pushed open the kitchen door.

I sniffed the air. "What's that?" I asked.

Now I noticed that the kitchen was ablaze with light, sound, color, scent. I paused in the doorway, trying to separate out the different stimuli. Selene walked over to the stove to stir something, and I realized she had a small, three-legged cast-iron cauldron bubbling on the burner of her range. The odd thing was how normal it looked somehow.

She caught my glance and said, "Usually I do all this outside. But this autumn has been so awful, weatherwise." She stirred slowly with a long wooden spoon, then leaned over and inhaled, the steam making her face flush slightly.

"What are you making?" I asked, moving closer.

"This is a vision potion," she explained. "When ingested by a knowledgeable witch, it aids with scrying and divination."

"Like a hallucinogen?" I asked, a little shocked. Images of LSD and mushrooms and people freaking out flashed through my mind.

Selene laughed. "No. It's just an aid, to make it easier to find your visions. I only make it every four or five years or so. I don't use it that often, and a little goes a long way."

On the gleaming granite counter I saw labeled vials and small jars and, at one end, a stack of homemade candles.

"Did you do all this?" I asked.

Selene nodded and brushed her dark hair away from her face. "I always go through a flurry of activity around this time of year. Samhain is over, Yule hasn't begun—I suppose I just itch for something to do. Years ago I started making many of my own tinctures and essential oils and infusions—they're always fresher and better than what you can buy in the store. Have you ever made candles?"

"No."

Selene looked around the kitchen, at the bustle and clutter, and said, "Things you make, cook, sew, decorate—those are all expressions of the power and homages to the Goddess." Busily she stirred the cauldron, deasil, and then tasted a tiny bit on the end of her spoon.

At any other time I would have found this impromptu lesson fascinating, but at the moment I was too keyed up to focus on it. "Will Cal be okay?" I blurted out.

"Yes," Selene said. She looked directly at me. "Do you want to talk about Hunter?"

That was all it took, and suddenly I was crying silently, my shoulders shaking, my face burning. In a moment she was beside me, holding me. A tissue appeared, and I took it.

"Selene," I said shakily, "I think he's dead."

"Shhh," she said soothingly. "Poor darling. Sit down. Let me give you some tea."

Tea? I thought wildly. I think I *killed* someone, and you're offering me *tea*?

But it was witch tea, and within seconds of my first sip I felt my emotions calm slightly, enough to get myself under control. Selene sat across the table from me, looking into my eyes.

"Hunter tried to kill Cal," she said intently. "He might have tried to kill you, too. Anyone standing there would have done what you did. You saw a friend in danger, and you acted. No one could blame you for that."

"I didn't mean to hurt Hunter," I said, my voice wavering.

"Of course you didn't," she agreed. "You just wanted to stop him. There was no way to predict what would happen. Listen to me, my dear. If you hadn't done what you did, if you hadn't been so quick thinking and loyal, then it would be Cal now in the river, and I would be mourning him and possibly you, too. Hunter came here looking for trouble. He was on our property. He was out for blood. You and Cal both acted in self-defense."

Slowly I drank my tea. The way Selene put it, it sounded reasonable, even inevitable. "Do you—do you think we should go to the police?" I asked.

Selene cocked her head to one side, considering. "No," she said after a moment. "The difficulty is that there were no other witnesses. And that knife wound in Hunter's neck would be hard to explain as self-defense, even though you and I both know that's the truth of it."

A fresh wave of dread washed over me. She was right. To the police, it would probably look like murder.

I remembered something else. "And his car," I said. "Did you move it?"

Selene nodded. "I spelled it to start and drove it to an

abandoned barn just outside of town. It sounds premeditated, I know, but it seemed the prudent thing to do." She reached out and covered my hand with her own. "I know it's hard. I know you feel that your life will never be the same. But you must try to let it go, my dear."

I swallowed miserably. "I feel so guilty," I said.

"Let me tell you about Hunter," she said, and her voice was suddenly almost harsh. I shivered.

"I've heard reports about him," Selene went on. "By all accounts he was a loose cannon, someone who could not be trusted. Even the council had their doubts about him, thought he had gone too far, too many times. He's been obsessed with Woodbanes all his life, and in the last few years this obsession had taken a deadly turn." She seemed quite serious, and I nodded.

A thought occurred to me. "Then why was he going after Cal?" I asked. "You guys don't know what clan you are, right? I heard Hunter call Cal Woodbane—did he think Cal . . . wait—" I shook my head, confused. Cal had told me that he and Hunter probably had the same father. And Sky had said Cal was Woodbane like his father. Which made both Cal and Hunter half Woodbane? I couldn't keep all this straight.

"Who knows what he thought?" said Selene. "He was clearly crazy. I mean, this is someone who killed his own brother."

My eyebrows knitted. I vaguely remembered Cal throwing that accusation at Hunter last night. "What do you mean?"

Selene shook her head, then started as her cauldron

hissed and spat on the stove, almost boiling over. She hurried over to adjust the flame. For the next few minutes she was very busy, and I hesitated to interrupt her.

"Do you think I could see Cal?" I asked finally.

She looked back at me regretfully. "I'm sorry, Morgan, but I gave him a drink to make him sleep. He probably won't wake up until tonight."

"Oh." I stood up and retrieved my coat, unwilling to pursue the story about Hunter if Selene didn't want to tell me. I felt a thousand times better than I had, but I knew instinctively the pain and guilt would return.

"Thank you for coming," Selene said, straining a steaming mixture over the sink. "And remember, what you did last night was the right thing. Believe that."

I nodded awkwardly.

"Please call me if you want to talk," Selene added as I headed for the door. "Anytime."

"Thank you," I said. I pushed through the door and headed home.

3.
Dread

April 2000

    Scrying doesn't always mean you see a picture—it can be more like receiving impressions. I use my lueg, my scrying stone. It's a big, thick chunk of obsidian, almost four inches at its widest and tapering to a point. It was my father's. I found it under my pillow the morning he and Mum disappeared

    Luegs are more reliable than either fire or water Fire may show you pasts and possible futures, but it's hard to work with. There's an old Wiccan saying that goes: Fire is a fragile lover, court her well, neglect her not; her faith is like a misty smoke, her anger is destructive hot. Water is easier to use but very misleading. Once I heard Mum say that water is the Wiccan whore, spilling her secrets to any, lying to most, trusting few.

    Last night I took my lueg and went down to the kill that flows at the edge of my uncle's property. This was where we swam in the summer, where Linden and I caught minnows, where Alwyn used to pick gooseberries.

I sat at the water's edge and scryed, looking deep into my obsidian, weaving spells of vision.

After a long, long time, the rock's face cleared, and in its depths I saw my mother. It was my mother of all those years ago, right before she disappeared. I remember the day clearly. An eight-year-old me ran up to where she knelt in the garden, pulling weeds. She looked up, saw me, and her face lit, as if I was the sun. Giomanach, she said, and looked at me with love, the sunlight glinting off her bright hair. Seeing her in the lueg, I was almost crushed with longing and a childish need to see her, have her hold me.

When the stone went blank, I held it in my hand, then crumpled over and cried on the bank of the kill.

—Giomanach

My birthday dinner was like a movie. I felt like I was watching myself through a window, smiling, talking to people, opening presents. I was glad to see Aunt Eileen and her girlfriend, Paula Steen, again—and Mom and Mary K. had worked hard to make everything special. It would have been a great birthday, except for the horrific images that kept crashing into my brain. Hunter and Cal grappling in the churned, bloody snow. Myself, sinking to my knees under Cal's binding spell, then me looking down at the athame in my hand and looking up to see Hunter. Hunter, rivulets of blood on his neck, going over the edge of the cliff.

"Hey, are you all right?" Mary K. asked me as I stood by the window, gazing out into the darkness. "You seem kind of out of it."

"Just tired," I told her. I added quickly, "But I'm having a great time. Thanks, Mary K."

"We aim to please." She flashed me a grin.

Finally Aunt Eileen and Paula left, and I went upstairs and called Cal. His voice sounded weak and scratchy.

"I'm okay," he said. "Are you okay?"

"Yes," I said. "Physically."

"I know." He sighed. "I can't believe it. I didn't mean for him to go over the edge. I just wanted to stop him." He laughed dryly, a croaking sound. "Helluva seventeenth birthday. I'm sorry, Morgan."

"It wasn't your fault," I said. "He came after you."

"I didn't want him to hurt you."

"But why did you put binding spells on me?" I asked.

"I was afraid. I didn't want you to jump into the middle of it and get hurt," Cal said.

"I wanted to help you. I hated being frozen like that. It was awful."

"I'm so sorry, Morgan," Cal breathed. "Everything was happening so fast, and I thought I was acting for the best."

"Don't ever do that to me again."

"I won't, I promise. I'm sorry."

"Okay. I called 911 when I got home," I admitted softly. "And I sent Sky an anonymous witch message, telling her where to look for Hunter."

Cal was silent for a minute. Then he said, "You did the right thing. I'm glad you did."

"It didn't help, though. I saw Sky at the river this morning. She said Hunter didn't come home last night. She was sure I knew something about it."

"What did you tell her?"

"That I didn't know what she was talking about. She said she didn't feel Hunter's presence or something like that. And she called me a lying Woodbane."

"That bitch," Cal said angrily.

"Could she find out about what happened somehow? Using magick?"

"No," said Cal. "My mom put warding spells around the whole place to block anyone from scrying and seeing what happened. Don't worry."

"I am worried," I insisted. A bubble of panic was rising in my throat again. "This is horrible. I can't stand it."

"Morgan! Try to calm down," said Cal. "It will all be okay, you'll see. I won't let anything happen to you. The only thing is, I'm afraid Sky is going to be a problem. Hunter was her cousin, and she's not going to let this rest. Tomorrow we'll spell your house and your car with wards of protection. But still—be on your guard."

"Okay." Dread settled more heavily on my shoulders as I hung up. Wherever this is going, I thought, there's no way it can end well. No way at all.

On Monday morning I got up early and grabbed the morning paper before anyone else could see it. Widow's Vale doesn't have its own daily paper, just a twice-monthly publication that's mostly pickup articles from other papers. I quickly paged through the *Albany Times Union* to see if there was any mention of a body being fished out of the Hudson. There wasn't. I gnawed my lip. What did that mean? Had his body not been found yet? Or was it just that we weren't close enough to Albany for them to cover the story?

I drove with Mary K. to school and parked outside the building, feeling like I had aged five years over the weekend.

As I turned off the engine, Bakker Blackburn, Mary K.'s boyfriend, trotted up to meet her. "Hey, babe," he said, nuzzling her neck.

Mary K. giggled and pushed him away. He took her book bag from her, and they went off to meet their friends.

Robbie Gurevitch, one of my best friends and a member of my coven, strolled up to my car. A group of freshman girls stared admiringly at him as he passed them, and I saw him blush. Being gorgeous was new to him—until I'd given him a healing potion a month ago, he'd had horrible acne. But the potion had cleared up his skin and even erased the scars.

"Are you going to fix your car?" he asked me.

I looked at my broken headlight and smashed nose and sighed. A few days ago I'd thought someone was following me, and I had skidded on a patch of ice and crunched my beloved behemoth of a car, fondly known as Das Boot, into a ditch. At the time it had seemed utterly terrifying, but since the events of Saturday night, it felt more in perspective.

"Yep," I said, scanning the area for Cal. That morning I'd noticed the Explorer was gone from my block, but I didn't know if he'd be back at school today.

"I'm guessing it'll cost at least five hundred bucks," Robbie said.

We walked toward the old, redbrick former courthouse that was now Widow's Vale High. I was striving for normalcy, trying to be old reliable Morgan. "I wanted to ask you—did you go to Bree's coven's circle on Saturday?" Bree Warren had been my other best friend since childhood—my closest friend—until we fought over Cal. Now she hated me. And I . . . I didn't know what I felt about her. I was furious at her. I didn't trust her. I missed her fiercely.

"I did go." Robbie held the door open for me. "It was small and kind of lame. But that English witch, Sky Eventide, the one who leads their circles . . ." He whistled. "She had power coming off her in waves."

"I know Sky," I said stiffly. "I met her at Cal's. What did you guys do? Did Sky mention me or Cal?"

He looked at me. "No. We just did a circle. It was interesting because Sky does it slightly differently than Cal. Why would she mention you or Cal?"

"Different how?" I pressed, ignoring his question. "You guys didn't, um, do anything scary, did you? Like call on spirits or anything?"

Robbie stopped walking. "No. It was just a circle, Morgan. I think we can safely say that Bree and Raven are not having their souls sucked out by the devil."

I gave him an exasperated look. "Wiccans don't believe in the devil," I reminded him. "I just want to make sure that Bree isn't getting into anything dangerous or bad." *Like I did.*

We walked to the basement stairs, where our coven, Cirrus, usually hung out in the morning. Ethan Sharp was already there, doing his English homework. Jenna Ruiz sat across from him, reading, her fair, straight hair falling like a curtain across her cheek. They both looked up and greeted us.

"Bad?" Robbie repeated. "No. Sky didn't strike me as bad. Powerful, yes. Sexy—absolutely." He grinned.

"Who's this?" Jenna asked.

"Sky Eventide," Robbie reported. "She's the blood witch that Bree and Raven have in their new coven. Oh, guess their coven's name." He laughed. "Kithic. It means 'left-handed' in Gaelic. Raven picked out that name from something she read, without knowing what it meant."

The rest of us smiled. After our fight, Bree had split off from Cirrus to start her own coven with Raven. To me it seemed both of them were just playing at being Wiccan, doing it to look cool, to get back at me for winning Cal, or just to do something different. Widow's Vale is a small town, and there aren't that many entertainment opportunities.

Or maybe I was selling them short. Maybe they were really sincere in their commitment. I sighed and rubbed my forehead, feeling like I didn't know anything anymore.

In homeroom people were already planning their Thanksgiving holidays, which would start at noon on Wednesday. It would be a relief not to have to go to school for a few days. I've always been an A student (well, mostly), but it was getting harder and harder to keep my mind on schoolwork when so many more compelling things were taking up my time and energy. Nowadays I just flashed through my physics and trig homework and did the bare minimum in other classes so I would have more time to study spells, plan my future magickal herb garden, and read about Wicca. Not only that, but just reading the Book of Shadows written by my birth mother, which I'd found in Selene's library over a week ago, was like a college course in itself. I was stretched very thin these days.

In homeroom I opened my book *Essential Oils and Their Charms* under my desk and started reading. In the spring I would try to make some of my own, the way Selene did.

When Bree came into class, I couldn't help looking up. Her face was as familiar as my own, but nowadays she had another layer to her, a layer that didn't include me. She wore mostly black, like Raven did, and although she hadn't adopted any of Raven's gothy piercings or tattoos, I wondered if it was just a matter of time.

Bree had always been the beautiful one, the one boys flocked around, the life of the party. I had been the plain friend that people put up with because Bree loved me and was my best friend, but then Cal had come between us. Bree had even lied and told me they'd slept together. We'd quit speaking, and then Cal and I started going out.

After being like conjoined twins for eleven years, I'd found the last few Breeless weeks bizarre and uncomfortable. She still didn't know I was adopted, that I was a blood witch. She didn't know about what had happened with Hunter. At one time she had been the only person in the world I might have told.

I couldn't resist looking at her face, her eyes the color of coffee. For just a second she met my gaze, and I was startled by the mix of emotions there. We both looked away at the same time. Did she miss me? Did she hate me? What was she doing with Sky?

The bell rang, and we all stood. Bree's dark, shiny hair disappeared through the doorway, and I followed her. When she turned the corner to go to her first class, I was seized by a spontaneous desire to talk to her.

"Bree."

She turned, and when she saw it was me, she looked surprised.

"Listen—I know that Sky is leading your coven," I found myself saying.

"So?" No one looked imperious like Bree looked imperious.

"I just—it's just that Sky is dangerous," I said quickly. "She's dangerous, and you shouldn't hang out with her."

Her perfect eyebrows rose. "Do tell," she drawled.

"She has this whole dark agenda; she's caught up in this whole program that I bet she hasn't told you about. She's— she's evil, she's bad, and dangerous." I realized in despair that I sounded melodramatic and muddled.

"Really." Bree shook her head, looking like she was trying not to laugh. "You are too much, Morgan. It's like you get off on lying, raining on people's parades."

"Look, I heard you and Raven last week in the bathroom," I admitted. "You were talking about how Sky was teaching you about the dark side. That's dangerous! And I heard you saying you gave Sky some of my hair! What was that about? Is she putting spells on me?"

Bree's eyes narrowed. "You mean you were spying on me?" she exclaimed. "You're pathetic! And you have no idea what you're talking about. Cal is filling your head with ridiculous crap, and you're just sucking it up! He could be the devil himself, and you wouldn't care because he's the only boy who ever asked you out!"

Before I realized what was happening, my hand had shot out and smacked Bree hard across the face. Her head snapped sideways, and within seconds the pink outline of my palm appeared on her cheek. I gasped and stared at her as her face twisted into anger.

"You bitch!" she snarled.

Out of lifelong habit, I started to feel remorseful, and then I thought, Screw that. I took a deep breath and called on my own anger, narrowing my eyes. "You're the bitch," I snapped. "You can't stand the fact that I'm not your puppet anymore, that I'm not your charity case, your permanent audience. You're jealous of *me* for once, and it's eating you up. I have a fantastic boyfriend, I have more magickal power than you'll ever dream about, and you can't stand it. Finally I'm better than you. I'm amazed your head doesn't explode!"

Bree gaped at me, her eyes wide, her mouth open. "What are you talking about?" she practically shrieked. "You were never my audience! You make it sound like I was using you! This is what I'm talking about! Cal is brainwashing you!"

"Actually, Bree," I said coldly, "you'd be amazed at how little we talk about you. In fact, your name hardly comes up."

With that, I swept off, my teeth clenched so tight, I could feel them grinding together. I didn't think I'd ever had the last word in an argument with Bree before. But the thought didn't make me feel any better. Why had I talked to her? I had just made everything worse.

4.
Haven

May 2000

I remember it rained the day Mum and Dad disappeared. When I woke up that morning they were already gone. I had no idea what was going on. Uncle Beck called late that day, and I told him I couldn't find Dad, or Mum either. Beck called around, to get a neighbor to stay overnight with us until he could get there, and he couldn't find anyone still around. In the end, I was in charge all that long day and night, and the three of us—me, Linden, and Alwyn—stayed in our house alone, not knowing what was happening to us, to our world.

Now I know that twenty-three other people besides my parents either died or disappeared that night. Years later, when I went back, I tried asking around. All I got were cautious mumbles about a dark wave, a cloud of fury and destruction.

I've heard rumors of a dark wave destroying a Wyndenkell

coven in Scotland. I'm on my way there. Goddess, give me strength.

   —Giomanach

After my fight with Bree, I was so upset that I couldn't concentrate on anything. My trig teacher had to call my name three times before I responded, and then I answered his question incorrectly—which almost never happened to me under normal circumstances. During lunch period I sneaked off to Cirrus's hangout spot to be by myself. I scarfed down my sandwich and a Diet Coke, then meditated for half an hour. Finally I felt calm enough to deal with the rest of my day.

I slogged through my afternoon classes. When the last bell rang, I went to my locker, then followed the crush of students outside. The snow was turning rapidly to slush, and the sun flowed down with an Indian-summerish warmth. After weeks of freezing weather, it felt wonderful. I raised my face to the sun, hoping it would help heal the pain I carried inside, the guilt over what I'd done to Hunter, the terror of being found out.

"I'm getting a ride home with Bakker, okay?" Mary K. bounced up to me as I took out my car keys, her cheeks flushed pink, her eyes clear and shining.

I looked at her. "Are you going home, or . . ." Don't go anywhere with him alone, I thought. I didn't trust Bakker—not since I'd caught him pinning Mary K. down on her bed and practically forcing himself on her two weeks earlier. I couldn't believe she'd forgiven him.

"We're going to get a latte first, then home," she said, her eyes daring me to say something.

"All right. Well, see you later," I said lamely. I watched her climb into Bakker's car and knew that if he hurt her, I would have no problem doing to him what I had done to Hunter. And in Bakker's case I wouldn't feel guilty.

"Whoa. I'm glad you're not looking at me like that," said Robbie, loping up to me. I shook my head.

"Yeah, just watch your step." I tried to sound light and teasing.

"Is Cal sick? I didn't see him all day," said Robbie. He smiled absentmindedly at a sophomore who was sending flirtatious looks his way.

"Morgan?" he prompted.

"Oh! Um, yes, Cal is sick," I said. I felt a sudden jangle of nerves. Robbie was a close friend, and I had told him about being adopted and a blood witch. He knew more about me than Bree did now. But I could never tell him about all that had happened on Saturday night. It was too horrible to share, even with him. "I'm going to call him right now—maybe go see him."

Robbie nodded. "I'm on my way to Bree's. Who knows, today might be the day I go for it." He wiggled his eyebrows suggestively, and I smiled. Robbie had recently admitted to me that he was totally in love with Bree and had been for years. I hoped she wouldn't break his heart the way she did with most of the guys she got involved with.

"Good luck," I said. He walked off, and I dumped my backpack in Das Boot and headed back to the pay phone in the school lunchroom.

Cal answered after four rings. His voice sounded better than it had the night before.

"Hi," I said, comforted just to talk to him.

"I knew it was you," he said, sounding glad.

"Of course you did," I said. "You're a witch."

"Where are you?"

"School. Can I come see you? I just really need to talk to you."

Groaning, he said, "I would love that. But some people just came in from Europe, and I've got to meet with them."

"Selene's been having people over a lot lately, it seems."

Cal paused, and when he spoke, his voice had a slightly different tone to it. "Yeah, she has. She's kind of been working on a big project, and it's starting to come together. I'll tell you about it later."

"Okay. How are your wrists?"

"They look pretty bad. But they'll be okay. I really wish I could see you," Cal said.

"Me too." I lowered my voice. "I *really* need to talk to you. About what happened."

"I know," he said quietly. "I know, Morgan."

In the background on Cal's end I heard voices, and Cal covered his mouthpiece and responded to them. When he came back on, I said, "I won't keep you. Call me later if you can, okay?"

"I will," he said. Then he hung up. I hung up, too, feeling sad and lonely without him.

I walked through the hall and out the door, got in Das Boot, and drove to Red Kill, to Practical Magick.

*   *   *

The brass bells over the door jingled as I pushed my way in. Practical Magick was a store that sold Wiccan books and supplies. Although I hadn't realized it until now, it was also becoming the place I went to when I didn't want to go anywhere else. I loved being there, and I always felt better when I left. It was like a Wiccan neighborhood bar.

At the end of the room the checkout desk was empty, and I figured Alyce and David must be busy restocking.

I began reading book titles, dreaming of the day I would have enough money to buy whatever books and supplies I wanted. I would buy this whole store out, I decided. That would be so much more fun than being a relatively poor high school junior who was about to wipe out her whole savings to pay for a crumpled headlight.

"Hi, there," came a soft voice, and I looked up to see the round, motherly figure of Alyce, my favorite clerk. As my eyes met hers, she stood still. Her brows drew together in a concerned look. "What's the matter?"

My heart thudded against my ribs. *Does she know?* I wondered frantically. *Can she tell just by looking at me?*

"What do you mean?" I asked. "I'm fine. Just a little stressed. You know, school, family stuff." I shut my mouth abruptly, feeling like I was babbling.

Alyce held my gaze for a moment, her eyes probing mine. "All right. If you want to talk about it, I'm here," she said at last.

She bustled over to the checkout counter and began to stack some papers. Her gray hair was piled untidily on top of her head, and she wore her usual loose, flowing clothes. She moved with precision and confidence: a woman at ease with herself, her witchhood, her power. I admired her, and it broke my heart to think how horrified she would be if she knew what I had done. How had this happened? How had this become my life?

I can't lose this, I thought. Practical Magick was my haven. I couldn't let the poison of Hunter's horrible death seep out and taint my relationships with this place, with Alyce. I couldn't bear it.

"I can't wait for spring," I said, trying to get my mind back on track. It wasn't even Thanksgiving yet. "I want to get started on my garden." I walked up the book aisle to the back of the store and leaned against a stool by the counter.

"So do I," Alyce agreed. "I'm already dying to be outside, digging in the dirt again. It's always a struggle for me to remember the positive aspects of winter."

I looked around at the other people in the store. A young man with multiple earrings in his left ear came up and bought incense and white candles. I tentatively sent out my senses to see if I could tell if he was a witch or not, but I couldn't pick up on anything unusual.

"Morgan, good to see you again."

I turned to see David stepping through the faded orange curtain that separated the small back room from the rest of the store. A faint scent of incense wafted in with him. Like Alyce, David was also a blood witch. Recently he'd told me that he was from the Burnhide clan. I felt honored to have gained his confidence—and terrified of losing it again if he ever found out what I'd done, that I'd killed someone.

"Hi," I said. "How are you?"

"I'm all right." He held a sheaf of invoices in his hand and looked distracted. "Alyce, did the latest batch of essential oils come? The bill is here."

She shook her head. "I have a feeling the shipment is lost somewhere," she said as another person checked out. This woman was buying a Wiccan periodical called *Crafting Our Lives*. I picked up on faint magickal vibrations as she passed me and was once again naively amazed that real witches existed.

I wandered around the store, fascinated as always by the candles, incense, small mirrors the shop contained. Slowly the place emptied, then new people came in. It was a busy afternoon.

Gradually the sunlight faded from the high windows, and I began to think about heading home. Alyce came up as I was running my fingers around the rim of a carved marble bowl. The stone was cool and smooth, like river stones. The stones Hunter had probably hit when he fell hadn't been smooth. They had been jagged, deadly.

"Marble is always thirteen degrees cooler than the air around it," Alyce said at my side, making me jump.

"Really? Why?"

"It's the property of the stone," she said, straightening some scarves that customers had rumpled. "Everything has its own properties."

I thought about the chunks of crystal and other stones I had found in the box containing my mother's tools. It seemed like ages ago—but it had actually been less than a week.

"I found Maeve's tools," I said, surprising myself. I hadn't planned to mention it. But I felt the need to confide *something* in Alyce, to make her feel I wasn't shutting her out.

Alyce's blue eyes widened, and she stopped what she was doing to look at me. She knew Maeve's story; it had been she who'd told me of my birth mother's awful death here in America.

"Belwicket's tools?" she asked unbelievingly. Belwicket had been the name of Maeve's coven in Ireland. When it was destroyed by a mysterious, dark force, Maeve and her lover, Angus, had fled to America. Where I'd been born—and they had died.

"I scryed," I told Alyce. "In fire. I had a vision that told me the tools were in Meshomah Falls."

"Where Maeve died," Alyce remembered.

"Yes."

"How wonderful for you," Alyce said. "Everyone thought those tools were lost forever. I'm sure Maeve would have been so happy for her daughter to have them."

I nodded. "I'm really glad about it. They're a link to her, to her clan, her family."

"Have you used them yet?" she asked.

"Um—I tried the athame," I admitted. Technically, since I was uninitiated, I wasn't supposed to do unsupervised magick or use magickal tools or even write in Cirrus's Book of Shadows. I waited for Alyce to chide me.

But she didn't. Instead she said briskly, "I think you should bind the tools to you."

I blinked. "What do you mean?"

"Wait a minute." Alyce hurried off and soon came back with a thick, ancient-looking book. Its cover was dark green and tattered, with stains mottling its fabric. She leaned the book on a shelf and flipped through pages soft and crumbling with age.

"Here we go." She pulled a quaint pair of half-moon glasses from her sweater pocket and perched them on her nose. "Let me copy this down for you." Then, just like the women at my church exchange recipes and knitting patterns, Alyce copied down an age-old Wiccan spell that would bind my mother's tools to me.

"It will be almost as if you're part of them and they are part of you," Alyce explained as I folded the paper and put it in my inside coat pocket. "It will make them more effective for you and also less effective for anyone else who tries to use them. I really think you should do this right away." Her gaze, usually so mild, seemed quite piercing as she examined me over the rims of her glasses.

"Um, okay, I will," I said. "But why?"

Alyce paused for a moment, as if considering what to say. "Intuition," she said finally, shrugging and giving me a smile. "I feel it's important."

"Well, all right," I said. "I'll try to do it tonight."

"The sooner the better," she advised. Then the bells over the door rang as a customer came in. I hastily said good-bye to Alyce and David and went out to Das Boot. I flipped on my one headlight, blasted the heater, and headed for home.

5.
Bound

June 2000

Two covens in Scotland were wiped out: one in 1974 and one in 1985. The first was in the north, the second, toward the southeast. Now the trail is leading into northern England, so I am making plans to go. I have to <u>know</u>. This started out being about my parents. Now it's a much bigger picture.

I've heard that the council is seeking new members. I've put my name in. If I were a council member, I would have access to things that are usually not publicized. It seems the fastest way to have my questions answered. When I come back from the north, I'll learn of their decision.

I applied to become a Seeker. With a name like mine, it seems almost inevitable.

—Giomanach

Mary K. breezed in halfway through dinner. Her cheeks were pink. There was also something wrong with her shirt. I gazed in puzzlement at the two flaps of the hem. They didn't meet—the shirt was incorrectly buttoned. My eyes narrowed as I thought about what that meant.

"Where have you been?" Mom asked. "I was worried."

"I called and let Dad know I'd be late," my sister said, sitting down at the table. Seated, her telltale shirt wasn't so obvious. "What's that?" she asked, sniffing the serving platter.

"Corned beef. I made it in the Crock-Pot," Mom said.

Dad had glanced up at the sound of his name, pulled back to reality for a moment. He's a research-and-development guy for IBM, and sometimes he seems more comfortable in *virtual* reality.

"Hmmm," said Mary K. disapprovingly. She picked out some carrots, cabbage, and onions and conspicuously left the meat. Lately she'd been on a major vegetarian kick.

"It's delicious," I said brightly, just to needle her. Mary K. sent me a look.

"So I think Eileen and Paula have decided on the York Street house, in Jasper," my mom said.

"Cool," I said. "Jasper's only about twenty minutes away, right?" My aunt and her girlfriend had decided to move in together and had been house hunting with my mom, a real estate agent.

"Right," Mom said. "An easy drive from here."

"Good." I stood up and carried my plate to the kitchen, already anxious for my family to be asleep. I had work to do.

The spell for binding tools to oneself was complicated but not difficult, and it didn't involve any tools or ingredients that I didn't have. I knew I would need to work undisturbed, and I didn't want to do it outside. The attic seemed like a good place.

At last I heard my parents turn in and my sister brush her teeth noisily in the bathroom we shared. She poked her head into my room to say good night and found me hunched over a book discussing the differences between practicing Wicca on your own and within a coven. It was really interesting. There were benefits—and drawbacks—to both ways.

"Night," said Mary K., yawning.

I looked at her. "Next time you're late, you might want to make sure your shirt is buttoned right," I said mildly.

She looked down at herself, horrified. "Oh, man," she breathed.

"Just . . . be careful." I wanted to say more but forced myself to stop there.

"Yeah, yeah, I will." She went into her room.

Twenty minutes later, sensing that everyone was asleep, I tiptoed up the attic stairs with Maeve's tools, the spell Alyce had written out for me, and four white candles.

I swept one area clean of dust and set the four candles in a large square. Inside the square I drew a circle with white chalk. Then I entered the circle, closed it, and set Maeve's tools on one of my old sweatshirts. Theoretically, it would be full of my personal vibrations.

I meditated for a while, trying to release my anguish over Hunter, trying to sink into the magick, feeling it unfold before me, gradually revealing its secrets. Then I gathered Maeve's tools: her robe, her wand, her four element cups, her athame, and things I wasn't sure were tools but that I'd found in the same box: a feather, a silver chain with a Claddagh charm on it, several chunks of crystal, and five stones, each one different.

I read the ritual chant.

"Goddess Mother, Protectress of Magick and Life, hear my song. As it was in my clan, so shall it be with me and in my family to come. These tools I offer in service to you and in worship of the glory of nature. With them I shall honor life, do no harm, and bless all that is good and right. Shine your light on these tools that I may use them in pure intent and in sure purpose."

I laid my hands on them, feeling their power and sending mine into them.

The same way it had happened in the past, a song in Gaelic came to my lips. I let it slip quietly into the darkness.

> *"An di allaigh an di aigh*
> *An di allaigh an di ne ullah*
> *An di ullah be nith rah*
> *Cair di na ulla nith rah*
> *Cair feal ti theo nith rah*
> *An di allaigh an di aigh."*

Quietly I sang the ancient words again and again, feeling a warm coil of energy circling me. When I had sung this before, it had drawn down an immense amount of power—I'd felt like a goddess myself. Tonight it was quieter, more focused, and the power flowed around and through me like water, going down my hands into the tools until I couldn't tell where the tools left off and I began. I couldn't feel my knees where I was kneeling, and giddily I wondered if I was levitating.

Suddenly I realized that I was no longer singing and that the warm, rich power had leached away, leaving me breathing hard and flushed, sweat trickling down my back.

I looked down. Were the tools bound to me now? Had I done it correctly? I had followed the instructions. I had felt the power. There was nothing else on the paper Alyce had given me. Blinking, feeling suddenly incredibly tired, I gathered everything up, blew out the candles, and crept downstairs. Moving silently, I unscrewed the cover for the HVAC vent in the hallway outside my room and put my tools, except the athame, back into my never-fail hiding place.

Back in my room, I changed into my pajamas and brushed my teeth. I unbraided my hair and brushed it a few times, too tired to give it any real attention. Finally, with relief, I got into bed with Maeve's Book of Shadows and opened it to my bookmark. Out of habit I held my mother's athame, with its carved initials, in my hand.

I started to read, sometimes pointing the athame to the words on the page, as if it would help me decipher some of the Gaelic terms.

In this entry Maeve was describing a spell to strengthen her scrying. She mentioned that something seemed to be blocking her vision: "It's as if the power lines are clouded and dark. Ma and I have both scryed and scryed, and all we get is the same thing over and over: bad news coming. What that means, I don't know. A delegation is here from Liathach, in northern Scotland. They, like us, are Woodbanes who have renounced evil. Maybe with their help we can figure out what's going on."

I felt a chill. *Bad news coming.* Was it the mysterious dark force that had destroyed Belwicket, Maeve's coven? No, it couldn't be, I realized; that hadn't happened until 1982. This entry had been written in 1981, nearly a year earlier. I tapped the athame against the page and read on.

"I have met a witch."

The words floated across the page, written in light within the regular entry. I blinked and they were gone, and I stared at Maeve's angular handwriting, wondering what I had seen. I focused, staring hard at the page, willing the words, the writing to appear again. Nothing.

I took the athame, passing it slowly over the blue ink. Splashes, pinpricks of light, coalescing into words. "I have met a witch."

I drew in my breath, staring at the page. The words appeared beneath the athame. When I drew it away, they faded. I passed the knife over the book again. "Among the group from Liathach, there is a man. There is something about him. Goddess, he draws me to him."

Oh my God. I looked up, glanced around my room to make sure I was awake and not dreaming. My clock was ticking, Dagda was squirming next to my leg, the wind was blowing against my windows. This was all real. Another layer of my birth mother's history was being revealed: she had written secret entries in her Book of Shadows.

Quickly I flipped to the very beginning of the book, which Maeve had started when she was first initiated at fourteen. Holding the athame close to each page, I scanned the writing, seeing if other hidden messages were revealed. Page after page I ran the knife down each line of writing, each spell, each song or poem. Nothing. Nothing for many, many pages. Then, in 1980, when Maeve was eighteen, hidden words started appearing. I began reading, my earlier fatigue forgotten.

At first the entries were things Maeve had simply wanted to keep hidden from her mother: the fact that she and a girlfriend were smoking cigarettes, about how Angus kept pressuring her to go "all the way" and she was thinking about it, even sarcastic, teasing remarks or observations about people in the village, her relatives, other members of the coven.

But as time went on, Maeve also wrote down spells, spells that were different from the others. A lot of what Maeve and Mackenna and Belwicket had done was practical stuff: healing potions, lucky talismans, spells to make the crops perform. These new spells of Maeve's were things like how to communicate with and call wild birds. How to put your mind into an animal's. How to join your mind to another person's. Not practical, perhaps. But powerful and fascinating.

I went back to the passage I had found a few minutes ago. Slowly, word by word, I read the glowing letters. Each entry was surrounded by runes of concealment and symbols I didn't recognize. I memorized what they looked like so I could research them later.

Painstakingly I picked out the message.

"Ciaran came to tea. He and Angus are circling each other like dogs. Ciaran is a friend, a good friend, and I won't have Angus put him down."

Angus Bramson had been my birth father. Ciaran must be the Scottish witch Maeve had just met. Previous entries had detailed Maeve and Angus's courtship—they'd known each other practically forever. When Belwicket had been destroyed, Maeve and Angus had fled together and settled in America. Two years later I had been born, though I don't think they ever married. Maeve had once written about her sadness that Angus wasn't her *mùirn beatha dàn*—her preordained life partner, her soul mate, the person who was meant for her.

I believed Cal was mine. I'd never felt so close to anyone before—except Bree.

"Today I showed Ciaran the headlands by the Windy Cliffs. It's a beautiful spot, wild and untamed, and he seemed just as wild and untamed as the nature surrounding him. He's so different from the lads around here. He seems older than twenty-two, and he's traveled a bit and seen the world. It makes me ache with envy."

Oh, God, I thought. Maeve, what are you getting into?

I soon found out.

"I cannot help myself. Ciaran is everything a man should be. I love Angus, yes, but he's like a brother to me—I've known him all my life. Ciaran wants the things I want, finds the same things interesting and boring and funny. I could spend days just talking to him, doing nothing else. And then there's his magick—his power. It's breathtaking. He knows so much I don't know, no one around here knows. He's teaching me. And the way he makes me feel . . .

"Goddess! I've never wanted to touch anyone so much."

My throat had tightened and my back muscles had tensed. I rested the book on my knees, trying to analyze why this revelation shook me so much.

Is love ever simple? I wondered. I thought about Mary K.

and Bakker, boy most likely to be a parolee by the time he was twenty; Bree, who went out with one loser after another; Matt, who had cheated on Jenna with Raven. . . . It was completely discouraging. Then I thought about Cal, and my spirits rose again. Whatever troubles we had, at least they were external to our love for each other.

I blinked and realized my eyelids were gritty and heavy. It was very late, and I had to go to school tomorrow. One more quick passage.

"I have kissed Ciaran, and it was like sunlight coming through a window. Goddess, thank you for bringing him to me. I think he is the one."

Wincing, I hid the book and the athame under my mattress. I didn't want to know. Angus was my birth father, the one who had stayed by her, who had died with her. And she had loved someone else! She'd betrayed Angus! How could she be so cruel, my mother?

I felt betrayed, too, somehow, and knowing that I was perhaps being unfair to Maeve didn't help. I turned off my light, plumped my pillow up properly, and went to sleep.

6.
Knowledge

I'm going to have these scars forever. Every time I look at my wrists, I feel rage all over again. Mom has been putting salves on them, but they ache constantly, and the skin will never be the same.

Thank the Goddess Giomanach won't bother us anymore.

—Sgàth

"If you hum that song one more time, I may have to kick you out of the car," I informed my sister the next morning.

Mary K. opened the lid of her mug and took a swig of coffee. "My, we're grumpy today."

"It's natural to be grumpy in the morning." I polished off the last of my Diet Coke and tossed the empty can into a plastic bag I kept for recyclables.

"Tornadoes are natural, but they're not a *good* thing."

I snorted, but secretly I enjoyed the bickering. It felt so . . . normal.

Normal. Nothing would ever be normal again. Not after what Cal and I had done.

There'd been no mention of a body in the river in this morning's paper, either. Maybe he'd sunk to the bottom, I thought. Or snagged on a submerged rock or log. I pictured him in the icy water, his pale hair floating around his face like seaweed, his hands swaying limply in the current. . . . A sudden rush of nausea almost made me retch.

Mary K. didn't notice. She looked through the windshield at the thin layer of clouds blotting out the morning sun. "I'll be glad when vacation starts."

I forced a smile. "You and me both."

I turned onto our school's street and found that all my usual parking spaces were taken. "Why don't you get out here," I suggested, "and I'll go park across the street."

"Okay. Later." Mary K. clambered out of Das Boot and hurried to her group of friends, her breath coming out in wisps. Today it was cold again, with a biting wind.

Across the street was another small parking lot, in back of an abandoned real estate office. Large sycamores surrounded the lot, looking like peeling skeletons, and several shaggy cypresses made it feel sheltered and private—which was why the stoners usually hung out there when the weather was warmer. No one else was around as I maneuvered Das Boot into a space. Wednesday, after school let out at noon, I had an appointment to take it to Unser's Auto Repair to have the headlight repaired.

"Morgan." The melodious voice made me jump. I whirled to see Selene Belltower sitting in her car three spaces away, her window rolled down.

"Selene!" I walked over to her. "What are you doing here? Is Cal okay?"

"He's much better," Selene assured me. "In fact, he's on his way to school right now. But I wanted to talk to you. Can you get in the car for a moment, please?"

I opened the door, flattered by her attention. In so many ways, she was the witch I hoped someday to be: powerful, the leader of a coven, vastly knowledgeable.

I glanced at my watch as I sank into the passenger seat. It was covered with soft brown leather, heated, and amazingly comfortable. Even so, I hoped Selene could sum up what she had to say in four minutes or less since that was when the last bell would ring.

"Cal told me you found Belwicket's tools," she said, looking excited.

"Yes," I said.

She smiled and shook her head. "What an amazing discovery. How did you find them?"

"I saw Maeve in a vision," I said. "She told me where to find them."

Selene's eyebrows rose. "Goodness. You had a vision?"

"Yes. I mean, I was scrying," I admitted, flushing. I didn't know for sure, but I had a feeling scrying was another thing I wasn't supposed to do as an uninitiated witch. "And I saw Maeve and where the tools might be."

"What were you scrying with? Water?"

"Fire."

She sat back, surprised, as if I had just come up with an impossibly high prime number.

"Fire! You were scrying with fire?"

I nodded, self-conscious but pleased at her astonishment. "I like fire," I said. "It . . . speaks to me."

There was a moment of silence, and I started to feel uneasy. I had been bending the rules and following my own path with Wicca practically from the beginning.

"Not many witches scry with fire," Selene told me.

"Why not? It works so well."

"It doesn't for most people," Selene replied. "It's very capricious. It takes a lot of power to scry with fire." I felt her gaze on me and didn't know what to say.

"Where are Maeve's tools now?" Selene asked. I was relieved that she didn't sound angry or disapproving. It felt very intimate in the car, very private, as though what we said here would always be secret.

"They're hidden," I said reassuringly.

"Good," said Selene. "I'm sure you know how very powerful those tools are. I'm glad you're being careful with them. And I just wanted to offer my services, my guidance, and my experience in helping you learn to use them."

I nodded. "Thank you."

"And I would hope, because of our close relationship and your relationship with Cal, that you might want me to see the tools, test them, share my power with them. I'm very strong, and the tools are very strong, and it could be a very exciting thing to put our strengths together."

Just then a familiar gold Explorer rolled into the parking lot. I saw Cal's profile through his smoked window, and my heart leapt. He glanced toward us, pausing for a moment before pulling into a spot and turning off the engine. Eagerly I rolled down my window, and as I did, I heard the morning bell ring.

"Hi!" I said.

He came closer and leaned on the door, looking through the open window. "Hi," he said. His injured wrists were covered by his coat sleeves. "Mom? What are you doing here?"

"I just couldn't wait to talk to Morgan about Belwicket's tools," Selene said with a laugh.

"Oh," said Cal. I was puzzled by the flat tone in his voice. He sounded almost annoyed.

"Um, I feel like I should tell you," I said hesitantly. "I, uh, I bound the tools to me. I don't think they'll work too well for anyone else."

Cal and Selene both stared at me as if I had suddenly announced I was really a man.

"What?" said Selene, her eyes wide.

"I bound the tools to me," I said, wondering if I had acted too hastily. But Alyce had seemed so certain.

"What do you mean, you bound the tools to you?" Cal asked carefully.

I swallowed. I felt suddenly like a kid called in front of the principal. "I did a spell and bound the tools to me, sending my vibrations through them. They're part of me now."

"Whoa. How come?" Cal said.

"Well," I said, "you know, to make it harder for others to use them. And to increase my power when I use them."

"Heavens," said Selene. "Who told you how to do that?"

I opened my mouth to say, "Alyce," but instead, to my surprise, what came out was, "I read about it."

"Hmmm," she said thoughtfully. "Well, there are ways to unbind tools."

"Oh," I said, feeling uncertain. Why would she want me to unbind them?

"I would love to show you some hands-on ways to use them." Selene smiled. "You can't get everything from books."

"No," I agreed. I still felt uncertain and indefinably uneasy. "Well, I'd better get going."

"All right," said Selene. "Congratulations again on finding the tools. I'm so proud of you."

Her words warmed me, and I got out of the car feeling better.

I looked at Cal. "You coming?"

"Yeah," he said. He hesitated as if he were about to say something else, then seemed to change his mind, calling merely, "Talk to you later, Mom."

"Right," she said, and the window rolled up.

Cal set off for school. His strides were so long that I practically had to run to keep up. When I glanced at his profile, I could see that his jaw was set. "What's wrong?" I asked breathlessly. "Are you upset about something?"

He glanced at me. "No," he said. "Just don't want to be late."

But I didn't need my witch senses to see that he was lying. Was he angry at me because I'd bound the tools to me and now no one else could use them?

Or was he angry with Selene? It had almost seemed like he was. But why?

My day went downhill from there. While I was changing classes at fourth period, I accidentally walked in on Matt Adler and Raven Meltzer making out in an empty chem lab. When our eyes met, Matt looked like he wanted to vaporize himself, and Raven looked even more smug than usual. Ugh, I thought. Then it occurred to me that I could never judge anyone again about anything because what I had done was so terrible, so unnatural. And as soon as I thought that, I went into the girls' bathroom and cried.

At lunchtime Cal and I sat with Cirrus at our usual table. The group was quiet today. Robbie was tight faced, and I wondered how it had gone at Bree's house yesterday. Probably not well since Bree was across the lunchroom sitting on Chip Newton's lap and laughing. Great.

Jenna was even paler than usual. When Cal asked her where Matt was, she said, "I wouldn't know. We broke up last night." She shrugged, and that was that. I was surprised and impressed by how calm she seemed. She was stronger than she looked.

Ethan Sharp and Sharon Goodfine were sitting next to each other. After months of flirting, they were looking into each other's eyes as if they'd finally realized the other was a real person and not just a clever simulation. Sharon shared her bagel with him. It was the only cheerful thing that happened.

Somehow I slogged through the afternoon. I kept thinking about Selene teaching me to use Maeve's tools. One minute I would want to do it, and the next minute I would remember Alyce's warning and decide to keep them to myself. I couldn't make up my mind.

When the final bell rang, I gathered up my things with relief. Only half a day tomorrow, thank the Goddess, and then a four-day weekend. I walked outside, looking for Mary K.

"Hey," said my sister, coming up. "Cold enough for

you?" We glanced up at the striated clouds that scudded slowly across the sky.

"Yeah," I said, hitching up my backpack. "Come on. I'm parked over in the side lot."

Just as I turned, Cal came up. "Hey, Mary K.," he said. Then he ducked his head and spoke only to me. "Is it okay if I come over this afternoon?" There was an unspoken message—we had tons to talk about—and I nodded at once.

"I'll meet you there."

He touched my cheek briefly, smiled at Mary K., then walked beside us to his own car. My sister raised an eyebrow at me, and I shot her a glance.

Once we were in Das Boot and I was cranking the engine, Mary K. said, "So, have you done it yet?"

I almost punched the gas, which would have slammed us right into a tree.

"Good God, Mary K.!" I cried, staring at her.

She giggled, then tried to look defiant. "Well? You've been going out a month, and he's gorgeous, and you can tell *he's* not a virgin. You're my sister. If I don't ask you, who can I ask?"

"Ask about what?" I said irritably, backing out.

"About sex," she said.

I rested my head for a second against the steering wheel. "Mary K., this may surprise you, but you're only fourteen years old. You're a high school freshman. Don't you think you're too young to worry about this?"

As soon as the words were out of my mouth, I wished I could take them back. I sounded just like my mom. I wasn't surprised when my sister's face closed.

"I'm sorry," I said. "You just . . . took me by surprise. Give me a second." I tried to think quickly and drive at the same time. "Sex." I blew out my breath. "No, I haven't done it yet."

Mary K. looked surprised.

I sighed. "Yes, Cal wants to. And I want to. But it hasn't seemed exactly right yet. I mean, I love Cal. He makes me feel unbelievable. And he's totally sexy and all that." My cheeks heated. "But still, it's only been a month, and there's a lot of other stuff going on, and it just . . . hasn't seemed right." I frowned at her pointedly. "And I think it's really important to wait until it *is* exactly right, and you're totally comfortable and sure and crazy in love. Otherwise it's no good." Said the incredibly experienced Morgan Rowlands.

Mary K. looked at me. "What if the other person *is* sure and you just want to trust them?"

Note to self: Do a castration spell on Bakker Blackburn. I breathed in, turned onto our street, and saw Cal in back of us. I pulled into our driveway and turned off the engine but stayed in the car. Cal parked and walked up to the house, waiting for us on the porch.

"I think you know enough to be sure for yourself," I said quietly. "You're not an idiot. You know how you feel. Some people date for years before they're both ready to have sex." Where was I getting this stuff? Years of reading teen magazines?

"The important thing," I went on, "is that you make your own decisions and don't give in to pressure. I told Cal I wasn't ready, and he was majorly disappointed." I lowered my voice as if he could hear us from twenty feet away, outside the car. "I mean, *majorly*. But he accepted my decision and is waiting until I'm ready."

Mary K. looked at her lap.

"However, if for some reason you think it might happen, for God's sake use nine kinds of birth control and check out his health and be careful and don't get hurt. Okay?"

My sister blushed and nodded. On the porch I saw Cal shifting his feet in the cold.

"Do you want me to send Cal home so we can talk some more?" Please say no.

"No, that's okay," said Mary K. "I think I get it."

"Okay. I'm always here. I mean, if you can't ask your sister, who can you ask?"

She grinned, and we hugged each other. Then we hurried inside. Twenty minutes later Mary K. was doing her homework upstairs and Cal and I were drinking hot tea in the kitchen. And I hoped my sister had taken my words to heart.

7.
Self

July 2000

The council called me to London upon my return from the North. I spent three days answering questions about everything from the causes of the Clan wars to the medicinal properties of mugwort. I wrote essays analyzing past decisions of the elders. I performed spells and rituals.

And then they turned me down. Not because my power is weak or my knowledge scanty, nor yet because I am too young, but because they distrust my motives. They think I am after vengeance for Linden, for my parents.

But that's not it, not anymore. I spoke to Athar about it last night. She's the only one who truly understands, I think.

"You aren't after vengeance. You're after redemption," she told me, and her black eyes measured me. "But, Giomanach, I'm not sure which is the more dangerous quest."

She's a deep one, my cousin Athar. I don't know when she grew to be so wise.

I won't give up. I will write to the council again today. I'll make them understand.

—Giomanach

Our kitchen was about one-sixth the size of Cal's kitchen, and instead of granite counters and custom country French cabinets, we had worn Formica and cabinets from about 1983. But our kitchen felt homier.

I rested my legs over Cal's knees under the table and we leaned toward each other, talking. The idea that maybe someday we would have our very own house, just us two, made me shiver. I looked up at Cal's smooth tan skin, his perfect nose, his strong eyebrows, and sighed. We needed to talk about Hunter.

"I'm really shaken up," I said quietly.

"I know. I am, too. I never thought it would come to that." He gave a dry laugh. "Actually, I thought we would just beat each other up a bit, and the whole thing would blow over. But when Hunter pulled out the braigh—"

"The silver chain he was using?"

Cal shuddered. "Yes," he said, his voice rough. "It was spelled. Once it was on me, I was powerless."

"Cal, I just can't believe what happened," I said, my eyes filling with tears. I brushed them away with one hand. "I can't think about anything else. And why hasn't anyone found the body yet? What are we going to do when they do find it? I swear, every time the phone rings, I think it's going to be the police, asking me to come down to the station and answer some questions." A tear overflowed and ran down my cheek. "I just can't get over this."

"I'm so sorry." Cal pushed his chair closer to mine and put his arms around me. "I wish we were at my house," he said quietly. "I just want to hold you without worrying about your folks coming in."

I nodded, sniffling. "What are we going to do?"

"There's nothing we can do, Morgan," Cal said, kissing my temple. "It was horrible, and I've cursed myself a thousand times for involving you in it. But it happened, and we can't take it back. And never forget that we acted in self-defense. Hunter was trying to kill me. You were trying to protect me. What else could we have done?"

I shook my head.

"I've never been through anything like this before," Cal said softly against my hair. "It's the worst thing in my life. But you know what? I'm glad I'm going through it with you. I mean, I'm sorry you were involved. I wish to the Goddess that you weren't. But since we were in it together, I'm so glad I have you." He shook his head. "This isn't making sense. I'm just trying to say that in an awful way, this has made me feel closer to you."

I looked up into his eyes. "Yeah, I know what you mean."

We stayed like that, sitting at the table, our arms around each other, until my shoulder blades began to ache from the angle and I reluctantly pulled away. I had to change the subject.

"Your mom seemed really excited about my tools," I said, taking a sip of my tea.

Cal pushed his hands through his raggedy dark hair. "Yeah. She's like a little kid—she wants to get her hands on every new thing. Especially something like Belwicket's tools."

"Is there something special about Belwicket in particular?"

Cal shrugged, looking thoughtful. He sipped his tea and said, "I guess just the mystery of it—how it was destroyed, and how old the coven was and how powerful. It's a blessing the tools weren't lost. Oh, and they were Woodbane," he added as an afterthought.

"Does it matter that they were Woodbane since Belwicket had renounced evil?"

"I don't know," said Cal. "Probably not. I think it probably matters more what you *do* with your magick."

I breathed in the steam from my tea. "Maybe I bound the tools to me without thinking it through too well," I said. "What would happen if another witch tried to use them now?"

Cal shrugged. "It's not predictable. Another witch might subvert the tools' power in an unexpected way. Actually, it's pretty unusual for someone to bind a coven's tools only to themselves." He looked up and met my glance.

"I just felt they were mine," I said lamely. "Mine, my birth mother's, her mother's. I wanted them to be all mine."

Nodding, Cal patted my leg, across his knee. "I'd probably do the same thing if they were mine," he said, and I adored him for his support.

"And then Mom would kill me," he added, laughing. I laughed, too.

"Your mom said I was an unusually powerful witch, this morning in the car," I said. "So witches have different strengths of power? In one of my Wiccan history books it talks about some witches being more powerful than others. Does that mean that they just know more, or does it mean something about their innate power?"

"Both," Cal said. He put his feet on either side of mine under the table. "It's like regular education. How accomplished you are depends on how intelligent you are as well as how much education you have. Of course, blood witches are always going to be more powerful than humans. But even among blood witches there's definitely a range. If you're naturally a weak witch, then you can study and practice all you want and your powers will be only so-so. If you're a naturally powerful witch, yet don't know anything about Wicca, you can't do much, either. It's the combination that matters."

"Well, how strong is your mother, for example?" I asked. "On a scale of one to ten?"

Laughing, Cal leaned across and kissed my cheek. "Careful. Your math genes are showing."

I grinned.

"Let's see," he mused. He rubbed his chin, and I saw a flash of bandage on his wrist. My heart ached for the pain he had gone through. "My mother, on a scale of one to ten. Let's make it a scale of one to a hundred. And a weak witch without much training would be about a twelve."

I nodded, putting this mythical person on the scale.

"And then someone like, oh, Mereden the Wise or Denys Haraldson would be up in the nineties."

I nodded, recognizing the names Mereden and Denys from my Wiccan history books. They had been powerful witches, role models, educators, enlighteners. Mereden had been burned at the stake back in 1517. Denys had died in 1942 in a London bomb blitz.

"My mom is about an eighty or an eighty-five on that scale," Cal said.

My eyes widened. "Wow. That's way up there."

"Yep. She's no one to mess with," Cal said wryly.

"Where are you? Where am I?"

"It's harder to tell," Cal said. He glanced at his watch. "You know, it'll be dark soon, and I'd really like to put some spells on your house and car while Sky's still in town."

"Okay," I agreed, standing up. "But you really can't say where we are on the Cal scale of witch power? Which reminds me: is it Calvin or just Cal?"

He laughed and brought his mug over to the sink. From upstairs we heard Mary K. blasting her latest favorite CD. "It's Calhoun," he said as we walked into the living room.

"Calhoun," I said, trying it out. I liked it. "Answer my question, Calhoun."

"Let me think," said Cal, putting on his coat. "It's hard to be objective about myself—but I think I'm about a sixty-two. I mean, I'm young; my powers will likely increase as I get older. I'm from good lines, I'm a good student, but I'm not a shooting star. I'm not going to take the Wiccan world by storm. So I'd give myself about a sixty-two."

I laughed and hugged him through his coat. He put his arms around me and stroked my hair down my back. "But you," he said quietly, "you are something different."

"What, like a twenty?" I said.

"Goddess, no," he said.

"Thirty-five? Forty?" I made my eyes look big and hopeful. It made me happy to tease and joke with Cal. It was so easy to love him, to be myself, and to like who I was with him.

He smiled slowly, making me catch my breath at his beauty. "No, sweetie," he said gently. "I think you're more like a ninety. Ninety-five."

Startled, I stared at him, then realized he was joking. "Oh, very funny," I said, laughing. I pulled away and put on my own coat. "We can't *all* be magickal wonders. We can't *all* be—"

"You're a shooting star," he said. His face was serious, even grave. "You *are* a magickal wonder. A prodigy. You could take the Wiccan world by storm."

I gaped, trying to make sense of his words. "What are you talking about?"

"It's why I've been trying to get you to go slowly, not rush things," he said. "You have a tornado inside you, but you have to learn to control it. Like with Maeve's tools. I wish you'd let my mother guide you. I'm worried that you might be getting into something over your head because you're not seeing the big picture."

"I don't know what you mean," I said uncertainly.

He smiled again, his mood lightening, and dropped a kiss on my lips. "Oh, it's no big deal," he said with teasing sarcasm. "It's just, you know, you have a power that comes along every couple of generations. Don't worry about it."

Despite my confusion, Cal really wouldn't talk about it anymore. Outside, he concentrated on spelling Das Boot and my house with runes and spells of protection, and once that was done, he went home. And I was left with too many questions.

That night after dinner my parents took Mary K. to her friend Jaycee's violin recital. Once they were gone, I locked all the doors, feeling melodramatic. Then I went upstairs, took out Maeve's tools, and went into my room.

Sitting on my floor, I examined the tools again. They felt natural in my hands, comfortable, an extension of myself. I wondered what Cal had meant about not seeing the big picture. To me, the big picture was: these had been my grandmother's tools, then my mother's; now they were mine. Any other big picture was secondary to that.

Still, I was sure Selene could teach me a lot about them. It was a compelling idea. I wondered again why Alyce had urged me to bind them to myself so quickly.

I was halfway through making a circle before I realized what I was doing. With surprise, I looked up to find a piece of chalk in my hand and my circle half drawn. My mother's green silk robe, embroidered with magickal symbols, stars, and runes, was draped over my clothes. A candle burned in the fire cup, incense was in the air cup, and the other two cups held earth and water. Cal's silver pentacle was warm at my throat. I hadn't taken it off since he'd given it to me.

The tools wanted me to use them. They wanted to come alive again after languishing, unused and hidden, for so long. I felt their promise of power. Working quickly, I finished casting my circle. Then, holding the athame, I blessed the Goddess and the God and invoked them.

Now what?

Scrying.

I looked into the candle flame, concentrating and relaxing at the same time. I felt my muscles ease, my breathing slow, my thoughts drift free. Words came to my mind, and I spoke them aloud.

"I sense magick growing and swelling.
I visit knowledge in its dwelling.
For me alone these tools endure,
To make my magick strong and sure."

Then I thought, I am ready to see, and then . . . things started happening.

I saw rows of ancient books and knew these were texts I needed to study. I knew I had years of circles ahead of me, years of observing and celebrating the cycles. I saw myself, bent and sobbing, and understood that the road would not be easy. Exhilarated, I said, "I'm ready to see more."

Abruptly my vision changed. I saw an older me leaning over a cauldron, and I looked like a children's cartoon of a witch, with long, stringy hair, bad skin, sunken cheeks, hands like claws. It was so horrible, I almost giggled nervously. That other me was conjuring, surrounded by sharp-edged, dripping wet stone, as if I stood in a cave by a sea. Outside, lightning flashed and cracked into the cave, shining on the walls, and my face was contorted with the effort of working magick. The cave was glowing with power, that other Morgan was giddy with power, and the whole scene felt awful, bizarre, frightening, yet somehow seductive.

I swallowed hard and blinked several times, trying to

bring myself out of it. I couldn't get enough air and was dimly aware that I was gaping like a fish, trying to get more oxygen to my brain. When I blinked again, I saw sunlight and another, older Morgan walking through a field of wheat, like one of those corny shampoo commercials. I was pregnant. There was no dramatic power around me, no ecstatic conjuring, just peace and quiet and calm.

Now I was breathing quickly, and every time my eyes closed, I alternated between the two images, the two Morgans. I became aware of a deep-seated pain in my chest and throat, and I started to feel panicky and out of control.

I want to get out of this, I thought. I want to get out. Let me *out!*

Somehow I managed to wrench my gaze away from the candle flame, and then I was leaning over, gasping on my carpet, feeling dizzy and sick. I was flooded with sensation, with memories and visions I couldn't interpret or even see clearly, and suddenly I knew that I was about to vomit. I staggered to my feet, breaking my circle, and lurched drunkenly to the bathroom. I yanked off my robe, slid across the tiled wall until I hovered over the toilet, and then I threw up, almost crying with misery.

I don't know how long I was in there, but it was a long while, and finally I started to cry, aching, deep sobs. I sat there till the sobs subsided, then shakily got to my feet, flushed the toilet, and crept to the sink. Splashing my face with cold water helped, and I brushed my teeth and washed my face again and changed into my pajamas. I felt weak and hollow, as if I had the flu.

Back in my room, Dagda sat in the middle of the broken circle, gazing meditatively at the candle. "Hi, boy," I whispered, then cupped my hand and blew out the candle. My hands trembling, I dismantled everything, storing the tools in their metal box, folding my mother's robe, which seemed alive, crackling with energy. The very air in my room felt charged and unhealthy. I flung open a window, welcoming the twenty-five-degree chill.

I vacuumed up my circle and hid the toolbox again, spelling the HVAC vent with runes of secrecy. Soon after that, the front door opened and I heard my parents' voices. The phone rang at the same moment. I sprang over to the hall extension and said breathlessly, "Hi. I'm glad you called."

"Are you okay?" Cal said. "I suddenly got a weird feeling about you."

He would not be thrilled to hear about my using my mother's tools in a circle. Lack of experience, lack of knowledge, lack of supervision. And so on.

"I'm okay," I said, trying to slow my breathing. I did feel much better, though still a bit shaky. "I just—missed you."

"I miss you, too," he said quietly. "I wish I could be there with you at night."

A cool breeze from my room gave me a quick shiver. "That would be wonderful," I said.

"Well, it's late," he said. "Sleep tight. Think of me when you're lying there."

I felt his voice in the pit of my stomach, and my hand tightened on the phone.

"I will," I whispered as Mary K. started coming upstairs loudly.

"Good night, my love."

"Good night."

8.
Symbols

September 2000

    I'm in Ireland. I went to the town of Ballynigel, where the Belwicket coven once was. It was wiped out around Imbolc in 1982, along with most of the town. So far it's the only Woodbane coven I've found that the dark wave has destroyed. But everyone knows Belwicket renounced evil back in the 1800s and had kept to the council's laws since the laws were first written. Did that have something to do with it? When I stood there and saw the bits of riven earth and charred stones that are all that's left, it made my heart ache.

    Tonight I am meeting with Jeremy Mertwick, from the second ring of the council. I have written them a letter every week, appealing their decision. I still hope to make them see reason. I am strong and sure, and my pain has made me older than they know.

    —Giomanach

"C'mon, last day before break," Mary K. coaxed, standing over my bed. She waved a warm Toaster Strudel under my nose. I sat up, patted Dagda, and then staggered unhappily to the shower.

"Five minutes," Mary K. called in warning. Then I heard her say, "Come on, little guy. Auntie Mary K. will feed you."

Her voice faded as the hot spray needled down my skin, making me feel semihuman.

Downstairs, my sister handed me a Diet Coke. "Robbie called. His car won't start. We need to pick him up on the way."

We headed out and detoured over to Robbie's house. He was waiting out front, leaning against his red Volkswagen.

"Battery dead again?" I greeted him as he climbed into Das Boot's backseat.

He nodded glumly. "Again." We drove on in companionable morning silence.

At school Mary K. was met as usual by Bakker.

"Young love," Robbie said dryly, watching them nuzzle.

"Ugh," I said, turning off the engine.

"Thanks for the ride," Robbie said. Something in his voice made me turn and look at him.

"So I kissed Bree on Monday," he said.

I sat back, taking my hand off the door handle. I had been so wrapped up in my own misery that I had forgotten to check in with Robbie about Bree. "Wow," I said, examining his face. "I wondered what had happened. I, um, I saw her yesterday with Chip."

Robbie nodded, scanning the school grounds through the car window. He said nothing, and I prompted him: "So?"

He shrugged, his broad shoulders moving inside his army surplus parka. He gave a short laugh. "She let me kiss her. It blew my mind. She just laughed and seemed into it, and I thought, All *right*. And then I came up for air and said that I loved her." He stopped.

"*And?*" I practically screeched.

"She wasn't into *that*. Dropped me like a stone. Practically pushed me out the door." He rubbed his forehead, as if he had a headache. Silently I offered him my soda, and he finished it off and wiped his mouth with the back of his hand.

"Hmmm," I said. I didn't trust Bree anymore. Before, she might have done the same thing to Robbie, but now I couldn't help wondering how her involvement in Kithic had affected her actions.

"Yeah. Hmmm."

"But the making out worked?" I asked.

"Worked fabulously. Hot, hot, hot." He couldn't help grinning at the memory.

"Okay, I don't need to know," I said quickly.

I took a minute to think. Was Bree capable of using Robbie for some dark purpose, or was she just toying with him in her usual way? I didn't know. I decided to take a chance.

"Well, my advice to you is," I said, "just make out with her. Don't talk to her about your feelings. Not yet, anyway."

He frowned. Outside the car, we saw Cal crunching toward us through the leftover snow, his breath puffing like a dragon's. As usual, my heart lurched when I saw him.

"Hey, I *love* her. I don't want to use her like that."

"No. My point is, let *her* use *you* like that."

"Like a boy toy?" He sounded outraged, but I saw a fleeting interest cross his face.

"Like someone who knocks her off her feet," I pointed out. "Someone who gives her something she can't get from Chip Newton or anyone else."

Robbie stared at me. "You are *ruthless*." I heard admiration in his voice.

"I want you to be happy," I said firmly.

"I think, deep down, you want *her* to be happy, too," Robbie said, unfolding his long frame from the backseat. "Hey, Cal," he said, before I could respond to his remark.

Cal leaned into the open door. "Getting out anytime soon?"

I looked at him. "How about you get in, we take off, and just keep driving until we run out of gas?" I checked my gauge. "Got a full tank." I was only half joking.

When I glanced up, I was startled by the look in his eyes. "Don't tempt me," he said, his voice rough. For a long moment I hung there, suspended in time, pinned by the fierce look of desire and longing. I remembered how it had felt, making out on his bed, touching each other, and I shuddered.

"Hey, Cal," said Ethan from the sidewalk, waving at us as he went into the building.

Cal sighed. "Guess we better go in."

I nodded, not trusting myself to speak.

Cal and I joined the other Cirrus members at the top of the basement stairs.

"Talk about brutal weather," said Jenna as we walked up. She hugged her Nordic sweater closely around her, looking ethereal. I wondered how her asthma was lately and if I could use my tools to help her breathing.

"It's not even officially winter yet. This is the third-coldest autumn on record," Sharon complained, and snuggled closer to Ethan, who looked pleased. Hiding a smile, I sank down on a step, and Cal sat next to me and twined his hand through mine.

"Oh, this is cozy," said Raven's voice. Her dark head appeared over the staircase, followed by another dark head: Matt's. He sat down on a step, the picture of guilt, and she stood there smiling down at us, the Wicked Witch of the Northeast.

"Hi, Raven," said Cal, and she looked him up and down with her shining black eyes.

"Hello, Cal," she drawled. "Having a coven meeting?" She didn't bother lowering her voice, and some students walking past glanced up, startled. And this was Bree's new best friend.

"How's *your* coven going?" I heard myself ask. "Everything okay with Sky?"

Raven's eyes focused on me. Her silver nose ring glinted, her full lips were painted a rich purple, and I was struck by her presence: she was bizarre and luxurious, silly and compelling at the same time.

"Don't talk about Sky," Raven said. "She's a better witch than you'll ever be. You have no idea what you're up against." She stroked two fingers along Matt's smooth cheek, making him flinch, and walked off.

"Well, that was fun," said Robbie when she was gone.

"Matt, why don't you just join Kithic?" Jenna said abruptly, her jaw tight.

Matt frowned, not raising his eyes. "I don't want to," he mumbled.

"Okay, we only have a minute," said Cal, getting down to business. "We have a circle coming up this Saturday, our first in two weeks, and I have an assignment for you."

"I'm sorry, Cal, I won't be here," said Sharon.

"That's okay," he said. "I know you have plans with your family. Do these exercises on your own, and tell us about it the next time we see you. Now, one of the basic platforms of Wicca is self-knowledge. One of my teachers once said, 'Know yourself, and you know the universe,' and that may have been overstating it a bit, but not entirely."

Jenna and Sharon nodded, and I saw Ethan gently massaging Sharon's shoulder.

"I want you to work on self-Imaging," Cal went on. "You're going to find your personal correspondences, your own . . . what's the word? I guess *helpers* or *connectors* sort of comes close. They're the things that speak to you, that feel like you, that awaken something in you. Objects or symbols that strengthen your connection to your own magick."

"Not following you here," said Robbie.

"Sorry—let me give you some examples. Things like stones, the four elements, flowers, animals, herbs, seasons, foods," said Cal, ticking them off on his fingers. "My stone is a tigereye. I often use it in my rituals. My element is fire. My metal is gold. My personal rune is—a secret. My season is autumn. My sign is Gemini. My cloth is linen."

"And your car of choice is Ford," Robbie said, and Cal laughed.

"Right. No, seriously. Think especially about elements, stars, stones, seasons, and plants. Define yourselves, but don't limit yourselves. Don't force anything. If nothing speaks to you, don't worry about it. Just move on to something else. But explore your connection to earthly things and to unearthly things." Cal looked around at us. "Any questions?"

"This is so cool," said Sharon.

"I already know your correspondences," Ethan told her. "Your metal is gold, your stone is a diamond, your season is the post-Christmas sale season . . . ouch!" he said as Sharon clipped him smartly on the head. He laughed and raised his hands to defend himself.

"Very funny!" said Sharon, trying not to smile. "And your element is *dirt,* and your metal is *lead,* and your plant is *marijuana!*"

"I don't smoke anymore!" Ethan protested.

We were all laughing, and I felt almost lighthearted in a way that I hadn't since Hunter—

The first bell rang, and suddenly the halls were filled with students swarming to their homerooms. We gathered our various belongings and went our separate ways. And I wondered how much longer I could take this inner darkness.

After the school bell rang at noon, I waited for Cal and Mary K. by the east entrance. It was snowing again. Footsteps sounded behind me, and I turned to see Raven and Bree heading toward the double doors. Bree's face hardened when she saw me.

"So, what are you guys doing for Thanksgiving?" I blinked in surprise as the words left my mouth. Two pairs of dark eyes locked in on me as if I were glowing like a neon light.

"Um, well, gee," Raven said. "I guess I'm celebrating a day of wonder and thankfulness in the arms of my loving family. How about you?"

Since I knew her loving family consisted of a mother who had too many boyfriends and an older brother who was away in the army, I guessed she didn't have plans.

I shrugged. "Family. Turkey. A pumpkin pie gone wrong. Keeping my cat off the dining-room table."

"You have a cat?" Bree asked, unable to help herself. She had a major weakness for cats.

I nodded. "A gray kitten. He's incredibly adorable. Totally bad. Bad and adorable."

"This is delightful"—Raven sighed as Bree opened her mouth to speak—"but we really must be going. We have things to do, people to see."

"Sky?" I asked.

"None of your business," Raven said with a smirk.

Bree was silent as they thumped down the stairs in their matching heavy boots.

A second later Mary K. ran up to say she was going to Jaycee's and Mom had said it was okay, and then Cal came up and asked if I could come over and of course I wanted to. I called Unser's Auto Shop and canceled Das Boot's repair appointment. Then I followed Cal to his house, where we could be alone.

Cal's room was wonderful. It ran the whole length and breadth of the big house since it was the attic. Six dormer windows made cozy nooks, bookcases lined the walls, and he had his own fireplace and an outside staircase leading down to the back patio. His bed was wide and romantic looking, with white bed linens and a gauzy mosquito net looped out of the way. The dark wooden desk where he did his homework had rows of cream-colored candles lining its edge. I had never been in here without envying him this magickal space.

"Want some tea?" he asked, gesturing to the electric kettle. I nodded, and we didn't speak, enjoying the silence and safety of his room.

Two minutes later Cal put a cup of tea into my hand, and I adjusted its temperature and took a sip. "Mmm."

Cal turned away and stood looking out the window. "Morgan," he said. "Forgive me."

"For what?" I asked, raising my eyebrows.

"I lied to you," he said quietly, and my heart clutched in panic.

"Oh?" I marveled at how calm my voice sounded.

"About my clan." The words had almost no sound.

My heart skipped a beat, and I stared at him. He turned to me, his beautiful golden eyes holding promises of love, of passion, of a shared future. And yet his words . . .

He took a sip of tea. The pale light from the window outlined the planes of his cheekbones, the line of his jaw. I waited, and he came close to me, so that his shirt was almost brushing mine and I could see the fine texture of his skin.

Cal turned toward the window again and pushed his fingers through his hair, holding it back from his left temple. I caught a glimpse of a birthmark there, beneath the hair. I reached up and traced its outline with my fingers. It was a dark red athame, just like the one I had under my arm. The mark of the Woodbane clan.

"Hunter was right," Cal went on, his voice low. "I am Woodbane. And I've always known it."

I needed to sit down. I had been so upset when I first found out about my heritage, and Cal had said it wasn't so terrible. Now I saw why. I put down my tea and walked across the room to the futon couch. I sank onto it, and he came to kneel at my side.

"My father was Woodbane, and so is my mother," he said, looking more uncomfortable than I'd ever seen him. "They're not the Belwicket kind of Woodbanes, where everyone renounces evil and swears to do good." He shrugged, not looking at me. "There's another kind of Woodbane, who practices magick traditionally, I mean traditionally for their clan. For Woodbanes that means not being so picky about how you get your knowledge and why you use your power. Traditional Woodbanes don't subscribe to the council's edict that witches never interfere with humans. They figure, humans interfere with us, we all live in the same world, not two separate universes, so they're going to use their powers to take care of problems they might have with humans, or to protect themselves, or to get what they need. . . ."

I was unable to take my eyes off his face.

"After my dad married my mother, I think they started to go different ways, magickally," Cal continued. "Mom has always been very powerful and ambitious, and I think my father disagreed with some of the things she was doing."

"Like what?" I asked, a little shocked.

He waved an impatient hand. "You know, taking too many risks. Anyway, then my dad met Fiona, his second wife. Fiona was a Wyndenkell. I don't know if he wanted a Wyndenkell alliance or he just loved her more. But either way, he left my mother."

I was finally getting some answers. "But if Hunter was right and your father was also *his* father, then wasn't he half Woodbane himself?" This sounded like some awful soap opera. *The Young and the Wiccan.*

"That's the thing," said Cal. "Of course he was. So it made no sense for him to persecute Woodbanes. But he seemed to have a thing about them, like Mom said. An obsession. I wondered if he blamed my father—our father— for what happened to his parents and their coven, for some reason, and so decided to get all Woodbanes. Who knows? He was unhinged."

"So you're Woodbane," I said, still trying to take it all in.

"Yes," he admitted.

"Why didn't you tell me before? I was *hysterical* about being Woodbane."

"I know," he said, sighing. "I should have. But Belwicket was a different kind of Woodbane, a completely good Woodbane, above reproach. I wasn't sure you would understand my family's heritage. I mean, it isn't like they're all evil. They don't worship demons or anything like that. It's just—they do what they want to do. They don't always follow rules."

"Why are you telling me now?"

At last he looked at me, and I felt the pull of his gaze. "Because I love you. I trust you. I don't want any secrets to come between us. And—"

The door to his room suddenly flew open. I jumped about a foot in the air. Selene stood there, dressed beautifully in a dark gold sweater and tweed pants.

Cal stood with swift grace. "What the hell are you doing?"

I had never heard anyone speak to their mother this way, and I flinched.

"What are *you* doing?" she countered. "I felt—what are you talking about?"

"None of your business," he said, and Selene's eyes flashed with surprise.

"We discussed this," she said in a low voice.

"Mom, you need to leave," Cal said flatly. I was embarrassed and confused and also worried: no way did I want to get in between these two if they were fighting.

"How—how did you know he was telling me anything?" I ventured.

"I felt it," Selene said. "I felt him say Woodbane."

This was really interesting. Creepy, but interesting.

"Yes, you're Woodbane," I said, standing up. "I'm Woodbane, too. Is there a reason I shouldn't know your clan?"

"Mom, I trust Morgan, and you need to trust me," Cal said thinly. "Now, will you get back to your work and leave us alone, or do I have to spell the door?"

My lips curved into an involuntary smile, and a second later the tension on Selene's face broke. She breathed out. "Very nice. Threaten your mother," she said tartly.

"Hey, I'll make it so you'll *never* find your way up here again," Cal said, his hands on his hips. He was smiling now, but I felt he wasn't entirely joking. I thought of Selene walking in on us when we were rolling around on Cal's bed and secretly decided maybe spelling the door wouldn't be such a bad idea.

"Forgive me," Selene said at last. "I'm sorry. It's just— Woodbanes have a terrible reputation. We're used to guarding our privacy fiercely. For a moment I forgot who Cal was talking to—and how extraordinary and trustworthy you are. I'm sorry."

"It's okay," I said, and Selene turned around and left. Quickly Cal stepped to the door and snapped the lock behind her, then traced several sigils and runes around the frame of the door with his fingers, muttering something.

"Okay," he said. "That will keep her out." He sounded smug, and I smiled.

"Are you sure?"

The answering look he gave me took my breath away. When he held out his hand, I went to him immediately, and next we tumbled onto his wide bed, the white comforter billowing cozily beneath us. For a long time we kissed and held each other, and I knew that I felt even closer to him than before. Each time we were alone together, we went a little further, and today I needed to feel close to him, needed to be comforted by his touch. Restlessly I pushed my hands under his shirt, against his smooth skin.

I never wore a bra, having a distinct lack of need, and when his hands slipped under my shirt and unerringly found their way to my breasts, I almost cried out. One part of my mind hoped the spell on his door was really foolproof; the other part of my mind turned to tapioca.

I pulled him tightly to me, feeling his desire, hearing his breathing quicken in my ear, amazed at how much I loved him.

This time it was Cal who gradually slowed, who eased the fierceness of his kisses, who calmed his breathing and so made me calm mine. Apparently today would not be the day, either. I was both relieved and disappointed.

After our breathing had more or less returned to normal, he stroked my hair away from my face and said, "I have something to show you."

"Huh?" I said. But he was rolling off the bed, straightening his clothing.

Then he held out his hand to me. "Come," he said, and I followed him without question.

9.
Secrets

It's odd to be the son of a famous witch. Everyone watches you, from the time you can walk and talk—watches you for signs of genius or of mediocrity. You're never offstage.

Mom raised me as she saw fit. She has plans for me, my future. I've never really discussed them with her, only listened to her tell me about them. Until recently, it never crossed my mind to disagree. It's flattering to have someone prepare you for greatness, sure of your ability to pull it off.

Yet since my love came into my life, I feel differently. She questions things, she stands up for herself. She's so naive but so strong, too. She makes me want things I've never wanted before.

I remember back in California—I was sixteen. Mom had started a coven. It was the usual smoke and mirrors—Mom using her circle's powers as sort of an energy boost so she wouldn't have to deplete her own—but then to our surprise she unearthed a very strong witch, a woman about twenty-five or so, who had no idea of her blood-lines. During circles she blew us away. So Mom asked me to get close to her. I did—it was surprisingly easy. Then Mom extinguished her during the Rite of Dubh Siol. It upset me, even though I'd known that it might happen.

It won't come to that this time. I'll make sure.

—Sgàth

As Cal led me down his outside steps to the back patio, the last flakes of falling snow brushed my face and landed on my hair. I held tightly to the iron rail; the metal stairs were slick with snow and ice.

Cal offered me his hand at the bottom of the stair. I crunched onto the snow, and he began to lead me across the stone patio. We were both cold; our coats had been in the downstairs foyer, and we hadn't gotten them.

I realized we were heading toward the pool. "Oh, God, you can't be thinking about going skinny dipping!" I said, only half joking.

Cal laughed, throwing back his head as he led me past the big pool. "No. It's covered for the winter, underneath that snow. Of course, if you're willing . . ."

"I'm not," I said quickly. I had been the lone holdout from a group swim at our coven's second meeting.

He laughed again, and then we were at the little building that served as the pool house. Built to look like a miniature version of the big house, its stone walls were covered with clinging ivy, brown in winter.

Cal opened a door, and we stepped into one of the small dressing rooms. It was decorated luxuriously, with gold hooks, spare terry-cloth robes, and full-length mirrors.

"What are we doing here?" I looked at my pale self in the mirror and made a face.

"Patience," Cal teased, and opened another door that led to a bathroom, complete with shower stall and a rack of fluffy white towels. Now I was really confused.

From his pocket Cal took a key ring, selected a key, and opened a small, locked closet. The door swung open to reveal shallow shelves with toiletries and cleaning supplies.

Cal stood back and gently swept his hands around the door frame, and I saw the faint glimmer of sigils tracing its perimeter. He muttered some words that I couldn't understand, and then the shelves swung backward to reveal an opening about five feet high and maybe two feet wide. There was another room behind it.

I raised my eyebrows at Cal. "You guys have a thing for hidden rooms," I said, thinking of his mother's concealed library in the main house.

Cal grinned. "Of course. We're witches," he said, and ducked through the door. I followed, stepping through, then straightening cautiously on the other side.

Cal stood there, expectant. "Help me light candles," he said, "so you can see better."

I glanced around, my magesight immediately adjusting to the darkness, and found myself in a very small room, perhaps seven feet by seven feet. There was one tiny, leaded-glass window set high up on the wall, beneath the unexpectedly high ceiling.

Cal started lighting candles. I was about to say it wasn't necessary, I could see fine, but then I realized he wanted to create an effect. I looked around, and my gaze landed on the burnt wick of a thick cream-colored pillar candle. I need fire, I thought, then blinked as the wick burst into flame.

It mesmerized me, and I leaned, timelost, into the wavering, triangular bloom of flame swaying seductively about the wick. I saw the wick shrivel and curl as the intense heat made the fibers contract and blacken, heard the roar of the victorious fire as it consumed the wick and surged upward in ecstasy. I felt the softening of the wax below as it sighed and acquiesced, melting and flowing into liquid.

My eyes shining, I glanced up to see Cal staring at me almost in alarm. I swallowed, wondering if I had made one of those Wiccan faux pas I was so good at.

"The fire," I murmured lamely in explanation. "It's pretty."

"Light another one," he said, and I turned to the next candle and thought about fire, and an unseen spark of life jumped from me to the wick, where it burst into a bloom of light. He didn't have to encourage me to do more. One by one, I lit the candles that lined the walls, covered the tiny bookcase, dripped out of wine bottles, and guttered on top of plates thick with old wax.

The room was now glowing, the hundreds of small flames lighting our skin, our hair, our eyes. In the middle of the floor was a single futon covered with a thin, soft, oriental rug. I sat on it, clasped my arms around my knees, and looked around me. Cal sat next to me.

"So this is your secret clubhouse?" I asked, and he chuckled and put his arm around me.

"Something like that," he agreed. "This is my sanctuary."

Now that I wasn't lighting candles, I had the time to be awestruck by my surroundings. Every square inch of wall and ceiling was painted with magickal symbols, only some of which I recognized. My brows came together as I tried to make out runes and marks of power.

My mathematician's brain started ticking: Cal and Selene had moved here right before school started—the beginning of September. It was almost the end of November now: that left not quite three months. I turned to look at him.

"How did you do all this in three months?"

He gave a short laugh. "Three months? I did this in three weeks, before school started. Lots of late nights."

"What do you do in here?"

He smiled down at me. "Make magick," he said.

"What about your room?"

"The main house is full of my mother's vibrations, not to mention those of her coven members. My room is fine for most things; it's no problem for us to have circles there. But for my stuff alone, sensitive spells, spells needing a lot of energy, I come here." He looked around, and I wondered if he was remembering all the warm late-summer nights he had been in here, painting, making magick, making the walls vibrate with his energy. Bowls of charred incense littered the floor and the bookshelves, and the books of magick lined up behind them were dark and faded, looking immeasurably old. In one corner was an altar, made of a polished chunk of marble as big as a suitcase. It was draped with a purple velvet cloth and held candles, bowls of incense, Cal's athame, a vase of spidery hothouse orchids, and a Celtic cross.

"This is what I wanted to show you," he said quietly, his arm warm across my back. "I've never shown this to anyone, although my mother knows it's here. I would never let any of the other Cirrus members see this room. It's too private."

My eyes swept across the dense writing, picking out a rune here and there. I had no idea how long we had been sitting there, but I became aware that I was sweating. The room was so small that just the heat of the candles was starting to make it too warm. It occurred to me that the candles were burning oxygen, and Practical Morgan looked for a vent. I couldn't see one, but that didn't mean anything. The room was so chaotic that it was hard to focus on any one thing.

I realized in surprise that I wouldn't be comfortable making magick in this room. To me it was starting to seem claustrophobic, jangling, as if all my nerves were being subtly irritated. I noticed that my breath was coming faster.

"You're my soul mate," Cal whispered. "Only you could handle being here. Someday we'll make magick here, together. We'll surprise everybody."

I didn't know what to think of that. I was starting to feel distinctly ill at ease.

"I think I'd better get home," I said, gathering my feet beneath me. "I don't want to be late."

I knew it sounded lame, and I could sense Cal's slight withdrawal. I felt guilty for not sharing his enthusiasm. But I really needed to get out of there.

"Of course," Cal said, standing and helping me to my

feet. One by one he blew out the candles, and I could hear the minuscule droplets of searing wax splatting against the walls. One candle at a time, the room grew darker, and although I could see perfectly, when the room was dark, it felt unbearable, its weight pressing in on me.

Abruptly, not waiting for Cal, I stepped back through the small door, ducking so I wouldn't whack my head. I didn't stop till I was outside in the blessedly frigid air. I breathed in and out several times, feeling my head clear, seeing my breath puff out like smoke.

Cal followed me a moment later, pulling the pool-house door closed behind him.

"Thank you for showing it to me," I said, sounding stiff and polite.

He led me back to the house. My nerves felt raw as I collected my coat from the front foyer. Outside again, Cal walked me to my car.

"Thanks for coming over," he said, leaning in through the car window.

I was chilled in the frosted air, and my breath puffed out as I remembered the things we had done in his bedroom and the sharp contrast with how I had felt in the pool house.

"I'll talk to you later," I said, tilting my head up to kiss him. Then I was pulling out, my one headlight sweeping across a world seemingly made of ice.

10.
Undercurrents

October 2000

I came home from Ireland this week for Alwyn's initiation. It's hard to believe she's fourteen: she seems both younger, with her knobby knees and tall, coltish prettiness, and somehow also older—the wisdom in her eyes, life's pain etched on her face.

I brought her a russet silk robe from Connemara. She plans to embroider stars and moons around its neck and hem. Uncle Beck has carved her a beautiful wand and pounded in bits of malachite and bloodstone along the handle. I think she'll be pleased when she sees it.

I know my parents would want to be here if they could, as they would have wanted to see my initiation and Linden's. I'm not sure if they're still alive. I can't sense them.

Last year I met Dad's first wife and his other son at one

of the big coven meetings in Scotland. They seemed very Woodbane: cold and hateful toward me. I had wondered if perhaps Dad still kept in touch with Selene—she's very beautiful, very magnetic. But his name seemed to set off a storm within them, which is not unreasonable, after all.

I must go—Alwyn needs help in figuring the positions of the stars on Saturday night.

—Giomanach

That night, after the house was quiet, I lay in bed, thinking. I had been disturbed by Cal's secret room. It had been so intense, so strange. I didn't really like to think about what Cal had done to make the room have those kinds of vibrations, vibrations I could only begin to identify.

And now I knew that Cal was Woodbane. So Hunter had been speaking the truth when he told me that. I understood why Cal and Selene would want to hide it—as Selene said, Woodbanes have a bad reputation in the Wiccan community. But it bothered me that Cal had lied to me. And I couldn't help remembering how he had said that he and Selene were "traditional" Woodbanes. What exactly did that mean?

Sighing, I made a conscious effort to set aside thoughts about my day and immerse myself in Maeve's BOS. Almost every entry in this section was overwritten with an encoded one, and painstakingly I made my way through several days' worth. I already knew that my birth mother had met a witch from Scotland named Ciaran and had fallen in love with him. It was horrible to read about, knowing the whole story of her and Angus. So far it didn't seem like she had slept with Ciaran—but still, the feelings she had for him must have broken Angus's heart. Yet Maeve and Angus had ended up together. And they'd had me.

At last I hid the book and the athame under my mattress. It was the night before Thanksgiving. Hunter's face rose once more before my eyes, and I shuddered. It would be hard, this year, to give thanks.

Downstairs the next morning the kitchen was a crazed flurry: a turkey on the counter, boiling cranberries spitting deep pink flecks of lavalike sauce, Dad—entrusted with only the simplest tasks—busily polishing silver at the kitchen table. Mary K. was wiping the good china, my mother was bustling about, flinging salad, hunting for the packages of rolls, and wondering out loud where she had put her mother's best tablecloth. It was like every other Thanksgiving, comforting and familiar, yet this year I felt something lacking.

I managed to slip outside without anyone noticing. The backyard was serene, a glittering world of icicles and snow, every surface blanketed, every color muted and bleached. What an odd, cold autumn it had been. Kneeling beneath the black oak, I made my own Thanksgiving offering, which I had planned almost a week ago, before the nightmarish events of the weekend. First I sprinkled birdseed on the snow, seeing how the smaller seeds pelted their way through the snow's crust but the large sunflower nuts rested on top. I hung a pinecone smeared with peanut butter from a branch. Then I put an acorn squash, a handful of oats, and a small group of pinecones at the base of the tree.

I closed my eyes and concentrated. Then I quietly recited the Wiccan Rede, which I had learned by heart. I was about to go inside to tell Mom that for some reason, she had left the bags of rolls in the hall closet, when my senses prickled. My eyes popped open, and I looked around.

Our yard is bordered on two sides with woods, a small parklike area that hadn't been developed yet. I saw nothing, but my senses told me someone was near, someone was watching. Using my magesight, I peered into the woods, trying to see beyond the trees.

I feel you. You are there, I thought with certainty, and then I blinked as a flash of darkness and pale, sun-colored hair whirled and disappeared from sight.

Hunter! Adrenaline flowed into my veins and I stood, taking a step toward the woods. Then I realized with a sick pang that it couldn't be him. He was dead, and Cal and I had killed him. It must have been Sky, with that hair. It was Sky, hiding in the woods outside my house, spying on me.

Walking backward, scanning the area around me intently, I moved toward the house and stumbled up the back steps. Sky thought I had killed her cousin. Sky thought Cal was evil and so was I. Sky was planning to hurt me. I slipped into the steamy, fragrant kitchen, soundlessly muttering a spell of protection.

"Morgan!" my mom exclaimed, making me jump. "There you are! I thought you were still in the shower. Have you seen the rolls?"

"Uh—they're in the hall closet," I mumbled, then I picked

up a silver-polishing cloth, sat down next to my dad, and went to work.

Thanksgiving was the usual: dry turkey, excellent cranberry sauce, salty stuffing, a pumpkin pie that was an odd, pale shade but tasted great, soft, store-bought rolls, everyone talking over each other.

Aunt Eileen brought Paula. Aunt Margaret, Mom and Eileen's older sister, had finally broken down and started speaking to Aunt Eileen again, so she and her family joined us. She spent most of the evening silently but obviously stewing over the fact that her baby sister was going to roast in hell because she was gay. Uncle Michael, Margaret's husband, was jovial and good-natured with everyone; my four little cousins were bored and only wanted to watch TV; and Mary K. kept making faces at me behind our cousins' backs and giggling.

All par for the course, I guessed.

By nine o'clock people started trickling homeward. Sighing, Mary K. plunked down in front of the TV with a slice of pie. I went upstairs to my room, and I heard Mom and Dad turn in early and then the click of the TV turning on in their room.

I turned off my bedroom light, then crept to the window and looked out. Was Sky still out there, haunting me? I tried to cast out my senses, but all I got was my own family, their peaceful patterns in the house. Using my magesight, I looked deeply past the first line of trees and saw nothing unusual. Unless Sky had shape-shifted into that small owl on the third pine from the left, everything was normal.

Why had she been there? What was she planning? My heart felt heavy with dread, thinking about it. I turned my light back on, pulled down my shades, and twitched my curtains into place.

I hadn't talked to Cal all day, and I both wanted to and didn't want to. I longed for him, yet whenever I thought of his secret room, I felt unsettled.

I climbed into bed and took out one of my Wiccan books. I was working my way through about five Wiccan-related books at one time, reading a bit each day. This one was an English history of Wicca, and it was dry going sometimes. It was amazing that this writer had managed to suck the excitement out of the subject, but often he had, and only a determination to learn everything about everything Wiccan kept me going.

I made myself read the history for half an hour, then spent another hour memorizing the correspondences and values of crystals and stones. It was something I could spend years doing, but at least I was making a start.

Finally, my eyes heavy, I had earned the reward of reading Maeve's BOS.

The first section I read described a fight she'd had with her mother. It sounded awful, and it reminded me of the fights I'd had with my parents after I'd found out I was adopted.

Then I found another hidden passage. "September 1981. Oh, Goddess," I read. "Why have you done this? By meeting Ciaran, I have broken a heart that's true. And now my own heart is broken, too.

"Ciaran and I joined our hearts and souls the other

night, on the headland under the moonlight. He told me about the depth of his love for me . . . and then I found out about the depth of his deception, too. Goddess, it's true he loves me more than anything, and I feel in my heart he's my soul mate, my one life love, my second half. We bound ourselves to each other.

"Then he told me another truth. He is already wed, to a girl back in Liathach, and has got two children with her."

Oh, no, I thought, reading it. Oh, Maeve, Maeve.

"Married! I couldn't believe it. He's twenty-two and has been married four years already. They have a four-year-old boy and a three-year-old girl. He told me he'd been forced to marry the girl to unite their two covens, which had been at war. He says he cares for her, but not the way he loves me, and should I give him the word, he would leave her tomorrow, break up his marriage, to be with me.

"But he will never be mine. I would never ask a man to desert his woman and children for me! Nor can I believe that he would even offer. Thank the Goddess, I kept a few of my wits and did not do anything that might see me with my own child by him!

"For this I broke Angus's heart, went against my ma and da, and almost changed the course of my life."

I rested the BOS on my comforter. Maeve's anguished words glowed beneath the blade of the athame, and I felt her pain almost as keenly as if it were my own. It was my own, in a way. It was part of my history; it had changed my future and my life.

I turned the page. "I have sent him away," I read. "He will go back to Liathach, to his wife, who is the daughter of their high priestess. Goddess, he was sickened with pain when I sent him away. If I willed it, he would stay. But after a night of talk we saw no clear path: this is the only way. And despite my fury at his betrayal, my heart tonight is weeping blood. I will never love another the way I love Ciaran. With him I could have drunk the world; without him I will be dosing runny-nosed children and curing sheep my whole life. If it were not a sin, I would wish I were dead."

Oh, God, I thought. I pictured Cal and me being split apart and missed him with a sudden urgency. I looked at the clock. Too late to call. It would have to wait till morning.

I hid the athame and the Book of Shadows, which lately was seeming like a Book of Sorrows, turned out the light, and went to sleep.

My last thought before drifting off was something about Sky, but in the morning I couldn't remember what it was.

On Friday morning I was blessedly alone in the house. I showered and dressed, then ate leftover stuffing for breakfast. My parents had gone to see some old friends of my mom's who were in town for the weekend. Bakker had already picked up Mary K. He had looked less than enthusiastic about Mary K.'s plan to hit the mall for some early Christmas shopping.

After they left, I made an effort to sort through my troubled thoughts. Okay, number one: Hunter. Number two: Cal's secret room. Number three: The fact that Cal lied to me about his Woodbane heritage. Number four: Selene being upset that Cal had told me about their being

Woodbane. Number five: Everything Maeve had gone through with Ciaran and my father. Number six: Sky spying on my house yesterday.

When the phone rang, I knew it was Cal.

"Hi," I said.

"Hi." His voice was like a balm, and I wondered why I hadn't wanted to talk to him earlier. "How was your Thanksgiving?"

"Pretty standard," I said. "Except I made an offering to the Goddess."

"We did, too," he said. "We had a circle with about fifteen people, and we did Thanksgiving-type stuff, witch style."

"That sounds nice. Was this your mom's coven?"

"No," said Cal, and I picked up an odd new tone in his voice. "These are some of the same people who have been coming and going for the last couple of weeks. People from all over. They're Woodbane, too."

"Wow, they're all over the place," I exclaimed, and he laughed. "You can't shake a stick around here without hitting a Woodbane," I added, enjoying his amusement.

"Not in my house, at least," Cal agreed. "Which is why I'm calling, actually. Besides just wanting to hear your voice. There are people here who really want to meet you."

"What?"

"These Woodbanes. Kidding aside, pure Woodbanes are few and far between," said Cal. "Often when they find out about others, they look them up, get together with them, exchange stories and spells and recipes and clan lore. Stuff like that."

I realized I was hesitating. "So they want to meet me because I'm Woodbane?"

"Yes. Because you're a very, very powerful pureblood Woodbane," Cal coaxed. "They're dying to meet the untrained, uninitiated Woodbane who can light candles with her eyes and help ease asthma and throw witch fire at people. And who has the Belwicket tools, besides."

Run, witch, run.

"What?" asked Cal. "Did you say something?"

"No," I murmured. My heart kicked up a beat, and I started breathing as if I had just run up a flight of stairs. What was wrong? Glancing around the kitchen, everything looked fine, the same. But a huge, crashing wave of fear had slammed into me and was now engulfing me and making me shake.

"I feel odd," I said faintly, looking around the room.

"What?" said Cal.

"I feel odd," I said, more strongly. Actually, I felt like I was losing my mind.

"Morgan?" Cal sounded concerned. "Are you all right? Is someone there? Should I come over?"

Yes. No. I don't know. "I think I just need to, um, splash water on my face. Listen, can I call you back later?"

"Morgan, these people really want to meet you," he said urgently.

As he spoke, I was sucked under the swell of fear, so that I wanted to crawl under the kitchen table and curl into a ball. Ask him for help, a voice said. Ask Cal to come over. And another voice said, No, don't. That would be a mistake. Hang up the phone. And run.

Cal, I need you, I need you, don't listen to me.

Now I *was* under the kitchen table. "I have to go," I

forced out. "I'll call you later." I was shaking, cold, flooded with so much adrenaline that I could hardly think.

"Morgan! Wait!" said Cal. "These people—"

"Love you," I whispered. "Bye." My trembling thumb clicked the off button, and the phone disconnected. I waited a second and hit talk, then put the phone on the floor. If anyone tried to call now, they'd get a busy signal.

"Oh my God," I muttered, huddled under the table. "What's wrong with me?" I crouched there for a moment, feeling like a freak. Trying to concentrate, I slowly took several deep breaths. For a minute I stayed there, just breathing.

Slowly I began to feel better. I crawled out from under the table, my knees covered with crumbs. Dagda gazed owlishly down at me from his perch on the counter.

"Please do not tell anyone about this," I said to him, standing up. By now I felt almost back to normal physically, though still panicky. Once more I glanced around, saw nothing different, wondered if Sky was putting a spell on me, if someone was doing something

"Dagda," I said shakily, stroking his ears, "your mother is losing her mind." The next thing I knew, I was putting on my coat, grabbing my car keys, and heading outside. I ran.

11.
Link

I've been studying formally since I was four. I was initiated at fourteen. I've taken part in some of the most powerful, dangerous, ancient rites there are. Yet it's very difficult for me to kindle fire with my mind. But Morgan . . .

Mom wants her desperately. (So do I, but for slightly different reasons.) We're ready for her. Our people have been gathering for weeks now. Edwitha of Cair Dal is staying nearby. Thomas from Belting. Alicia Woodwind from Tarth Benga. It's a Woodbane convention, and the house is so full of vibrations and rivulets of magick that it's hard to sleep at night. I've never felt anything like this before. It's incredible.

The war machine is starting to churn. And my Morgan will be the flamethrower.

—Sgàth

Outside of Practical Magick, I parked Das Boot and climbed out, not seeing the Closed sign until I was pushing on the door. Closed! Of course—it was the day after Thanksgiving. Lots of stores were closed. Hot tears sprang to my eyes, and I furiously blinked them back. In childish anger I kicked the front door. "Ow!" I gasped as pain shot through my toes.

Dammit. Where could I go? I felt weird; I needed to be around people. For a moment I considered going to Cal's, but another strange rush of fear and nausea swept over me, and gasping, I leaned my head against Practical Magick's door.

A muffled sound from within made me peer inside the store. It was dark, but I saw a dim light on in the back, and then the shadow moving toward me metamorphosed into David, jingling his keys. I almost cried with relief.

David opened the front door and let me in. He locked the door behind me, and we stood for a moment, looking at each other in the dimness.

"I feel odd," I whispered earnestly, as if this would explain my presence.

David regarded me intently, then began to lead me to the small room behind the orange curtain. "I'm glad to see you," he said. "Let me get you a cup of tea."

Tea sounded fabulous, and I was so, so glad I was there. I felt safe, secure.

David pushed aside the curtain and stepped into the back room. I followed him, saying, "Thanks for let—"

Hunter Niall was sitting there, at the small round table.

I screamed and clapped my hands over my mouth, feeling like my eyes were going to pop out of my head.

He looked startled to see me, too, and we both whirled

to stare at David, who was watching us with a glint of amusement in his hooded eyes. "Morgan, you've met Hunter, haven't you? Hunter Niall, this is Morgan Rowlands. Maybe you two should shake hands."

"You're not dead," I gasped unnecessarily, and then my knees felt weak, just like in mystery novels, and I pulled out a battered metal chair and sank onto it. I couldn't take my eyes off Hunter. He wasn't dead! He was very much alive, though even paler than usual and still bearing scrapes and bruises on his hands and face. I couldn't help looking at his neck, and seeing me, he hooked a finger in his wool scarf and pulled it down enough for me to see the ugly, unhealed wound that I had made by throwing the athame at him.

David was pouring me a steaming mug of tea. "I don't understand," I moaned.

"You understand parts of it," David corrected me. He pulled up another chair and sat down, the three of us clustered around a small, rickety table with a round plywood top. "But you haven't quite got the big picture."

It was all I could do not to groan. I had been hearing about the big picture since I'd first discovered Wicca. I felt I would never be clued in.

I felt a prickle of fear. I disliked and distrusted Hunter. I'd grown to trust David, but now I thought of how he used to disturb me. Could I trust anyone? Was anyone on my side? I looked from one to the other: David, with his fine, short, silver hair and measuring brown eyes; Hunter, his golden hair so like Sky's but with green eyes where hers were black.

"You're wondering what's going on," said David. It was a massive understatement.

"I'm afraid," I said in a shaking voice. "I don't know what to believe."

As soon as I started speaking, it was as if a sand-bagged levee had finally collapsed. My words poured out in a torrent. "I thought Hunter was dead. And . . . I thought I could trust *you*. Everything is upsetting me. I don't know who I am or what I'm doing." Do not cry, I told myself fiercely. Don't you *dare* cry.

"I'm sorry, Morgan," said David. "I know this is very hard for you. I wish it could be easier, but this is the path you're on, and you have to walk it. My path was much easier."

"Why aren't you dead?" I asked Hunter.

"Sorry to disappoint you," he said. His voice was raspier than before. "Luckily my cousin Sky is an athletic girl. She found me and pulled me out of the river."

So Sky had gotten my message. I swallowed. "I never meant to—hurt you that badly," I said. "I just wanted to stop what you were doing. You were killing Cal!"

"I was doing my *job*," Hunter said, his eyes flaring into heat. "I was fighting in self defense. There was no way Cal would go to the council without my putting a braigh on him."

"You were killing him!" I said again.

"He was trying to kill me!" Hunter said. "And then *you* tried to kill me!"

"I did not! I was trying to stop you!"

David held up his hands. "Hold it. This is going nowhere. You two are both afraid, and being afraid makes you angry, and being angry makes you lash out."

"Thank you, Dr. Laura," I said snippily.

"I'm not afraid of *her,*" Hunter said, like a six-year-old, and I wanted to kick him under the table. Now that I knew he was actually alive, I remembered just how unpleasant he was.

"Yes, you are," David said, looking at Hunter. "You're afraid of her potential, of her possible alliances, of her power and the lack of knowledge she has concerning that power. She threw an athame into your neck, and you don't know if she'd do it again."

David turned to me. "And you're afraid that Hunter knows something you don't, that he might hurt you or someone you love, that he might be telling the truth."

He was right. I gulped my tea, my face burning with anger and shame.

"Well, you're both right," said David, drinking from his mug. "You both have valid reasons to fear each other. But you need to get past it. I believe things are going to be very tough around here very soon, and you two need to be united to face them."

"What are you *talking* about?" I asked.

"What would it take for you to trust Hunter?" David asked. "To trust me?"

My mouth opened, then shut again. I thought about it. Then I said, "Everything I know—almost everything—seems to be secondhand knowledge. People *tell* me things. I ask questions, and people answer or don't answer. I've read different books that tell me different things about Wicca, about Woodbanes, about magick."

David looked thoughtful. "What do you trust?"

In a conversation I'd had once with Alyce, she'd said that

in the end, I really had to trust myself. My inner knowledge. Things that just *were*.

"I trust *me*. Most of the time," I added, not wanting to sound arrogant.

"Okay." David sat back, putting his fingertips together. "So you need firsthand information. Well, how do you suggest getting it?"

On my birthday Cal and I had meditated together, joining our minds. Standing, I walked around the table, next to Hunter. I saw the tightening of his muscles, his wariness, his readiness for battle if that was what I offered.

Setting my jaw, focusing my thoughts, I slowly reached out my hand toward Hunter's face. He looked at it guardedly. When I was almost touching him, pale blue sparks leapt from my fingers to his cheek. We all jumped, but I didn't break the contact, and finally I felt his flesh beneath my curled fingertips.

In the street a couple of weeks ago I had brushed past him, and it had been overwhelming: a huge release of emotions so powerful that I had felt ill. It was something like that now, but not as gut-wrenching. I closed my eyes and focused my energy on connecting with Hunter. My senses reached out to touch his, and at first his mind recoiled from me. I waited, barely breathing, and gradually I felt his defenses weaken. His mind opened slightly to let me in.

If he chose to turn on me, I was cooked. Connected like this, I could sense how vulnerable we were to each other. But still I pressed on, feeling Hunter's suspicion, his resistance, and then very slowly his surprise, his acquiescence, his decision to let me in further.

Our thoughts were joined. He saw me and what I knew of my past, and I saw him.

Giomanach. His name was Giomanach. I heard it in Gaelic and English at the same time. His name meant Hunter. He really was a member of the High council. He was a Seeker, and he'd been charged to investigate Cal and Selene for possible misuse of magick.

I almost pulled back in pain, but I stayed with Hunter, feeling him searching my mind, examining my motives, weighing my innocence, my connection to Cal. I felt him wonder if Cal and I had been lovers and was embarrassed when he was relieved that we hadn't.

Our breathing was slight and shallow, noiseless in the deep silence of the little room. This connection was deeper still than the one I had forged with Cal. This was bone deep, soul deep, and we seemed to sift through layer upon layer of connection, and suddenly I found myself in the middle of a sunny, grassy field, sitting cross-legged on the ground, with Hunter by my side.

This was nice, and I smiled, felt the sun heat warm my face and hair. Insects buzzed around us, and there was the fresh, sweet smell of clover.

I looked at Hunter, and he at me, and we needed no words. I saw his childhood, saw him with his cousin Athar, who I knew as Sky, felt the agony of his parents' leaving. The depth of his anguish over his brother's death was almost unbearable, though I saw that he had been tried and found not guilty. This was something about which Cal didn't know the truth.

Hunter saw my normal life, the shock of finding out I was a blood witch, the growing sweetness of my love for Cal, the disturbing feelings I'd had about his secret room. I couldn't hide my concern about Mary K. and Bakker, my love for my family, my sorrow over the sadness of my birth mother's life and her unsolved death.

Gradually I realized it was time to go, and I stood up in the field, feeling the grass brush against my bare legs. Hunter and I didn't smile as we said good-bye. We had achieved a new level of trust. He knew I hadn't meant to kill him and that I wasn't part of any larger, darker plan. In Hunter, I had seen pain, anger, even vengefulness, all surrounded by a layer of caution and mistrust—but still, I hadn't seen what I had looked for. I hadn't seen evil.

When I came out of it, I felt light-headed, and David's hand guided me back to my chair. Shyly I glanced up to meet Hunter's eyes.

He looked back at me, seeming as shaken as I was.

"That was interesting," said David, breaking the silence. "Morgan, I didn't know you knew how to join with Hunter's mind, but I suppose I shouldn't be surprised. What did you learn?"

I cleared my throat. "I saw that Hunter wasn't—bad or anything."

Hunter was looking at David. "She ought not to be able to do that," he said in a low voice. "Only witches with years of training—she got right inside my mind—"

David patted his hand. "I know," he said ruefully.

I leaned across the table toward Hunter. "Well, if you're not evil," I said briskly, "why have you and Sky been stalking me? I saw you two in my yard a week ago. You left sigils all over the place. What were they for?"

Hunter twitched in surprise. "They're protection spells," he said.

Just then the back door, a door I had barely noticed, opened. Its short curtain swung in, and a blast of cold air swirled into the room.

"You!" Sky snapped, staring at me from the doorway. She looked quickly at Hunter, as if to make sure I hadn't been trying to kill him in the last twenty minutes. "What is she doing here?" she demanded of David.

"Just visiting," David said with a smile.

Her black eyes narrowed. "You shouldn't be here," she snarled. "You almost killed him!"

"You made me think I *had* killed him!" I snapped back. "You knew what had happened, you knew he was alive, yet you let me think he was dead. I've been sick about it!"

She made a disbelieving face. "Not sick enough."

"What were you doing at my house yesterday? Why were you spying on me?"

"Spying? Don't flatter yourself," she said, flinging down her black backpack. "I've had more important things to do."

My eyes widened. "Liar! I saw you yesterday!"

"No, that was me," Hunter put in, and Sky and I both turned to stare at him.

He shrugged. "Keeping tabs."

His arrogance was infuriating. He might not be evil, but he was still a horrible person.

"How dare you—" I began, but Sky interrupted me.

"Of course he's keeping tabs on you!" she snapped. "He's on the council, and you tried to kill him! If another witch hadn't seen what you'd done and sent me a message to go get Hunter, he would have died!"

I exploded, leaping to my feet. "What other witch? *I* was the one who sent you the message that night! *I* was the one who told you to go get him! And I called 911, too!"

"Don't be ridiculous," Sky said. "You couldn't have sent that message. You're nowhere near strong enough."

"Oh, yes, she is," Hunter said mournfully, leaning his chin on his hand. "She just flushed out my brain. I have no secrets anymore."

Sky gaped at him as if he'd been speaking in tongues. He took careful sips of his tea, not looking at her. "What are you talking about?" Sky asked.

"She did tàth meanma," Hunter said, his accent thickening with the Gaelic words. A shiver went down my spine, and I knew instinctively he'd referred to what we had done, the thing I thought of as the "Vulcan mind meld."

Sky was taken aback. "But she can't do that." She stared at me, and I felt like an animal in a zoo. Abruptly I sat down again.

"You're Athar," I said, remembering. "Athar means Sky. Cousin Athar."

No one had much to say to that.

"She's not in league with Cal and Selene," Hunter offered finally. I got angry again.

"*Cal* and *Selene* aren't in league with Cal and Selene, either!" I said. "For your info, Cal and I have done . . . tàth menama—"

"Meanma," Hunter corrected.

"Whatever. And he wasn't evil, either!"

"Did he lead it or did you?" Hunter asked.

Nonplussed, I thought back. "He did."

"Did you go as deep as with me?" he pressed. "Did you see childhood and future, wake and sleep?"

"I'm not sure," I admitted, trying to think.

"You need to be sure," David told me, almost impatiently.

I looked at all three of them. They seemed to be waiting for my response, and I had nothing to give them. I loved Cal, and he loved me. It was ridiculous to think he might be evil.

A picture of the little room in the pool house suddenly rose in front of my mind's eye. I pushed it angrily away. My mind seized on something else.

"I heard Bree and Raven talking about how you were teaching them about the dark side," I accused Sky.

"Of course I was," she countered, black eyes flashing. "So they could recognize it and fight it! It seems someone should have been teaching you the same thing!"

I stood again, overwhelmed with anger. "Thanks for the tea," I told David. "I'm glad you're not dead," I growled at Hunter. Then I stalked out the back door.

As I stomped down the alley and back to my car, my brain pounded with possibilities. Hunter wasn't dead! It was a huge relief, and waves of thankfulness washed over me. And he wasn't evil! Just—misguided. Unfortunately, Sky was still a total bitch and leading Bree and Raven and the rest of Kithic into what seemed to me to be a gray area.

But first things first. Hunter was alive!

12.
The Bigger Picture

October 2000

Alwyn's initiation went well. I was so proud of her, giving her answers in her clear, high voice. She will grow up Wyndenkell and, we hope, marry within Vinneag, Uncle Beck's coven.

For one moment, as Uncle Beck pressed his athame to her eye and commanded her to step forward, I wondered if her life would be better had she not been born a witch. She would be just a fourteen-year-old girl, giggling with her friends, getting a crush on a boy. As it is, she's spent the last six years memorizing the history of the clans, tables of correspondences, rituals and rites; going to spell-making classes; studying astronomy, astrology, herbs, and a thousand other things along with her regular schoolwork. She's missed school functions and friends' birthdays. And she lost her parents when she was only four.

Is it better for her this way? Would Linden still be alive if he hadn't been a witch? I know our lives would have held less pain if we had been born just human.

But it's pointless to consider. One cannot escape one's destiny—if you hide from it, it will find you. If you deny it, it will kill you. A witch I was born, and my family, too, and witches we'll always be, and give thanks for it.

—Giomanach

When I got home, I found a note saying that Cal had stopped by while I was gone. I ran upstairs, brought the phone into my room, and called Cal's house. He answered right away.

"Morgan! Where have you been? Are you okay?"

"I'm fine," I said, the familiar feeling of warmth coming over me at the sound of his voice. "I don't know what was wrong with me this morning. I just felt so weird."

"I was worried about you. Where did you go?"

"To Practical Magick. And you'll never guess who I saw there."

There was silence on Cal's end, and I felt his sudden alertness. "Who?"

"Hunter Niall," I announced. I pictured Cal's eyes widening, his face showing astonishment. I smiled, wishing I could see him.

"What do you mean?" Cal asked.

"I mean he's alive," I said. "I saw him."

"Where has he been all this time?" Cal asked, sounding almost offended.

"Actually, I didn't ask," I said. "I guess he's been with Sky. She found him that night and brought him home."

"So he wasn't dead," Cal repeated. "He went over that cliff with an athame in his neck, and he wasn't dead."

"No. Aren't you thrilled?" I said. "The weight of this has been so awful. I couldn't believe I had done something so terrible."

"Even though he was killing me," Cal said flatly. "Putting a braigh on me. Trying to take me to the council so they could turn me inside out." I heard the bitterness in his voice.

"No, of course not," I said, taken aback. "I'm glad I stopped him from doing that. We *won* that battle. I don't regret that at all. But I thought I had killed someone, and it was going to be a shadow over my life forever. I'm really, really glad that it won't."

"It's like you've forgotten that he was trying to kill me," Cal said, his tone sharpening. "Do you remember what my wrists looked like afterward? Like hamburger. I'm going to have scars for the rest of my life."

"I know, I know," I said. "I'm sorry. He was—more than wrong. I'm glad I stopped him. But I'm also glad I didn't *kill* him."

"Did you talk to him?"

"Yes." I was getting so weirded out by how Cal sounded that I decided not to tell him about the tàth menima— mamena—whatever. "I also saw his charming cousin, Sky, and we got into an argument. As usual."

Cal laughed without humor, then was quiet. What was he thinking? I felt the need to meld with his mind again, to feel his inner self. But I wanted to lead it myself this time.

That was a disturbing thought. *Did* I have doubts about Cal?

"What are you thinking about?" he asked softly.

"That I want to see you soon," I said. I felt guilty at the partial truth.

"I wanted to see you today," he said. "I asked you, and you said no, and then you went to Practical Magick. You weren't even home when I came by to see if you were all right."

"I'm really sorry," I said. "I just—this morning I felt so strange. I think I was having a panic attack. I wasn't thinking clearly and just wanted to get out of here. But I'm sorry—I didn't mean to blow you off."

"There were people here who wanted to meet you," he said, sounding slightly mollified.

All the hairs on the back of my neck stood up. "I'm sorry," I said again. "I just wasn't up to it today."

He sighed, and I pictured him running a hand through his thick, dark hair. "I've got to do a bunch of stuff tonight, but we've got a circle tomorrow at Ethan's house. So I'll see you there, if not during the day."

"Okay," I said. "Give me a call if you can get away."

"All right. I missed you today. And I'm worried about Hunter. I think he's psycho, and I was relieved when I thought he couldn't hurt either of us anymore."

I felt a sudden twinge of alarm. I hadn't even considered that. I'd have to talk to Hunter and make sure he didn't try to go after Cal again. We'd have to find a way to straighten out all these—misunderstandings or whatever they were— without violence.

"I have to go. I'll see you soon." Cal made a kissing noise into the phone and hung up.

I sat on my bed, musing. When I talked to Cal, I hated the whole idea of Hunter. But today, when Hunter and I were doing the tàth thing, he'd seemed okay.

I sighed. I felt like a weather vane, blowing this way and that, depending on the wind.

After dinner Mary K. and I were in the kitchen, cleaning up. Doing mundane things like working in the kitchen felt a little surreal after my conversation with Cal.

For the hundredth time I thought, Hunter is alive! I was so happy. Not that the world necessarily needed Hunter in it, but now I didn't have his death on my conscience. He was alive, and it felt like a thousand days of sunshine, which was bizarre, considering how I couldn't stand him.

"Any plans for tonight?" I asked Mary K.

"Bakker's picking me up," she answered. "We're going to Jaycee's." She made a face. "Can't you talk to Mom and Dad, Morgan? They still say that I can't go out on dates by myself, I mean, just me and Bakker. We always have to be with other people if it's at night."

"Hmmm," I said, thinking that it was probably a good idea.

"And my curfew! Ten o'clock! Bakker doesn't have to be home till midnight."

"Bakker's almost seventeen," I pointed out. "You're fourteen."

Her brows drew together, and she dropped a handful of silverware into the dishwasher with an angry crash.

"You hate Bakker," she grumbled. "You're not going to help."

Too right, I thought, but I said, "I just don't trust him

after he tried to hurt you. I mean, he held my sister down and made her cry. I can't forget that."

"He's changed," Mary K. insisted.

I didn't say anything. After I'd scraped the last plate, I went up to my room. Twenty minutes later I picked up on Bakker's vibrations, and then the doorbell rang. I sighed, wishing I could protect Mary K. from afar.

Up in my room, I studied my book on the properties of different incenses, essential oils, and brews that one can make from them. After an hour I turned to Maeve's Book of Shadows once more, dreading what I would find out and yet compelled to keep reading. It was so full of sadness right now, of anguish over Ciaran. Even though he had concealed his marriage and proved ready to desert his wife and children, she still felt he was her mùirn beatha dàn. It was hard for me to understand how she could still love him after learning all that. It reminded me of Mary K. and Bakker. If someone had held me down and almost raped me, I knew there was no way I would ever forgive him or take him back.

Who's there? I looked up, my senses telling me that another person's energy was nearby. I scanned the house quickly. I did that so often and was so familiar with my family's patterns that it took only a second to know that my parents were in the living room, Mary K. was gone, and a stranger was in the yard. I flicked off my bedroom light and looked out my window.

I peered down into the darkest shadows behind the rhododendron bushes beneath my window, and my magesight picked out a glint of short, moonlight-colored hair. Hunter.

I ran downstairs and through the kitchen, grabbing my

coat off the hook by the door. Boldly I crunched through the snow across the backyard, then down the side, where my bedroom window was. If I hadn't been looking for him, if I didn't have magesight, I never would have seen Hunter blending with the night's shadows, pressed against our house. Once again I got a strong physical sensation from his presence—an uncomfortable, heightened awareness, as if my system was being flooded with caffeine over and over.

Hands on hips, I said, "What the hell are you doing here?"

"Can you see in the dark?" he asked conversationally.

"Yes, of course. Can't every witch?"

"No," he said, stepping away from the house, dusting off his gloves. "Not every witch has magesight. No uninitiated witch does, except you, I suppose. And not even every full-blood witch has it. It does seem to run strongly in Woodbanes."

"Then you must have it," I said. "Since you're half Woodbane."

"Yes, I do," he said, ignoring the challenge in my voice. "In me it developed when I was about fifteen. I thought it had to do with puberty, like getting a beard."

"What are you doing here?"

"Redrawing the protection sigils on your house," he said, as if he was saying, Just neatening up these bushes. "I see Cal laid his own on top of them."

"He was protecting me from you," I said pointedly. "Who are *you* protecting me from?"

His grin was a flash of light in the darkness. "Him."

"You're not planning to try to bind him again, are you?" I asked. "To put the braigh on him? Because you know I won't let you hurt him."

"No fear, I'm not trying that again," Hunter said. He touched his neck gingerly. "I'm just watching—for now, anyway. Until I get proof of what he's up to. Which I will."

"This is great," I said, disgusted. "I'm tired of both of you. Why don't you two leave me out of whatever big picture you're playing out?"

"I wish I could, Morgan," said Hunter, sounding sober. "But I'm afraid you're part of the picture, whether you want to be or not."

"But why?" I cried, fed up.

"Because of who you are," he said. "Maeve was from Belwicket."

"So?" I rubbed my arms up and down my shoulders, feeling chilled.

"Belwicket was destroyed by a dark wave, people said, right?"

"Yes," I said. "In Maeve's Book of Shadows, she said a dark wave came and wiped out her coven. It killed people and destroyed buildings. My dad went to look at the town. He said there's hardly anything left."

"There isn't," said Hunter. "I've been there. The thing is, Belwicket wasn't the only coven destroyed by this so-called dark wave. I've found evidence of at least eight others, in Scotland, England, Ireland, and Wales. And those are only the ones where it was obvious. This—force, whatever it is—could be responsible for much more damage, on a smaller scale."

"But what is it?" I whispered.

"I don't know," Hunter said, snapping a small branch in frustration. "I've been studying it for two years now, and I still don't know what the hell I'm dealing with. An evil force of some kind. It destroyed my parents' coven and made my parents go into hiding. I haven't seen them in almost eleven years."

"Are they still alive?"

"I don't know." He shrugged. "No one knows. My uncle said they went into hiding to protect me, my brother, my sister. No one's seen them since."

The parallels were clear. "My birth parents went into hiding, here in America," I said. "But they were killed two years later."

Hunter nodded. "I know. I'm sorry. But they're not the only ones who have died. I've counted over a hundred and forty-five deaths in the eight covens I know about."

"And no one knows what it is," I stated.

"Not yet." His frustration was palpable. "But I'll find out. I'll chase it till I know."

For a long minute we stood there, not speaking, each lost in our thoughts.

"What happened with Linden?" I asked.

Hunter flinched as if I'd struck him. "He was also trying to solve the mystery of our parents' disappearance," he said in a low voice. "But he called up a force from the other side, and it killed him."

"I don't understand," I said. A chill breeze riffled my hair, and I shivered. Should I ask Hunter in? Maybe we could hang in the kitchen or family room. It would be warm there.

"You know, a dark spirit," Hunter said. "An evil force. I'm guessing the dark wave is either an incredibly powerful force like that or a group of many of them, banded together."

This was too much for me to take in. "You mean, like a dead person?" My voice squeaked. "A ghost?"

"No. Something that's never been alive."

I shivered again and wrapped my arms around myself. Before I knew it, Hunter was rubbing my back and arms, trying to warm me up. I glanced up at his face in the moonlight, at his carved cheekbones, the green glitter of his eyes. He was beautiful, as beautiful as Cal in his own way.

This is who hurt Cal, I reminded myself. He put a braigh on Cal and hurt him.

I stepped away, no longer wanting to ask him inside. "What will you do with this dark force when you find it?" I asked.

"I won't be able to do anything to it," he said. "What I hope to do is to stop the people who keep calling it into existence."

I stared at him. He held my gaze; I saw him glance at my mouth.

"And then," he said quietly, "maybe then people who have been hurt by this, like you, like me . . . will be able to get on with their lives."

His words fell like quiet leaves onto the snow as I stood, trapped by his eyes. My chest hurt, as if I had too much emotion inside, and to let it all out was unthinkable: I wouldn't know where to begin.

Frozen, I watched Hunter lean closer to me, and then his hand was on my chin, and it was cold, like ice, and he tilted up my face. Oh, Goddess, I thought. He's going to kiss me. Our eyes were locked on each other, and again I felt that connection with him, with his mind, his soul. A small spot of heat at my throat reminded me that I wore Cal's silver pentacle on a cord around my neck. I blinked and heard a car drive up and realized what we were doing, and I stepped back and pushed against him with my hands.

"Stop that!" I said, and he looked at me with an unfathomable expression.

"I didn't mean to," he said.

A car door opened, then slammed shut, then opened, and Mary K.'s voice said, "Bakker!" Her tone was shrill, alarmed.

Before the door slammed shut again, I was running across the yard to find Mary K., with Hunter right behind me.

Bakker had parked in front of our house. Inside the dark car I caught glimpses of arms and legs and the auburn flash of my sister's hair. I yanked the car door open, spilling Mary K. on her back into the snow, her legs up on the car seat.

Hunter reached down to help Mary K. up. Tear tracks were already frosting on my sister's face, and one of her jacket's buttons had been ripped. She was starting to cry and hiccup at the same time. "M-M-Morgan," she stammered.

I leaned into the car to glare at Bakker.

"You stupid bastard," I said in a low, mean voice. I felt cold with rage. If I'd had an athame right then, I would have stabbed him.

"Stay out of it," he said, sounding upset. He had scratch marks on one cheek. "Mary K.!" he called, shifting in his seat as if he would get out. "Come back—we need to talk. "

"If you ever look at, touch, talk to, or stand next to my sister again," I said very softly, "I'll make you sorry you were ever born." I didn't feel at all afraid or panicky: I wanted him to get out of the car and come after me so I could rip him apart.

His face turned red with anger. "You don't scare me with all that witch crap," he spat.

An evil smile snaked across my face. "Oh, but I should," I whispered, and watched the color drain from his cheeks. I narrowed my eyes at him for a second, then drew out of the car and slammed the door shut.

Hunter was watching us from a few feet away. Mary K. was holding his arm, and now she blinked up at him, saying, "I know you."

"I'm Hunter," he said as Bakker peeled away, burning rubber.

"Come on, Mary K.," I said, taking her arm and leading her toward the house. I didn't want to look at Hunter—I was still trying to process that almost kiss.

"Are you okay?" I asked, hugging Mary K. to my side as we went up the steps.

"Yes," she said shakily. "Just get me upstairs."

"Will do."

"I'll see you later, Morgan," said Hunter. I didn't reply.

13.
The Circle

Giomanach is alive. Back from the dead. Dammit! Having the council's dog breathing down our necks could ruin everything. I need to take care of him. It's my responsibility.

I'll put the braigh on him, around his neck, and he can see how it feels.

—Sgàth

The next day Mary K. came into the family room as I was researching correspondences on the computer. There were dozens of Wiccan sites on-line, and I loved cruising from one to another.

"Morgan?"

"Yeah? Hey." I turned to look at her. Head hanging down, she looked uncharacteristically drawn and defenseless. I stopped what I was doing and pulled her into a tight hug.

"Why did he do it?" she whispered, her tears making

my cheeks wet. "He says he loves me. Why does he try to hurt me?"

A rage began to boil in me. Was there some kind of spell I could do to Bakker that would teach him a lesson?

"I don't know," I told her. "He can't take no for an answer. Somehow he doesn't mind hurting you."

"He *does* mind," Mary K. cried. "He doesn't want to hurt me. But he always does."

"If he can't control himself, he needs help," I said slowly and carefully. "He needs to be in therapy. He's going to end up killing someone someday, a girlfriend or a wife." I pulled away and looked my sister in the eyes. "And Mary K.? That person will not be you. Understand?"

She looked at me helplessly, her eyes awash with tears. I shook her shoulders gently, once, twice, until she nodded.

"It won't be me," she said.

"It's over this time," I said. "Right?"

"Right," she said, but her eyes slid away, and I swore to myself.

"Do you want to tell Mom and Dad about him, or should I?" I said briskly.

"Oh, uh . . ."

"I'll tell them," I said, setting off to find them. In my opinion, keeping this a secret only made it more likely it would happen again. If my folks knew, Mary K. would have a harder time forgiving Bakker and going back to him again.

My parents did not take it well. They were angry with me for not telling them sooner, furious with Mary K. for continuing to see Bakker after the first time, and almost murderous in their rage toward Bakker, which cheered me up. In the end there was a big group hug, complete with tears and sobbing.

Half an hour later I paced off a small plot in the backyard, where my parents had agreed I could have a garden. The ground was too hard to dig, but I hammered in stakes and string to show where next spring's herbs would be. Then I sat on the snowy ground and tried to meditate for a while, clearing my mind and sending good thoughts into the earth below me, thanking it for being receptive to my garden. Feeling refreshed, I went back inside to look for a spell to put on Bakker.

Technically, of course, I wasn't supposed to do spells. I wasn't initiated, and I'd been a student for barely a couple of months. So I wasn't *committed* to spelling Bakker. But if the necessity arose . . .

Once more we had turkey sandwiches for dinner. I was approaching my saturation point with turkey and was glad to see the carcass was almost bare.

"Any plans for tonight?" my mom asked me.

"Cal's going to pick me up," I said "Then we're going to Ethan's." Mom nodded, and I could almost see her weighing my boyfriend against Mary K.'s. On the one hand, Cal was Wiccan. On the other hand, he had never hurt me.

By the time Cal rang our doorbell, I had dressed in faded gray cords and the purple batik blouse he had given me for my birthday. I'd French braided my hair to the nape of my neck, then let the rest hang down. In the mirror I looked excited, pink cheeked, almost pretty: a vastly different creature than the Morgan I had been two months ago and a different Morgan than just two days ago. Now I knew I wasn't a murderer. I knew I wasn't guilty. I could breathe again, and enjoy life, without Hunter's death hanging over me.

"Hi!" I greeted Cal, shuffling into my coat. I said goodbye to my parents, and we walked down the salt-strewn pathway to the Explorer. In the dark car he leaned over and kissed me, and I welcomed his familiar touch, the faint scent of incense that clung to his jacket, the warmth of his skin.

"How's Mary K.?"

"So-so." I rocked my hand back and forth. I'd told him the gist of what had happened last night, omitting the Hunter part. "I've decided to fix it so that every time Bakker speaks, a toad or snake will slither from his mouth."

Cal laughed and turned onto the main street that would take us to Ethan's. "You are one bloodthirsty woman," he said. Then he flicked me a serious glance. "No spells, okay? Or at least, please talk to me about them first."

"I'll try," I said with exaggerated virtue, and he laughed again.

He parked in back of Robbie's red Beetle outside Ethan's house and turned to me again. "I haven't seen you in days, it feels like." He looped his hand around my neck and pulled me closer for a breathless kiss.

"Just one day," I answered, kissing him back.

"I wanted to ask you—what did you think about my seòmar?"

"What's a shomar?"

"Seòmar," Cal corrected my pronunciation. "It's a private place, usually used by one witch alone, to work magick. Different from a place where you meet with others."

"Does every witch have one?" I asked.

"No. Quit evading the question. What did you think of *mine?*"

"Well, I found it sort of disturbing," I said. I didn't want to hurt his feelings, but I couldn't lie, either. "After a while I wanted to get out of there."

He nodded, then opened the car door and got out. We walked up the pavement to Ethan's small, split-level brick rambler. "That's natural," he said, not sounding offended. "I'm the only one who's worked there, and I've done some intense stuff. I'm not surprised it seemed a little uncomfortable." He sounded relieved. "You'll get used to it pretty fast."

He rang the doorbell while I wondered if I even wanted to get used to it.

"Hey, man," said Ethan. "Come on in."

This was the first time I'd been to Ethan's house: before we were coven mates, we'd never socialized in or out of school. Now I saw that his house was modest but tidy, the furniture worn but cared for. Suddenly two small apricot bundles skittered around the corner from the hall, barking wildly, and I backed up a little.

Jenna laughed from the couch. "Here, pup dogs," she called. The two doglets ran toward her, panting happily, and Jenna gave them each a tortilla chip. She'd obviously been here before and knew Ethan's dogs. Another surprise.

"I never figured you for Pomeranians," Cal told Ethan with a straight face.

"They're my mom's," Ethan said, scooping one under each arm and carrying them back down the hall.

Robbie came out of the kitchen, munching a chip. Matt arrived last, and we went downstairs to the basement, which had been finished to be a large family room.

"Is Sharon still out of town?" I asked, helping Ethan push back furniture.

"Yeah. In Philly," he said. He pushed one of his straggly ringlets out of his eyes.

Once the furniture was out of the way, Cal started unpacking his leather satchel, taking out his Wiccan tools.

"Hey, Jenna," Matt said, since she had ignored him upstairs. His usual pressed appearance had taken a downslide in the last few days: his hair was no longer brushed smooth, his clothes looked less carefully chosen.

Jenna met his gaze squarely, then turned away from him with no expression on her face. Matt flinched. I'd always thought of Jenna as being kind of needy and dependent on Matt, but now I was beginning to suspect that she'd always been the stronger one.

"Last Wednesday, I asked you to choose your correspondences," Cal said as we settled on the floor around him. "Did anyone have any success?"

Jenna nodded. "I think I did," she said, her voice firm.

"Let us have it," said Cal.

"My metal is silver," she said, showing us a silver bracelet on her wrist. "My stone is rose quartz. My season is spring. My sign is Pisces. My rune is Neid." She lifted her hand and drew Neid in the air. "That's all I have."

"That's plenty," said Cal. "Good work. Your rune, standing for delay and the need for patience, is very apt."

He fished in his satchel and took out a squarish chunk of rose quartz the size of an egg. It was pale pink, mostly clear, not milky, and inside were cracks and flaws that looked like broken windowpanes, trapped inside. I thought it looked like pink champagne, frozen in time. Cal handed it to Jenna. "This is for you. You'll use it in your spells."

"Thanks," Jenna said, looking deeply into it, pleased.

"Your rune, Neid, will also become important. For one thing, you can use it as a signature, either on your spells or even in notes and letters."

Jenna nodded.

I sat forward, excited. This was cool stuff—this was what I really loved about Wicca. In my Wicca books the use of quartz in various spells had come up again and again. It had been used religiously for thousands of years. In particular, pink or rose quartz was used to promote love, peace, and healing. Jenna could use all three.

"Robbie?" Cal asked.

"Yeah," he said. "Well, I'm a Taurus, my rune is Eoh, the horse, which also symbolizes travel or change of some kind. My metal is copper. My herb is mugwort. My stone is emerald."

"Interesting." Cal grinned at us. "This is really interesting. You guys are doing a great job of feeling your way to your essences. Robbie, I didn't even associate emerald with you, but as soon as you said it, I thought, yeah, of course." He reached into his bag, rejecting several stones, then brought one out.

"This is a rough emerald," he said, holding it toward Robbie. It was about the size of a pat of butter, a dark, greenish lump in his hand. Robbie took it. "Don't get excited—it's not gem quality. No jeweler would buy it from you. Use it in good health," said Cal, and I was oddly reminded of taking communion at church. Cal went on, "Emerald is good for attracting love and prosperity, to strengthen the memory, to protect its user, and also to improve the eyesight."

Robbie turned and wiggled his eyebrows at me. Until about a month ago, he'd worn thick glasses. My healing potion had had the unexpected side benefit of perfecting his vision.

"So do you just have every stone possible in that bag?" Ethan asked.

Cal grinned. "Not every one. But I have one or two of the most typical."

I had been wondering the same thing myself.

"Okay, Matt?" Cal prompted

Matt swallowed. "I'm a Gemini," he said. "My rune is Jera. My stone is tourmaline."

"Jera, for karma, a cyclical nature, the seasons," said Cal. "Tourmaline."

"The kind with two colors," Matt said.

"They call that watermelon tourmaline," said Cal, and took one out. It looked like a hexagonal piece of quartz, about an inch and a half long and as thick as a pencil. It was green on one end, clear in the middle, and pink on the other end. Cal handed it to Matt, saying, "Wearing this balances the user. Use it in good health."

Matt nodded and turned the stone over in his hand.

"I can go next," said Ethan. "I know what Sharon's are— should I tell them to you?"

Cal shook his head. "She can tell us at the next circle or at school."

"Okay, then, mine," said Ethan. "I'm a Virgo. My season is summer. My stone is brown jasper. I don't have a plant or anything. My favorite jellybean flavor is sour apple."

"Okay," said Cal, smiling. "Good. I think I have a piece of brown jasper . . . hang on." He looked at the stones in his bag and pulled out one that looked like solidified root beer. "Here you go. Brown jasper is especially good for helping you keep your feet on the ground."

Ethan nodded, looking at his stone.

"I think for your rune, you should use . . ." Cal considered Ethan thoughtfully while we all waited. "Beorc. For new beginnings, a rebirth. Sound okay?"

"Yeah," Ethan said. "Beorc. Cool."

Cal turned to me with a special look. "Last but not least?"

"I'm on the Scorpio-Sagittarius cusp," I said. "Mostly Sagittarius. My herb is thyme. My rune is Othel, which stands for an ancestral home, a birthright. My stone is bloodstone."

I might have been the only one to see Cal's pupils dilate and then contract in an instant. Was my choice wrong? Maybe I should have run my ideas by him first, I thought uncertainly. But I had been so sure.

Cal let a stone drop unseen into his bag; I heard it click faintly. "Bloodstone," he said, trying it out. I met his gaze as he looked at me. "Bloodstone," he repeated.

"What are its properties?" Jenna asked.

"It's very old," said Cal. "It's been used in magick for thousands of years to give strength to warriors in battle, to help women through childbirth. They say it can be used to break ties, open doors, even knock down barriers." He paused, then reached into his bag again, rummaged around, and pulled out a large, dark green stone, smooth and polished. When he tilted it this way and that, I could see the dark, blood-colored flecks of red within its darkness.

"Bloodstone," repeated Cal, examining it. "Its ruling planet is Mars, which lends it qualities of strength, healing, protection, sexual energy, and magick involving men."

Jenna grinned at me, and I felt my cheeks flush.

"It's a fire stone," Cal went on, "and its associated color is red. In spells you could use it to increase courage, magickal power, wealth, and strength." His eyes caught mine. "Very interesting." He tossed me the stone, and I caught it. It felt smooth and warm in my hand. I had come across another bloodstone among the things in Maeve's toolbox. Now I had two.

"Okay, now let's make a circle," said Cal, standing. He quickly drew a circle, and we all helped cast it: purifying it, invoking the four elements and the Goddess and God, linking hands within it. Without Sharon there were only six of us. I looked around and realized that I was starting to feel like these people were my second family.

Each of us held our stones in our right palm, sandwiched with the left palm of the person next to us. We moved in our circle, chanting. Looking forward to the rush of ecstatic energy I always got in a circle, I moved around and around, watching everyone's faces. They were intent, focused, perhaps more so than during other circles: their stones must be at work. Jenna looked lovely, ethereal as delight crossed her features. Wonderingly she glanced at me, and I smiled at her, waiting for my own magick to take me away.

It didn't. It was a while before I realized I was deliberately holding it down, not letting it go, not letting myself give in to the magick. It occurred to me: I didn't feel safe. There was no reason I could think of not to, but I simply didn't. My own magick stayed dampened, not the enormous outpouring of power that it usually was. I let out a deep breath and put my trust in the Goddess. If there was danger here that I couldn't see, I hoped she would take care of me.

Gradually Cal took us down, and as we slowed, my coven members looked at me expectantly. They were used to me having to ground myself after a circle, and this time, when I shook my head, they seemed surprised. Cal gave me a questioning look, but I just shrugged.

Then Jenna said, "I feel kind of sick."

"Sit down," Cal said, moving to her side. "Ground yourself. All of you may feel some increased sensations because of your stones and the inner work you did over the week."

Cal helped Jenna sit cross-legged on the carpeted floor, her forehead touching the floor, both hands out flat. He took her chunk of pink quartz and placed it on the back of her slender neck, exposed because her ash blond hair had slipped down on both sides.

"Just breathe," he said gently, keeping one hand on her back. "It's okay. You're just getting in touch with your magick."

Robbie sat down, too, and assumed the same position. This was amazing. The others were finally picking up on the kind of magickal energy I'd been overwhelmed by since the beginning. Forgetting about my own weird feelings, I met Cal's eyes and smiled. Our coven was coming together.

An hour later Cal ended the circle. I stood and got my coat from the hall.

"It was a great circle tonight, guys," Cal said, and everyone nodded enthusiastically. "School starts again Monday, and we'll all be distracted again, so let's try to keep focused. I think you'll find it's easier to do now that you have your working stones. And just remember, we have a rival coven, Kithic. Kithic is working with witches who are untrustworthy, who have an agenda. For your own sake, I want you all to stay away from anyone associated with them."

I looked at Cal in surprise. He hadn't mentioned his intention of telling us this, but I supposed it was only natural, given the connection between Hunter and Sky, Sky and Kithic.

"We can't just be friends with them?" asked Jenna.

Cal shook his head. "It might not be safe. Everyone, be careful, and if anything feels strange or you feel things you can't figure out, please tell me right away."

"You mean like spells?" Ethan asked with a frown. "Like if they put spells on us?"

"I don't think they will," Cal said quickly, raising his hands. "I'm just saying be alert and talk to me about everything and anything, no matter how small."

Robbie looked impassively at Cal. I doubted he planned to quit seeing Bree. Matt looked completely depressed—he didn't seem to have a choice about seeing Raven or not: she wanted to see him, and so far he hadn't been able to say no.

Cal and I went out to the car, and I was silent with thought.

14.
Finding

December 2000

My petition to become a Seeker has gone to the top. Yesterday I met with the seven elders of the council. They once again turned me down. What to do now?

I must curb my anger. Anger cannot help me here. I will ask Uncle Beck to intercede on my behalf. In the meantime I am taking classes with Nera Bluenight, of Calstythe. With her guidance I can school my emotions more and petition the council once again.

—Giomanach

On Sunday morning I realized that one week ago today I had turned seventeen. Looking back, it had been an intensely unhappy day: trying to appear normal while reliving the horror of watching Hunter go over the ledge, the dismay over Cal's wounds, the temporary loss of my magick.

This week was going better. Thank the Goddess and God, Hunter was alive. I felt reassured by knowing that he wasn't inherently evil—and neither was I.

Yet there were still huge, unresolved issues in my life. Questions about Cal and the things he might or might not be hiding from me, questions about myself and the depth of my commitment to Cal, to Wicca itself . . .

I went to church with my family because I knew my mother would make a fuss if I tried to duck out for the second week in a row, and I just wasn't ready to fight that battle. I sleepwalked through the service, my mind churning ideas incessantly. I felt I was two people: Catholic and not Catholic. Part of my family and not part of my family. In love with Cal, yet holding back. Loathing Hunter and yet full of joy that he was alive. My whole life was a mishmash, and I was being divided in two.

When the time for communion approached, I slipped out of our pew as if I was heading for the bathroom. I stood in the drafty hall behind the organist's cubby for a couple of minutes, then came back and fell in line with the people who had just taken communion. I took my seat, dabbing my lips as if I'd just sipped from the chalice. My mother gave me a questioning look but didn't say anything. Leaning back, I let my thoughts drift away once again.

Suddenly Father Hotchkiss's booming voice startled me. From the pulpit he thundered, "Does the answer lie within or without?"

It was like a bolt of lightning. I stared at him.

"For us," Father Hotchkiss went on, gripping the pulpit, "the answer is both. The answers lie within yourselves, as

your faith guides you through life, and the answer lies without, in the truth and solace the church offers. Prayer is the
key to both. It is through prayer we connect with our Maker,
through prayer we reaffirm our belief in God and in ourselves." He paused, and the candles glowing behind him
seemed to light the whole nave. "Go home," he went on,
"pray thoughtfully to God, and ask him for guidance. In
prayer will be your answer."

"Okay," I breathed, and the organ started playing, and we
stood to sing a hymn.

After church my family had lunch at the Widow's Diner
as usual, then headed home. Up in my room I sat on my bed.
It was time to take stock of my life, decide where I was
going. I wanted to follow the path of Wicca, but I knew that
it wouldn't be easy. It would need more commitment from
me than the things I was doing. It had to be woven into the
everyday cycles of my life. I needed to start living mindfully
in every moment.

Serious Wiccans maintain small altars at home, places to
meditate, light candles, or make offerings to the Goddess
and God, like the one in Cal's seòmar. I wanted to set one
up for myself as soon as possible. Also, I had been meditating a bit, but I needed to set aside time to do it every day.

Making these simple decisions felt good—they would be
outward manifestations of my inner connection to Wicca
and my witch heritage. Now for another outward manifestation. Quickly I changed into jeans and a sweatshirt. When
the coast was clear, I retrieved Maeve's tools from behind
the vent and threw my coat over the box.

"I'm going for a drive," I told Mom downstairs.

"Okay, honey," she replied. "Drive carefully."

"Okay." Out in Das Boot, I put my coat on the seat beside me and cranked the engine. A few minutes later I was approaching the edge of town.

Surrounding Widow's Vale are farmlands and woods. As soon as we had gotten our driver's licenses the year before, Bree and Robbie and I had gone on many day trips, exploring the area, looking for swimming holes and places to hang out. I remembered one place not too far out of town, a large, undeveloped tract that had been cleared for lumber back in the 1800s and was now covered with second-growth trees. I headed there, trying to remember the turns and forks, looking for familiar landmarks.

Soon I saw a field I remembered, and I pulled Das Boot over and put on my coat. I left the car on the shoulder of the road, took Maeve's box, and set off across the field and into the woods. When I found the stream I remembered, a sense of elation came over me, and I blessed the Goddess for leading me there.

After following the stream for ten minutes, I came upon a small clearing. Last summer, when we'd found it, it had seemed a magickal place, full of wildflowers and damselflies and birds. Robbie and Bree and I had lain on our backs in the sun, chewing on grass. It had been a golden day, free of worries. Today I had come back to partake of the clearing's magick again.

The snow here was deep—it had never been plowed, of course, and only faint animal tracks disturbed it. With each step I sank in over my ankles. A boulder at the edge of the clearing made a convenient table. I set Maeve's box there

and opened it. Cal had said that witches wore robes instead
of their everyday clothes during magickal rites because their
clothes carried all the jangled, hectic vibrations of their lives.
When I had worn Maeve's robe and used her tools a few
days ago, I had felt nauseated, confused. It had occurred to
me today that perhaps it was because of the clashing vibrations of my life and my magick.

Father Hotchkiss had advised us to pray, to look within
for answers before we tackled outside problems. I was going
to take his advice. Witch style.

Luckily for me, it was another one of those weird,
warm days. The air was full of tiny dripping sounds as
snow melted around me. I shucked my coat, sweatshirt,
and undershirt.

It might have been warm for late autumn, but still, it
wasn't summer. I began to shiver, and quickly pulled Maeve's
robe over my head. It fell in folds to midcalf. I untied my
boots, took off my jeans, and even my socks.

Miserably I peered down at my bare ankles, my feet
buried in the snow. I wondered how long I would have the
guts to stick this out.

Then I realized I no longer felt even the tiniest bit cold.

I felt fine.

Cautiously I lifted one foot, it looked pink and happy, as if
I had just gotten out of the bath. I touched it. Warm. As I
was marveling about this, I felt a focused spot of irritation at
my throat. I touched it and found the silver pentacle Cal had
given me weeks ago. I was so used to wearing it that I hardly
noticed it anymore, but now it felt prickly, irritating, and
regretfully I took it off and put it on the boulder with my

other things. Ah. Now I was completely comfortable, wearing nothing but my mother's robe.

I wanted suddenly to sing with joy. I was completely alone in the woods, enveloped in the warm, loving embrace of the Goddess. I knew I was on the right path, and the realization was exhilarating.

I set up the four cups of the compass. In one I put snow, then took out a candle. Fire, I thought, *flame,* and the charred wick burst into life. I used that candle to melt the snow into water. It was harder to find earth, but I dug a hole in the snow and then scraped at the frozen ground with my athame. I'd brought incense for air, and of course I used the candle for fire.

I made a circle in the snow with a stick, then invoked the Goddess. Sitting on the snow, as comfortable as an arctic hare, I closed my eyes and let myself sink through layer upon layer of reality. I was safe here; I could feel it. This was a direct communion between me and nature and the life force that exists within everything.

Slowly, gradually, I felt myself joined by other life forces, other spirits. The large oak lent me its strength, the pine, its flexibility. I took purity from snow and curiosity from the wind. The frail sun gave me what warmth it could. I felt a hibernating squirrel's small, slow heartbeat and learned reserve. A fox mother and her kits rested in their den, and from them I took an eager appetite for survival. Birds gave me swiftness and judgment, and the deep, steady thrumming of the earth's own life force filled me with a calm joy and an odd sense of expectation.

I rose to my feet and stretched my bare arms outward.

Once again the ancient song rose in me, and I let my voice fill the clearing as I whirled in a circle of celebration.

Both times before, the Gaelic words had seemed like a call to power, a calling down of power to me. Now I saw that it was also a direct thread that connected me to Maeve, Maeve to Mackenna, Mackenna to her mother, whose name, it came to me, had been Morwen. For who knows how long I whirled in a kaleidoscope of circles, my robe swirling, my hair flying out in back of me, my body filled with the power of a thousand years of witches. I sang, I laughed, and it seemed that I could do it all at once, could dance and sing and think and see so startlingly clearly. Unlike the last time, I felt no unease, no illness, only an exhilarating storm of power and connection.

I am of Belwicket, I thought. I am a Riordan witch. The woods and the snow faded around me, to be replaced by green hills worn smooth by time and weather. A woman strode forward, a woman with a plain, work-lined face. Mackenna. She held out tools, witch's tools, and a young woman wearing a clover crown took them. Maeve. Then Maeve turned and handed them to me, and I saw my hand reaching out to take them. Holding them, I turned again and held them out to a tall, fair girl, whose hazel eyes held excitement, fear, and eagerness. My daughter, the one I would have one day. Her name echoed in my mind: Moira.

My chest swelled with awe. I knew it was time to let the power go. But what to do with it, where to direct this power that could uproot trees and make stones bleed? Should I turn it inward, keep it within myself for a time when

I might need it? My very hands could be instruments of magick; my eyes could be lightning.

No. I knew what to do. Planting my feet in the churned snow beneath me, I flung my arms outward again and came to a stop. "I send this power to you, Goddess!" I cried, my throat hoarse from chanting. "I send it to you in thanks and blessing! May you always send the power for good, like my mother, her mother, her mother before her, and on through the generations. Take this power: it is my gift to you, in thanks for all you have given me."

Suddenly I was in the vortex of a tornado. My breath was pulled from my lungs, so that I gasped and sank to my knees. The wind embraced me, so that I felt crushed within strong arms. And a huge clap of thunder rang in my ears, leaving me shaken and trembling in the silence that followed, my head bowed to the snow, my hair wet with perspiration.

I don't know how long I crouched there, humbled by the power I myself had raised. I had left this morning's Morgan behind, to be replaced by a new, stronger Morgan: a Morgan with a newfound faith and a truly awesome power, gifted by the Goddess herself.

Slowly my breathing steadied, slowly I felt the normal silence of the woods fill my ears. Both drained and at peace, I raised my head to see if the very balance of nature had shifted.

Before me sat Sky Eventide.

15.
Visions

February 2001

They have accepted me at last. I am the council's newest member—and its youngest, the most junior member of the third ring. I'm one of more than a thousand workers for Wiccan law. But my assigned role is that of Seeker, as I requested. I've been given my tools, the braigh and the books, and Kennet Muir has been assigned as my mentor. He and I have spent the past week going over my new duties.

Now I have been given my first task. There is a man in Cornwall who is accused of causing his neighbor's milk cows to sicken and die. I'm going down there today to investigate.

Athar has offered to come with me. I didn't tell her how glad I was of her offer, but I could see that she understood it nonetheless. She is a good friend to me.

—Giomanach.

Sky was perched on a snow-covered log about fifteen feet away from me. Her eyes were almond-shaped pools of black. She looked pale with cold and very still, as if she had been waiting a long time. Kicking in after the fact, my senses picked up on her presence.

She casually brushed off one knee, then clasped her gloved hands together.

"Who are you?" she said conversationally, her English accent as crisp and cool as the snow around us.

"Morgan," I was startled into replying.

"No. Who *are* you?" she repeated. "You're the most powerful witch I've ever seen. You're not some uninitiated student. You're a true power conduit. So who are you, and why are you here? And can you help me and my cousin?"

Suddenly I was chilled. Steam was coming off me in visible waves. My skin was damp and now turning clammy with sweat, and I felt vulnerable, *naked* beneath my robe.

Keeping one eye on Sky, I dismantled my circle swiftly and packed away my tools. Then I sat on the boulder and dressed, trying to act casual, as if getting dressed in front of a relative stranger in the woods was an everyday thing. Sky waited, her gaze focused on me. I folded Maeve's robe and put it back in my box, and then I turned to face Sky again.

"What do you want?" I demanded. "How long have you been spying on me?"

"Long enough to wonder who the hell you are," she said. "Are you really the daughter of Maeve of Belwicket?"

I met her eyes without responding.

"How old are you?"

A harmless question. "I just turned seventeen."

"Who have you been studying with?"

"You know who. Cal."

Her eyes narrowed. "Who else? Who before Cal?"

"No one," I said in surprise. "I only started learning about Wicca three months ago."

"This is impossible," she muttered. "How can you call on the Power? How can you use those tools without being destroyed?"

Suddenly I wanted to answer her, wanted to share with her what I had just experienced. "I just—the Power just comes to me. It *wants* to come to me. And the tools . . . are mine. They're for me to use. They *want* me to use them. They beckon me."

Sky sighed.

"Who are *you?*" I asked, thinking it was time she answered some questions herself. "I know you're Sky Eventide, you're from England, you're Hunter's cousin, and he calls you Athar." I thought back to what I had learned during the tàth thing with Hunter. "You grew up together."

"Yes."

"What are you doing with Bree and Raven?" I demanded.

After a pause she said, "I don't trust you. I don't want to tell you things only to have you tell Cal and his mother."

I crossed my arms over my chest. "Why are you even here? How did you know where to find me? Why do you and Hunter keep spying on me?"

Conflicting emotions crossed Sky's face.

"I felt a big power draw," she said. "I came to see what it was. I was in my car, heading north, and suddenly I felt it."

"I don't trust you, either," I said flatly.

We looked at each other for long minutes, there in the woods. Sometimes I heard clumps of snow falling off branches or heard the quick flap of a bird's wings. But we were in our own private world, Sky and I, and I knew that whatever happened here would have far-reaching consequences.

"I'm teaching Bree, Raven, Thalia, and the others basic Wiccan tenets," Sky said stiffly. "If I've told them about the dark side, it was only for their protection."

"Why are you in America?"

She sighed again. "Hunter had to come here on council business. He told you he's been doing research about the dark wave, right? He's combining his research with his duties as a Seeker. I get worried about him—all our family does. He's treading on dangerous ground, and we didn't want something bad to happen to him. So I offered to keep him company."

Remembering what Hunter's council duties were, I felt my fists clench. "Why is he investigating Cal and Selene?"

Sky regarded me evenly. "The council suspects they've been misusing their powers."

"In what way?" I cried.

Her dark eyes gazed deeply into mine. "I can't tell you," she whispered. "Hunter believes you're not knowingly involved with their plan. He saw that when you two were in tàth meanma. But I'm not so sure. Maybe you're so powerful that you can hide your mind from others."

"You can't believe that," I said.

"I don't know what to believe. I do know that I don't trust Cal and Selene, and I fear they're capable of more evil than you can imagine."

"Okay, you're pissing me off," I said.

"You need to face the facts. So we need to figure out the facts first. Hunter thinks Selene has a big plan that you're a key element of. What do you think they'll do to you if you don't want to be part of it?"

"Nothing. Cal loves me."

"Maybe he does," Sky said. "But he loves living more. And Selene would stop at nothing to have you—not even her own son."

I shook my head. "You're crazy."

"What does your heart tell you?" she asked softly. "What does your mind tell you?"

"That Cal loves me and accepts me and has made me happy," I said. "That I love him and would never help you hurt him."

She nodded thoughtfully. "I wish you could scry," she said. "If you could see them . . ."

"Scry?" I repeated.

"Yes. It's a somewhat precarious method of divination," Sky explained.

I nodded impatiently. "I know what it is. I scry with fire."

Her eyes opened so wide, I could see the whites around her black irises.

"You don't."

I just looked at her.

Disbelieving, she said, "Not with fire."

Not answering, I shrugged.

"Have you scryed to see what's happening in the present?"

I shook my head. "I just let the images come. It seems to be mostly the past, and sometimes I see possible futures."

"You can guide scrying, you know. You focus your energy

on what you want to see. With water you'll see whatever your mind wants to see. A stone is the best, most accurate, but it offers less information. Do you think you could control scrying with fire?"

"I don't know," I said slowly, my mind already leaping with possibilities.

Ten minutes later I found myself in a situation I never could have dreamed up. Sky and I sat cross-legged, our knees touching, our hands on each other's shoulders. A small fire burned on a flat stone I had unearthed in the snow. It crackled and spat as the snow in the cracks of the burning branches boiled. I'd lit it with my mind, and had felt a stealthy surge of pride at the way Sky's eyes widened in shock.

Our foreheads touched; our faces were turned to the fire. I took a deep breath, closed my eyes, and let myself drift into meditation. I tuned out the fact that my jeans were getting wet and my butt would probably never thaw again. I had never scryed while doing the Vulcan mind meld, but I was into trying it.

Gradually my breathing deepened and slowed, and sometime later I sensed that Sky and I were breathing in unison. Without opening my eyes I reached out to touch her mind, finding the same suspicious brick wall that I had with Hunter. I pushed against it, and I felt her reluctance and then her slow acceptance. Cautiously she let me into her mind, and I went slowly, ready to pull out if this was a trap, if she tried to attack. She was feeling the same fear, and we paused instinctively until we both decided to let down our guards.

It wasn't easy. She had always rubbed me the wrong way, and she just about hated me. Surprisingly, it hurt to see the depth of her dislike for me, the rage she felt over what I had done to Hunter, her suspicion of my powers and their possible sources. I didn't realize witches could transfer their powers to another until I saw her worry that Selene had done this to me.

We breathed together, locked in a mental embrace, looking deeply into each other. She loved Hunter dearly and was very afraid for his safety. She missed England and her mother and father terribly. In her mind I saw Alwyn, Hunter's younger sister, who looked nothing like him. I saw her memory of Linden, how beautiful he had been, how tragic his death was.

Sky was in love with Raven.

What? I followed that elusive thought, and then it was there, in the forefront, clear and complete. Sky was in love with Raven. Through Sky's eyes I saw Raven's humor, her strength, her gutsiness, her determination to study Wicca. I felt Sky's frustration and jealousy as Raven chased Matt and flirted with others and had no reaction to Sky's tentative overtures. To Sky, slender, blond, restrained English Sky, Raven was almost unbearably lush and sexy. The bold way she spoke, her vivid appearance, her brash attitude all fascinated Sky, and Sky wanted her with a frank desire that took me aback and almost embarrassed me.

Then Sky was leading me, asking questions about Cal. Together we saw my love for him, my humiliating relief that someone finally wanted me, my awe at his beauty and respect for his power. She saw my uncertainty about and fascination with Selene and my discomfort about Cal's seòmar. As Hunter had, she saw that Cal and I hadn't made love yet. She saw that Hunter had almost kissed me, and she nearly broke off contact in surprise. I felt like she was paging through my private diary and began to wish I'd never agreed to this. My mind told Sky I had been shocked to find out I was Woodbane and extra shocked just four days ago to learn Cal was Woodbane also.

Now, together, she thought, and I opened my eyes. After looking at each other for a moment, weighing what we had learned, we turned, staying connected, and looked into the fire.

Fire, element of life, Sky thought, and I heard her. Help us see Cal Blaire and Selene Belltower as they are, not as they show themselves to us.

Are you ready to see? I heard the fire whisper back to us seductively. Are you ready, little ones?

We are ready, I thought, swallowing hard.

We are ready, Sky echoed.

Then, as it had for me in the past, the fire created images that drew us in. I felt Sky's awe and joy: she had never scryed with fire before. She strengthened her mind and concentrated on seeing the here and now, seeing Cal and Selene. I followed her example and focused on that also.

Cal, I thought. Selene. Where are you?

An image of Cal's huge stone house formed within the flames. I remembered how I could never project my senses through its walls and wondered if that applied to scrying. It didn't. The next time I blinked, I found myself in Selene's circle room, the huge parlor where she regularly held her coven's circles. It had once been a ballroom and now seemed like a grand hall of magick. Selene was there, in her yellow witch's robe, and I recognized Cal's dark head standing out from a group of people I didn't recognize.

"Do we really need her?" a tall, gray-haired woman with almost colorless eyes asked.

"She's too powerful to let go," said Selene.

An icy trickle down my back told me they were speaking of me.

"She's from Belwicket," a slender man pointed out.

"Belwicket is gone," Selene said. "She'll be from anywhere we want her to be."

Oh, God, I thought.

"Why haven't you brought her to us?" asked the gray-haired woman.

Selene and Cal met eyes, and to me it felt like they fought a silent battle.

"She'll come," said Cal in a strong voice, and inside me I felt a piercing pain, as if my heart were being rent. "But you don't understand—"

"We understand that it's past time for action," another woman said. "We need this girl on our side now, and we need to move on Harnach before Yule. You had an assignment, Sgàth. Are you saying you can't bring her to us?"

"It will be done," said Selene in a voice like marble. Again her gaze seared Cal, and his jaw set. He gave an abrupt nod and left the room, graceful in his heavy white linen robe.

I can't see anymore, I thought, and then I said the words aloud. "I can't see anymore."

I felt Sky pulling back as I did, and I shut my eyes and deliberately came back to the snowy woods and this moment. Opening my eyes, I looked up to see that the sky was darkening with late afternoon, that my jeans were soaked through and miserably uncomfortable, that the trees that had made a circle of protection around me now seemed black and threatening.

Sky's hands slid off my shoulders. "I've never done that," she said in a voice just above a whisper. "I've never been good at scrying. It's—awful."

"Yes," I said. I looked into her black eyes, reliving what I had just seen, hearing Selene's words again. Shakily I uncoiled and stood, my leg muscles cramped, my butt beyond feeling, and an unsettling feeling of nausea in my stomach. As Sky stood, stretching and groaning under her breath, I knelt and scooped up some clean snow, putting it in my mouth. I let it melt and swallowed the cold trickle of water. I did this again, then rubbed snow on my forehead and on the back of my neck under my hair. My breath was shallow, and I felt shaky, flooded with fear.

"Feel ill?" Sky asked, and I nodded, eating more snow.

I stayed on all fours, melting small mouthfuls of snow while my brain worked furiously, trying to process what we had seen. When Bree and I had fought over Cal and I had realized that we were no longer friends after eleven years, it had been shockingly painful. The sense of betrayal, of loss, of vulnerability had been almost unbearable. Compared to what I was feeling now, it had been a walk in the park. Inside, my mind screamed, No, no, no!

"Were those images true?" I choked out.

"I think so," Sky said, sounding troubled. "You heard them mention Harnach? That's the name of a Scottish coven.

The council sent Hunter here to investigate evidence that Selene is part of a Woodbane conspiracy that's trying, basically, to destroy non-Woodbane covens."

"She's not the dark wave?" I cried. "Did she destroy Belwicket?"

Sky shrugged. "They don't see how she could have. But she's been linked to other disasters, other deaths," she said, hammering my soul with each word. "She's been moving around all her life, finding new Woodbanes wherever she goes. She makes new covens and ferrets out blood witches. When the coven is solid, she breaks it up, destroying the non-Woodbane witches and taking the Woodbanes with her."

"Oh my God," I breathed. "She's killed people?"

"They believe so," Sky said.

"Cal?" I said brokenly.

"He's been helping her since he was initiated."

This was all too much for me to take in. I felt frantic. "I have to go," I said, looking around for my tools. It was now almost dark. I grabbed Maeve's box and shook some of the snow off my boots.

"Morgan—" Sky began.

"I have to go," I said, more strongly.

"Morgan?" she called as I took the first step into the woods. I turned back to look at her, standing alone in the clearing. "Be careful," she said. "Call me or Hunter if you need help."

Nodding, I turned again and made my way back to my car. Inside, my heart began screaming again: No, no, no . . .

16.
Truth

I've always wondered if my mother killed my father. After all, he left her, not the other way around. And then he had two more kids right away with Fiona. That really freaked Mom out.

Dad "disappeared" when I was almost nine. Not that I'd seen anything of him before that. I was the forgotten son, the one who didn't matter.

When Mom got the phone call, she just told me that Dad and Fiona had vanished. She didn't say anything about them being dead. But as the years have worn on and no one's heard from him—that I know about, anyway—it seems safe to assume he's dead. Which is convenient, in a way. It means Giomanach doesn't have Dad's power behind him. But still, I wish I knew what really happened. . . .

—Sgàth

The sun had faded away. My wheels crunched ice on the road as I drove past old farms, fields of winter wheat, silos.

Cal and Selene. Selene was evil. It sounded melodramatic, but what else do you call a witch who works on the dark side? Evil. Woodbane.

No! I told myself. I'm Woodbane. I'm not evil. Belwicket wasn't evil; my mother wasn't. My grandmother wasn't. But somewhere along the line, my ancestors had been. Was that why Selene wanted me? Did she see the potential for evil in me? I remembered the vision I'd had of myself as a gnarled crone, hungry for power. Was that my true future?

I choked back a sob. Oh, Cal, I screamed silently. You betrayed me. I loved you, and you were just playing a *part*.

I couldn't get over this. It was a physical pain inside me, an anguish so devastating that I couldn't think straight. Tears rolled down my cheeks, leaving hot tracks and tasting of salt when they touched the edges of my lips. A thousand images of Cal bombarded my brain: Cal leaning down to kiss me, Cal with his shirt open, Cal laughing, teasing me, offering to help me with Bakker, making me tea, holding me tight, kissing me hard, harder.

I was flying apart inside. I began to pray desperately that the scrying had been a lie, that Sky had tricked me, made me see things that weren't there, she had lied, had lied. . . .

I needed to see him. I needed to find out the truth. I'd had my questions answered by Hunter and by Sky, and now only Cal remained to fill me in on the big picture, the dangers I was blundering into, the reasons I needed to be careful, to watch myself, to rein in my power.

But first—I had to hide my mother's tools. With all my heart, I hoped that Cal would convince me of his innocence, convince me that Sky was wrong, convince me that our love was true. But the mathematician in me insisted that nothing is one hundred percent certain. I had bound my mother's tools to me, they were mine, and now I had to make sure no one would take them away or make me use them for evil.

But where to stash them? I couldn't go home. I was already almost late for dinner, and if I went home, I wouldn't be able to turn around and leave. Where?

Of course. Quickly I made a right turn, heading to Bree's house. Bree and I were enemies: no one would suspect I would hide something precious in her yard.

Bree's house looked large, immaculately kept, and dark. Good—no one was home. I popped the trunk on my car and took out the box. Whispering, "I am invisible, you see me not, I am but a shadow," I slunk up the side yard, then quickly ducked beneath the huge lilac bush that grew outside the dining-room window. It was mostly bare this time of year, but it still hid the opening to the crawl space beneath Bree's house. I tucked the toolbox out of sight behind a piling, traced some fast runes of secrecy, and stood up.

I was opening my car door when Bree and Robbie drove up in Bree's BMW. They pulled up beside me and stopped.

Ignoring them, I started to swing into the driver's seat of my car. The passenger window scrolled down smoothly. Crap, I thought.

"Morgan?" said Robbie. "We've been looking for you. We were talking to Sky. You've got to—"

"Gotta go," I said, climbing in and slamming the door shut before he could say anything else. I had already talked to Sky, and I knew what she'd said.

Robbie opened his door and started toward me. I peeled off, watching him get smaller in the rearview mirror. I'm sorry, Robbie, I thought. I'll talk to you later.

On the way toward the river, thoughts of exactly what I would say to Cal raced through my mind. I was in the middle of my ninth hysterical scenario when—

Morgan.

My head whipped around. Cal's voice was there, right beside me, and I almost screamed.

Morgan?

Where are you? my mind answered frantically.

I need to see you. Please, right away. I'm at the old cemetery, where we had our circle on Samhain. Please come.

What to do? What to think? Had everything he'd told me been a lie? Or could he explain it all?

Morgan? Please. I need you. I need your help.

Just like that night with Hunter, I thought. Was he in trouble? Hurt? Blinking, I wiped away some stray tears with the back of my sleeve and peered through the windshield. At the next intersection I turned right instead of left, and then I was on the road leading north, out of town. Oh, Cal, I thought, a new wave of anguish sweeping over me. Cal, we have to have it out.

Five minutes later I turned down a side road and parked in front of the small Methodist church that had once shepherded the people who now lay in its graveyard.

Shuddering with leftover sobs, I sat in my car. Then I felt Cal, coming closer. He tapped gently on my window. I opened the door and got out.

"You got my message?" he said. I nodded. He examined

my face more closely. Then he caught my chin in his hands and said, "What's wrong? Why were you crying? Where were you? I tried going by your house."

What should I say?

"Cal, is Selene trying to hurt me?" I asked, my words like shards of ice in the night air.

Everything in him became still, centered, and focused. "Why would you say that?"

I felt his senses reaching out to me, and quickly I shut myself down, refusing him entrance.

"Is Selene part of an all-Woodbane coven that wants to erase non-Woodbanes?" I asked, pushing my hair out of my face. Please tell me it's a lie. Please convince me. Tell me anything.

Cal gripped my hair in his hand, making me look at him. "Who have you been talking to?" he demanded. "Dammit, has that bastard Hunter been—"

"I scryed," I said. "I saw you with Selene and other people. I heard them talking about your 'assignment.' Was I your assignment?"

He was silent for a long time. "Morgan, I can't believe this," he said at last. "You know you can't believe stuff you see in scrying—it's all nebulous, uncertain. Scrying shows you only possibilities. See, this is why I always want you to wait until I guide you. Things can be misunderstood—"

"Scrying showed me the possibility of where my mother's tools were," I said, my voice stronger. "It's not always lies—otherwise no one would use it."

"Morgan, what's this all about?" he asked in a loving voice. He gently pulled me to him so that my cheek rested against his chest, and it felt wonderful and I wanted to sink into him. He kissed my forehead. "Why are you having doubts? You know we're mùirn beatha dàns. We belong together; we're one. Tell me what's wrong," he said soothingly.

With those words the pain in my chest intensified, and I took deep breaths so I wouldn't cry again. "We're not," I whispered, as the truth broke over me like a terrible dawn. "We're not."

"Not what?"

I tilted back my head to look into his gold eyes, his eyes full of love and longing and fear. I couldn't bring myself to say it outright.

"I know you slept with Bree," I lied instead. "I *know* it."

Cal looked at me. Before Bree and I had broken our friendship, she had been chasing Cal hard, and I knew from past experience that she always got whatever guy she wanted. One day she had been happy, saying she and Cal had finally gone to bed, so now they were going out. But they hadn't started going out, and he had come after me. I'd asked him about it before, and he had denied sleeping with her, with my best friend. Now I needed to know the truth of it, once and for all, even as I was being hit with other painful truths from every direction.

"Just once," Cal said after a pause, and inside, I felt my heart cease its pumping and slowly clog shut with ice.

"You know what Bree's like," he went on. "She won't take no for an answer. One night, before I really knew you, she jumped on me, and I let her. To me it was no big deal, but I guess she was hurt that I didn't want more."

I was silent, my eyes locked on his, seeing in their reflection all my dreams exploding, all my hopes for our future, all shattering like glass.

"The only powers she had were reflections coming from you," he said, the barest trace of disdain in his voice. "Once I realized you were the one, Bree was just . . . unimportant."

"Realized I was the one what?" My voice sounded tight, raspy, and I coughed and spoke again. "The one Woodbane around? The Woodbane princess of Belwicket?" I pushed him away. "Why do you keep lying to me?" I cried in anguish. "Why can't you just tell me who you are and what you want?" I was practically screaming, and Cal winced and held up his hands.

"You don't love me," I accused him, still pathetically hoping he would prove me wrong. "I could be *anyone,* young or old, pretty or ugly, smart or stupid, as long as I was *Woodbane.*"

Cal flinched and shook his head. "That isn't true, Morgan," he said, a note of desperation in his voice. "That isn't true at all."

"Then what *is* true?" I asked. "Is anything you've told me true?"

"Yes!" he said strongly, raising his head. "It's true that I love you!"

I managed a credible snort.

"Morgan," he began, then stopped, looking at the ground. His hands on his hips, he went on. "This is the truth. You're right. I was supposed to find a Woodbane, and I did."

I almost gasped with pain.

"I was supposed to get close to her, and I did."

How could I still be standing, I wondered in a daze.

"I was supposed to make her love me," he said quietly. "And I did."

Oh, Goddess, oh, Goddess, oh, Goddess.

He raised his head and looked at me, my eyes huge and horrified.

"And you were the Woodbane, and you didn't even know it. And then you turned out to be from the Belwicket line, and it was like we'd hit gold. You were the one."

Oh, Goddess, help me. Help me, please, I beg you.

"So I got close to you and made you love me, right?"

I had no answer. My throat was closed.

Cal gave a laugh laced with bitterness. "The thing is," he said, "no one said I had to love you back. No one expected me to, including me. But I do, Morgan. No one said I had to fall for you, but I did. No one said I had to desire you, enjoy your company, admire you, take pride in your strength, but I do, dammit! I do." His voice had been rising, and he stepped closer to me. "Morgan, however it started, it isn't like that now. I feel like I've always loved you, always known you, always wanted a future with you." He put his hand on my shoulder, gently kneading and squeezing, and I tried to back up. "You're my mùirn beatha dàn," he said softly. "I love you. I want you. I want us to be together."

"What about Selene?" My voice sounded like a croak.

"Selene has her own plans, but they don't have to include us," he said, stepping closer still. "You have to understand how hard it is to be her son, her only son. She depends on me—I'm the heir to the throne. But I can have my own life, too, with you, and it doesn't have to include her. It's just— first I have to help her finish some things she's been working on. If you help us, too, it will all go so much faster. And then we can be free of her."

I looked at him, feeling a cold, deadly calm replacing the panic and wretchedness inside me. I knew what I had seen in my vision, and I knew Cal was either lying or kidding himself about Selene's plans. They didn't include letting him—or me—be free.

"I'm free of her now," I said. "I know that Selene needs me for something. She's counting on you to sign me up. But I'm not going to, Cal. I'm not going to be part of it."

His expression looked like he had just watched me get hit by a car.

"Morgan," he choked out, "you don't understand. Remember our future, our plans, our little apartment. Remember? Please just help us with this one thing, and then we can work out all the details later. Trust me on this. Please."

My heart was bleeding. I said, "No. Selene can't have me. I won't do what she wants. I won't go with you. It's all over, Cal. I'm leaving the coven. And I'm leaving you."

His head snapped up as if I had hit him, and he stared at me. "You don't know what you're saying."

"I do," I said, trying to make my voice strong, though I really wanted only to crumple in misery on the ground. "It's over. I won't be with you anymore." Each word scarred my throat, etching its pain in acid.

"But you love me!"

I looked at him, unable to deny it even after all this.

"I love *you,*" he said. "Please, Morgan. Don't—don't force my hand. Just come with me, let Selene explain everything herself. She can make you understand better than I can."

"No."

"Morgan! I'm asking you, if you love me, come with me

now. You don't have to do anything you don't want to. Just come and tell Selene herself that you won't be part of her coven. That's all you need to do. Just tell her to her face. I'll back you up."

"You tell her."

His eyes narrowed with anger, then it was gone. "Don't be unreasonable. Please don't make me do anything I don't want to do."

Fear shot through me. "What are you talking about?"

His face had a strange look, a look of desperation. I was suddenly terrified. The next second I whirled, broke into a run, and was digging my car keys out of my pocket. I ripped open the car door, hearing Cal right behind me, then he yanked the door open, hard, and shoved me in.

"Ow!" I cried as my head hit the door frame.

"Get in!" he roared, pushing against me. "Get in!"

Goddess, help me, I prayed as I scrambled to let myself out the other side. But when I grabbed the door handle, Cal put his hand on my neck and squeezed, muttering words that I didn't understand, words that sounded ancient and dark and ugly.

I tried to counter with my Gaelic chant, but my tongue froze in my mouth and a paralyzing numbness swept over me. I couldn't move, couldn't look away from him, couldn't scream. He had put a binding spell on me. Again.

I'm so stupid, I thought ridiculously as he started Das Boot with my keys.

17.
The Seòmar

February 2001

I did it. I put a witch under the braigh.

The fellow in Cornwall was mad, there is no question of that. When I came to question him he first tried to evade me, then when he saw that I would not give up, he flew into a frenzy. He gibbered about how he would curse me and my whole family, that he was one of the Cwn Annwn, the hounds of Hell. He began to shout out a spell and I had to wrestle him to the ground and put the braigh on him. Then he began to weep and plead. He told me how it burned him, and begged me to let him go. At last his eyes rolled back in his head and he lost consciousness.

I put him in the car, and Athar drove us to London. I left him with Kennet Muir. Kennet told me I'd done well; the man might be mad but he also had true power and was therefore dangerous. He said my task was done, and now it was the seven elders' job to determine the man's future.

I left, and then Athar and I went to a pub and got very drunk. Later, she held me while I wept.

—Giomanach

"You just don't get it, do you?" Cal said angrily, taking a corner too fast. I slumped against the car door helplessly. Inside, my mind was whirring like a tornado, a thousand thoughts spinning out of control, but the binding spell he had put on me weighted my limbs as thoroughly as if I were encased in cement.

"Slow down," I managed to whisper.

"Shut up!" he shouted. "I can't believe you're making me do this! I love you! Why can't you listen to me? All I need is for you to come talk to Selene. But no. You can't even do that for me. The one thing I ask you to do, you won't. And now I have to do this. I don't want to do this."

I slanted my eyes sideways and looked at Cal, at his strong profile, his hands gripping Das Boot's steering wheel. This was a nightmare, like other magickal nightmares I'd had before, and soon I would wake up, panting, in my own bed at home. I just needed to wake up. Wake up, I told myself. Wake up. You'll be late for school.

"Morgan," Cal said, his voice calmer. "Just think this through. We've been working with witchcraft for years. You've only been doing it a couple of months. At some point you'll just have to trust us with what we're doing. You're only resisting because you don't understand. If you would calm down and listen to me, it would all make sense."

Since I was in essence deadweight right now, his telling

me to calm down seemed particularly ironic. Cal kept on talking, but my brain drifted away from his monologue. Focus, I thought. Focus. Get it together. Make a plan.

"I thought you would be loyal to me always," Cal said. My eyes were just above the window ledge, and I saw that we were just entering Widow's Vale. Were we going to Cal's house? It was so secluded—once he got me there, I'd never get out. I thought about my parents wondering where I was and wanted to cry. Focus, dammit! Think your way out of this. You're the most powerful witch they've ever seen; surely there must be something you can do. Think!

Cal flew through a red light at the edge of town, and involuntarily I flinched as I heard the squeal of brakes and an angry horn. I realized he hadn't even put my seat belt on me, and in my present helpless state I couldn't do it myself. Fresh, cold fear trickled down my spine when I pictured what would happen to me in an accident.

Think. Focus. Concentrate.

"You should have just trusted me," Cal was saying. "I know so much more than you do. My mother is so much more powerful than you. You're a student—why didn't you just trust me?"

My door was locked. If I could open it, I could maybe tumble out somehow. And get crushed beneath the wheels since I probably couldn't leap out of the way. Could I unroll my window and shout for help? Would anyone in town recognize my car and wonder why I wasn't driving it?

I tried to clench my right hand and saw with dismay that I could barely curl up my first knuckle.

The night of my birthday, when Cal had put the binding

spells on me, I had somehow managed to break free. I had—
pushed, with my mind, like tearing through plastic, and then I
had been able to move. Could I do that now?

We raced through downtown Widow's Vale, the three
stoplights, the lit storefronts, the cars on their way home. I
peered up over my window, hoping someone, anyone, would
see me. Would Cal get stopped for speeding? I almost cried
as a moment later we passed through downtown and were
on the less traveled road that led toward Cal's house. Panic
threatened to overtake me again, and I stamped it down.

Bree's face floated suddenly into my mind. I seized on it.
Bree, Bree, I thought, closing my eyes and concentrating. Bree,
I need your help. Cal has me. He's taking me to Selene. Please
come help me. Get Hunter, get Sky. I'm in my car. Cal is desperate. He's going to take me to Selene. Bree? Robbie? Hunter,
please help, Hunter, Sky, anyone, can you hear me?

Working this hard mentally was exhausting, and my
breath was coming in shallow pants.

"You don't understand," Cal went on. "Do you have any
idea what they'd do to me if I showed up without you?" He
gave a short, barking laugh. "Goddess, what Hunter did to
me that night was child's play compared to what they would
do." He looked at me then, his eyes glittering eerily. He
looked belovedly familiar and yet horribly different. "You
don't want them to hurt me, do you? You don't know what
they could do to me. . . ."

I closed my eyes again, trying to shut him out. Cal had
always been so in control. To see him this way was sickening,
and a cold sweat broke out on my forehead. I swallowed and
tried to go deep inside myself, deep to where the power

was. Bree, please, I'm sorry, I thought. Help. Help me. Save me. Selene is going to kill me.

"Stop that!" Cal suddenly shouted, leaning over and shaking my shoulder hard.

I gasped, opening my eyes. He glared at me in fury.

"Stop that! You don't contact anyone! Anyone! Do you hear me?" His angry voice swelled in the car's interior, filling my ears and making my head hurt. One hand shook me until my teeth rattled, and I clenched my jaws together. I felt the car making big swerves on the road and prayed to the Goddess to protect me.

"Don't you wreck this car," I said, unclenching my lips enough to speak.

Abruptly he let go of me, and I saw the glare of headlights coming at us and then the long, low blare of a truck horn blowing. It swept past us as I drew in a frightened breath.

"Shit!" Cal said, jerking the steering wheel to the right. Another horn blared as a black car screeched to a halt just before ramming my side. I started to shake, slumped against my door, so afraid, I could hardly think.

You, afraid? part of me scoffed. You're the Woodbane princess of Belwicket. You could crush Cal with the power in your little finger. You have the Riordan strength, the Belwicket history. Now, save yourself. Do it!

Okay, I could do this, I told myself. I was a kick-ass power conduit. Letting my eyes float closed again, trying not to think about the chaos raging around me, I let the music come to me, the timeless music that magick sent. *An di allaigh an di aigh,* I thought, hearing the tune come to me as if borne on a breeze across clover-covered hills.

An di allaigh an di ne ullah. Was that my voice, singing in a pure ribbon of glorious sound that only I could hear? My fingers tingled, as if coming awake. *An di ullah be nith rah.* I drew in a deep, shuddering breath, feeling my muscles twitch, my toes curl. I am breaking this binding spell, I thought. I am smashing it. I am tearing it like wet tissue. *Cair di na ulla nith rah, Cair feal ti theo nith rah, An di allaigh an di aigh.*

I was myself. I had done it. I stayed exactly where I was, opening my eyes and gazing around. With a flare of alarm I recognized the tall hedges that surrounded Cal's property. He swung Das Boot into a side road, skidding a bit, and we began to crunch on icy gravel.

Bree, Sky, Hunter, Robbie, anyone, I thought, feeling my radiating power. Alyce, David, any witch, can you hear me?

The side road to Cal's driveway was long, with tall, overhanging trees. It was pitch-black except where moonlight glistened off snow. The dashboard clock said six-thirty. My family was sitting down to eat. At the thought I felt a surge of anger so strong it was hard for me to hide it. I couldn't accept the possibility that I might never see them again, Mom, Dad, Mary K., Dagda. I would escape. I would get out of this. I was very powerful.

"Cal, you're right," I said, making my voice sound weak. I couldn't even feel the effects of the binding spell anymore, and a surge of hope flamed in my chest. "I'm sorry," I said. "I didn't realize how important this was to you. Of course I'll go talk to your mom."

He turned the wheel and paused, reaching out his left hand and pointing it ahead of him. I heard the metallic rumbling of heavy gates, heard them swing on hinges and clunk open with a bang.

Then, as if he had finally heard me, Cal looked over. "What?" He stepped on the gas, and we rolled through the gate. Ahead of me was a dark roofline, and I realized we were in the backyard, and the building in front of me was the little pool house. Where Cal had his seòmar.

"I said, I'm sorry," I repeated. "You're right. You're my mùirn beatha dàn, and I should trust you. I do trust you. I just—felt unsure. Everyone keeps telling me something different, and I got confused. I'm sorry."

Das Boot rolled slowly to a halt, ten feet from the pool house. It was dark, with the car's one headlight shining sadly on the dead brown ivy covering the building.

Cal turned off the engine, leaving the keys in the ignition. He kept his eyes on me, where I leaned awkwardly against the door. It was all I could do to keep my hand from grasping the door handle, popping the door, and running with all my might. What spell could I put on Cal to slow him down? I didn't know any. Suddenly I remembered how his pentacle had burned at my throat when I used Maeve's tools. I'd felt better without it on. Was it spelled? Had I been wearing a spell charm all this time? I wouldn't doubt it at this point.

With agonizingly slow movement, I slipped my right hand down into my pocket and pulled out Cal's pentacle. He hadn't noticed I wasn't wearing it yet, and I let it slip from my fingers to the floor of the car. As soon as it left my hand, my head felt clearer, sharper, and I had more energy. Oh, Goddess, I was right. The pentacle had been spelled all this time.

"What are you saying?" Cal said, and I blinked.

"I'm sorry," I repeated, making my voice a little stronger. "This is all new to me. It's all confusing. But I've been thinking about what you said, and you're right. I should trust you."

His eyes narrowed, and he took hold of my hand. "Come on," he said, opening his door. His grip on my hand was crushing, and I dismissed the possibility that I could slip out suddenly and run. Instead he pulled me out the driver's side door and helped me stand. I pretended to be weaker than I was and leaned against him.

"Oh, Cal," I breathed. "How did we get into such a fight? I don't want to fight with you." I made my voice soft and sweet, the way Bree did when she talked to guys, and I leaned against Cal's chest. Seeing the mixture of hope and suspicion cross his face was painful. Suddenly I pushed hard against him, shoving with every bit of strength in my arms, and he staggered backward. I raised my right hand and shot a spitting, crackling bolt of blue witch fire at him, and this time I didn't hold anything back. It blasted Cal right in the chest, and he cried out and sank to his knees. I was already running, my boots pounding heavily toward the metal gates that were swinging closed.

The next thing I knew my knees had crumpled and I was falling in slow motion to land heavily, facefirst, on the icy gravel. The breath left my lungs in a painful whoosh, and then Cal stood over me, cradling one arm against his chest, his face a mask of rage.

I tried to roll quickly to shoot witch fire again, the only defensive weapon I knew, but he put his boot on my side and pressed down, pinning me to the cold ground. Then he grabbed one of my arms, hauled me to my feet, and squeezed the back of my neck, muttering another spell. I screamed, "Help! Help! Someone help me!" but of course no one came. Then I sagged, a deadweight.

"An di allaigh," I began in a choking voice as Cal hauled me toward the pool house. I knew where we were going, and I absolutely did not want to go there.

"Shut up!" Cal said, shaking me, and he pushed open the changing-room door. Bizarrely, he added, "I know you're upset, but it will all be okay. Everything will be all right soon."

Reaching out, I grasped the door frame, but my limp fingers brushed it harmlessly. I tried to drag my feet, to be an awkward burden, but Cal was furious and afraid, and this fed his strength. Inside we lurched through the powder room, and Cal let me slump to the floor while he unlocked the closet door. I was trying to crawl away when he opened the door to his seòmar, and I felt the darkness come out of it toward me, like a shadow eager to embrace.

Goddess, I thought desperately. Goddess, help me.

Then Cal was dragging me by my feet into his room. With my magesight I saw that it had been cleared of everything, everything I could have used for a weapon, everything I could have used to make magick. It was bare, no furniture, no candles, only thousands and thousands of dark spells written on the walls, the ceiling, the floor. He'd prepared my prison in advance. He'd known this would happen. I wanted to gag.

Panting, Cal dropped my feet. He hovered over me, then narrowed his eyes and grabbed at the neck of my shirt. I tried to pull away, but it was too late.

"You took off my charm," he said, sounding amazed. "You don't love me at all."

"You don't know what love is," I croaked, feeling ill. I

raised my hands over my eyes and clumsily brushed my hair out of the way.

For a moment I thought he was going to kick me, but he didn't, just looked down at me with the devastating face that I had adored.

"You should have trusted me," he said, sweat running down his face, his breathing harsh.

"You shouldn't have lied to me," I countered angrily, trying to sit up.

"Tell me where the tools are," he demanded. "The Belwicket tools."

"Screw you!"

"You tell me! You should never have bound them to you! How arrogant! Now we'll have to rip them away from you, and that will hurt. But first you tell me where they are—I didn't feel them in the car."

I stared at him stonily, trying to rise to my feet.

"Tell me!" he shouted, looming over me.

"Bite me," I offered.

Cal's golden eyes gleamed with hurt and fury, and he shot out his hand at me. A cloudy ball of darkness shot right at me, hitting my head, and I crashed headlong to the floor, sinking into a nightmarish unconsciousness, remembering only his eyes.

18.
Trapped

June 2001

Litha again. It's now fully ten years since my parents disappeared. When they left, I was a boy, concerned only with building a working catapult and playing Behind Enemy Lines with Linden and my friends.

At the time we were living in the Lake District, across Solway Firth from the Isle of Man. For weeks before they left, they were in bad moods, barking at us children and then apologizing, not having the time to help us with our schoolwork. Even Alwyn started coming to me or Linden to help her dress or do her hair. I remember Mum complaining that she felt tired and ill all the time, and none of her usual potions seemed to help. And Dad said his scrying stone had stopped working.

Yes, something was definitely oppressing them. But I'm sure they didn't know what was really coming. If they had, maybe things would have turned out differently.

Or maybe not. Maybe there is no way to fight an evil like that.

—Giomanach

When I awoke, I had no idea how much time had passed. My head ached, my face burned and felt scraped from the gravel, and my knees ached from when I had fallen on them. But at least I could move my limbs. Whatever spell Cal had used on me, it wasn't a binding one.

Cautiously, silently, I rolled over, scanning the seòmar. I was alone. I cast out my senses and felt no one else near. What time was it? The tiny window set high on one wall showed no stars, no moon. I crawled up on my hands and knees, then unfolded myself and stood slowly, feeling a wave of nausea and pain roll over me.

Crap. As soon as I stood, I felt the weight of the spelled walls and ceilings pressing in on me. Every square inch of this tiny room had runes and ancient symbols on it, and without understanding them, I knew that Cal had worked dark magick here, had called on dark powers, and had been lying to me ever since the day I met him. I felt incredibly naive.

I had to get out. What if Cal had left only a minute ago? What if even now he was bringing Selene and the others back to me? Goddess. This room was full of negative energy, negative emotions, dark magick. I saw stains on the floor that had been hidden by the futon the first time I was here. I knelt and touched them, wondering if they were blood. What had Cal done here? I felt sick.

Cal had gone to get Selene, and they were going to put

spells on me or hurt me or even kill me to get me to tell them where Maeve's tools were. To get me to join their side, their all-Woodbane clan.

No one knew where I was. I had told Mom I was going for a drive more than six hours ago. No one had seen me meet Cal at the cemetery. I could die here.

The thought galvanized me into action. I got to my feet again, looking up at the window, gauging its height. My best jump was still two feet short of the window ledge. I pulled off my jacket, balled it up, and flung it hard at the window. It bounced off and clumped to the floor.

"Goddess, Goddess," I muttered, crossing to the door. Its edge was almost invisible, a barely seen crack that was impossible to dig my nails into. In the car I had my Swiss Army knife—patting my pockets quickly yielded me nothing. Still I tried, wedging my short nails into its slit and pulling until my nails split and my fingers bled.

Where was Cal? What was taking so long? How long had it been?

Panting, I backed up across the room, then launched myself shoulder first at the small door. The impact made me cry out, and then I slid down to the floor, clutching my shoulder. The door hadn't even shuddered under the blow.

I thought of how my parents had been so devastated when I took up Wicca, how afraid they had been for me after what happened to my birth mother. I saw now that they'd had good cause to worry.

An unwanted sob choked my throat, and I sank to my knees on the wooden floor. The back of my head ached sickeningly. How could I have been so stupid, so blind? Tears edged from my eyes and coursed down my bruised and dirty cheeks. Sobs struggled to break free from my chest.

I sat cross-legged on the floor. Slowly, knowing it was pointless, I drew a small circle around myself, using my index finger, wetting the floor with my tears and my blood. Shakily I traced symbols of protection around me: pentacles, the intersected circles of protection, squares within squares for orderliness, the angular runic þ for comfort. I drew the two-horned circle symbol of the Goddess and the circle/half circle of the God. I did all these things with only the barest amount of thought, did them by rote, over and over, all around me on the floor, all around me in the air.

Within moments my breathing calmed, my tears ceased, my pain eased. I could see more clearly, I could think more clearly, I was more in control.

Evil pressed in around me. But I was not evil. I needed to save myself.

I was the Woodbane princess of Belwicket. I had power beyond imagining.

Closing my eyes, I forced my breathing to calm further, my heartbeat to slow. Words came to my lips.

"Magick, I am your daughter"
"I am following your path in truth and righteousness.
Protect me from evil. Help me be strong.
Maeve, my mother before me, help me be strong.
Mackenna, my grandmother, help me be strong.
Morwen, who came before her, help me be strong.
Let me open the door. Open the door. Open the door."

I opened my eyes then and gazed before me at the spelled and locked door. I looked at it calmly, imagining it opening before me, seeing myself pass through it to the outside, seeing myself safe and gone from there.

Creak. I blinked at the sound but didn't break my concentration. I was unsure whether I had imagined it, but I kept thinking, Open, open, open, and in the darkness I saw the minuscule crack widen, just a hair.

Elation, as strong as my earlier despair had been, lifted my heart. It was working! I could do this! I could open the door!

Open, open, open, I thought steadily, my focus pure, my intent solid.

I smelled smoke. That fact registered only slightly in my brain as I kept concentrating on opening the door. But I realized that my nose was getting irritated, and I kept blinking. I came out of my trance and saw that the seòmar was becoming hazy, and the scent of fire was strong.

I stood up within my circle, my heart kicking up a beat. Now I could hear the joyful crackling of flames outside, smell the acrid odor of burning ivy, and see the faint, amber light of fire reflected in the high window.

They were burning me alive. Just like my mother.

As my concentration broke, the door clicked shut again.

Panic threatened to drown me. "Help!" I screamed as loud as I could, aiming my voice at the window. "Help! Help! Someone help me!"

From outside, I heard Selene's voice. "Cal! What are you doing?"

"Solving the problem," was his grim response.

"Don't be stupid," Selene snapped. "Get away from there. Where are the tools?"

I thought fast. "Let me out and I'll tell you, I promise!" I shouted.

"She's lying," said another voice. "We don't need her, anyway. This isn't safe—we have to get out of here."

"Cal!" I screamed. "Cal! Help me!"

There was no answer, but I heard muffled voices arguing outside. I strained to hear.

"You promised she would join us," someone said.

"She's just an uneducated girl. What we really need is the tools," said someone else.

"I'll tell you!" I shouted. "They're in the woods! Let me out and I'll take you there!"

"I'm telling you, we have to leave," someone said urgently.

"Cal, stop it!" said Selene, and suddenly the sound of flames was louder, closer.

"Let me out!" I screamed.

"Goddess, what is he doing? Selene!"

"Get back or I'll torch the whole place with all of us in it," said Cal, sounding steely. "I won't let you have her."

"The Seeker will be here any minute," said a man. "There's no way he won't come for this. Selene, your son—"

I heard more arguing, but I was choking now, the smoke stinging my eyes, and then I heard the popping of the wooden rafters up above. I pressed my ear to the wall and listened, but there were no more voices. Had they all just gone away? If I died in the fire, they would never find Maeve's tools. That wasn't true, I realized. They could scry to find them; they could do spells to find them. The simple concealment runes I had traced around the box wouldn't deceive any of them. They wanted me to tell them only to save time. They didn't really need me at all.

I tried once again to open the door with my mind, but I couldn't focus. I kept coughing and my mind was starting to feel foggy. I slumped against the wall in despair.

It had all been for *nothing*: Maeve hiding her tools to keep them safe, coming to me in a vision to tell me where they were, my finding them with Robbie, my learning how to use them. For nothing. Now they would be in Selene's hands, under her control. And maybe the tools were so old that they had been used by the original members of Belwicket— before the clan promised to forsake evil. Maybe the tools would work just as well for evil as they could for good.

Maybe this was all my fault. This was the big picture everyone kept talking about. This was the danger I was blundering into. This was why I needed guidance, a teacher.

"Goddess, forgive me," I muttered, lying belly down on the smooth wooden floor. I pulled my jacket over my head. I was going to die.

I was very tired. It was hard to breathe. I was no longer panicking, no longer full of fear or hysteria. I wondered how Maeve had faced her death by fire, sixteen years before. With each moment that passed, I had more in common with her.

19.
Burn

June 2001

Here's an interesting thing: I went today to Much Bencham, which is the little town in Ireland next to where Ballynigel used to be. No one there wanted to talk to me, and I got the feeling the whole village was anti-witch. Having seen their closest neighbors turn to dust all those years ago, I'm not surprised. But as I was leaving the town square, an old woman caught my eye. She was probably on the dole—making ends almost meet by selling homemade pasties. I bought one, and as I bit into it she said, very quietly, "You're the lad's been asking questions about the town next door." She didn't name Ballynigel, but of course that was what she meant.

"Aye," I said, taking another bite. I waited.

"Odd things," she murmured. "Odd doings in that town, sometimes. Whole town wiped off the face of the earth. It's not natural."

"No," I agreed. "Not natural at all. Did no one survive, then?"

She shook her head, then frowned as if remembering something. "Though that woman last year said as how some did survive. Some escaped, she said."

"Oh?" I said, though inside my heart was pounding. "What woman was this?"

"She were a beauty," said the old woman, thinking back. "Dark and exotic. She had gold eyes, like a tiger. She came here asking about them next door, and someone—I think it was old Collins, at the pub—he told her they were dead, all of them, and she said no, she said that two made it away to America."

"Two people from Ballynigel went to America?" I said, to make certain. "After the disaster, or before?"

"Don't know, do I," said the woman, starting to lose interest. "She just said that two from there had gone to New York years ago, and that's in America, isn't it."

I thanked her and walked away, thinking. Damn me if that tiger woman didn't sound like Dad's first wife, Selene.

So now I am on my way to New York. Is it really possible two witches from Belwicket escaped the disaster? Could they be in New York? I won't rest until I know.

—Giomanach

Dying from smoke inhalation is not the worst way to go, I thought sleepily. It's uncomfortable and gives you a drowning sort of feeling, but it must be better than being shot or actually burned to death or falling off a cliff.

It wouldn't be long now. My head ached; smoke filled my lungs and made me cough. Even lying on the floor, with my head covered by my jacket, I wouldn't last much longer. Was this how it had been for Maeve and Angus?

When I heard the voices calling my name from outside, I figured I was hallucinating. But the voices came again, stronger, and I recognized them.

"Morgan! Morgan! Are you in there? Morgan!"

Oh my God, it sounded like Bree! Bree and Robbie!

Sitting up was a mistake because even a foot above me, the air was heavier. I choked and coughed and sucked in air, and then I screamed, "I'm in here! In the pool house! Help!" A spasm of coughing crushed my chest, and I fell to the floor, gasping.

"Stand back!" Bree shouted from outside. "Get away from the wall!"

Quickly I rolled to the wall farthest away from her voice and lay there, huddled and coughing. My mind dimly registered the familiar, powerful roar of Das Boot's engine, and the next thing I knew, the wall across from me was hit with a huge, earthshaking crash that made the plaster pop, the window shatter and rain glass on me, and the wall bulge in. I peeped out from under my coat and saw a crack where smoke was rising, pouring out into the sky, grateful for release. I heard the roar of the engine, the squeal of wheels, and the whole building shook as my car rammed the wall violently once more. This time the stone and plaster broke, studs snapped, and then the crumpled, ash-strewn nose of my car was perched in the wall, opening like the mouth of a great white shark.

The driver's door opened, and then Bree was scrambling over rubble, coughing, and I reached out to her, and she grabbed my arms and hauled me out over the wreckage. Robbie was there outside, waiting for us, and as my knees buckled he ran over and caught me. I bent over, coughing and retching, while he and Bree held me.

Then we heard the nearing sounds of wailing fire sirens, and in the next few minutes three fire trucks appeared, Sky and Hunter arrived, and Cal's beautifully manicured lawn was ruined.

And I was alive.